RED CLAY

AND

ROSES

Many thanks for your time and support, Daniel. Sincerely, S. K. Nicholls

S. K. Nicholls

Copyright © 2013 by S. K. Nicholls
Ark Books
All rights reserved.
ISBN: 0989568695
ISBN-13: 9780989568692

Cover Image Design by: create-imaginations.com

While visiting my grandparent's farm in my youth,
an elderly African American man told me,

"If your children can look at my grandchildren and
not see color, then we have made progress."

This book is dedicated to him, the progress
that we have made, and to my loving and
supportive husband, Greg.

"We are, each of us angels with only one wing, and
we can only fly by embracing one another."
~Luciano de Crescenzo

RED CLAY AND ROSES

A "Faction" Novel

S. K. Nicholls

Table of Contents

Introduction: A Trip Back to Georgia 2012

12 April 2012

Before I left for Georgia, my daughter, grand-daughter, and myself, went to visit "Belinda's Dream", a rose bush that we had planted in the little garden of an apartment complex where my daughter and I had once shared a unit. Someone had added a white trellis behind the bush and a small angelic cherub had been placed at its base. The bush wasn't bloom-ing, but was blanketed in clusters of small buds that would soon burst forth clouds of frilly fragrant pink blossoms. It was February and over eighty degrees. My two year old granddaughter, a gorgeous mixed race child, was fascinating herself in the shade by tossing pebbles into the tiny koi pond in the corner. The cool water was pumped over slippery stones to appear as if it ran from a stream that bubbled up out of the earth. The rose bush was planted by the two of us a few years ago when we were moving away as a remembrance. The birds were singing. It was a beautiful day in Orlando. My thoughts were on self-will, destiny and God's plan.

On that same day, a couple of days before Valentine's Day, I received a call from my dad's wife. My dad was at Emory Hospital in Atlanta. He already had four stents in his heart and was scheduled for a double coronary bypass graft. Daddy is 74 years old but he looks all of 50 years. He has always been handsome. He was voted "Cutest" in his high school annual, with his black hair and blue eyes, and the graying at his temples has really done him no disservice. His wife (number four) was frantic, as was my half-sister (by a different wife), because they had rescheduled his surgery twice. They needed me there, not only because I am Henry Hamilton's daughter, but also because I am a Registered Nurse. I had more than five hundred miles in front of me and did not know if I would be gone a week or a month. I would leave in a couple of days.

We have had an unusually warm winter in Florida this year. The mild cold has not harmed our tropical plants. The brugmansia is about to trumpet golden. The hibiscus, bird of paradise, allamanda, and peace lilies are splashing their multi-colors between the palms around the pool. The pool itself is most inviting, but I have work to do in packing. My husband of four years, Gary, does not want to see me go,

especially on Valentine's Day, but he is most supportive, as he is always.

Orlando is almost always green. When I first moved
here, some fourteen or fifteen years ago, I was thirty-six
years old. While in Georgia, I would sometimes pause
when writing a check until the clerk told me the date.
A few months after arriving in Florida I was at the grocery store. When I paused, the clerk told me the date.
I stood still, paused yet again, and then asked, "What
month is this?" They seemed to all be the same. She
laughed and asked me how long I had been in Florida
and I told her, "Only a few months." She said, "Just
wait until you get to Key West. When I worked down
there people asked me, 'What year is this?'"

That is how it is, perpetually green. There are
subtle changes with the seasons, a mild graying as
fall blends into spring. There is no winter. There is
summer. I had to remind myself what February in
the Georgia Mountains near the river might be like
as I packed for the trip. Not knowing the length of
my stay, I decided to layer my clothes. I threw practically everything I owned into two bags, grabbed
a cooler of sodas and a bag of chips, and left for
"home". My thoughts were on how my granddaughter's life would be so very different from my own as I
set off on my journey.

❧

I was born Hannah Hamilton at LaGrange City County Hospital in Georgia, November of 1960, to Henry and Carol Hamilton. That was four wives ago for my dad. My early childhood was quite tumultuous.

As a very small child, I recalled being raised by someone else. That is to say, regardless of having a mother or not, there was always a maid or a nanny. June of 1965, while staying at my maternal Grandma's house after my baby sister had been born, my older sister and I were playing with our dolls on the big screened porch. A summer storm rolled in suddenly. I had never been afraid of thunderstorms. The wind was whipping up. Gusts sent broken tree limbs crashing across the roof. Lightening cracked in the darkened sky and our nanny, Wylene, a great big buxom black woman who smelled of baby powder, sweat, and peppermint came charging onto the porch. I was only four years old. She bellowed at us, "You young'uns better get into this here house, ifin you don't, you gwan t'be struck by lightenin, and be black as I is!" For more years than I am ashamed to admit, I seriously believed that black people had become black by being struck by lightning. During that time, many white families in the South employed black nannies who became like family members to the children. I loved my nannies as much as I could love my own mother.

My parents divorced when I was seven years old. Mama was a smart dresser and a very pretty lady.

Her name, Carol, meant, "Song of Joy", and it was her way to carry joy with her. She read to us every night, and despite her long hours away at work, she devoted every minute she could to us. She sang like a flower opening up to the sunshine in the spring-time. Her voice was lilting and sweet. Her mood never seemed to reflect the despair that she must have been feeling. She had planned to become a professional ballerina in her youth, but God had other plans for her. She had become a housewife instead. She had us three girls and was only able to dance as a hobby.

After my parent's divorce, Mama moved us to Atlanta, briefly. She was alone in a big city with three young daughters. She danced in performances for the community ballet and practiced for hours. She had taken a job as a waitress in a small café on Peachtree Street. She frequently sang there on weekends when she was not dancing. There was also church, where she sang in the choir. Sometimes, because our nanny had weekends off, Mama would take us downtown to sit on blankets outside of the café with the hippies who played their guitars, played their flutes, braided our hair, taught us how to make flower leis, and fluffed each other's afros. We would help them make posters, "MAKE LOVE, NOT WAR", and "BLACK POWER". It was often Peter, Paul, and Mary, The Mamas and the Papas, and other such folksy music. Other times the

"Jazz Men" would join in with melodic soft saxophone while we drifted off to sleep in some stranger's lap. Late in the evening we came home and she would put albums on the stereo: Diana Ross and the Supremes, Herb Alpert and the Tijuana Brass, Johnny Mathis or Petula Clark. Her music interests were varied, and she would sing along or dance to the music. Our mother also sold her blood at the Blood Bank downtown so someone else might live, and so we could have eggs with our toast at breakfast.

We returned to Chipley, GA due to financial hardship. By February of 1969, Mama was eternally gone from us in this life, having taken her own life. There are things about the night of her death that I do not wish to remember, but cannot forget.

We spent a brief time in Pine Mountain, (formerly Chipley), GA with our maternal Grandma. At Chipley Elementary School, there were two grades in my classroom, second and third. Despite that the U.S. Supreme Court ruled that segregation of schools violated the 14th amendment in 1954, and Jim Crow Law was repealed in 1965, schools in the Deep South were not integrated until much later in a child's life. I had three black students in my class in the third grade. They were Brenda and Linda Brooks, identical twins who were both very smart, and Adolphus Hightower, a boy who could turn his eyelids inside out and stuff his ears inside of his head. Adolphus had a knack for keeping us all quite amused when the teacher was out of the room.

There was Dunbar Elementary School on the far side of town, where we sent our schoolbooks after they were used a few years. Dunbar was the black school. Our mother had insisted on us saying, "Negro," or "colored people", but the blacks at that time simply preferred, "black." Mama also never had allowed us to say, "Ain't." It was, "Isn't," or it was, "Am not," and it was not, "Cheap," it was, "More affordable." Men did not, "Cut the grass," they, "Mowed the lawn," and we didn't come to meals, meals were served, at the table and with proper utensils that we were taught how to use properly.

There was turmoil following Mama's death, but serenity was found in family and farm. Our paternal Grandparents had a huge farm in rural Harris County where we gathered with cousins on weekends, holidays, and summers. They were happy and wholesome times. We went to their churches and Sunday schools. We learned to appreciate the seasons and all they offered. We learned to attend to livestock, to plant, tend to gardens, and harvest crops. We learned to hunt and fish. We learned to sew, cook, can and freeze vegetables, dry apples and grind sausage. But Grandmother and Grandfather were already elderly and to live there permanently was never an option.

I cannot deny that my perceptions in life as an adult are, like anyone else's, affected by my perceptions as a child. I know that I did not have a "normal" childhood...who really has a normal childhood? I suppose that whatever occurs in society becomes what is considered "normal" at some point in history based on somebody's statistics somewhere. As I told you, I had more than five hundred miles in front of me and that gave me much personal time alone to reflect over the years. The Turnpike is a long stretch of highway, and I-75 to Tifton is longer still. I was forced to get out and stretch my legs from time to time, and expected this to be a six to eight hour journey, depending on the traffic.

To say we were orphans would not be entirely true, and yet, it would be.

After my mother passed, we three girls eventually moved to LaGrange, GA to live with my dad and his second wife. She had a daughter, and twin two year olds, a boy and a girl. We also had a housekeeper, and my step-mother did not work outside of the home. She was loving toward me and my older sister, but rather hard on my younger three year old sister. I suppose she wanted her to grow up instantly, as managing three toddlers was quite the challenge, I am sure. Those were our "Brady Bunch" and "Wonder Years" in, seemingly, quiet suburbia. We rode our bicycles all around the neighborhood making new friends and exploring the creeks and woods. We were largely unaffected by the Vietnam War, except that an occasional neighbor friend would lose an older brother, and my older sister's music was highly influenced. Initially, we only had three major network channels, CBS, ABC, and, NBC and then there was PBS. We had to go outside to turn the antennae north-south for NBC and PBS, or east west for CBS and ABC. The Vietnam War, Civil Rights and protest stories dominated the news. Then we got one cable channel, # 17, that broadcast lots of reruns of 1950s & 60s shows.

Our dad was out of town often, or working late into the evening. We lived in a nice house in a nice neighborhood, and new houses were constantly under construction. This meant that new people were constantly being added to the mix, but it was an exclusively "white" neighborhood. On a springtime night with an early full moon, I had my first kiss in the midst of a rain of swirling pink crabapple petals, from my puppy love crush, a musician's son. His dad sang in a band called, "The White Soul Movement." Curious about romance, I recall asking my paternal Grandmother why she had married my Grandfather. I was fully anticipating long and lusty stories about moonlit buggy rides and romantic poetry. No such luck. Grandmother had simply looked away. She shrugged her shoulders, and flatly replied, "Twernt much to choose from."

When I started into the fifth grade in 1971, the schools had just fully integrated. This meant that a good number of children from the east side of town had to go to school on the west side of town and vise-a-verse. The black schools were closed down. The black children were dispersed throughout all of the white schools. Still, the children seldom mixed because the single grades were divided up according to achievement levels and based on the achievement tests, most of the black students trailed behind. Not because they were less intelligent, but because the achievement tests were constructed by white standards. Many of these black students were raised in families that had taught them to hate the whites, and many whites were taught to hate the blacks, and the violence that they brought to school with them was often out of control. Fear was something students seemed to strive to achieve in groups against their classmates; it wasn't something that any individual decided to do, it was how society had forced itself over generations.

Being a book nerd placed me into many advanced classes, but not all. There were the "Goody Two Shoes" who were in all advanced classes. These included all of the "popular" kids. And there were the "Slow Learners" who were in all remedial classes. These included a large number of black kids. Everything in-between was "Average", and I considered myself average. To be anything worse would have meant an ass-whipping with a belt. I was tolerated by the popular kids because my grades were fairly good, and I was tolerated by the black kids because I could run like the wind, and was often picked on teams at recess for this reason. The days of water-skiing on the lake and running through the woods on the farm had helped me develop strong muscles and a swift pace.

∾

I was almost to Tifton, GA. I pulled into the Dairy Queen to get a bite to eat and to stretch my legs. I went to the counter to place my order. The girls behind the counter were laughing and playing. A tall thin girl with obsidian skin took my order. She had to be barely sixteen and obviously pregnant. After I placed my order, she quipped, "Diduwonmutidondat?" I had no idea what she just said to me.

"I'm sorry; could you repeat that, perhaps a little more slowly?"

She drawled out, "I daid, did du won't mutid on dat?"

"Oh yes, mustard, I do want mustard, thank you," I responded, a bit bewildered by the fact that everything changes, and yet, everything remains quite the same.

I was startled at the reminder of the reality of where I was going. This wasn't an eloquent Caribbean, Jamaican, or Haitian black woman. This wasn't an urban sophisticated African-American woman. This was a rural Georgia black girl in 2012. I was more than half way "home".

I have made this trip to LaGrange at least a dozen times over the past fifteen years. I took my exit onto the highway from the Interstate. It is easier now that there are at least four lanes of highway all the way home. This stretch between Tifton and Albany is a notorious speed trap, with the speed limit changing from 65 mph to 35 mph in the blink of an eye and back again just as quickly. It is dotted with little towns, more like villages, along the way. There are vast stretches of nothing but peanut farms and pine forest.

This is the highway that brings back the fondest memories of my youth. Along the highway there are farmhouses and barns that sit in the midst of freshly plowed fields with a few shade trees around, broad spanning oaks to curtain their windows. The first sign of being nearer to "home" is the red clay that juts up out of the green grass embankments along the carved out highway. The color is surrealistic. It appears as if someone accidently dipped their paint-brush in the red instead of the brown while painting some country scene, but decided to continue paint-ing in shades of red and orange. I had forgotten. Wildflowers bloom in the foreground and the road begins to meander around sharp curves and flow up and down high hills.

My granddaughter's heritage through me is quite simple really. My grandmother and her sisters had been as thick as molasses. When she married my grandfather, two of her sisters married his two first cousins who were brothers. They all shared the same party-line phone with my great auntie. Most had lived within two miles of each other. There was Great Auntie, a school teacher who had remained a spinster, Aunt Lizzy and Uncle Billy, Aunt Mary Mae and Uncle Bob, and my grandparents. Another Great Aunt lived in Montgomery. Only one Uncle had moved away to Macon. The Methodist Church that Grandmother's family had started was on one end of the property, and the Baptist Church that Grandfather's family has started was on the other end of the property. There was farm land and cous-ins all in-between. They had all been so close. Why did modern times mean everything has to be so very different, so complicated? We are all so scattered now. My granddaughter may never come to know her cousins.

I skirted Albany, and passed over the Flint River. The hills and curves are exaggerated as the fault line (called the fall line, by locals) to the Appalachian Mountains is approached. There are roadside signs offering boiled peanuts, fried apple pies, crispy peanut brittle, pecans, and other such local treats. As the hills steepen and the sun begins to drop in the sky, the forest closes in casting lacy shadows over the road. The smell of burnt underbrush is thick, but there is no smoke, only filtered sunlight and blue sky. The temperature begins to drop severely. Eighty six miles left to Columbus through Fort Benning.

When I left Florida for Georgia, I took along a Spanish language CD that I had planned to listen to on this trip. Instead, I fought with the radio stations to find something remotely appealing. I needed to stop again.

I pulled into Merritt Pecan Company. This is one of the most nostalgic tourist traps in the area. There is every jam or jelly imaginable, muscadine, scuppernong, (both wild grapes), every berry known to mankind, a dozen varieties of pepper jellies, and even a moonshine jelly. Relishes from habanera pepper to cabbage and corn. There are baskets and wreaths made from wild grape vines. There are gorgeous ceramic pieces made by local artists. The best pecan and peanut candies are found here, from brittles to divinities and chocolates. I decided to wait until my trip home to purchase anything.

Darkness settled as I passed through Fort Benning near Columbus. I stopped briefly on the side of the road before turning onto the interstate. I took a short walk with a flashlight to stretch my legs again. A young man pulled over to ask if I was having car trouble and I waved him on. On this warmer winter night the crickets and spring peepers were all that I could hear. They were a strong indicator of the coming season. It was otherwise quiet on the country roadside. The terrain here is steep and hilly for a while, and then swampy and low for a while so close to the Chattahoochee River.

I returned to my car after my short walk. Soon, I was off of the highway and onto I-185. Cities never sleep. The tall steel walls on either side of the interstate block the view of Columbus State University, (formerly Columbus College), my alma mater. Cars whizz by me with important places for their drivers to be. I am not going to rush. There will only be Richard, the butler, to let me into the house.

We call him Richard the butler, but he wasn't hired as such. He is an older man with no family, who had nowhere to go, so they took him in. He does all of the house and yard work, and frequently answers their phone. Richard does all that he can to make my dad's and his wife's lives easier. My dad's wife remains at the hospital in Atlanta where they have postponed his surgery until tomorrow.

My husband has texted me pictures of the roses, teddy bear and chocolates that I was supposed to have been home to receive today. He is such The Sweetheart. I miss him already. It won't be a lonely trip though, as I am hoping to see and visit with some cousins on this trip that I have not seen in a long while. I will also see my two younger half-sisters.

It is not far now, forty three miles. After passing through Columbus the traffic thins to next to nothing. This is country land and forest for the rest of the trip home. Harris County, just north of Columbus, is fast becoming the bedroom to Muscogee County. There are subdivisions and convenience stores where nothing but trees once stood. For the most part, the inhabitants are still country folk who have moved closer to the city to lessen commutes.

Passing through Harris County, I was reminded of the joy that my former husband and I had in raising our three children, both on the farm and along the river. A couple of deer made their way lazily across the highway as I slowed. I have traveled this strip a myriad of times in running the children from place to place; for school, soccer practice, horse-back riding lessons, Boy Scout and Girl Scout activities, karate lessons, softball, cheerleading, gymnastics, music lessons, Youth Group activities, and any number of other events. I also struggled to get from home to work to nursing school to home to work again, up and down this road, in-between all of those events. My former husband had adopted my oldest son and we had given life to two more children, a daughter and another son. We had stayed married for eighteen years.

I think back on that life and wonder how we were all able to manage. The flurry of rampant demands was tempered by the peace of laying my head on my pillow to hear the sounds of the whippoorwills or horse hooves pounding on the pasture, if only for a little while.

I took my exit off of the interstate and turned north up highway #27, and passed Rosemont Baptist Church on my left. This was not the quickest route to my dad's home, but I wanted to come into LaGrange from the south, as I had so many times from Pine Mountain (formerly Chipley). I passed the penitentiary on my left, the Georgia State Trooper's building on my right, and Troup High School on my left. Up and down the hills, into and out of the curves.

The four lanes narrowed to two lanes as I came into LaGrange proper. The road is lined with shabby old mill houses on either side, where children play in the street, sometimes after dark.

There is a very high point by this route, where you drive around an extremely sharp westerly curve, to see the charming town of LaGrange spread out before you. The town square sits high on a hill surrounded by dales in all four directions, with the brightly lit First Baptist Church steeple standing sentinel. It looks like something out of a post card from another era. As I turned this curve, I saw that the "Colored People's Old Folks Home" sign had finally been replaced by a sign that read, "D.K.'s Rose Garden", on the front of the old stone building in the foreground. The building looked abandoned, no light shone from within.

I came to the intersection and crossed over the railroad tracks to ascend to the square. I saw that the old theater had been remodeled with a white and shining dome for a roof. So many buildings and store fronts stood empty. The economy is so terrible right now, and this is a town that has relied on industry for much longer than I have been alive.

I made my way slowly to the square at the town's center. Gone were the venues of my youth. The large fountain in the center of the square seemed to spray forth the water of hope, always active.

The Court House was new. There was no more Rexall Drugs on the corner. The Dime Store, Behr's, the Mercantile Co., the old Ice Company, Kay Bee's Jewelers, Johnson's Feed & Seed, Miss Dorothy's Diner, Sam's Shoe Repair Shop, and the Pawn, Radio and Bicycle Repair had all long been gone. Charlie Joseph's Hot Dogs and Mansour's Department Store were about all that remained, and there was a sign in Mansour's that read, "This Building for Lease," as history was becoming history. Those two establishments, and the row of offices on the north side of the square where businessmen like my dad struggled to remain afloat, were about all that were familiar.

I turned left onto Lafayette Parkway that becomes Vernon Road. Lafayette was waving from his place in the center of the fountain. I remembered the time before he was there. A thirty foot high gold tinsel tree would be erected over the fountain each Christmas, and colored lights would cast red and green beams into the water. Mama would take us to the square to drink hot chocolate, or hot apple cider, and to sing with the carolers who would gather there.

Down the corridor past LaGrange College and the old antebellum mansions, grand and stately they had once seemed. The old homes were spared by the efforts of the "Nancy Harts", a women's militia in April of 1865. The women had trained for three years and defended their homes against advancing Union soldiers just before the Civil War ended. They had been named in honor of Nancy Hart, a Georgia Revolutionary War heroine, who had single-handedly defended her home against a group of invading British soldiers. "Bellevue," home of Senator Benjamin Harvey Hill, had remained unscathed, and others, as well. How haunted they appeared in the dark of the night. The Callaway Mansion, "Hills and Dales" completed in 1916, was mysteriously hidden by the glossy green leaves of magnolia to my right. After living in Florida with its multitude of McMansions on every corner, these all seemed so tiny and frail.

I drove on past the hospital, where I had my first Nursing job, out toward West Point Lake where my father, his wife, and Richard now lived. Upon my arrival, as expected, Richard let me in and continued his chore of attending to Daddy's laundry. I brought in my bags and proceeded to unpack.

I spent the first couple of days at the hospital with my dad after his surgery, so his wife could return home to return to work. She is more than twenty years his junior. Her employer, the new Kia plant, has given the local economy a mild boost that it desperately needed. She had less than ninety days in her new job and was worried that she might be terminated for missing too many days during her probationary period.

My dad, at 74 years of age, is a most shrewd businessman. I don't believe that he will ever retire again. He tried that once and it lasted about a year before he was back in the saddle with his own business. I believe that he will simply go to work one day and not come home. I remember how he helped me when I was in L.P.N. school back in 1983-84.

I had left college shortly after Katherine was born in order to spend some time with her and also because we could not afford gas or tuition. I had decided to get my vocational school degree, which would afford us more income and me more experience and I would return to Columbus College at a later date. The program was only a year. I had become a member of the Vocational-Industrial Clubs of America (V.I.C.A.) in an effort to make myself worthy of a scholarship from the local hospital. I was participating in a fund raiser and going about things entirely the wrong way. I was going from store to store in downtown LaGrange, asking for money. In return, the contributors would receive an acknowledgement in the local paper, but nobody was donating much more than a dollar or two. It was a slow and nearly fruitless venture.

I stopped by my dad's office and told him of my plight and my results. He said, "Oh hell, this is what you do. You go to Mr. Mallory's office and tell him that you have been to Mr. Hudson's office and Mr. Hudson has donated $75.00, and couldn't he at least top that? Then, you go to Mr. Hudson's office and tell him that Mr. Mallory has donated $75.00 and couldn't he at least top that? Then, you go to every businessman in town, lawyer's offices, insurance company offices, real estate offices, and call the owners by name and repeat that process and I guarantee that you will get results. They are always trying to one-up each other."

He was absolutely right. I did just that and had accumulated more money in a day than I had in two weeks by my method. At the end of the fund raiser, I had raised more money than anyone. I earned a scholarship, and I would not have to worry about books or tuition again. I could work as a Licensed Practical Nurse and have my further education paid. I worked as an L.P.N. in the Extended Care facility of the local hospital until Donald was born, and again, after I returned to Columbus College, I worked at the local hospital as an L.P.N. on the Med-Surg and Oncology floors.

I had been estranged from my dad during my teen years. We reconciled after I was married, and I was glad that my children could know their grandfather. It was good to have reconciled with my dad after his divorce from wife number three, and his next wife was so very different from the ones we had known in childhood, but then, so was he.

Daddy came home with me from the hospital in Atlanta and began his convalescence, which was no easy feat for him. He was up at 8:00 am every morning for breakfast and meds with his oxygen tubing trailing behind him. He was biting at the bit to be able to drive and to return to the office. He was on the phone with the office often. In a matter of days he was strong enough to sit at the office for a few hours each day. It had been decided that I would stay for 5-6 weeks of his recuperative period so that I could drive him to and from his many appointments and to and from the office as his doctor had not cleared him to drive.

We spent hours chatting about his work, his wife's work, my work, and my husband's work, the children's and grandchildren's work. To say that my dad is a workaholic would be an understatement. Every morning and afternoon we walked around the neighborhood, him pulling his oxygen bottle behind him, talking all the while.

We also spent hours with him relating stories from his youth, who he was with when this or that event took place. He talked about what he had done, the people he had known, the places he had been, and how things were, "Back in the day." For days into weeks, he talked and I listened. I suppose a

near death experience is a good qualifier for review-
ing one's life.

Many of the stories I had heard before, but many
I had not. Some, we had shared in, but recalled dif-
ferently. Early on, Daddy told me something that I
did not know. Our cousin, Sybil, Daddy's 1st cousin
and a few years older than him, was still alive and living alone in a little apartment on North Greenwood
Street. He told me that I should call her and go by
to visit with her while I was up there. He felt that she
would like the company, saying that he did not get
by there often enough, and felt bad for it. I agreed
to call her.

The next day, I got my dad's breakfast and medicine ready, and gave Sybil a call. She said she would
be happy for me to come by anytime. I took my dad
to his office and dropped him off with Richard and
one of my half-sisters. He was planning to spend a
few hours there. If all went well, he would be doing
so every day.

After leaving the office, I drove to the humble
apartment complex on North Greenwood St. where
Sybil was living. She was happy to see me and wel-
comed me into her home. The apartment was small
and tidy, and the first thing I noticed was the computer sitting on a desk by the sliding glass door to
the patio. There were pictures on the walls, mostly
black and whites of her in her youth surrounded

by girlfriends and guyfriends. A few were of her in seductive poses dressed in strapless gowns. It was a small space, decorated in primary red and black, with zebra throw pillows and tasseled red velour throws over a black leather sofa and chair. A posh white fur rug lay in the floor at the center of the room and there was no coffee table, only black lacquered end tables to each side of the sofa. There was a kitchenette at the right of the entry that opened into the L-shaped living/dining room combination. I guessed it had one bedroom and one bath by the doors.

Sybil's scent was Shalimar, and she wore cosmetics, most likely Merle Norman, with her thin arched brows penciled, her lips outlined and filled with a becoming shade of wine red. She was older than Daddy by about six years, but she didn't look it, at 80 years old she could have easily passed for 60 or younger. She was a tall five foot ten, slender build and had an air of sophistication about her, even at her age. I could only hope to age so gracefully. Her hands were soft and her nails were long and polished in a French manicure. She was dressed in a beige pantsuit. Jewelry adorned her. Everything about her was refined and polished, yet she had spunk and a brassy demeanor.

Her face, though slightly freckled, truly did not show her age in the least. The only ways that she showed her age were by the wrinkles at her knuckles and under her neck. Nobody her age could have such a white and bright smile. Certainly, she had to wear dentures. Her hair showed no sign of gray, as she was as blonde as I could recall from my childhood. It was waved in curl around her face, which served to soften her sharp features. With Aunt Lizzy and Uncle Billy's blue eyes, she sparkled.

We passed the black lacquered dining table and went into the living room. "I see you are keeping up with the latest technology," I said, waving in the direction of the computer. "Daddy finally put them in his office several years ago. He had to do it; no company would do business with him if he didn't."

Sybil smiled, "I just couldn't live without one. I have friends all over the world now and this thing is just a Godsend. I do all of my business and banking and such online now, not to mention, my online dating!"

"So you are still dating, at what age now?" I quickly apologized, "Don't tell me, I don't mean to be rude."

"Oh, I don't mind saying I'm eighty years old, damn proud of it, earned every day of it."

I asked, "So what is your secret to staying so beautiful?"

"I'd hardly call myself beautiful, but if you insist, I'll tell you. Break all the rules before you are forty!

Drink, smoke, curse like a sailor, sleep around, of course with protection, and don't give a bloody rotten damn about what other people think. Think for yourself. Don't think too much of yourself. Wash your own laundry. Be loyal to your friends. Travel anywhere you are asked to go, and when you are not asked, ask someone to join you. Appreciate the small things in life, and be humbled by the large. Live frugal, but party with expense. Pamper yourself, and I don't mean with diapers. At forty, know that you are saved by the Grace of God and pray every day for His continued blessings and forgiveness, and pray with gratitude in your heart. Don't worry so much about what the next day might bring, just know that God has a plan, and it will be revealed to you in due time. And, most importantly, never, ever miss an opportunity. I don't know if it is a formula for success, but it's worked for me."

I liked her already, and felt like I had known her for years, although I had not seen her in more than twenty. She offered me a glass of sweet iced tea. I took the iced tea and followed her out to the patio. It was an early spring. The days were warming and the azaleas were just beginning to bud open. We sat there on comfortable patio cushions and talked for hours.

Inquiries were made about this cousin or that, and she learned about my own family. She remembered my mother, in much the way that I did, except to say that she was popular and had "oodles" of girlfriends both before and after she had married my dad. She said that she and my mother had once fancied going off to Hollywood, California, to try to be in the movies, them and ten million other girls. Her mind was sharp and her memory as much so. She asked me to come back anytime and said that she thought it would be peachy if we could visit each day until I returned home to Florida. So that became the routine. I would drop Daddy off at the office, and then visit with Sybil.

Sybil was a marvelous story teller. She filled in a lot of blanks from the stories my dad told me. She knew everything about everybody, and described all of the details. Over the weeks, we became quite intimate in our conversations and I learned that Sybil was a nonconventional woman in her time, almost a feminist, yet a genuine romantic at heart. She had no reservations when she spoke. She talked for hours relating both her joy and her sorrow. When it came time for me to go, we exchanged e-mail addresses and promised to keep in touch. She offered me three books, all diaries that she had kept over the years. I asked her why she felt I should have the books, and she told me that diaries are no good unless someone eventually reads them. I told her that they were good for refreshing memories. She said that at her age, most of what was written years ago was best forgotten.

When I went back to my dad's home that last evening in Georgia, I reminded him of the time when Sybil had called him to say that she had sold Aunt Lizzy and Uncle Billy's old home place to a group of investors from Atlanta. It was 1992, and the investors were planning to tear down the old house and she had wanted my dad to go out and see if there was anything at the house that he might want to keep before it was demolished and hauled away. I was coming back from school in Columbus that day and agreed to meet him at the old house, but by the time we got out there, the place had been stripped of anything of any value.

The next day, I had stopped again on my return from school. The walls lay in a heap of debris. I picked through the debris to see if there was any good wood that my husband could come back for with the truck, anything that we might need for the farm or the house. As I was pulling out boards of the tongue and groove wood, I found an old ledger stuck between two walls. How did it get there and why, I wondered?

When I found the ledger, titled simply, "The Good Doctor", and told my dad about it, he told me to burn it or throw it away. I was curious about it as it seemed to be an accounting of transactions between a physician of some sort and his patients who often bartered with chickens and produce for services rendered. Twenty years ago, I made a startling discovery about the ledger. Twenty years later, Sybil revealed its origin.

Sybil's stories over the past few weeks provided some sense of closure. As much as she had to say, I felt that she was holding back something important. As soon as I was home, I would set about reading the Diaries of Sybil. I left my dad's feeling like I could lose him any day, and there was so much more I wanted to learn from his generation. I thought about the patients I had cared for over the years.

Every nurse has those few patients that stand out to never be forgotten. During my time with Sybil, two such patients came to mind: Beatrice Handley, wife of The Good Doctor and town chiropractor who had died decades earlier, and Moses Grier, his handyman, who had recalled the tragedy of his daughter, Althea, to me back in 1993. Hearing the history of the ledger, and the families it involved, is crucial to understanding Sybil's story.

On my drive out of town to return to Florida, I felt compelled to stop at The Colored People's Old Folks Home and pay my respects. Moses is gone now, but the rose bush we had planted survives to this day on the edge of a park that overlooks the city of LaGrange. I walked along the edge of the park to the rose garden behind what was once The Colored People's Old Folks Home. Althea's rose bush wasn't blooming, but was blanketed in clusters of small buds that would soon burst forth clouds of frilly fragrant pink blossoms. I placed a small angelic cherub beside the bush, a guardian angel.

PART ONE

HANNAH HEARS THE HISTORY OF THE LEDGER

1992-1993

1

THE GOOD DOCTOR

The ledger was thick and titled, "The Good Doctor". The inside cover read, "The records of Dr. David Handley and wife Beatrice 1950-66." Dr. Handley had been a chiropractor, and chiropractic medicine had been most controversial at that time. There had been an ongoing battle between the American Medical Association and the American Chiropractic Association on whether or not Chiropractics could use the title of Doctor. I had been given an assignment in political science class and was tasked with writing an essay on a controversial subject. I thought that I might study the ledger and use it in writing my paper.

The book seemed to be filled with dates, names, addresses, and phone numbers of Dr. Handley's clients and their methods of payment, which I found rather interesting. "Services rendered at town office…..$15.00, Services rendered at town office……$30.00; Services rendered at home office……$50.00, Services rendered at home office……$100.00. It seemed that his home office calls were far more expensive than his town office calls, and I noticed that while some of the town office appointments were for women, most of the town office calls were for men, and all of his home office calls were for women. I could see men going to Dr. Handley's office in town during the day hours, while they were in town, and the women coming to the home office in the evenings after their husbands were home, perhaps to watch over the children. There were about 4-8 entries a day at the town office and 2-4 entries a day at the home office.

The ledger had other interesting entries. "Services rendered……at home office……2 setting hens and a basket of cabbages, Services rendered……at home office…..a small heifer and 2 piglets." It seemed as if some clients had bartered for his services. There was even one entry, "Services rendered……at home office….haircuts and shaves for one year."

There were other curiosities about the ledger. For example, there were notes scribbled almost illegibly in the margins by some of the names. Some were in pencil and some were in red ink. Notes like: "Tell Jerome not to bring Selma by until dark;" and, "Abnormal bleeding." I had thought it rather odd to have notes such as these in a chiropractic medicine doctor's ledger.

I called my dad and told him about the ledger. He told me that I needed to burn that thing and forget I had ever found it. His comments only served to peak my investigative curiosity further. I asked my cousin, Sybil, about it and I got only silence. The book was forty-two years old, and listed sixteen years of content, but I thought that there might be a chance that some of these people were still around and might shed some light on their experiences with The Good Doctor.

I made a list of all the names that had phone numbers beside them. I decided that I would call and introduce myself as a political science student writing on the subject of chiropractic medicine, and had discovered a ledger from thirty to forty years ago. I would tell them that I would like their opinions on the advances of medicine, and whether they now regarded chiropractic medicine as real science or quackery. I would see if they volunteered any information.

There were sixteen years of names and dates in that thick book, hundreds of men and women. I wondered if I would be able to reach any of them. There were family names that I recognized in that book, some prominent family names; surely some would still be in the area, maybe even with the same phone number. I was pleasantly surprised when the first number that I called was answered by a soft spoken lady who identified herself as the person whose name appeared in the ledger. She had never married and she had seen Dr. Handley for an abortion in 1952. She had believed herself to be one of The Good Doctor's first patients, "But certainly not his last."

Her lover had been killed in the Korean War before she had even determined that she was pregnant. He had been stationed at Ft. Benning briefly when she met him. It was a whirlwind romance and she could not bear to have his child as an unwed mother at that time. Maybe it would have been different had they been married, but they weren't. She said that she had no regrets. She said that she would do things all over again the same way given the same set of circumstances. When asked if she considered herself an anti-abortion supporter, or a pro-choice supporter, she responded that she would never wish her burden on anyone, but she felt strongly that a woman should be allowed to decide what to do in her own personal circumstances. I thanked her for her candidness and her willingness to speak with me on the subject. She said she felt some sense of relief in having had our little talk. I expressed my sorrow for her loss. We ended the conversation.

She had had an *abortion* in 1952, when to do so *anywhere* was purely *criminal,* unless to preserve the life of the mother. That was an arbitrary law open to interpretation and was vehemently challenged over the previous laws wherein abortion was only allowed in cases of rape, incest, if the mother was retarded, or her physical life were at stake, and finding a doctor who would perform one was difficult. Abortion had been legal and widespread in the 18th Century and was first criminalized in 1821. By 1967, abortion was classified a *criminal felony* in 49 states and Washington, D. C. I was so very surprised that she talked with me, so very openly, and me a stranger. She did not give me her age, but I could tell that she must be up in her years. To make a chiropractic visit for an abortion had to have been a last resort and certainly was in no way legal.

It was 1974 when Roe versus Wade had resulted in the decriminalization of abortion. It had barely been legal when I had my abortion in 1978, and I had thought it necessary to go to the big city to find an authorized doctor prepared to perform a legal, aseptically, relatively safe procedure. I had to marvel at the lady's courage to present to the local chiropractic for such. Those were definitely more difficult times. To my knowledge, The Good Doctor never went down on charges of "*criminal abortion*". I wanted to know more.

Most of those remaining phone numbers were out of service. The next few people I managed to get in touch with where not so very cordial. Some acknowledged who they were, but quickly denied they were the person whose name was in the ledger once I told them the purpose of my call. Some just hung up, others yelled at me that it was none of my business and I should never call their number again.

So very many that I was able to reach were evasive about their experience but were willing to state their position on the controversy of AMA (American Medical Association) versus ACA (American Chiropractic Association) debate, as well as the matter of pro-choice versus anti-abortion. I was tactful in my approach, but knew well that I was speaking on sensitive matters with most.

There were some, out of hundreds, who outright spoke praises of The Good Doctor Handley and had no reservations at all about telling me of the options of women in those times and how fortunate they themselves felt. "At least he was somewhat *medically aseptic*, about the procedure." Many of these women were quick to say that they vehemently supported a woman's right to choose a relatively safe procedure. Some had been single and some had been married at the time of their experience with Dr. Handley. Most were unwilling to elaborate on their personal stories.

I kept a notebook on their comments. Of the contacts that I had been able to make, the ones who had been able or willing to speak with me at the very least in sharing an opinion, they were split down the middle. About fifteen were opposed to abortion in any form, and about fifteen were in favor of a woman's right to choose.

In terms of dollars and cents, it appeared that The Good Doctor, on average, performed at least two to four abortions each day. While some of the home visits could have been legitimate chiropractic visits, I hardly believed so. He was seeing women from as far away as Atlanta, Franklin, Newnan, Columbus, Albany, Macon and Montgomery. On the women's home visits alone, if he was charging roughly $50.00 to $100.00 each visit, on the low end he was raking in $12,500.00, and on the high end $100,000.00 in **tax free** dollars each year, and that wasn't chump change back in the 50's and 60's. I imagined that the exact number fell somewhere in-between.

By comparison, in 1969, my dad had built our nice three bedroom brick home for $13,000.00 and earned, on average, $4000.00-$8,000.00 per year selling insurance depending on whether business was good or bad.

Business was obviously good for The Good Doctor in those days and *the pill*, with its convenience of use, did not arrive on the market until 1960, and few had access to it initially. The methods of contraception consisted of abstinence, the pull out method or rhythm methods, the sometimes painful and dangerous I.U.D.s, diaphragms with messy spermicidal creams and ointments, and the age old sheaths which also offered some protection against sexually transmitted disease. There were other cultures in the world where women stuffed their vaginas with unsanitary rags of silk and sponges, or worse, practiced infanticide.

In 1992, the Good Doctor had been long dead. So, I thought to look up his wife, whom I found to be living in the same home in which those "Home Visits" had been made.

Mrs. David G. Handley was most agreeable on the phone. She seemed overjoyed that someone was interested in her husband's work. I told her the same thing that I had told the others, "I am working on an assignment for Political Science class regarding the ongoing controversy surrounding chiropractic medicine." I did not mention abortion. Mrs. Handley told me how to get to her home and we established what time would be convenient for both of us. I was taking our daughter to her dressage lessons where she would be riding Sassy Lassie out at Big Bear Farms. That would give me a couple of hours to spend with Mrs. Handley. I was still in uniform from my job at Florence Hand Home, but I had no classes this afternoon.

I dropped my daughter off and went down Hwy. # 18 to the Whitesville Road, turned and looked for the red brick house that she had described. I saw it, just off the road, down a red dirt drive scattered with gravel. I was not sure that I was in the right place. The windows were boarded up as if no one lived inside. The house had a high roof with an attic and white gables.

As I pulled down the drive and around to the back, which was the only place to go, I saw an old gray barn in a clearing beyond the woods. The woods came nearly up to the house in the back. The barn was leaning to one side, as if it could topple over any second. The old corral around the barn had already rotted and could barely be defined, but there had most definitely been a corral. Beyond the barn, high on a hill back in the thickest part of the woods, I could see what remained of a small wooden house. There was only darkness where windows and doors once were. It was almost smothered in brambles.

The back of the red brick house was two stories, with the ground floor being earth bermed at its front. There was a rickety wooden stair to the second floor with a screened porch at its top. I did not wish to enter from the rear of the house, and it did not seem that I was getting any sort of welcome party, no dogs on the property, so I parked my car next to a green sedan that was parked in the drive and got out.

It had been raining earlier and was beginning to sprinkle rain again. I walked up the incline to a little sidewalk, stepped off and wiped the red clay from my shoes onto the grass, and continued up the little walk around to the front of the house. As I came around the house I heard music, something low, yet jazzy, with trumpet sounding. I noticed the rose gardens, long left untended, a mass of thorny stems. Two red buds were struggling to survive. Thunder rumbled and I thought poor Katherine would be shut up in the stables grooming horses or cleaning tack.

I thought it odd that a house so large and grand not have a grand porch. There wasn't even an awning to hold away the weather. Before I could knock, the door swung opened, "You must be Hannah, have to be, because we weren't expecting anyone else. Do come in."

"Good afternoon, yes I'm Hannah, Hannah Schmidt; I am a nurse and a nursing student. I'm sorry to bother you so very late in the afternoon, but I work days in LaGrange and take classes some evenings in Columbus."

"Oh, don't you worry, you are no bother. Schmidt, now," she went on to inquire, "That is a German name, isn't it?"

"It's a married name," I responded, not feeling it was necessary to give her my family name.

"So you married a kraut, well, then. We don't get much company, so we are rightfully glad to have you, aren't we Trudy?" She invited me in and asked why I wasn't wearing any coat, and I told her that I only had a white lab coat and did not want to get it dirty. After all, it was early summer, and nearly 80 degrees outside.

"Trudy, wake up," she snapped.

"You know it rains every day between 4 & 5 pm, you can just about set your clock by it," she remarked.

I nodded in Trudy's direction. Trudy was seated on a sofa in what appeared to be an old dining room converted into a den of sorts. There was an old television on the back wall and two sofas were arranged to face it at angles. A large round coffee table sat between them, littered with newspapers, tissues and bottles of creams and lotions. Trudy was a plump woman, with grey-blonde short hair and a ruddy complexion, about 60 years old, and seemed to be sleeping. She was dressed in a white polyester uniform with white shoes and support hose. Her pants rode high above her ankles. She didn't get up, but opened her eyes and smiled at me, leaning on her right arm.

The living room was to my left, as I faced the den, and was sparsely furnished in old period pieces, turn of the century stuff, not quite antique. There was an upright piano in the far left corner, and an old console stereo where the music was coming from. The one thing I noticed quite immediately was that the bamboo tile parquet ceiling was missing some tiles. It was a low dark ceiling, and made the rooms look smaller. It had sagging sections that appeared as if they might fall any time. The floor was covered in thick Asian rugs.

Mrs. Handley was a red-haired woman, though not much hair was left. Thin places were seen between tightly wound pin curls. She stooped so low that she had to turn her neck to look up at me. She was arthritic and twisted, with gnarled fingers. She had a broad smile with slightly bucked straight teeth, yellowed and trimmed in gold. She looked as if she had been a pretty woman in her prime, bright blue eyes and lean figure. Her step was spry. She wore a navy plaid dress with a white sweater sitting over her shoulders. There was a white full apron tied around her small waist. Her yellowed slip was hanging out from under her knee-length dress, and her shoes were flat with soft soles. There was something finished about her, yet askew.

She looked in Trudy's direction, "Trudy's not a real nurse, you know, she's only a sitter. She just sits, and that's all she does. Gets paid to sit, and to sleep. She has a night job, so she just sits and sleeps

because my doctor thinks I need a sitter...like a baby
sitter, only worse because she sleeps. I could be
dead back in the kitchen for hours and she wouldn't
know. Isn't that right, Trudy, humph?"

Trudy said nothing, and pretended she hadn't
been addressed.

"Probably sleeps on her night job too," Mrs. Handley
went on, as if she really expected no response from
Trudy, "You know you could offer our guest some tea,
you could, but she won't because all she does is sitting."

"I'll get it myself, of course I will, because you
can't get good help anymore, you just can't," she
continued, as she made her way to the back of the
house where the very large kitchen was located. I
followed.

She put the kettle on to boil and proceeded to
tell me all about the house. "The Good Doctor and
I, we built this place, designed it, and had it built
just like we wanted it. That's bamboo on the ceiling,
came all the way from the Philippines. And these
floors, this isn't pine, you know, it's mahogany. You
can't even get this anymore, all that rainforest pres-
ervation and such. We were one of the first couples in this area to build our house out of brick. I
know everybody does it now, the newer homes, but
nobody did it back then around here, no, just stick-
built houses with clapboard walls or some artificial
siding, back then. Yes, we bought the best red brick,

and these walls, no; they aren't stick built like today. Today, they throw up stick built walls and insulated siding and then slap the brick right over it. No, these walls are all poured concrete with steel reinforcement inside. I watched them put it up myself, we did. We were staying in the little house out back and I watched them build every inch of this house, and lay every brick. The Good Doctor, he had a colored boy move into that old place out back with his family. There's nobody, but the spirits, living out there now, though. Do you believe in spirits?"

"Yes well, sort of, I don't think I have really given it much thought but I do believe in a spiritual presence," I said.

"Well, you should."

The kettle had begun to boil and she set out three cups and saucers. She steadied her right hand with her left hand as she poured the hot water and set the saucers to steep the tea.

I asked, "What music is that playing on the stereo?"

"Oh that's Freddie Hubbard's album, 'Red Clay'. I think Negros play the best music. They always have. I'll turn it down a bit. Music is the best thing to keep bad angels away. I like the Big Bands too. I have a tremendous album collection, 45s, 33 1/3rds, goes way back to some 78s that my mother had. Tommie Dorsey, Glenn Miller, Benny Goodman, I liked it 'sweet' and 'hot'. Like Bean and Prez. We were swing dancers back in those days and man weren't we good. I was a little bitty thing and whipped right over the backs of my beaus back then. You can't see it now though, can you?" Her broad smile faded. She stepped into the den and went toward the living room to turn down the stereo.

Trudy stood up and stretched, and stacked some of the newspaper across the top of her head. "Well, Ms. Bea, since you have your own real nurse here today, I guess I'll head on back to the house."

Beatrice didn't respond to her with words. She looked in my direction and said, "She's supposed to stay until seven, but I put myself to bed." She walked to the living room door and that's when I saw all of the brass on the door. She opened the door wide and Trudy made her exit. Beatrice closed the door behind her and reached into her apron for a large ring of keys. She bolted three deadbolts and slid across three chains and one bar lock. "There," she announced, "We'll be safe enough in here now. I have to keep the fairy babies out, you know, they are everywhere when it rains. The rains spook them up out of the leaves in the woods and they come scratching at the windows and doors."

"Fairy babies," I asked, "are they sprits too?"

"Oh yes, of a sort. Real, they are, but possessed and much more annoying than most spirits. They aren't dangerous, just annoying. They do bite and sting when you swat at them. You hear their wings humming before you can see them, worse than mosquitoes, they are, and much bigger, too. They will buzz holes in the glass. That's why the windows are boarded, yes, to keep the fairy babies out. When they bite, I can feel it right down to my bones, I can."

I inquired, "Have you told your doctor about the fairy babies and bad spirits?"

"Oh yes, he knows, Dr. Baxter, he says it's just nerves and the rheumatism, but he's wrong. I can see them outright, with their insect-like tails and their gossamer wings. I believe that you have to possess a certain talent to be able to see them."

"Oh, I'm sure you do," I reflected.

She pushed a large side chest in front of the door, and I saw that all of the furniture in the rooms had wheels, no doubt, to make it easier for her to push it around. She pulled the piano out from the living room wall so that it covered the boarded up window, and stacked light furniture atop the stereo beneath the front window. When she seemed satisfied that her work was complete, she made her way back to the den and motioned for me to follow. Through the den we went, to the kitchen for the tea, and back to the den. She set her tea on the table with trembling hands so that the cup rattled on its saucer. We seated ourselves on the sofa.

She offered me sugar or cream, which I declined. She told me that she couldn't have sugar in her tea because her pancreas was failing her. That's what Doctor Baxter had said.

"It's quite a fortress you have here," I remarked.

"Oh, it's all necessary. Dr. Baxter prescribed a tranquilizer that he said would keep them away, but it didn't, so I don't take it anymore. He gives me pills for everything, pills for the rheumatism, two pills for my blood pressure, a potassium pill, and a water pill, a pill to slow and strengthen my heart, why he throws a new pill at me every year. He thinks a pill should be able to ward off spirits and fairy babies. I think he thinks I ought to be in a home, you know. A home where they sit in wheelchairs all day and drool on themselves, and church people come in to sing hymns of salvation and gospel music is all you ever get to listen to, because they all think you're on the way to see Jesus. They come to sing because they are more worried about their souls than yours, they are, you know."

"No doubt," I returned, half laughing. She was amusing in her own way. "Have you ever had any, well, any mental treatment, besides Dr. Baxter's pills?"

"Oh, it's funny that you ask me that! When I was a young girl, about nineteen, that was back in 1935, or so, so very long ago, my mother was carrying on

behind my father's back. He was a military man
and gone most of the time, and my mother had all
sorts of affairs. He fought in the First World War.
They, my parents, had met in Europe during that
war. That's probably when I was conceived. Well by
the time I was just about grown, I was old enough
to know what was going on back then, yes, she was
out all night with men, married or not, having her
affairs. Some women were driving automobiles by
then, you know, and she would be gone for days.
Not that I wasn't old enough to stay by myself, but it
just wasn't proper. And I knew what she was doing
and threatened to tell my papa in a letter if she
didn't stop it. We got into a real fight, my mama
and me. She drove me all the way to Milledgeville
tied up like a wrangled bull; she did, in the back seat
of our 1932 Ford Model B, the same motor car she
carried her men-folk around in. It was the very one
papa had bought when he was home on leave, so
she could get around after he left again. He trusted
her. They weren't poor you know, and her family,
the Mercers, they had money too. So she decided
to leave me there at Milledgeville with orders that
I wasn't to be allowed to write to anyone. It wasn't
on account that I was a lunatic or insane, she just
didn't want me around anymore, I know that. They
only kept me there four days and sent her a wire that
she was to come get me, but she didn't. I hitched a

ride to my grandmother's home near Savannah on a sweet potato truck. I did that very thing, and stayed with my grandmother on my mother's side until I met my husband. Oh yes, you are here to hear about him, not me, enough about me."

"I understand that your husband had both a home office and an office downtown in LaGrange," I moved along.

"Yes he did, he was such a good man, and a hardworking man. He would be at the office downtown by seven in the morning, come home, and work until as late as ten or eleven at night. He died twenty years ago this spring, at only 58, massive stroke they said. He was a hardworking man, yes he was. He helped a lot of folks. You know mill work is hard work. During and after WWII, women had started working in those mills. Sometimes they showed up just crying in pain, I know they were. By the time they left, they were just fine. I tell you he could make an adjustment and then we wouldn't see them for a very long time, sometimes never. All they needed was one adjustment. That's how chiropractic is, no long treatments with pills and chemicals, just a few adjustments. Now, sometimes they required major adjustments and I would hear them just cry out, but they were better when he was done. He was real good. He had men who had tried every doctor in town and then some, without any success in relieving their pain, and The Good Doctor, that's what they called him, he would see them a few times and there wasn't any more pain. That's what people called him, The Good Doctor. He even got to where he was calling himself The Good Doctor."

I supposed, "His work was quite valuable then?"

"Of course it was, but sometimes, folk didn't have any money to pay so he took his pay on barter for just about anything. He was a good provider that man. The best. Even before we were married, he let the military hold onto his pay until he got out of the service so he would have some kind of future. That's the money we bought this land on. He hardly ever reported to the paymaster. He joined the Army at 18 years of age in 1932. He and his father had some sort of disagreement and his father disowned him, but that's okay. He did well on his own and stayed in the Army for twelve years. Combat Medic he was in the war, but I don't think that's how he started. Said he couldn't be a pencil pusher when guys were dying in the fields.

We met when he was in Savannah. I was working at a foundry there during the War, in the office. I could type real well. These old hands aren't as nice as they once were. Most of the girls worked for the Southeastern Shipyard, but I carried important papers to the shipping clerks and that's how we met. I never knew exactly what he was doing there but he was around for three months, always in uniform. He looked so sharp in his uniform. But then, he reenlisted for another three years to get a 5% increase in pay. That was March 1942, when he shipped out again. He was all hush, hush and secrets, a real mysterious character. He got both longevity pay and Foreign Service pay. I know that much. He had already been to Japan. He knew every muscle, ligament and bone by its Latin name, spoke French too, so that's where he went next, to France.

In April of 1945, he was about to reenlist and I just wouldn't have it. We had been corresponding by mail, and he had been promoted many times after the War started, but I was so in love. I just didn't want him to become a casualty of that war. So he got out. Felt like a traitor almost, he did, but he loved me too. I don't think he thought I would wait for him much longer."

I encouraged her to continue, "So, he bought this place and you got married?"

"Well, we got married first in Savannah in 1945. I was 29 and he was 31. By then, the war was coming to an end and the factories and ship building and all in Savannah was slowing down. He worked there for a shipping company in medical supplies, for about a year in exports. We had this money saved up, mine and his, and he thought he could try his hand at farming. A friend of his at Ft. Benning told him about this place and we came over and built this house.

He raised some cows, and pigs, but he studied his books all the time. Had a mule and a plow, and he tried to grow a garden, but we ended up buying most of our produce from the peddler. Old man use to come by here with a horse and cart. He made his rounds to all the farms. This old red clay ain't good for farming unless you feed it. The Good Doctor didn't take to farming like he thought he might.

He was a real scientist, always studying. Got his Chiropractic through the mail in 1950, just like we use to develop all our pictures through the mail. We would send in the film and the Jackrabbit Co. would send back our photographs. Sent his Authorization of Completion of Course of Study just one year after he started. I did all of his correspondences too. Opened his offices in 1951, both of them. Started off doing well. Would you like to see his office?"

"Yes, I very much would. Thank you," I agreed.

"Hope you're not squeamish, there are things down there," she muttered, "but no, you're a nurse, I guess you've just about seen it all."

We got up and she led the way through the kitchen, "You don't mind if I feed the cats first, do you?"

She busied herself pulling out bags of cold biscuits, and obtained from the cupboard a great bowl of cold gravy, which she mashed together into two large roasting pans that she had retrieved from beneath the table.

She tossed in two handfuls of dry cat food. "Trudy usually does this, but I like to get the cats up to the house whenever I have to go down to the basement." She wiped her hands on her apron.

"We don't have to, if you'd rather not," I offered to withdraw my agreement.

"Oh no, I'm fine with it. There's a door to the basement from the outside downstairs, but it's all boarded up, so we have to go out on the porch anyway." She picked up one pan and I took the other. We walked out onto the screened back porch. The rain had stopped, but the stairs were wet. "Set these pans there at the bottom of the stairs." And she called at the top of her voice, "Here kitty, kitty, kitty, here kitty, kitty!"

I took the two pans and went down the stairs. Within seconds, two dozen or more cats, some with suckling kittens trailing behind them, came running to devour their dinner.

I made my way back up the stairs where Mrs. Handley was fidgeting with her large ring of keys. She dropped it.

"Let me get that for you Mrs. Handley, just show me which key," I bent to pick up the keys.

"It's Ms. Bea, everybody calls me Ms. Bea. That's Bea, for Beatrice. You don't have to call me Mrs. Handley. I hardly know what to make of that, now you just take this key right here and jiggle it a little to the left."

The deadbolt clacked and the door was opened. Ms. Bea switched on the light over the stairs and we descended the inside stairs from the porch to the basement. "I've left it just as he left it. Haven't touched a thing, no I wouldn't. It's just as it was in 1972 when he died, God rest his soul. Just come down here now and again to change a light bulb. I keep it lit all the time, except for these stairs here, you know, because… "

"…Because of the fairy babies, yes, I know," I finished her sentence.

"Yes, and dark angels, they won't come into a lighted room, you know," she added.

The first room was a dark wood paneled office, not unlike any businessman might have in his home. A desk, file cabinets, a lamp, a few chairs, comfortable chairs. The lamp was on and the room was unremarkable, except for two model planes on the desk and a fridge behind the desk chair.

Then, we passed into the next, most institutional looking room with bright florescent light. An exam table of yellow porcelain covered steel was the glaring centerpiece of this room, and I could not help but notice the stirrups that were still in place. The walls were industrial green, and a microscope sat on the counter. There were trays of large and small pieces of chrome and surgical steel tools and blades, instruments of all sizes strewn about the countertop;

duck-bill speculums, curettes, and forceps. There were curved and pointed instruments, some looking very sharp. There was also some large machine with a fan and rubber fittings. I didn't quite know what to make of it, but it was pulled close to the table. I wondered if Ms. Bea had ever given a thought to the strangeness of the devices and instruments. I did not see one device that would appear to be a massager or an exercise gadget of any sort. There was an ominous sense of foreboding in this room.

We passed into yet another room, again with industrial green walls. There were shelves and shelves of books on anatomy and physiology, stacks of magazines, "Chiropractic Economics", and others. The room was dusty and cobwebs clung to the shelves. Then I saw them, a vast collection of bottled contents. Big pickle jars and quart jars. They held a fetal calf, fetal pigs, and all manner of animals at all stages of development. One small jar was most certainly human. I reached to pick it up.

"I'm certain that one is a fairy baby." Ms. Bea started, "I don't know where he found it. He never told me about it, but I'm sure that's what it is. It hasn't yet developed its wings and I'm not exactly sure if they are hatched or born, but that's definitely what this is, a fairy baby. I can tell from its insect like tail. He must have caught one and was trying to identify it. That's what he did down here for hours, you know, when he didn't have patients, he would sit and study these things. I would send them to the college for other students to study. I have no use for them, of course. Do you know somebody, maybe, that could put them to use? I'm afraid I might break them if I did anything at all with them, you know, with these hands. They're all filled with formaldehyde; I'd sure hate to break one."

"Ms. Bea, I'll ask, but I really don't think so, it's all old and murky, maybe, I'll ask Dr. Birkhead, if he's interested. He comes out to our farm sometimes to tag snakes."

"Woo snakes," she shuddered, "I don't like snakes either. Yes, well let us go upstairs and I'll show you my trunk in the attic. I have a whole collection of memories in that trunk."

"Yes, let's do that," I answered, eager to get out of this morbid hole. There was a stench to it. It reeked of chemicals and pain. There was a profound sense of sadistic doom in these rooms.

On ascending the stairs I asked, "Ms. Bea, did you have any children, you and The Good Doctor?"

"Oh yes, we had two, two boys, almost right away. "One in '46' and one in '48', but we weren't close. Never really were and aren't today. They would lock me away somewhere if I let them. I know they would. That's why I have accountants and attorneys to deal with all of my business. They are both big shot lawyers now. One in Thomasville, and well, I don't rightly know where the other one is, they've been gone from here so long. I didn't raise them really. Eula Mae did most of the raising, until they went off to boarding school. She was our handyman's wife, a high yellow, young thing when she came here in '46'; she wasn't 32 years old but already had a boy 18. Grown, he was, and tall; handsome, you know, for a colored boy, and smart. Eula Mae was smart too. She had a girl also, about 8 years old; don't know what became of her. Girl, Althea, left here to go live with relatives somewhere up north at about 16 years old. She wasn't no count anyway, lazy girl. I never had a daughter; my heart aches sometimes, because I never had one. Now Eula Mae, she wasn't lazy. She cooked and cleaned; saw after my boys. Now her son, Nathaniel, The Good Doctor took an immediate liking to that one. You know he was grown, didn't have to come here with his paw, but he did, and he helped him on the farm those few years, but he was real smart. As a child, he was educated in Atlanta, so The Good Doctor, you know what he did? When the money got real good, he paid for his education to go all the way to Howard University in Washington, D.C., that's what he did. I'm telling you, my David was a good man."

Ms. Bea was wheezing after climbing those stairs and about to climb yet another set, and fumbling again in her apron for her keys to the attic door. I asked, "Would you like to rest and we'll do this on another day?"

But she was having none of it, and had found the key to the attic. She told me that she had kept these two rooms in the attic for her sons when they came home to visit on holidays, but she would also come up here sometimes just to think. She said that they had not been home for the holidays since they were just boys, and she wasn't certain whether or not she had any grandchildren and wouldn't know what to do with them if she did. Reflecting over such things, there was sadness in her eyes. She was lonely. She seemed to be so much older than her 76 years. Her husband had been everything to her. For the past twenty years it had just been her, some "sitter", and her own soul.

Her wheezing was absolutely atrocious. I begged her off of ascending the long stairwell in her condition. There were no rails to hold onto, and while she insisted that she could hold well to the walls because it was so very narrow, I likewise insisted that I really needed to leave to go pick up my daughter. I had seen enough for one day.

"I really do have to go now," I pleaded.

"Well then, you come back another day," she relinquished.

She saw me to the door and assured me that she always put herself to bed after supper. She would be, "Just Fine."

I promised her that I would return. I heard her fasten the locks behind me, and the furniture rolling in front of the door. Back down the drive to my car I went, wondering if she would be; "Just fine."

As I drove back to Big Bear Farm, I thought about this old lady living alone and how her life must be. Suffering as she does with nerve and joint pains, no doubt, which she perceives as bites and stings from fairy babies and dark angels. For twenty years after her husband's death she has fastened herself up against her haunting. That she is plagued by a fixed delusion and perhaps has some hallucinatory content is obvious, but she is not demented in any way. She is nostalgic, fully aware and functional. She has her wits about her. She adored her husband, but something affected her in a sinister way. Something she could not speak of, not even to herself. Something she has suppressed deep within her own soul. I could not mention the ledger.

2

Ms. Bea

Several days later, as promised, I went to the home of The Good Doctor and Ms. Bea. Trudy's car was nowhere to be seen, and I knocked hard on the door with a rock calling out for Trudy or Ms. Bea, but there was no answer. I would have feared that the old lady was trapped inside, somehow injured or sick, if it weren't for the daily visits of Trudy. Surely if something had happened, Trudy would have seen to her.

I returned several times, and one Saturday, in my jeans and t-shirt, decided that I would explore the old place. The house was locked up as tight as I had expected. I made my way through the stand of woods between the house and the clearing. There was no orchard, but a plum tree hung thick with green bitter fruit in front of the old abandoned house. There were boxes for laying hens mounted to the exterior walls. There was a stump with an old rusted axe still wedged into its surface just beside the steps.

With no door to block me, I made my way up the steps and entered the front room. It was bright with sunlight from the open windows that had no glass panes, and briars were growing in to invade its interior. Sunlight also filtered in through the floorboards, as there were no rugs of any sort. An old stone hearth and a fireplace that was filled with ash took up the south wall. The chimney rocks were crumbling to join the ashes. There was no furniture except for an old recliner in front of the fireplace. Rats or mice had made nests in the chair and the stuffing was scattered about on the floor in little cotton piles. It was only two rooms, but they were quite large. No kitchen and no running water, but an old cast iron cook top wood-burning stove sat in the far north corner of the front room. The spring-handle was still in a feed plate over one grate. A large sink, which drained directly to the ground below, sat next to this stove, and a wood box sat next to it. I was reminded of my own grandmother's wood stove. She never would let them take that old thing out, even after she had an electric stove. She continued to make her breakfasts and biscuits on that old thing. I turned around to examine the room and saw that a cord for electric light hung from the center of the room with a multifaceted plug-in between bulb and fixture. As I scanned the room, my attention was drawn to a small cross that hung on the wall. It was most intricately carved of cedar, and had been whittled along its edges to form scalloped ridges. Though roughly cut, it was polished, perhaps by loving hands. There was also a wooden wall-hanging next to the cross. It was a lacquered picture, a decoupage, of the Guardian Angel hovering over two small children who were precariously leaning out over the edge of a suspended bridge. I left the picture as it was, but took down the little cross. It did not seem right for the cross to be abandoned in that way.

I walked through the threshold to the next room. There was an old iron framed bed with mattress and springs against the west wall, and two smaller beds with mattresses along the east wall. Sunlight shone across the big bed and the vermin had obviously found refuge in this bed, as it was covered in pellets. Sunlight also filled the room from the north wall window. There were no closets, and no other furniture. Two cans from Vienna sausages lay in the floor, along with a soda can and an old cracker box, its contents long since eaten by mice or man.

With nothing else to see, I went back to the front room. It seemed that it was a lonely place and I thought of what it must have been like for the "colored boy", his wife, Eula Mae, and their two children when they first came here. I wondered what they must have left behind to find this place remotely hospitable. There was a breeze coming in from the front door and I turned back to face the back room before making my exit. For a second, I thought I saw a black girl, a teenager in a white slip, standing in the threshold with her arms folded across her chest and a defiant look on her face. I thought I heard singing. But no, I looked again and saw only a play in the shadows from the light and heard the wind from the breezes strumming across the empty window panes.

I held the small cross in my hand and heard the wind move the old leaning barn. It creaked and swayed as I went back to my car. The wind was picking up and clouds were beginning to roll in. It was about to be storming by the time I reached my own home. The early summer storms came up fast and furious. It was hot, and the humidity hung thick in the air. I placed the wooden cross into the glove box. Lightning flashed and thunder cracked. The bottom fell out and the rains came pouring as I reached our front door, and I was glad that I had not stayed any longer at the home of Ms. Bea and The Good Doctor.

Sunday came and went and Monday morning I was at work by 6:30 am. West Georgia Medical Center was a newly constructed six -story building attached to the front of the old City-County Hospital. The operating suites, critical care and surgical intensive

care units were in the old building. This old building was attached to the newly built Florence Hand
Home, where I was assigned after graduation. I had
worked in the new building, in the hospital section
as an L.P.N., but had only worked in the extended
care unit since graduation from R.N. school. I was
assigned to the south hall that was attached to the
hospital by a breezeway. This breezeway, as well as the
dayroom area, had floor to ceiling windows of glass
that looked out over the gardens that the Callaway
Foundation had planted. Sometimes, you could see
rabbits around the gazebo, or birds gathered at the
feeders. Lovely flowers bloomed almost year round.

Finishing up my 2 pm med pass, I was about to
move my med cart when the automatic doors to the
breezeway opened. I was scarcely paying attention.
I stepped into the last room on my list. A young man
was wheeling a wheelchair through the breezeway
door and past my cart. The occupant of the wheelchair was screaming at the top of her lungs, "Turn
this thing around. I'm not crazy. I'm not going to
stay here, I'll tell you that!"

The young man attempted to console her, "This
is only temporary; Dr. Baxter told you that, I was
right there."

The woman continued to yell, "Oh go to hell!
You're a liar just like he is, Dr. Baxter my ass, why I'm
younger than he is, you know that don't you?"

When the young man reached the nurse's station and parked the wheelchair, I saw the red hair. It was definitely Ms. Bea, and she wasn't at all happy about her predicament. A nursing assistant passed by the station, "Nurse! Nurse! Come here and make this man release me. He's got my hands tied. I'm being held against my will, I say come here girl!"

I made my way to the station with my cart and another nurse appeared at the station, "Lucky you," she said, "I've got west hall today and it looks like I'm not going home anytime soon."

"Ms. Bea. Why don't you let these nice ladies help you to your room?" I tried to plea, "They need to help you get settled. I've been worried about you."

"Why Hannah, I was wondering where you might possibly be," she said, as she turned in my direction.

Looking down, I saw that her wrists were restrained and she had a bleeding skin tear on her right forearm. "Look here, you're bleeding; let's fix this up, shall we?" I took her hand in mine. I asked the west hall nurse, "What room is she going to?" I released the restraint on her right wrist.

Beatrice continued to wail, "I'm not about to go to any room. Look here, they are holding me against my will. I didn't agree to this, they are crazy, all of them, I'm not the crazy one. They have me bound like some sort of lunatic, they do. I'll not stand for this!"

She had started to cry and I handed her a tissue, doused her wound with saline and covered it with a piece of sterile gauze, "Let them take you to a room and I'll come right away with a bandage for this, no need to cry now."

She calmed, at least for a little while, and the nursing assistant wheeled her down to her room. When I came to the room she was engaged in an argument with the nurse's aide, "You absolutely must cover that window, the fairy babies can get in here."

"Look, this glass doesn't even open, it's locked. You're on the second floor. Nobody can get in from up here," the aide calmly explained.

Beatrice shouted, "Don't you know that fairies have wings?"

I motioned for the aide to leave the room. I untied the remainder of her restraints and attended to her skin tear. When that was done, I helped her up and to bed. I encouraged her to process. "Why don't you tell me what happened, Ms. Bea?"

"Hannah, sweet one, they came to me in the night, after Trudy was gone, the fairy babies were biting me all over and stinging me about my legs and arms. I had fallen asleep with my glasses on, the ones with the cord around my neck, and the dark angel was trying to choke me with it. I couldn't breathe. I tell you, if I didn't have a phone by my bed, I'd be with that dark angel now."

"So you called for help?" I added, "That's a good thing,"

"I don't know what I did, next thing I know all these men were around and there were needles and everybody pushing and pulling. They put me on a gurney and wheeled me out of my house and then they brought me here all tied up. They kept me tied up in a room for days. They wouldn't even let me go to the bathroom, said I had a tube in my bladder. Then Dr. Baxter comes in all puffed up and said I had to come here. I know what this is, it's a Nursing Home. They call it 'an extended care facility'. They planned it that way, telling me I had to change rooms again, like I'm some stupid child. I knew they were bringing me here, and I won't stand for it. Dr. Baxter said only for a little while, but I know they will try to keep me here until I die. I know they will. It happens all the time, Hannah, they trick people like that, telling them, 'Only for a little while,' next thing you know, they're shriveled up and force fed, while somebody eats up their money. That's what happens, Hannah. You have to help me."

"Well now, you see this cord right here. Push the little button on the end, it's soft like a little pillow, just squeeze it there. It calls the nurse's aide to come and take you to the bathroom. Can you push it? Try it, and see if you can use it. We don't want you to get up and fall and break a hip, now, do we? You'll be here much longer if that happens."

She gave a return demonstration in the use of the call system and I felt comfortable leaving her unrestrained. "You'll have to promise to do this for me, Ms. Bea, so they will leave the restraints off."

She was agreeable and seemed to be settling in fairly well. I placed the phone within her reach also. "Ms. Bea, I have to go, I have class in Columbus this afternoon, but I will be back tomorrow and I'll look in on you when I come to work."

"Hannah, would you do this one thing for me, please child? Would you take that set of keys there in the bag, take them and go by my house? There is an address book in my little night stand by my bed. There is a key here for the front door, and another here for my room downstairs. I need that address book. I tried to get Trudy to do it for me but she wouldn't. She's in with them, I know. I don't think she wants her job with me anymore. She's useless anyway. I should fire her."

I agreed to stop by her house to get her address book. I also told her that I had been by her house many times and didn't know what to make of her absence. I was glad to know that she was safe. I told her that I had taken the cross from the front room of the old house.

"You keep that. Crosses don't really work for warding off evil spirits. I have no use for it."

I graciously thanked her, and left for the day, knowing that I would have to hurry to be able to stop by her house on the way to Columbus. I couldn't pick up I-185 until I passed the crossroads to Hwy #18, if I was going to have to go down the Whitesville Road for such a long ways.

I stopped at her home and let myself inside. I unlocked the door to her room, and found the address book in her night stand. The bed was unmade. The furniture was all askew. I saw a photograph on her dresser. Mr. and Mrs. David G. Handley newly married. She was pretty in a flowing gown and he was handsome in his dress uniform. It looked like a grand palace around them. There was another photo of two little boys, her sons no doubt, splashing in a #3 wash tub in the back yard. They were fond memories for her.

As I was backing out of the front door, Trudy pulled up. "Just came to feed the cats," she called through her car window.

"I came, at Ms. Bea's request, to get her address book," I returned.

"You know, her son doesn't want her to stay here anymore," she called back.

"Well, that just might not be his prerogative," I concluded.

I went on to class and took the address book with me to work the next day. In report, I learned that Ms. Bea had been quite a character throughout the night and nobody could get her to stay in her room for more than fifteen minutes. She had screamed all night about fairy babies, wood sprites and evil angels. She refused to allow them to turn off the lights, and claimed she was being bitten and stabbed by creatures that no one else could see.

Mary Anne Monroe, the Director of Nursing, was the best. She was always willing to come onto the floor to help out when needed despite her many responsibilities. She asked me if I would be willing to change my assignment to the west hall. I flatly refused. Mary Anne said that she noticed I had a calming effect on Ms. Bea and she wanted me to have her on my assignment. Again, I flatly refused. Pushed, I had to tell her of my political science assignment and that I knew Ms. Bea and had been interviewing her about her husband, the chiropractic. It was a controversial topic regarding whether or not Chiropractic Medicine was a legitimate practice. Mary Anne agreed that I should not be assigned to her, but asked if I would be willing to help if needed.

After report, I took the address book to Ms. Bea. She was very grateful and told me all about her bad night, and how she would not spend another night in that place. She asked me to write down the name of the place she was at and the address, phone number and D.O.N.'s name along with her own room number, which I did, then left her alone and went about my assignment.

About noon, we were preparing to take patients downstairs to the main dining hall. I noticed a large group of men dressed in suits and a lady dressed in a skirt and blazer came walking out of Ms. Bea's room. They carried brief cases and notepads. I asked Mary Anne what was going on. She told me that she couldn't talk about it right then and that Dr. Baxter was on his way over. She asked me to show him downstairs to the administrative office whenever he arrived. Dr. Baxter came within minutes and I took him down the elevator to Mary Anne's office, where this large group of people had gathered in the big conference room.

In a short while, the group left. I was sitting in the dining hall with my coworkers having lunch. A taxi cab drove up under the portico. Ms. Bea walked over and the driver got out and opened the door for her. He took her light bag and tossed it into the cab and drove away, as simple as that. Ms. Bea was on her way home. Mary Anne later told me that Ms. Bea had left AMA, Against Medical Advice. She wasn't spending another night in that place, and I didn't blame her.

The next day after work, I skipped class to go by and check on Ms. Bea. I found Trudy remarkably alert and up dusting the furniture, while Ms. Bea had her feet elevated on pillows atop the coffee table in the den. Trudy had let me in without as much as a greeting. She motioned to the den where I found Ms. Bea in good spirits.

She went over her ordeal again with me. She told me how she had called her attorneys and had that matter taken care of in a flash. She thanked me again for bringing her address book. I had brought sugar free cookies with me and she went to get up to start the kettle to boil. I made her stay put and did this little chore myself, setting the tea to steep on the coffee table before us.

Ms. Bea recalled that we were about to go upstairs when I had to leave from my first visit with her. She asked me who my father was and I told her, Henry Hamilton. She said that she knew him, or of him, and that her husband had purchased a life insurance policy from him years ago, and she was mighty thankful that he did; well of course, The Good Doctor took care of her.

She went on to tell me that he had always taken good care of her, dead or alive, and she had assets, they called them, which would continue to grow for as long as she lived. She didn't understand all of that talk about stocks and annuities, but she knew that the house and land were paid for, the bills were paid, she had a credit card for expenses and plenty of cash, and the taxes were paid every year from her funds.

Speaking of taxes brought to her mind a tragic time in her husband's life. She said, "That's when he really did suffer, The Good Doctor, when the revenuers came around to hound him. You would have thought he was running moonshine stills, the way that they hounded him, and him not even a drinker. I have all of those newspaper clippings upstairs, everything about it. You know, it was quite a scandal it was, them trying to make him out to be some terrible monster when he was so set on helping folks anyway that he could. Let us go upstairs and I'll show you."

"Are you sure that you are up to it?" I did not want her emotionally stressed nor did I want her physically stressed from climbing the stairs. Her ankles appeared swollen.

"Oh, of course I am, and it's what I want to do." And we already knew that Ms. Bea did what she wanted to do.

Trudy threw her the set of keys and made a comment to that effect, and Ms. Bea was leading the way again. She unlocked the attic door and switched the stairwell light on. All the while she was talking. It was a narrow passage and had no handrail to hold onto, but she held to the walls as we ascended. At the top of the landing there was a door to the right and a door to the left, and a half bath in front of us. She took the door to the left. The room was well lit with an overhead light and two lamps.

Attempting to turn the subject away from tax issues I asked about Savannah and told her that I had seen her wedding picture on her dresser.

"The greater Savannah community was greatly involved in wartime production, through the conversion of the Port of Savannah into a military cargo port. Goods were shipped out of that port all over the world, and the officers were frequently seen along the waterfront. They were building ships, and port security was a top concern. Germans in submarines were sinking ships along the Atlantic Coast, sunk 70 of them in March of 1942. I was working at The Savannah Machine and Foundry Company when I met The Good Doctor around Christmas of 1941. He wasn't a doctor then, and I never knew rightly why he was there. I was just glad that he was. We received the Army-Navy "E" award for excellence in defense production at the Foundry. Now we, The Good Doctor and myself, often took lunch together on the town green. He gave me a gold locket with his picture in it for Valentine's Day, and I gave him a gold watch with my picture in it. We sometimes went to Tybee Island, just to get away from the War. There was a road back before Highway 80. We weren't supposed to travel it, but he didn't care, if he wanted to do something, he just went out and did it. It was all swamp and marsh back then on either side of the road. Then, when we reached the beach he would tease me that he had spotted submarines. I was most impressionable and genuinely frightened that the Germans might invade our port city. There were always museums and galleries to wander in Savannah. We had a nice time, and I'm glad that he wasn't a boozer like many men were at that time, drinking away their sorrows of war and loss. We were married August 5th, 1945. We had a church wedding because my grandmother insisted. Neither one of us was particular about the church. It was a grand church, a cathedral, with twin spires over 200 feet high, The Cathedral of Saint John the Baptist. Probably the only Catholic Church in Georgia at that time, unless you went to Atlanta and that would be hard to do every Sunday morning, wouldn't it? Have you ever been to Savannah? If not, you really should go just to see the grand churches and homes."

By now she had pulled from the closet a great dusty trunk, and was setting its contents onto the bed. "These are his medals and ribbons and things," she said, as she opened display case after display case. "This one here is really special, it's a Purple Heart…

and here are his bronze Oak Leaf Clusters, two of them. He had a limp, because of those wounds. Shrapnel was lodged in his back, and he had been shot in the leg above the knee once and again below the knee on the same leg. I just knew he wasn't coming home to me. Oh yes, and the letters, tons of letters, just see, this one is postmarked from France, Air Delivery."

Ms. Bea reached into her apron for her glasses and put them on. She began pulling out old envelopes and reading their content aloud. There was mention of his loyalty and his yearning to be near to her. She read like a schoolgirl all blushed and excited. He said that he would feel like a deserter to leave his men for home. Some letters were sad, when he spoke of the conditions of the men in his charge and in his care. He did not find it beneath him to cry or to hold a dying man in his arms. He was a young man, but he was wise beyond his years, and most mature.

"These are all very personal, Ms. Bea," I interjected.

"Yes well, let me set them aside." She piled the letters onto the bed. Then she brought out a cardboard box. She lifted the lid. Inside was a large stack of newspaper articles. Some disintegrated at her touch. They were yellowed and frayed. Some looked very old and some not so very old.

"He was such a romantic, all of his life, and took me on a Trans-Atlantic voyage in 1971, the year before he died. He was 57, and I was already an old lady at 55, but we toured Paris in springtime and took trains all over the country side where he told me all about his life in the War."

As I waited for her to rummage through the articles to find the ones of her interest, I noticed the plaques on the wall. There was a framed certificate from the National Chiropractic Association, and another from The Foundation for Accredited Chiropractic Education, and another from The Palmer College of Chiropractic. Then she brought up the first article that she intended to show me.

The article was dated 1952. "Here he is, shaking the hand of Mr. B.J. Palmer himself. That's me in my hat and gloves beside him there, all of the ladies wore hats and gloves back then. B.J. was the son of D.D. Palmer the founder of Chiropractic. He took over his father's schools. D.D. Palmer's theories revolved around the fact that the spine held the spinal cord and thus, the communication to all of the body was by way of the spine. He studied and taught magnetic healing and spinal adjustment to cure a variety of ailments, and he studied spiritual healing of the intellect. He knew that just about any ailment had to do with the nerves, because they were the pathways that carried sensations. He actually cured a man's deafness by adjusting his spine. In 1906, they threw him in jail for practicing medicine without a license. Well his son, Mr. B.J. Palmer studied under his father and went abroad to study also. They didn't always agree, and D.D. Palmer had set up schools of learning all over the west. These were all consolidated under one School of Chiropractic, a term he coined from Greek language. Now some people thought B.J. ran over his father with an automobile and killed him. But I think he died in Los Angeles of natural causes."

"We got to know B.J. real well over the years. I just never could see him doing anything to cause harm to another person, let alone his own father. We went to his home on St. Armands Key in Sarasota, Florida, many times. His wife, Mabel Heath, died in 1949, of a stroke, same as The Good Doctor in 1972, but that was before we met B.J. so we didn't know her. B.J. bought that home on St. Armands Key in 1951. It was a real pretty place and we traveled all over Florida back then too because that was the thing to do. Air-conditioning was new and there were resorts and springs everywhere, so we went to visit with B.J. every chance that we could. This picture was taken in Memphis when we went to a convention there.

We were all over the states at conventions and awards ceremonies. B.J. died in May of 1961, of cancer of the bowels. A good number of folk thought

chiropractic was quackery, but I know different.
I know The Good Doctor, B. J., and others that
studied like them, hundreds of them, they helped
people. The AMA was all up in arms because they
wanted all of the action. That's why they sent the
revenuers down here, claiming my husband wasn't
paying the government enough, and him an Army
man. It was a disgrace." She held up a newer article
dated 1967.

"This one tells the whole story. I can't read it,
you read it if you like," she said, wiping her glasses
with a tissue, and then wiping her eyes. "He was not
the only chiropractor in the area, but he was certainly the best, no matter what anyone had to say."

"I'm afraid I'm upsetting you, Ms. Bea, we don't
have to read anymore," I said, as I pushed the box aside.

"No you go ahead, and I'll just show you the rest
of this stuff," she replied, reaching into the trunk to
pull out a clown. It was a novelty. A clown was holding his stethoscope to a man's knee as he sat on an
exam table, bewildered.

"Not this, this was a gift from B.J, he loved clowns
and had quite a collection. I always thought them
scary and a bit disturbing. Now this," she went on, as
she pulled out a trophy, a glass torch. "This is something special. I ought to take it out of here and put
it downstairs. This was an achievement award The

Good Doctor received in 1964. This was before all
that scandal."

"It's very beautiful, and I think you should display it somewhere," I said, half observing her actions.
She placed the trophy on the chest of drawers.

I read several of the articles that she had in her
collection, and made many notes while she went
about explaining this nick-knack or that, souvenirs
she had collected over the years.

"I'm done here Ms. Bea," I somberly stated.

"Yes, well, I am too. You make your way downstairs and I'll be along in a minute. I need to stop
by the lavatory."

I put the articles into their cardboard box and
set it back into the trunk. Ms. Bea had replaced all
of the display cases, the clown, and the piles of letters in envelopes. I set the trunk back into its place
inside of the closet and closed the door.

When I got downstairs, Trudy says to me, "You
best be going now. I have called her son and he says
that you are to leave right away and not come back
here. He says if you do, I'm to call the sheriff and
have you arrested for trespass."

I heard the toilet flush upstairs and the sound of
Ms. Bea coming down the stairs. I was standing by
the front door when she came around to the living
room. She asked, "You will come back, won't you?"

"I will," I said tossing a glance in Trudy's direction. "But I am awful busy with school and work and family. It might be awhile."

"Well, that's just fine dear," and she reached to hug my neck.

Several months passed when I learned that Ms. Bea had passed away in her sleep. One of the nurses said that her housekeeper had found her dead in her bed. The housekeeper, apparently Trudy, went to her church. She said that Ms. Bea had an exacerbation of congestive heart failure and had refused to go to the hospital and her son told the housekeeper not to make her go.

The fairy babies had stung her and bit her and the dark angel had finally suffocated her to death. She was at peace.

One of the nursing assistants who overheard the conversation called me aside. She said that I needed to talk with a man she knew of at her other job. She told me that he knew, "All of the secrets of those people."

My curiosity was peaked. I asked her, "What secrets?"

"You know! Why she was so crazy, he knows all about it. You should talk to him, that man, he loves to talk." She handed me a name scrawled on a piece of paper. "Moses Grier". "He's at The Colored People's Old Folks Home out on Hwy. 27, just before that place you people call nigger town," she laughed and added, "I know you do! All of *you people* do."

3

MOSES

There was a bar next door to the Colored People's Old Folks Home in 1993, and there were men and women, all black, loitering there early in the day as I drove up and parked. I got looks and stares as I walked into the old stone building. A young boy on the sidewalk stopped beating a plastic bucket with sticks as I approached the door, and resumed his play after I entered.

We only had a couple of black patients at Florence Hand Home, the Royal Elaine was mixed, and the Colored People's Old Folks Home was all black. The lobby was clean, and a white haired black woman greeted me at the desk. I told her my name and that I would like to visit with Mr. Grier. She asked if Mr. Grier was expecting me and I told her that he wasn't, but I would love to speak with him if he was feeling up to visitors. She said that she would have to check. I seated myself.

She asked, "Are you with Social Services?"

"No, a friend of the family," I lied.

"Didn't know he had no family," she mumbled, as she left the lobby.

In few moments, she reappeared and asked me to follow her. There were large vases of flowers all about the nurse's station that looked as if they had come from altars of churches or from funerals. The fragrance was surprisingly fresh. This nurse's station opened to a large dayroom area. There was another sitting area that had windows to a garden on one side. The patient's rooms were directly off of the dayroom area. There were a few patients in wheelchairs. Two with lap trays and feeding tube poles with bags suspended above their heads. A woman was restrained in a Geri-chair, screaming out nonsense from time to time. There was a man seated on a sofa holding a pillow on top of his head saying, "Dodie, Dodie, Dodie," repeatedly. A frail woman was wandering and talking to herself or to no one in particular. The nurses, both of them black, paid us no mind. The nursing assistants were busy clearing away lunch trays for the ones they had fed that were gathered at a large round table.

There were wards of four beds each. The woman led me into one such ward. There were two empty beds, and two occupied beds. One was occupied by a comatose thin black man being feed through a tube in his nose. The other one near the window was occupied by a man with a trapeze over his bed. I could tell from the flatness of his linens that he was a double amputee.

"Moses, this is Hannah," she announced. She left the room, not waiting for his reaction.

Moses kept looking through the window as if I wasn't present in the room.

He asked, "What is it you come to see me fer?"

"I got to be friends with Ms. Bea last year, and she told me about you, and Eula Mae, coming out there to live and work back in 1946. I was wondering if you could tell me more about that, what it was like back then. I'm a student at Columbus College, and I'm looking to learn more about those days. I've brought a tape recorder, if you don't mind me recording?"

"Humph, can't imagine Ms. Bea having too many friends. Heard she passed last year, her more than a few years younger than me. Didn't reckon I'd out live'em both," he speculated. He paused a while.

"I don't suppose it would bother me none, you recordin," he added.

Then he looked in my direction. "Gotcha hair done up on yer head and dressed in a fine skirt and blouse, didn't have to do it all up on my account."

"It's an honor for me to be in your company, Mr. Grier. I heard that you worked for The Good Doctor for a good number of years."

"Rightly so, I did."

"Could you tell me more about it?" I asked sheepishly, fearing that he might be evasive, despite our mutual acquaintance professing him to be a big talker. I felt that he was suspicious.

"I could, sho'nuff tell ya'll 'bout it, but you would have to tell me what it is you won't to know 'bout it first," came his response.

"Let's start with you telling me a little about yourself, about Eula Mae and your children," I requested.

He told me that he had been a farm hand on the same farm his pappy was raised on. He said that his grandpappy had been a slave on that same farm, but his pappy had been born a free man. He said that he was born in Walton County near Monroe Georgia, and would be all of 86 years old on his next birthday. His pappy sent him to Atlanta in 1927 to find work, "'Cause men my age was sought after until the Black Tuesday of 1929, when weren't no work to be found by most of my people throughout the Great Depression til 'bout 1933-1935." He said that he firmly believed that, "It wasn't none of Roosevelt's New Deals that got us out of the Great Depression, it was, instead, the repeal of prohibition in 1933, and the taxation of booze that done that trick."

I asked, "Can you tell me what it was like growing up?"

"Well, I was born in 19 and 07, and we was dirt poor. My pappy, he had an old mule and 'bout forty acres of the driest land God ever made. Farmed tobbaci and sweet taters, whatever he could get to grow. Didn't have no irrigation, was dependent on the rain to make anythin grow. When it did, we had a few dollars, and when it didn't, we had nothin. There was eight of us boys and two girls, but 'bout half of my brothers what was older than me run off to work on the railroads out west somewheres.

We had a dirt yard, and we used to tie opossoms up to the front porch rail and fatten'em up on corn, and then they was dinner. My mammie, she just grew a little garden and gathered eggs from the hen nests. Them hens just run wild ever where. Mammie, she took off real sick and just up and died.

My pappy didn't want fer us to stay there, and my two sisters, they went off to live with they auntie in Macon. Didn't never hear from them again. Two of my brothers, they wanted to stay with Pappy and had taken to runnin moonshine with some white boys, blokes they were, from the farm what was right up the road a ways. None of us could read ner write. We had all learned 'bout how prosperous things were lookin in Atlanta, even after the big fire in 19 and 17. Even black folk owned businesses in Atlanta.

So one day in 1927, my pappy swore off farmin. We had worked all year on the crops, and at the end of it all had nothin. So he give me and my younger brother the mule and tol us to go to Atlanta and get us some real jobs. I was 19 year old, and my brother, he was 18. Now my younger brother, he didn't never part with our two brothers what was runnin moonshine, and he taken that mule from Atlanta and back home would come back into the city with liquor from the white boy's still and sell it to the speakeasies, juice joints and gentlemen's clubs what all served liquor under the table, ifin you know what I mean? Now they was joints all over Atlanta, mainly on the west side and it was all over the place, even though it were illegal. One day my brother come into town, and Atlanta weren't much bigger than LaGrange is now, and he took that mule all loaded down with whiskey and got caught by the law. I don't know where they took him, nor what happened to him nor to the mule. They was folk drivin breezers, and flivvers be stuck all over the roads back then, but a good mule, well, I don't rightly know what become of them."

"What were you doing in Atlanta?" I was most curious to know.

"Well me, now I had taken a job fer the Irishman. He weren't no Irishman, he was black same as me, but he bought his store from a Irishman, and so he

was called the Irishman. He didn't never change
the name on the store, and it were O'Neil's Grocer,
down off of The Boulevard in Bedford Pines in what
they now call the Old Forth Ward 'bout Midtown. I
had met up with some fellas what had a house they
rented nearby and we all stay together and go in on
the rent. The Irishman found that I could cut meat,
so he put me in a butcher shop back of the store.
Meat come in by the side almost dressed, and I done
it up, not wastin nothin. I made up a sausage that
everybody all 'round came to likin. So me and the
Irishman, we gotta long real good. Paid me good
money. Even after Black Tuesday in 1929, and all
through the Depression, he paid me wages."

I inquired, "Eula Mae, when and where did you
meet her?"

"That was 'bout a year after I were there. They
had street cars back then and I was all so very excited
'bout them electric lights and gasoliers, 'cause we
didn't have nothin like that back home. Had me
a bicycle and taken to runnin errands to deliver
groceries to folk, both white and black. When the
butcherin was done, I took orders and filled them,
couldn't read ner write but I knowed what the labels
were, and flour and meal, meat and produce.

So one day I was up to Chandler Park near Druid
Hills where a big shot lived who was writtin contracts
for the loggin people. That was a lot of how them

white folk what had land was a makin all kind of
dough, hand over fist, on loggin up in the mountains. Mrs. Kendrick, she was putin on a party and
ordered a mess of steaks cut thick and a mess of my
sausage, and I was to deliver to the back door, like we
always did, to they help, Ms. Mattie Lou.

'Bout time I topped the hill comin up to the
house I was to deliver to, three white boys jumped
outta the woods, 'cause it was all woods back up in
there then, not like it is now. These boys had base-
ball bats and sticks and said, 'Boy, what'cha got in
that there sack?' Now ya see, I was grown, and them
boys was younger than me by 'bout five-six years, but
me bein a nigger, they call me boy, and I knew best
not to argue with'em. I handed off my bag, knowin I
had Mrs. Kendrick's steaks in there. Them boys run
off with them steaks, all the meat just gone, and I
was lucky they didn't take my bicycle too. Them was
poor white boys, and didn't live nowhere close to
there. I didn't have nothin to do but to turn 'round
and go back to the store. I just knew the Irishman
was a goin to fire me on the spot. But he didn't, he
sent me right back up there with another mess of
meat.

Now, I was a runnin all kinds of late with this
meat, and I didn't know if Ms. Mattie Lou would still
be at they house or not. Could well I have to be
deliverin to Mrs. Kendrick herself, and I weren't too

happy 'bout it. But sure as I got there Ms. Mattie Lou,
old lady, she was a standin there on the back steps
a waitin on me. She took them steaks inside, and I
saw her, my Eula Mae, a standin there in the light of
the gas lamp post. She was just a baby vamp, a real
tomato, but I didn't know it then, 'cause she was all
filled out like a woman chil', and she were a wearin
a hat on top of her head and had on the purtiest sky
blue dress that matched her purse and her hat, and
she was a wearin white gloves. She had come to walk
her mama home. I was mighty pleased to meet her.
I didn't know then that she were just thirteen year
old. She could've been my age or older."

"So you were about twenty and she was thirteen
when you met?" I urged him to continue.

"Yes, and she had 'bout six older sisters and was
the baby of the bunch. Her mama had been a workin for Mrs. Kendrick all of her life and some of
them girls too, but baby vamp, no, she weren't fer
doin that kinda work at that time. Her papa and
her mama, they was well off, and her papa had a suit
coat and hat shop where he tailored down on Wheat
Street, in the thick of the Negro business section of
town. Mama, she didn't have to work but she did it
'cause she liked it.

So they had'em a nice house and all, but it
weren't painted white, 'cause that just weren't
done back then 'cause the poor whites, they taken

offense to it. Big new gray frame house, and her
sister, nearby, had a big house too. Her man was all
educated and taught at the colored folk's college. I
didn't even know they had a colored folk's college til
I met that one. Talked like a white boy, he did. Me
and Eula Mae and some of her sisters and they men
folk got to takin the carriage out to the speakeasies and sometimes we took it out alone, and fer you
know it I done got her knocked up.

Ifin she hadda had brothers; I might notta been
so lucky. Now it weren't so strange to knock up a
young darkie girl back then, but you was spected
to marry her, and that's what we did, got married
in a little Baptist Church. All them church ladies
were there. And that's how it was back then. The
gals, they went out all dolled up in they glad rags
and headdresses like flapper gals all sparkles on
Saturday night, got bent, and then showed up in
they Sunday best to pray fer forgiveness of they sins
on Sunday mornins. The depression hit not long
after Nathaniel was born."

I asked, "So you kept working through the
Depression?"

"I did, and it got real bad. Me and Eula Mae, we
was stayin at her sister's house. We couldn't afford
no place of our own. She had Nathaniel right off, in
1928, and it nearly scared her to death. She weren't
'bout havin no babies after that. Now they was places

where you could take a few liberties, with the white
folk, you know, socialize, and places where you had
to toe the line, tip your hat and walk on. Eula Mae's
brother-in-law, well he was all up with the white folk
and 'bout gettin Nathaniel educated proper, and
Eula Mae, she was just all for it. So he taken to get
Nathan, what we come to call'im, in school by the
time he were seven. He taken to his books real fine
and 'bout time he were eight, I think he's smarter
than me.

I kept workin on through the Depression with
the Irishman. They was a group called the Black
Shirts what sprung up offin the KKK during the
Depression. They was a threatenin people and tellin
white folk to fire all the black folk and they says that
all whites should have all the jobs before niggers
get hired, so we just took to stayin in our neighborhoods and not to go out at night like we had been.
In 1933, the Irishman, he went in debt to buy a truck
so we could deliver farther and keep the monies up.
That's when I learnt to drive.

Now 'bout this time, most of Eula Mae's sisters
had done moved off with they chillun and they man
folk, up to the cities up north, you know big cities
like Chicago and New York, and other places out
west, Houston and New Orleans. Seemed like everybody was a leavin Atlanta. Business fer her folks got
bad. Her folks was old in years and they both up and

died the same year. We didn't know that her papa
had put the house on a note. People was ridin trains
back to Atlanta fer visits, but the black folk had they
own cars on the trains, and the white folk, they had
better cars on the trains. When her sisters come fer
her Mama's funeral, well they found out the house
was owed to the bank, so they weren't no place fer us
to live like we was a plannin to do. Well, the sisters
all but one, Martha, left after a while, and Eula Mae's
brother-in-law and her sister, what had stayed, done
had 'bout three youngins and was spectin another,
and then also in 'bout 1933, they tol us we had to
find us a place.

My wages weren't nothin, but the Irishman give
me enough to rent a little place, shot gun house,
over to Cabbagetown along side of poor whites.
Nathan, who was light-skinned, like his mama, taken
to runnin with them white boys 'bout the time he
was ten. They was immigrant boys and didn't seem
to mind he was a darkie. Althea, she were born in
that house in 1938, and Eula Mae weren't but 24
year old. Nathan were right there when the mid-
wife come to deliver and mama, Eula Mae, she done
right well with that birth. Nathan, he was still goin
to school with his Uncle what picked him up and
carried him ever mornin and brung him home ever
afternoon. He would study his books and then go off
with them white boys.

The Depression was 'bout over, and they was juice joints opened up everywhere with prohibition bein over as well, but we was in the Bible Belt and all was quiet in most of the neighborhoods, 'cause most of the counties was supposed to be dry counties. I had taken to the gin mills after work, and I don't mean cotton, mostly just shooten the bull with men folk. Mama liked sippin gin, but she didn't like what I was goin out without her. Then one of her sisters sent a big box delivered right to the house. It was all things for the baby girl and a big heap of store bought dresses for Eula Mae.

Now after it come legal to sell liquor outright, a place opened up called The Top Hat in 1939, came to be called The Royal Peacock later on, where mostly blacks but some whites was to gather, all puttin on the Ritz, and Mama was fer 'bout showin off her store bought clothes. Now this was just on the edge of Sweet Auburn and mostly high class blacks come out there.

One night we had Nathan lookin after his sister and we went out to The Top Hat, to listen to the bands and dance a little, 'cause I danced back when I had the legs to do it, and mama, she was lookin like somebody's child, the cat's meow. We go'd up to The Top Hat and partied til 'bout two in the mornin. They was places all 'round where there was rooms to be had fer to be gettin some nookie.

Eula Mae had a friend, name was Penny, and she and Penny had slipped off to the ladies room. Now all the men folk, they was talkin 'bout War and fightin Germans and whether black folk ought to be fightin ifin it come to that, and I was all up in it, with the talk. I didn't rightly know how long they was gone, but Eula Mae and Penny come back all disheveled and wanted to go home and so we left.

It were another seven years gone by when Eula Mae tol me what happened that night. In 1946, the War was over and ever body had money to spend and things were pickin up in the neighborhood. Nathan was up and grown and graduatin Valedictorian from high school and that was a big deal fer a colored boy to get through high school in them days.

Eula Mae hadn't wanted to go out drinkin much after that night we was at The Top Hat, and took to tryin to get Althea raised. Althea was going on eight year old and still weren't in school and she didn't seem to take to book learnin. She was already bein razzed in the neighborhood fer bein a dummy, but she were pretty like her mama. By this time I had seen Atlanta go from 'bout horse and buggy to full on automobiles everywhere, even women was drivin. But Eula Mae, she didn't want to be drivin, and didn't want fer to be out alone anymore.

Well, we was to go out drinkin after Nathan's graduation. We was all dressed out in our Sunday best, and food was brought to the house from all over and we decided, that is, me and Nathan, decided that we was a goin to The Royal Peacock, 'cause he was drinkin age by now, and that was a swanky place then. Mama, Eula Mae, flew into a fit. I asked her why she wanted to be a wet blanket, you know, it was Nathan's party and all.

That's when she tol me 'bout how her and Penny had gone to the ladies room at The Top Hat, and slipped outside to get some fresh air, 'cause the club was all smoke filled. When they walked down the sidewalk a ways, two white boys pulled over to the curb and one got out whilst the other one was at the wheel. The one got out forced Penny and Eula Mae into the car and took'em off to the motel where they had their way with'em.

Now Eula Mae knowed that I had a good shiv an would'a been brought to knife them boys ifin I had known what had happened and I'd been up in the lynchin tree fer doin it, 'cause see, a black man could quick become strange fruit for just mouthin off at a white man then, and a black man surely would be put to death for strikin a white man. So I just held her. Was all I could do by then."

I clarified, and expressed my sympathy for his pain, "Eula Mae and Penny had been raped by two white boys? That's awful, it shouldn't happen to any woman."

"Naw ma'am, it shouldn't have. I had Nathan 18 year old and his sister, 8 year old, and me, I was 38 and Eula Mae was 'bout 31 or 32. The Irishman had taken a stall outside of the curb market that was built on Edgewood after the big fire, and I was a sellin surplus produce and changin money fer him, 'cause he trusted me that way. Most Saturdays, I run the stall and he run the store. Now the white folks, they could go inside to sell and shop, but the black folks had to put up on the street outside for shoppers. Nathan had taken the job of loadin cars fer folks fer tips and runnin the stall with me.

'Long come a day when a white woman come out of the market with a big sack and I saw Nathan go over, and I knowed what was 'bout to happen, but before I could say a thing, Nathan had done grabbed her sack and headed fer her car what was a waitin at the curb. Her husband was at the wheel of the car and he done jumped out and 'round the car 'bout ready to fight Nathan, 'cause see, Jim Crow Law was surely in place at that time and Nathan had done insulted this white woman. Why you couldn't even brush up 'gainst a white woman that somebody be done called you a rapist and had you hung. That man of her's was 'bout to fight him, callin him nigger boy, and he looked over at me and I come 'round to see could I stop things from escalatin. Nathan, he had been all 'round poor white women in our neighborhood and with the folks his uncle knew and he didn't have a clue what he done was wrong. So things got settled and they drove off without a fight, but poor Nathan, we had to talk real serious after that ifin he was a goin to help me there.

'Bout a week later, the Irishman, well he was goin on seventy years, and he taken the flu and got real sick. Next thing I knowed, his brother come by the grocer store and tol me to move everythin out to the curb at the market on Edgewood come Saturday, 'cause they was a closin up the store. He offered me a month's wages and said I was to keep all the proceeds for sellin out the business as they had no interest in it. Now that was real generous, but I didn't rightly know what I was to do after the store was closed and all was gone.

I thought to get me a loan and reopen the store on my own, but that would mean a big debt and Nathan, him wantin to go off to school. I didn't have no credit and I didn't have no one to vouch fer me. It didn't look like that was a goin to happen 'cause didn't nobody have the money fer school. Eula Mae had been writtin schools all over and so had Nathan and his teachers. Mama had her heart set on Nathan becomin a professor and workin right there in Atlanta. I wanted fer Nathan to go to school, but I didn't think Atlanta was the best place fer him. Nathan had been kinda sheltered from the worst of things and I worried 'bout him 'cause them white boys he was a runnin with was a goin over to the west side all the time and I know'd it was a matter of time fer they was in big trouble of some sort.

The first Saturday that we had hauled all the grocer goods out to market, a white man come 'long. He was a lookin fer somebody what might have a tractor to sell, and he was a talkin to everybody, black and white. He said he had come home from the War and bought himself a farm down in South Georgia. Now he was a gimp, that is to say that one leg was bad, he walked fine, but he had a bit of a limp. He went on to say that he needed a handyman and a housekeeper fer his wife; and he gotta talkin to me real serious. He said he had a heap of money saved up from the War and he would pay fer Nathan to go to school ifin me and the wife could come help him out. Talked all 'bout this big brick house he was a buildin and how he had an old farm house on the place what we could stay in fer free.

Lawd, ifin I knowed what trouble was to happen, I would have surely stayed right there in Atlanta with my own kind. Now this man was Mr. David G. Handley, and I guess you know we up and decided to come down here. It was mainly to get Nathan off to school and we wasn't spectin to stay too many years. But Mama, she thought it would be best to raise Althea out of the city and she was all 'bout livin a wholesome country life by this time, but she come to regret ever leavin Atlanta."

"Then you brought your family out of the city to come to LaGrange for country living." I paraphrased.

The nurse had come in to tell Moses that his supper tray was ready. Moses told me that he had kidney failure and that Dr. Ingram was about to start dialysis in a couple of weeks. He was going into the hospital to have a shunt put in. Moses said, "I don't know why they want to try to save these old wore out parts when half of me is gone already."

I turned off my tape recorder and thanked him for his time. He asked me to come back anytime. I told him that I sure would like to hear about his life out at the Handley place and he agreed to tell me all about it. He told me that there were good times and there were bad times, but he would be glad to tell me what he knew about it.

I started to take my leave of him and remembered the small cross in my purse. I pulled it out and handed it to him.

"Well, what do you know? I carved this thing outta solid piece of cedar from a tree we fell, and whittled it down real smooth. I thought this thing had gone out with the trash when old Ms. Bea moved me up in the housing projects, you know, after I lost my first leg. Well I'll be, don't that beat all. I made this when Mama was all up with the church ladies over at Union Baptist. I'll tell you more 'bout that later, if you come back to hear more."

I told him that I enjoyed his stories and I promised to come back. I told him that I wanted to know what *really* went on out there in the basement.

He cocked his head at me and looked me in the eye, "Sho' nuff? I can tell ya."

He also made me promise to bring him a can of Prince Albert and a pack of OCBs when I came back. He said that the boys next door, meaning the bar, would sometimes come in and check on all of the old boys and bring cigarettes, which they were allowed to smoke in the garden out back, but he preferred to roll his own. As I left by the front, I saw and heard that the club next door was going full swing. There was a new Cadillac parked out on the curb and a man with more gold jewelry and as big as Mr. T. was standing guard by the door. He didn't look like anyone that I would want to cross. He nodded at me and I nodded back. I got in my car, and headed to the grocery store. I did my grocery store shopping in LaGrange every Saturday and it became my routine to stop in to see Moses Grier every other Saturday and bring him a can of Prince Albert. I didn't know what his doctor would have thought of that, but Mr. Grier was just fine with it.

4

THE RELOCATION

Moses anticipated my visits and I would find him up and dressed, sitting in his wheelchair by about 11:00 am. He was always smiling and always happy to see me. We would go out to the garden where he had his smokes and he would tell me stories. One such story had to do with why Mr. Handley decided to quit his efforts at becoming a farmer. Ms. Bea had her opinion on the matter, but Moses had another. He didn't dispute her opinion; he just had more to the story than Ms. Bea was aware, or was telling.

Mr. Handley had brought them down from Atlanta in a truck with Nathan and Althea riding all the way from Atlanta in the truck bed with all of their things. When Eula Mae saw the big brick house the Handley's had, she was all impressed, but when she saw the little two room shack that they were to live in, not much better than their little shot gun house in Atlanta; worse in some ways because it didn't have any plumbing, well she was all into tears. Beatrice tried to make it better by bringing out a dresser with a mirror and a wardrobe with a full length mirror on the front, a nice wash stand and pitcher and basin. She gave her rugs and furniture and had the wood stove put in. Eula Mae never used it much except for special occasions, breakfast and heating. Whatever she was making for the Handley's, Eula Mae made extra to bring over for them.

Eula Mae had started waiting on the Handleys, cooking and cleaning, and took up with the two baby Handley boys over the next couple of years. Beatrice wasn't much for mothering, so Eula Mae nurtured the boys. At first, Althea was always helping her mama in the house. Eula Mae had also taken up with the church ladies and could read and write well enough to study her Bible. Althea was never into religion like her mama, and this pained Eula Mae, but Althea would attend Sunday services with her mama, so she could chat with her friends.

The country church ladies looked up to Eula Mae because she could read and write so very well, knew her scripture, and Eula Mae and Althea always came to church in nice store bought clothes that her sisters would send to them. She also received and wrote letters to her sisters all over the country. Althea wasn't good at reading and never developed a desire for learning from books and that also pained

Eula Mae. Back then, there were no laws enforced mandating that a colored girl had to attend school, so Althea was home most of the day.

Their first couple of years, the Handleys had several cows and a mule. Moses had built a corral in front of the old barn on the place. "Mr. Handley didn't know which end of the mule kicked ner which end of the bee stung," Moses said with a laugh.

They had some chickens in the yard and a few pigs in a sty back behind the barn. When the mule died, Mr. Handley bought a tractor. Moses would do all of the plowing and a couple of colored boys from a neighboring farm would come over and help Nathan with the planting. Althea had made friends with these two boys and had gotten to know their sisters from the church.

Along about the time Althea was ten years old, she came running to the field to get Moses from the tractor. Moses stopped the tractor and Althea told him that a heifer was down in the barn. They had been watching this cow for days because she was about to drop a calf. It was getting late in the day, almost dark, and Moses was afraid that the cow was trying to deliver breech, so he called Mr. Handley to the barn.

Mr. Handley came out to the barn and he was all distraught over the possibility of losing both the heifer and the calf. He asked Moses if there was any way they might save either one of them. Now, Moses had seen his own father deliver calves that were breech, but that was a very long time ago. He expected that he could recall enough of it to get the job done with Mr. Handley's help. Althea was sent away from the barn and Moses went about explaining to Mr. Handley how he was going to have to reach up in the cow's hind quarter with his hands and turn the calf, and then pull the calf out.

There wasn't enough time to call the local vet. Mr. Handley showed no reservation about it and put on a long pair of gloves and then, just like that, he reached up into the cow's hind quarters. Within a few minutes, he had pulled the little calf out and Moses said that Mr. Handley had an unnatural gleam in his eyes like he had done something quite spectacular. The cow was breathing heavy, but she was okay, and the little calf was set down beside her, all wet with birth. Mama cow was licking her clean, and as Moses held up the lantern so they could see better, he saw that Mr. Handley was just staring off, like in a trance, like he was in another world altogether.

Moses said that Mr. Handley lost interest in farming almost right after that incident and went about his studies real hard. He sold off the tractor and had Moses tending the barnyard. Eula Mae had made herself indispensable to Ms. Bea, looking after the children. They kept a few cows and a couple of pigs because meat was cheaper on the hoof than in the store. They had a big freezer and Moses would slaughter the animals and then butcher them right there, saving money on the processor who charged a big fee. They also sold a few calves at market every year.

I asked, "Moses, what was your most proud moment?"

"Well Nathan, Mr. Handley had taken a real likin to that boy 'cause he come down and worked hard for three or four years. He was a showin Nathan all his books on the human body, and how ever thing works and all. Nathan studied with him. Mr. Handley done bought a microscope and they would look at ever thing from pond water to bug wings with that thing and it just had Nathan's mind on science. He reckoned on goin to school to be a doctor by this time, and Mr. Handley seemed 'bout as proud as if he were his own son, and mama, she couldn't be happier. Mr. Handley had a friend up in Washington, D.C. what had tol him all 'bout Howard University, and they wrote. Nathan, he went up and he passed his exams, and he got accepted. He come home all smiles to tell it. Put him on the train come September of 1950. That was a proud day."

"That must have been a very proud day for all of you," I concurred. Moses agreed that it was, and went on to tell me about another incident in the barn.

Shortly after Nathan went off to school, Mr. Handley received a letter and a certificate in the mail that he had passed his chiropractic exams and could call himself a chiropractor, and Ms. Bea was all proud and showing it to everybody, and of course, Eula Mae was one of the first to see it. Mr. Handley considered himself a doctor by this time, even though chiropractors weren't considered real doctors.

When spring arrived in 1951, Mr. Handley came out to the barn to tell Moses that he wanted to butcher the old sow, and this didn't set right with Moses because it was unusually warm and pigs were always butchered on the coldest day of winter, because of parasites and disease. He also knew that the old sow was carrying a litter, and he told Mr. Handley. But given his orders he set out to slaughter the old sow.

Once the old sow was slaughtered, her throat slit and bled out, Mr. Handley appeared at the barn door about the time Moses was to cut her down her middle. Mr. Handley advised Moses to be careful to cut just through her skin so as not to disturb her innards. Moses took the sow down from where she was hanging to bleed, because he knew the pressure, once she was cut, would cause her innards to bail out. He laid her on the butchering table and slit a thin line down her middle. Mr. Handley put on his gloves and proceeded to pick through her with all manner of instruments that he had brought from the basement.

Moses stood back and observed as Mr. Handley inspected all of her organs. He saw Mr. Handley handle her swollen womb real careful and could see the little fetal piglets once Mr. Handley cut through the womb, ever so gentle. He took the tiny fetal piglets, six of them, and set them aside and continued to study over the old sow. He examined the heart, lungs, liver, and kidneys, and all of the blood vessels and where they went to. The bladder and all of the intestines, he lay out on the table. Then he told Moses to go get a bag of lime out of the barn and take the old dead sow out into the woods and bury her after throwing the lime in so she wouldn't stink. Moses got the wheel barrow and took the sow, and all of her innards, out past the barn into the woods and set about to digging a hole to bury her. He hated to lose all of that good meat, but he completed that project as ordered.

When Moses came back to the barn, an hour or two later, he saw Mr. Handley had put the little fetal piglets in separate jars of chemical that stunk up the whole barn. He was sitting there studying the contents of the jars and it was like a light went on in Mr. Handley's head. He looked up at Moses and said, "You know what these little fellas are, don't you?"

Moses answered, "Why they is unborn piglets, sir."

Mr. Handley said, "Nope, they are gravy, that's what they are. I believe I know now how I can make some extra cash."

Moses said to me, "Why I just knowed right then what The Good Doctor was a plannin to do!"

I asked him, "What was it then, that you supposed he planned to do?"

Moses just shook his head and said, "Lawd, have mercy woman, ifin you don't know I ain't 'bout to be tellin ya!"

We called it a day. I told him that he could tell me more about it later. Moses thumped his hand rolled cigarette butt into the rose bushes and I wheeled him back to his ward. I left, knowing that there was so much more to be learned from Moses.

On our next visit Moses began by telling me about a "secret" that he had to live because of Eula Mae. He told me how Eula Mae's sister in Atlanta was planning to move to Harlem and her sister from Harlem had come to Atlanta to help with the packing. This was Eula Mae's last sister living in Atlanta that was moving to Harlem. Moses didn't know what Eula Mae had been writing to her sisters about their lives in the employ of The Good Doctor and Ms. Bea, but he was about to find out that it wasn't all truth, whether Eula Mae was a devout Christian lady or not.

They had always taken phone calls at the brick house of the Handley's, and the sisters were aware that Eula Mae was keeping house for them. But Eula Mae had concocted some sort of story about Moses buying up pecan orchards and making money off of pecans, and how well off he was since he had made these investments. She had been telling these sisters how they owned lots of land all around for growing pecans and how they had built this big brick house.

"Now it was true, that we was surrounded by pecan groves, but me ner The Good Doctor owned none of them," Moses went about explaining.

"Eula Mae come a runnin from the house one day late in June 1955, had to be, 'cause Nathan done got into medical school and Althea she was already gone, and Eula Mae says to me, 'I done made a terrible error, Moses, they is a comin down on the train fer to see us.' Well, I didn't think it was all bad til Eula Mae went to tellin me all 'bout her lies she'd been feedin her sisters and what was we a goin to be able to do 'bout this?"

I questioned, "What did you do?"

"Coincidentally," he said, "the Handley's was a goin to Florida fer two weeks vacation 'long 'bout that time. Them two boys what Eula Mae had raised

had already gone off to boardin' school, and The
Good Doctor and his wife was a goin down to stay
a while, like they was doin from time to time. Eula
Mae done taken all they photographs off they walls
after they left and hid'em out to our house and when
her sisters come in on the train we picked'em up at
the train station and brought'em out here like it was
our own house, you know to the Handley's place."

"That's funny." Again, I questioned, "Did you
pull it off okay?"

"Course we did, we was all up in they house, and
Mama had set'em up a room each upstairs and was
cookin like it was her own kitchen, 'cause really it
was, you know, and they was a playin the piano and
singin, and Ms. Bea had all these records of black
folk music, 'cause she liked it, and they was just
like they was in our own home. They was a eatin
on the Handley's plates with they silverware, and a
usein they dishes like they belonged to us. That just
weren't done in them days. Black folk weren't served
with the same utensils as white folk. We didn't even
dine at the same tables nor in the same cafes. Early
in June in 1954, we had all went up to Washington
D.C. on the train to see Nathan graduate when he
received his B.S. degree. Eula Mae, me, Althea, Ms.
Bea and The Good Doctor, in separate cars, you
know, blacks and whites. We had separate hotels
even in different parts of the city," he laughed.

I laughed along with him, "I remember my grandmother on our farm once scolded me for serving our hired black lady with the wrong dipper from the water bucket. I was only six years old; even then I thought it kind of stupid to have a black people's dipper and a white people's dipper in the same water bucket. That was in about 1967."

"Then you know'd even then how things were. Why, them two weeks we was all sleepin in they own beds. Me and Eula Mae drove her kinfolk all 'round the countryside talking pecans and all. We took'em down to the widow lady's pond and took'em out on the boat 'round 'bout the pond like we owned it, we did. She made out like the widow lady's house was the Handley place. Took'em all 'cross the mountain top to see FDR's places, the Little White House and the stonework them C.C.C. boys had done all up at the Inn and the Liberty Bell pool."

I remarked, "So a fine time was had by all, and the Handley's were none the wiser?"

"Naw, they never knew 'bout it. Them two sisters both belonged to the National Association of Colored Women and they was a talkin 'bout Du Bois and Booker T. Washington. They was all against Washington's argument that the black folk should be subservient to the whites and gratefully so, and they tol Mama all 'bout how young Michael Luther King had done changed his name to Martin, a boy what growed up right in our neighborhood in Atlanta, who became a preacher like his paw, at the Ebenezer Baptist Church. Mama had been baptized in that church as a girl, and knew all of his people. That was *the* Dr. Martin Luther King, Jr.. Eula Mae's sister what was movin to Harlem said they was encouraged by papers and sermons of King and they was glad to be gettin up outta the south where they felt things weren't changin fast enough. They was awarned that things was a goin to be worse before things got better. All these conversations was a goin on in a white folk's house." Moses was laughing hard as he related his story.

"So this took place in 1955, and that was after Althea was gone?" I asked.

Moses' face dropped and his laughter subsided. It was a few moments before he spoke again.

"Yes, that was the year after the U.S. Supreme Court decided that segregation was unlawful, but you know, things didn't change 'round here for a long time afterwards. Well you know that, don'tcha?" he asked me, still looking a bit solemn.

"So, tell me about you and The Good Doctor," I urged. "How did he come by that name and how did his business get going?"

"Well, he opened up shop downtown first, in LaGrange, in 1951, and got a big name 'cause he was a treatin all manner of folk in the area what doctors couldn't give no relief to. I would go with him on Saturdays sometimes to mop and clean the place up. He had all types of tables, exercise devices, and electric massagers. I kept it all sparklin clean fer him. And he had this here office in his basement too, the same year."

"Tell me more about that. I know that he was performing abortions there. You knew about that, didn't you?" I asked this very abruptly because I did not want Moses to feel that he had to be evasive of me knowing what went on there. I wanted to know everything, and Moses was the one to tell me.

"I knew when first he started." He reminded, "As hired hand it was my job, well you know'd what I tol you 'bout the calf pullin and the piglets?"

"Yes, go on."

"It was my job to gather up scraps and slop the hogs, feed the chickens and the cows, and keep the barn in order. I was also cleanin the basement every Monday mornin. I polished his instruments and cleaned his tables with antiseptic cleaners and mopped in there like I did at the downtown office. One night, 'bout a month after he opened up, The Good Doctor asked me to go to the fridge that he kept in the basement and get the slop bucket out and take it to the hogs. Well I looked in there, was a slop bucket, like you kept under the bed fer peein in the night and like you slopped hogs with, and this bucket had a cover on it. Right up beside The Good Doctor's sandwiches and soda bottles, was this slop bucket. So I brung it out to the pig pen and took the cover off and right away I knew what it was, it was human what was in that bucket. I wasn't 'bout to be feedin that slop to the pigs what we was a goin to be eaten so I took it out to the field just past the little woods there between the house and the barn and dumped it out. I poured kerosene, even a little gasoline, all 'round and raked up dry leaves and put wood on to set it afire. Incinerate it like they did my old legs, you know, I thought that was the way it should be done."

"How come you never told the police what he was doing, for surely you had to know that it was criminal back then even for real doctors, and especially that he wasn't licensed as a medical doctor?" I asked, trying not to sound too accusing.

"Well, you probably don't remember John Wallace, and Murder in Coweta County, 'cause that was before your time. Took place not so very far from here. He went to the electric chair in 1950, for testimony that was given by two black boys. He was the richest man ever to get the death penalty and the first white man in Georgia to get the chair on testimony by a black man. They was all kinds of publicity on that trial and everythin 'bout it was sha-kin up white and black folk alike. I weren't 'bout to be startin up nothin like that. The Good Doctor, he was a good man and he helped outta lotta folk in them days, he did, and my family. Where would we have been off to ifin I did anythin like that?"

"I couldn't tell you Moses, I guess you had to get by the best you could," I answered.

"Yes ma'am, we did, and I took to a goin in that fridge ever week and a rakin me up a little pile of leaves, kindlin wood, and logs to set me a fire. Ms. Bea, she knew what was going on. She wouldn't have never tol it, but she knew. She would sometimes come stand beside me over that little fire and say not a word, but she knew. It's what nearly drove her crazy you know, the girls tol me from over at the hospital; she was 'bout crazy just before she died. The Good Doctor, he took to flushin that stuff later on. I was mighty glad he did."

I told Moses, "I visited with Ms. Bea a time or two. She told me all about The Good Doctor, but she never mentioned abortions, and I didn't think that she would."

"Naw, she wouldn't have said a word 'bout it, never." Moses asked me, "How did you come to know 'bout what all was going on?"

I told him about the Ledger, and how I had found it, and the notes written in the margins. I told him that I was learning about him and The Good Doctor because I felt strongly that "*Civil* Rights" went far beyond the black-white issues. "'The civility which money will purchase, is rarely extended to those who have none.'" I added, "That's a quote from Charles Dickens."

His reply, "'Just be careful the causes you stand for, 'cause the world has every intention of usin it against you,' somebody tol me that a long time ago."

I was preparing to leave when it occurred to me that I had not learned what happened to his children. Where were they now?

"You mentioned Althea was gone by 1955." I asked, "Gone where?"

"You come back again sometime and let me think on that," he answered.

I left him alone with his thoughts. Moses had shared a story not unlike "The Grapes of Wrath" in that he was forced by poverty to accept circumstances that were as bad as or worse than those he attempted to escape. I sensed that he was yet to tell me the worst of things.

5

THE TRAGEDY OF ALTHEA

A couple of weeks later I came back to visit and Moses was already sitting in the rose garden. He looked tired and said that the dialysis was taking a lot out of him. He had no appetite. He was losing weight and his face was sagging. He told me that it was too hot outside and he wanted to go back to his room. I started to push him in and he asked me to get one of the girls to do it. He told me that he wanted me to take my tape recorder back to my car. He said that he didn't want what he had to say to be known beyond me while he lived and breathed. His heart sounded heavy and, of course, I complied.

When I went to his room, he was all settled into his bed. He had the cross in his hands as he spoke, polishing both the cross and his words. He asked me to close the door, and I did. Then he began.

"I'm a goin to tell you this 'cause I haven't told another livin, breathin soul in all my long life and

I'm feelin like maybe I should. If I am to be for-
given, I must tell at least one other soul and my lord,
Jesus. Now I ain't never been baptized and I ain't
altogether sure 'bout heaven and hell, but I surely
don't want to go to hell if they is one. I done tol you
'bout a secret that we was a livin 'cause of Eula Mae
and what she done tol her folks, but it ain't the worst
secret we done kept."

I interrupted, "You know, Moses, you don't have
to tell anyone, as long as you are at peace with your
Lord, let it be in peace."

"That's just the thing, I ain't never been at peace
'bout it, so I figure if I tell someone, maybe you,
then maybe I'll have another shoulder for this burden and it won't seem so very big for an old man like
me to carry to his grave," he continued. "You asked
me 'bout Althea and I aim to tell you. Fer starters,
this is 1993, and all what was a goin on was back in
the 50s, like I tol you, things was different back in
them days, and ain't all that different 'round here
now, except that a black man can be behind a closed
door with a white woman and don't nobody much
be askin any questions. Them was days, back then,
when such wasn't so."

"Althea," he started, "she weren't too much fer
learnin her books, like I tol you, and she weren't too
much 'bout helpin Mama in the house neither after
a while. Mostly, 'bout the time she had just turned

sixteen in first of May 1954, she was 'bout hangin out at the juke joint up the road. Myself, I had been up there to talk with the old boys, but most of them was gone, and the young folk was a goin up there to sing and dance, and listen to the bands play.

Althea, she was takin to eatin white kaolin clay, what the colored girls ate to keep'em from havin babies, you know, mess'em up bad and didn't always work, that clay they would eat. Some of these colored girls would show up at The Good Doctor's doorstep pregnant and needin help, and back then he was a turnin'em away. He didn't start treaten colored girls til 'long 'bout 1964.

Well, Mama, she done figured Althea was 'bout not gettin pregnant by these nigger boys at the juke joints 'cause Althea she thought she was a goin off to sing. 'Bout all she could do well was sing and she had a dreamy-eyed notion that she was a goin off to Atlanta, NYC, or Chicago and get herself recognized fer her singin. She been watchin too much of Ms. Bea's television. She sang at the church on Sundays and she was to go to Atlanta to sing at Ebenezer with her Mama, but that day never come 'bout. Now they was a planin to catch the train to go stay with one of Eula Mae's old friends, Penny. Althea was to be singin in the church in Atlanta on that Sunday. The Friday night afore the Saturday that they was to leave on the train; somethin tragic happened to Althea."

Moses was choosing his words very carefully. His speech was pressured, and not nearly as fluid. He seemed agitated.

I asked him plainly, "You can be frank with me, Moses, what happened to Althea?"

"I'm 'bout to tell you! Come that Friday night, really 'bout 4:30 am Saturday mornin, Althea come home from the juke joint. Now she was usually home by 'bout 2:30 am 'cause it weren't but a mile down the road walkin, and they closed up 'bout 2:00 am. By then everybody be liquored up and on they way off. Most of all, I knowed that Althea just go there to sing 'cause she weren't one to do much drinkin, and most times she went, she rode back home in the car with the Moody sisters, 'cause I done tol her how dangerous it were to be a woman walkin on the road at that hour.

I was down in the bed already sleepin and Mama; she was a waitin in the front room. When I woke up, they was both a cryin and a carryin on. I went into the other room and they was a huggin and all upset. Althea, she was a shakin and a shiverin, and Mama was a holdin to her, tryin to get her to tell what done happened.

Althea was covered in scratches all 'long her face, arms and legs, with her face bleedin at the lip and her hair all matted and drippin wet. She was a rea-kin of urine. As she tol it, Althea done left the juke joint 'bout 2:00 am and sisters, they done gone on home without her 'cause she was a talkin to Joshua Williams, a colored boy what played in a band they put together. He gone on with the boys in the band and Althea took off walkin down the road. 'Long come a brand new Mercury Monterey pulled up 'long side of her. They was four white boys, all soldier boys in uniform greens from Ft. Benning, most likely.

She tried to ignore them, and kept to her walkin, but they was a whistlein at her and callin her 'Sugar Baby' and 'Hot Chocolate', and she left the road to get away from them thinkin that they would drive on by, but they didn't. They pulled off the road and she heard the car door slam and them boys got out and walked down in the woods after her. She went to runnin, but the underbrush was so very thick that she couldn't run far before they caught up with her. They bound her with they belts and then they all taken turns a rapin her.

When they was all done they just laughed and talked 'bout how them little college girls they was after wouldn't have put up such a good fight and it weren't near as much fun as a nigger girl could be. Now Althea thought she might never see her mama and papa again. She thought them boys was a goin to kill her on the spot, but they didn't. One boy, as she lay on the ground, relieved hisself right on her, and the other boys, not to be outdone, just did the same. They got their belts and went on off through the woods and back to the road. Althea waited til she heard'em drive off and then she took to the road a runnin to get home."

"That is tragic, Moses, no woman should have to endure such agony. First your wife, now your daughter." My efforts to console him were very ineffective. His face was flushed and his breathing rapid.

"Hell, I was fightin blood red angry, and it wouldn't have done me well to own a gun, but all I had was my knife and I had to just leave the house to let Mama take on cleanin her up proper. There has to be no more shame worse than for a woman to be raped, except maybe that of a father of one who has been. I was ashamed to even be a man a lookin at my daughter's pain."

"Moses, that was just awful, I'm so very sorry that happened," I offered, "I cannot imagine what you must have been feeling."

"Oh, that ain't the worst of things. I didn't know what I was 'bout to do, but I took off up the road with a rock in each hand. I figured I could at least throw'em at they new car should they come a ridin back by. I come back to the house 'bout sunrise and went to choppin wood. Ever swing of the axe was another white boy's head fer me. I must have chopped enough wood fer all of Atlanta that day. Mama come and tol me to come in fer breakfast, but I wasn't eatin. Mama tol me that Althea was restin and she had bruises and bite marks on her breasts and neck, and that was nothin what I needed to hear then. I just went on back to choppin wood.

The Good Doctor, he comes out of his house to go to LaGrange to his office and he seen me and my wood. I walked over to his car and tol him 'bout Althea. He asked me what I planned to do. I tol him it wasn't much I could do. He said the sheriff probably could not or would not do anythin bein as these boys was military and long gone. I knowed he meant to add, 'And Althea bein a colored girl,' but he didn't. He went on to his office and I finally went on in the house.

Mama sat at the table with her Bible in her lap, and she was a prayin for everybody; us, Althea, even them white boys what raped her daughter. Time went by and Mama quit her prayin so hard. Althea, she quit singin. She was healin all her scratches up, but she wasn't healin inside none. Mama kept tryin to get Althea to go to church with her, but she wasn't goin. The two began to argue, and not long after, Eula Mae began to argue with me. She was convinced that we should move back to Atlanta, to Chicago, Harlem, out West, or to Washington, D. C., where Nathaniel was in school, anywhere but where we was at. Like things would be different if we were, 'Back with our own kind,' she would say."

"It must have been real hard for her to feel like she was going through all of this without a female confidant." I asked, "Did she tell the church ladies or Ms. Bea what had happened?"

"I don't know that she tol Ms. Bea anythin, but she tol the church ladies at least one of 'em a while afterwards. She didn't tell her family much, 'cause she was too ashamed, and afraid they might come back at her up in arms to do somethin that Althea wasn't up to, ner Mama." Moses asked, "Who we a goin to prosecute, who we a goin after, the whole U.S. Army?"

I shrugged my shoulders, and shook my head.

Moses told me, "Things went from bad to worse."

"Good God, don't tell me she got pregnant!?" I half questioned, half exclaimed.

"Yes she was, and that made Mama's argument all the much stronger. We went up to Washington, D. C., 'bout a month after, for Nathan's graduation early in June of 1954, and that was one fine time. Everybody seemed to be so happy, except Althea. Even the Handleys came along. Afterwards, Mama was a beggin me to move back to the city. I was 'bout illiterate, and couldn't see me holdin no kinda job at my age what paid enough money to move us ner to live nowheres else. Eula Mae done tol one big lie to her sisters 'bout us bein so well off. Course, I didn't know 'bout it at the time, but she did. Was we to say we went under 'cause the pecan crop didn't come in, and sold all my property, and still didn't have nothin?

Well, 'bout a month and a half after Althea's tragedy which had occurred the first of May, one of the church ladies had invited us to a weddin in Columbus for her daughter. It was a June weddin and Mama got Althea to dress up pretty in lavender and did up her hair and we was a takin her to this weddin. We caught the train in Chipley and rode down to Columbus. The Korean War had been over 'bout a year and soldier boys was a crawlin all over the depot when we got there to Columbus. Althea was a shakin like a leaf on a tree. We went on to the weddin and come home by the train.

Pride, it is an awful thing. Had been a little colored boy with green eyes 'bout ten years old a sittin on the church steps and Eula Mae, not seein as he had nobody with him, asked him was he a comin inside and he tol us he wasn't allowed inside 'cause he was mullato. See, the blacks didn't fully accept'em and neither did the whites. They was lost children back then, and here we was with this woman child, carryin a child of rape would be mulatto. It seemed me and Mama we done took Althea from a bad place to a worse place with tryin to help her 'come accustomed again."

I attempted to console him, "You couldn't blame yourselves for what happened to Althea."

"We could, and we did. Althea was not eatin and Mama was a tryin to feed her oatmeal with a spoon, and it seemed Althea was set on starvin herself to death. She weren't talkin none at all. It seemed Althea's life was at stake. Mama and me, we had to have a serious discussion on what we was to do. I done spoke to The Good Doctor, a tryin to get him to consider an abortion for Althea. I tol him out loud that I knowed what he was a doin with them white women what come out there. He got all mad, as I spected he would, and he threatened to throw us off the place if I mentioned one word to him 'bout it again. I was 'bout goin to ask him fer some money so I could take Althea somewheres proper, but I could see he weren't up to no further to be said 'bout it. I would'a had to find a doctor or two would say Althea's life was at stake. Mama said they was places that could take care of such things if Althea's life was at stake, but that would'a meant tellin the whole story and we couldn't get Althea to open her mouth fer food ner talkin.

So, directly Mama tol the church ladies, at least one of them, and she up and produced a paper. It were a letter to her regardin one of her nieces that had found herself in some sucha predicament as Althea's. The letter was from Mayhayley Lancaster, the fortune teller in Heard County what came later to testify 'gainst John Wallace. Now this lady was a lawyer, and a teacher, so she was respected, even though she was a numbers runner and knew all the dark secrets of so many in her day.

The letter was dated 1946, that was long afore all that John Wallace stuff happened, where them black boys testified 'gainst that white man, and it was addressed to the church lady, Sister Martha. There was a map with the letter. Sister Martha tol Mama that she done taken her niece to see this woman, described in the letter by the name of Swamp Witch Wilma, what lived out near the river in a house she built herself on landlocked property in the middle of the swamp. Some said she built her house by herself, and some said she had the hoboes from the railroad build it and paid them with gold coins. This Swamp Witch Wilma was recommended by Mayhayley. Accordin to Sister Martha, this Witch Wilma would do spells and chants and give potions what would cause a woman to miscarry if it were the spirit's wish.

Well, Eula Mae done 'bout given up hope and her daughter was ailin and she woulda done 'bout anythin to bring her back 'round. They wasn't no time fer thinkin was it the right thing to do. Now

Mama, she inquired of others in the church what had been out to Swamp Witch Wilma's and found that it wasn't so uncommon. She was known to use such things as purple corn rust, ammonia, and other herbs and things to make the girls miscarry, and Mama, she thought it was safer than anythin else. Bein as the church ladies supported her, Mama; she thought she was a doin the right thing.

This Witch Wilma, she were a quadroon from Louisiana, and had a Creole background. She was French, Caucasian, Negro, and Spanish. Some said her paw's family owned this land, was given to her mother as a dowry. Others said she just claimed the land under the train trestles 'cause it weren't desirable to nobody else. Well, Swamp Witch Wilma come up and put claim to it, and didn't nobody contest her, so she went 'bout building her a house in the middle of the swamp. Now I don't rightly know why anyone would want fer to live in a swamp but we was 'bout to meet her. I didn't much like the thought of turnin my daughter's life over to anything called a 'Witch', but we was desperate.

We set out early fer the dirt loggin road supposed to take us directly to the Long Cane Creek. Back in them days, there wasn't a Lake West Point, and people didn't live 'long the river like they do now in they fancy houses. It was the backwaters to the Chattahoochee River and the marsh and swamp all 'round was deep and subject to floodin. The creeks were subject to floodin too, and wide and deep as the river in some places. We was to follow the creek to the railroad, and follow the railroad 'bout a mile deep into the swamp. Now some places you could step off the tracks and walk on dry land, and other places you had to walk the tracks over the trestles that rose up high over the swamp.

We made it down the loggin road as far as we could go, and come up 'long side of the creek. The rains had the creek swole up, and the marsh it were deep in places. The water was high and the creek was way up outta its bank. One good thing was ain't no alligators in this swamp, too cold fer'em, but it was snakes there and Eula Mae, she feared them most.

We held hands as we walked carefully 'cross the long trestle that we had come upon. Althea weren't talkin but she was a followin 'long, and fer long we come 'cross the tracks to find a wide place open and dry, like a island it were there in the swamp. Down and almost under the next trestle, there was the house. It were a nice log cabin, built of solid logs, and bigger and better than I imagined bein built by a woman. That cabin was 'bout a mile and a half through the swamp from the loggin road where we done parked the truck.

They was peacocks in the trees took to screamin as we come up. Now ifin you ain't never heard a peacock holler, well it sent chills up my spine. The house, it were raised up off the ground 'bout ten feet, on posts, solid as the walls, and I thought must be some strong woman what built this house. 'Bout that time, Swamp Witch Wilma, she comes out onto the porch with a big bibbed bonnet on her head, old timey one like the women used to wear.

I took off my hat, and I tol her, 'Mayhayley, she sent us.' She don't say nothin, but motioned fer us to come up and onto the porch. I could see this woman good now, and she had skin was fair as yorn, and eyes icy blue as the summer sky, but her hair was coarse and black as mine used to be, afore all this gray set in. She looked like she weren't one day shy of a hundred years old. She walk right over and took Althea by the hand and ain't said a word now, and took her into the house and us behind them followed.

They was a big front room and furniture, antiques fine as any white woman has ever owned, a kitchen there to the side, had bottles and all lined up 'long a great number of shelves. They was chicken feet strung up like chile peppers and onions a hangin from the ceilin all over, and baskets full of weeds a hangin all 'long the walls. The house it were damp and dusty, and smelled of mildew and camphor.

Miss Wilma shook her head and her bonnet slipped back and her hair come out, black with a white streak right down the center. She had all gold teeth, even the front ones. She started to talkin and I couldn't hardly make out a word she was a sayin, half French, half Spanish, and a few words in English. She took Althea into the bedroom and pulled back the covers and lay her down. Eula Mae, she done pulled up a chair aside of her. 'How long she is?' Miss Wilma asked, and Mama says, 'Bout two months.' Miss Wilma says, 'Alright then is good. Ella estara bien, vous lui sortir avec moi.'

Now I heard the words but didn't know what they was a sayin. I don't know no other language, but I remember what she said. She got Eula Mae by the arm fer to make her get up, but she was a holdin her baby girl by the hand and she wasn't goin nowheres. 'Miss Wilma,' I say, 'she ain't a movin if that's what you mean to say.' She says then to me, 'Very well, you go now, four to five day you come back.' I looked at Eula Mae and she looked back at Althea. I turned to go, then I turned back to give Althea a kiss and her mama too.

I got out onto the porch and I stood there a while with the door closed behind me. I heard all manner of tongues and chantin and it sounded like Eula Mae had done joined in with her. I made my way back to the truck what was a waitin at the loggin road and drove on home through the pine forest and down the highway. It didn't set right with me from the start, naw, but I done let it go on, and Mama seemed she was 'bout it bein okay and all.

When I drove into the drive, The Good Doctor had done come home fer lunch. He says, 'Where you been?' and I says, 'Done took Eula Mae and Althea to the train station fer to go stay with folks fer a spell,' another lie I done tol. The Good Doctor, he says, 'Good thing, boy, but that basement ain't goin to clean itself, and I got customers comin out to here this evenin!' I said, 'Yes sir, I'll get right on it.' So that's what I done.

I worked until dark and then sat on the steps. Ms. Beas's music was a playin, some jazzy scat tune. Lady come up in a Cadillac Coupe de Ville, all by herself. 'Bout a hour later I heard her yell out once. Then she come out lookin happier than a tick on a fat dog, and drove away. All I could think 'bout was my babies in the swamp. I didn't sleep much that night.

Next three days it was a rainin and a stormin, day and night, so bad I had to get pans out to catch the leaks. I thought 'bout them women in the swamp, but weren't no gettin to 'em. It was a real toad strangler. I felt 'bout like the poorest man alive. Thundered loud and lightnin crackin from the clouds to the ground all 'round. Then come a day with the rain slackened up. I knew that them creeks was a goin to be all swollen up. I barely got that old truck down the loggin road. Was slip sliddin in that wet red clay, had to get out and get myself unstuck twice. I couldn't get the truck in as far as I did the last time.

I took out to walkin the rest of the loggin road. By the time I was at the creek I was covered in so much red mud I 'bout had to get into the creek to clean myself up. Long Cane was a runnin fast and furious. I scraped off most of the slippery clay from my boots on the rocks and took off on the tracks through the swamp. Weren't many places I could step off the tracks. Was some places with gravel here and there. I come to the trestle and walked over knowin if I was to fall I'd go right out to the river. The water rushin out to the Chattahoochee seemed as if it would be 'bout to take the trestle with it.

I got to where I could see the house and it 'bout surrounded by water. Didn't hear no peacocks this time, but afore I stepped off the tracks good Swamp Witch Wilma was on the porch. I slid down the hill from the trestle and twisted my ankle some. It weren't real bad, but it was sore. She led me right into the house, without sayin a word, and Eula Mae come to me and said Althea was real sick. Said she been a bleedin bad, real bad, fer three days now, and that first night, after Witch Wilma give her the tonic, her face and tongue swells up bad and her breathin got off bad right away. She said her baby was a dyin and we needed to get her to the hospital.

Well, I was as scared as any man might be, and I didn't know how's we to get Althea to no hospital. The hospital weren't that far down the main highway, but gettin back to the loggin road with a sick girl what can't walk, well that just might not to be done. I give Swamp Witch Wilma a fifty dollar note and bent over to scoop Althea up in my arms. She was in a fever. She sounded awful, like death already had her, and her body as limp as a dish rag. Mama wrapped a blanket 'round her and we headed out the door. It was late afternoon and the sky was already darkened black from the storm clouds a rollin overhead and it had been mistin rain and now begun to sprinkle again like more was to come."

Moses stopped. He had become emotional and tears welled in his eyes. "I can excuse myself Moses, if you don't want to go on, I understand."

He seemed exhausted. He dropped the cross he had been fidgeting with from his hands. I handed him some tissues. He blotted his eyes. "No ma'am, just a minute. I want to tell it all." And he did, through tears of remorse and grief.

Moses and Eula Mae had set out up the hill to the trestle, with Althea in his arms. Moses's ankle was throbbing by this point. When they made it through the tall weeds and up to the trestle, his back was strained because Althea was no small child. The rain had started coming in heavy drops. Moses could hear his daughter's hard gurgling breaths. Across the trestle, above the swirling torrent twenty feet below, they stepped carefully to walk the ties. He had carried Althea about fifty yards on the trestle and had about fifty more yards to go. Then it stopped. The sound of her breathing was gone. He went to his knees in the midst of the track and Eula Mae sat down beside him and screamed, "No, not my baby! No!" They knew she was gone.

The blanket fell to the rushing water, and Althea's body was quickly slick with wetness. Moses could hardly stand, and his heart was wrenched as if someone had crushed it in a vice. They both held to her and Moses had to make Eula Mae let go if he was to be able to get her body down the track. They felt the train before they heard it. The rails began to tremble. The sound of a fast moving train was growing closer as they tried to hurry with their heavy load. Eula Mae grabbed to tug at her daughter again.

When they saw the light coming around the bend, they knew that they had to let go of Althea's body completely if they were going to make it to where they could safely get off of the track. As they watched her slip into the darkness of the fast moving water, lightning streaked across the sky and the rains began to pour. They ran down the trestle and made it off of the tracks, about the time the train came whizzing past. Their wailing could have probably been heard over the noise of the train had there been anyone to hear.

More lies. To The Good Doctor, Ms. Bea, and the church ladies, Althea had decided to stay with her family in the city, where people don't worry so much about other folk's business. To family, Althea had run off to see if she could get discovered for her singing talent, and if anyone were to hear about her or to see her, they were to call immediately. In that way, Eula Mae might have some sympathy from her family and the family could imagine hope. Eula Mae imagined Althea and her child had become angels in God's Heavenly Host.

I said a prayer with Moses; for the Lord to bless him and keep him and give him peace. I begged for the forgiveness of his sins and my own. I hugged his neck. He asked for his cross, which I handed back to him. He told me that Eula Mae nearly grieved herself to death, and died from a stroke at the young age of 47, but not before seeing her son become a *real doctor.* On my next and last visit with Moses at The Colored People's Old Folks Home, we went into the garden behind the building and planted a rose bush in memory of Althea Grier.

∾

I had spent weeks listening to the stories of my dad and my cousin, Sybil. I had five hundred miles in front of me. I thought about how much the world has changed over the course of their lives and my own. When I had told her what I had learned from Moses of Althea's tragedy, I watched her become emotional. Her sadness had a depth to it that I had not expected. She had no words. I had her diaries. I wanted to know the rest of her story.

PART TWO
SYBIL'S STORY
1953-1971

6

Sybil Meets a Stranger

It was near Christmas 1953, and coming back from Montgomery on the train had been a long ride for Sybil. There were delays in Auburn and Opelika with the students who were boarding the train to go home for Christmas break. Even with the delays, it was a shorter ride than going by automobile. Thank God she didn't have to go through Columbus, as the soldiers probably have the station packed this week. There were a few soldiers aboard. A man had been smoking a cigar. They ought to ban such behavior. It made Sybil want a smoke, but the air was too stuffy already. They had come through West Point across the river and would be at the station soon enough.

Sybil wished that she had made arrangements for someone to pick her up at the station once she reached LaGrange. There were pay phones at the station, but she wasn't sure who to call. She had lots of girlfriends who drove motor cars, but most were already out of town for the holidays or busy with their families, parties and such. She could take a taxicab. She wondered if any of her friends were going out to Red's next weekend for roller skating. Sybil had graduated from LaGrange College with a Bachelor in Arts in the spring of this year. Some of the girls had decided they were too old for roller skating, but Sybil enjoyed it, and enjoyed being around the younger people. Some people even called her Bohemian. She liked that word.

She had concentrated her studies in literature, theater and drama. Her mother thought that she should teach. Auntie was a teacher, the first in Harris County, and a spinster. Sybil saw herself more like Little Auntie in Montgomery. Aunt Minnie, whom they called Little Auntie, had wanted to become a nurse. Grandfather Holmes had flat refused her, and said that no decent woman would put herself in the position of handling men-folk. In the middle of the night, Little Auntie had hitched up her horse and rode all the way to Columbus to enroll in the nursing school. Auntie had given her the money to do it and Grandfather was furious. Little Auntie was the youngest child of six siblings, and Grandfather was too old to fight her on it, but she didn't stay a nurse long. She met Uncle Wing, and married right away.

Uncle Wing is a doctor from India, and a most exotic, soft spoken man. Their children are absolutely gorgeous, and both of them quite brilliant. It never set too well with Grandfather Holmes. So Aunt Minnie and Uncle Wing moved to Montgomery where he started a practice and bought a grand home. She thought Little Auntie had been a brave woman to both run off to nursing school and to have married a foreigner like that in her day. It just wasn't done, to disobey your parents or to marry out of your race.

Many of her girlfriends had married in 1949 and 1950, right out of high school, and a lot had dropped out of high school to get married. Most had been pregnant. It was the best way to keep your lover from going off to war. Sybil had graduated in 1949, and never had a real lover in high school. There were those boys who had made mirror warmers of her scarves in high school, but she had never jacketed with any of them. LaGrange College had become officially co-ed in her senior year there, but the few guys who were there were real closet cases, not very impressive. Most of them were hub caps or wet rags, anyway.

The fruitcake that Little Auntie had sent back for her parents felt heavy in her lap. She was just starting to adjust it, when the train whistle began to blow.

They must be nearing town now. The conductor announced the stop. It was already dark when the train slowed to a complete stop, but the depot was well lit. People scurried off the train, pushing for the opened doors. Sybil waited until the flurry passed. She was the last one out of the passenger car.

Sybil noticed him immediately. He stuck out like a sore thumb, the only colored man on this side of the station. The Negros were leaving their passenger car, claiming their baggage and making their way to the other side of the station. The whites had almost completely left the platform. Most had already found their rides with waiting loved ones. A couple of taxicabs were parked at the north end and a couple of taxicabs were parked at the south end. This man stood with his back to the counter, leaning on his elbow, and tipping his hat at the few people walking by. He was a tall man with moderately light skin, not too light or too dark, and dressed in a suit befitting an Ivy Leaguer.

Sybil had her small suitcase in one hand, her purse on her arm, and the fruitcake in the other hand. She walked to the counter, set the fruitcake down, and set down her suitcase, while she fumbled in her purse for her Parliaments.

She brought the cigarette to her lips while she continued to dig through her purse for her matches. The Negro gentleman offered to light her with a stunning silver lighter, and she begged off, "I'll save you a trip to the lynching tree with a penny pack of matches." It was a most intimate gesture for a man to light a woman's cigarette and Negros just didn't do that, light white women's cigarettes. She noticed his hands were fine, with no calluses and nails well-manicured. Sybil found her matches and fired up her Parliament.

"That's a beautiful lighter though," she added, almost apologetically.

"It was a gift, but I don't smoke. I just carry it for good luck."

"Has it gotten you lucky?" she inquired, and immediately apologized.

"No, that's quite alright, it has actually," he smiled.

He had the most perfect teeth, and his smile reminded her of Rudolf Valentino, a little curled.

"You don't talk like you are from around here. Where are you from?" Sybil found herself rather entranced.

"I was born in Atlanta, and I attend school in D.C., but I've just come from my auntie's in Harlem," he said proudly.

"Harlem, New York, then; that explains why you might have forgotten the rules."

"Oh I haven't forgotten any rules, just know that sometimes the risks of breaking the rules are worth the punishment," he smiled again.

Sybil blushed slightly, and then asked, "So what brings you down to these parts?"

"Why Christmas of course; I'm visiting with my parents who work out on the Handley place just outside of town in Whitesville."

"I know the place. I've taken a couple of lady friends out there for adjustments by The Good Doctor." Sybil wondered if he knew what sort of adjustments, she seriously doubted he would.

"Yes, I hear The Good Doctor has built up quite a reputation, with folks coming from all over...I'm sorry, my name is Nathaniel Grier." He had taken off his hat and held it in his hands.

"Sybil Hamilton," she replied in response. "My family lives on past there out in Harris County." She didn't know why she felt obliged to continue her conversation with this man, but felt she should cut it short, in case people were taking notice. Not that she cared what people noticed, but for his sake.

"I have to go now; the colored folk usually wait on the back side. I mean, if you are waiting on your folks, that's probably where they'll be. Sybil picked up her suitcase and headed for one of the awaiting cabs.

She had already opened the cab door when she heard, "Wait just a minute, your cake!" Nathaniel brought the cake to her. "My friends call me Nathan," he added.

The cab driver shouted, "Ma'am, is this Nigra a botherin you!"

"No sir!" Sybil shouted back.

"And thank you, Nathan," she added sweetly.

"118 ½ Doughtery Street," she told the cabby as Nathan closed the door. The cab driver sped away.

Sybil thought about this tall dark stranger at the train station. He was so very polite. He moved fluidly and gracefully. He was handsome and daring, refined and educated. He had traveled to places far removed from LaGrange, and wasn't like anyone she had ever met. He had poise and caliber above that of any man who had ever approached her. She had felt instantly infatuated by his charm.

Sybil lived off of Hill Street, just a short distance from the station. Her mama and papa had not liked the idea of her getting an apartment to herself. They thought she should at least have a roommate, another student from the College. Sybil had tried that initially, but it had not worked out. She had been alone in this little duplex for two years now and preferred to not bother with a roommate. She liked her privacy. She even detested the older widow who lived next door. It was more than she needed, with two bedrooms. She had a washer in the kitchen and a line for drying out back. It was a nice brick house, and very clean. There were huge picture windows in the front bedroom and the living room. She had a small dinette set in the kitchen. There were two stone planters on either side, with spindles to the ceiling dividing the kitchen and living areas.

Sybil paid the cabby two dollars. Upon entering her flat, she plugged in the Christmas tree and the window lights. She set the cake on the kitchen table and was about to finish signing her cards when there was a knock at the door.

Melba, the lady next door came over to tell her that her phone had been ringing off the hook for nearly two hours. "Well, I don't rightly know who it could be, Melba, but I am sorry if it disturbed you."

Sybil had to hurry. She was supposed to be at Auntie's house by seven to watch Miracle on 34th Street on Auntie's new television set. Auntie lived in Harris County west of Chipley out on the old home-place, not a stone's throw from Hamilton Farm. All of the aunties and cousins were supposed to be there, along with her sister, whom she had not seen in a year. Her sister had not seen her new red Studebaker Champion convertible. Well it wasn't brand new, it was a 1950 model, she had bought it used, but it was still new to her. She just hoped it cranked after having sat a week while she was in Montgomery.

Glad it wasn't raining, Sybil loaded the car with the fruitcake and her gifts, scarves and slips for the ladies and socks for the men. Working at Behr's

Women's Specialty Shop had its rewards. The car cranked up on the second try. She sat in the drive for a few minutes to let it warm up. She had told her sister about it over the phone. Her sister had scolded her for buying a convertible, but it was her graduation present to herself. She liked it. All summer and into fall she had been able to ride with the top down, with the breeze in her face, and her scarf trailing behind her. She just knew that she should be in the movies. She was far prettier, and just as talented, as Bette Davis in her mind. She was more like Doris Day with a bit of a zing.

It didn't bother her a bit that she might be regarded as a naughty girl, even if she had never had sex. She wasn't about to be driving some old jalopy. She put the car in gear and backed out of the drive. It was about a half hour to Auntie's house.

The first color movie Sybil had ever seen was "Gone with the Wind". Sybil was only eight years old, when Little Auntie had decided to drive to Atlanta to see the movie that had just premiered at The Fox Theater. Her older sister, Arlene, had been twelve. Little Auntie had come from Montgomery to show off her new automobile and insisted that Auntie, Mama, and her two girls come along for the long ride to the theater. They went to the Saturday matinee, and the movie was more than three hours long, but Sybil enjoyed every minute of it. There were "Felix the Cat" and "Mickey Mouse" cartoons. She thought of Scarlett as a naughty girl too, but a strong woman. The movie was grand. The theater was grand also with its colorful mosques and spires, and painted murals all covered in crystals and trimmed in gold. There had to be thousands of people in there that day. The ride home had not seemed so long as the ride up. That seemed such a long time ago.

Sybil pulled into the filling station and the attendant washed her windows and mirrors, checked her tire pressure, and checked her oil. She knew she was going to be late. Auntie liked promptness and Sybil would have to be quiet about the automobile until time to go if the movie was already playing on the television. She had seen televisions once.

She had been to Atlanta to Rich's with her girlfriends and they had them on display for sale. Most of the pictures were snowy and grainy but it was quite remarkable and she wondered at how they must work. Atlanta was too far away, and there weren't any broadcast companies in Columbus until this year when WDAK started broadcasting on television in addition to radio. Auntie had rung her up to say that she had bought one from a catalog and that she could receive this one CBS station with UHF rabbit ears in place. Auntie was not one to react too much, but she seemed genuinely enthralled. Auntie, a school teacher, had always been the first to embrace technology. She was the only one of the four local sisters to have a telephone for years, until they had the party line installed.

Her mother had married one of the two Hamilton brothers. Her Aunt Mary Mae, her mother's sister, had married his brother, and another sister, Aunt Barb, had married the Hamilton brothers' first cousin.

Sybil and her sister had been brought up in the country at Hamilton Farm. Arlene had married a mill worker right out of high school. He was already a plant manager and they had moved to Manchester. Arlene worked as an inspector in one of the mills. She had no desire to go off to school. They were hoping for children but, so far, had no success. After nearly eight years of marriage, they were considering adoption. With Sybil's school schedule and work, she wasn't able to visit her sister as often as she would like.

Sybil was glad that the war was over, and the fighting in Korea had stopped. She expected that there would be lots of eligible young men to marry now that this war was over. That was the hope for most young ladies Sybil's age. Their worst fears were to marry some drunken mill worker who beat his wife and kids. Sybil saw them in Behr's with their fading blue-yellow-green shiners and cut lips, dragging two or three bashful, dirty children in tow. The best a lady could do in these parts was to marry an officer and pray that she not become a widow too soon, or be whisked away to some foreign country. Sybil had been too busy with school to think too much about marriage. She took her studies seriously, but had no idea how she would make it to Hollywood.

When Sybil arrived at Auntie's, she saw Uncle Frank's truck. It was a quarter past seven and she timidly turned the bell while juggling her cake and packages. Auntie let her in and took the cake to the dining room. There was a roaring fire in the fireplace and all were gathered around the new Zenith. She set her packages under the tree. The fresh cedar tree was dressed in glass ornaments from all over the world that Auntie had collected for years, but it had no lights. She feared a fire and never burned any. After hugging her mama, daddy and sister, Sybil found a place on the rug in front of the television.

Of course it was black and white, and Miracle on 34th Street was a delightful showing, but they had not quite figured how to set the vertical hold and a black bar rolled past from time to time. It was a fairly clear picture, and aside from that one problem the movie had been a hit. Sybil still thought the box office theater was the best for viewing a movie. Television wasn't as spectacular as she had thought it might be.

They dined on a smorgasbord of pot-luck, with the Christmas dinner reserved for Christmas Day when everybody would stop in at Aunt Barb's after church. Aunt Barb was the best cook of all of the sisters. Sybil was quick to call Arlene, and Henry and Moe, her cousins, out to the yard to see her new motor car as soon as it appeared that they were done with their meal.

Henry was sixteen and Moe about eighteen. They thought it quite smashing and begged to take it for a spin. Sybil couldn't resist. Henry was fascinated that it had a radio and a heater factory installed. Moe called it a girly car, but he liked what he saw under the hood. He said that it looked easy to work on. Moe was joining the Army, and was expected to ship off after the first of the year. Their older brother, Frank Jr., who was almost grown when Moe and Henry were born, whom they called Bubba, was working in Atlanta and had already married a lady from Chattanooga and had a daughter and a son with another child on the way.

Uncle Frank and Aunt Barb were to carry Aunt Mary Mae, whom they all called Aunt Mae, home in the truck. Sybil was glad because Aunt Mae wore heavily adorned wide brimmed hats, gobs of bright red lipstick and reeked of cheap perfumes. Her papa and mama got into her car. She took them down the long dirt road to their house and waited for the lights to come on before driving away.   Looking at the old house, she was humbled.

None, except for Auntie, had indoor plumbing. Their only heat was from fireplaces they nurtured by day and by night with black coal and wood they had cut themselves.   Driving past Aunt Mae's she was reminded of times in her youth when her father, Uncle Frank and Uncle Bob would gather on Uncle Bob's porch to sing and play music.   Her father played the harmonica, fiddle, and also a saw.   Uncle Bob played the banjo.   Uncle Frank played a wash-board and spoons.   The children and women would eat watermelon and blueberries on these summer days, while the men made their music.   Uncle Bob dipped snuff and had died young of throat cancer, and Aunt Mae was all alone in her house.

Sybil turned on her radio.   She tuned in a station playing Bing Crosby's Christmas music.   She delib-erately or half consciously turned off the Old Salem Road and onto the West Point Road, she wasn't sure.   At Jones crossroads she took a right onto the Whitesville Road and past the Handley place.   It was nearly eleven.   All was dark.   She wondered why she had made that turn.   What had she expected to see?

When she got to her apartment she saw her neighbor's curtain move.   Her lights were on.   As she put the key in the door, she heard the telephone ringing. Who in this world would be calling at this late hour? She dropped her purse and grabbed the phone, "Hamilton residence," she announced.

"My God girl, where have you been?" It was her best friend Bonnie Jean.

Sybil was seriously concerned, "I just got in from my auntie's house in Harris County, why girl, what's the matter with you?"

"I knew you were coming back from Montgomery today and I was trying to hold it until we could talk face to face, but I just can't do it," Bonnie Jean whined.

Sybil directed, "Well you have me now. Don't have a cow; spit it out, whatever is eating you?"

"The rabbit didn't die, Sybil, I am as pregnant as a woman can be!" Bonnie Jean didn't sound very happy about the news and that she wasn't married was all the more cause for alarm.

"So you just tell Charles and you get married," Sybil reassured. She asked "How long have you been on the hook, two years?"

"It's not that simple, Sybil. I have another year of school and Charles has just gotten his business started. To make matters worse, we decided to cool it for a while. I mean we haven't had sex in over four months." Bonnie Jean ended with a long pause of silence and a deep breath.

Sybil didn't quite know what to make of that. Bonnie Jean and Charles had been a couple for a relatively long time.

"Sybil, do you know Sergio Martino?"

"Of Sergio's used cars? I know of him but we have never met." Sybil knew where this was going.

"He's that Latino fellow, you know, that was at Red's in his souped up hot rod when we were out there back in October. All of the high school girls were gathered around him and the boys too, checking out his rod," Bonnie Jean explained, but she didn't need to.

"So you hooked up with this guy?" she asked, as politely as she could.

"Exactly, it was just a one night stand. He came on with his hot-blooded Latin Lover charm, and I had been on the roost for over two months. It was such a screamer, that car! You have to pinky promise you won't say a thing to Charles. Oh tell me now, that you won't," she pleaded.

"Of course I won't," Sybil promised. She inquired, "But what do you plan to do?"

"I can't possibly tell Charles and pretend that I somehow magically got knocked up and now he *has* to marry me. We're not even engaged and never will be if he finds out. I could care less about Sergio at this point and couldn't see myself married to a used car salesman...geez Louise...not ever in a million years would my folks accept that of me, their only daughter…and forget about school. God knows if my older brother ever found out, Sergio would be a dead man. I'm as blonde as you and Charles is too, that would be a real hoot for me to show up with a black haired brown eyed child. I was so into him that night and he said that he was going out to Roanoke to watch the submarine races and asked me if I'd like to ride along. I couldn't resist. The moon was bright on the river and before you know it, we're at the Roanoke Inn. I phoned my mother that I was staying over with you, but I should have told you what I was planning to do. I knew that you would have talked me out of it. I had my diaphragm but I didn't use it. I was thinking, 'Maybe this one time wouldn't hurt a thing.' It was the wrong thing to do. That next morning when he took me to pick up my car at Red's I felt just about like dirt, and now this," she was sobbing as she rambled.

"Get a hold of yourself girly, this can all be worked out, I'm sure. When did you find out?" Sybil tried to get her to start thinking rationally.

"Last Monday, and the doctor says that I'm just two months along."

"Do you have a cousin, an Aunt, a friend you could trust to stay with for about seven months? My sister is thinking of adopting," Sybil offered.

"There's nobody, I just can't risk Charles finding out, he would surely want to see me. I couldn't possibly stay away from him for seven months, or even two or three."

"Honey it's getting late and I have to work tomorrow, I don't mean to cut you off, but could we meet tomorrow for lunch at Dorothy's Diner?"

"Oh no, I couldn't possibly discuss this in a public place. What time are you home?"

"Of course not, what was I thinking? I'm tired. It has been a really long day. Come over to my place around six. I have some errands to run but I should be done around dark. We'll talk more. Don't fret yourself to much about things, I am certain it will all work out," she assured.

"Good night, doll, you're such an angel. Thanks for listening."

Sybil knew that Bonnie Jean wasn't the first person she had taken out to see The Good Doctor, but, at twenty-one, she was the oldest.

7

COMING HOME

Nathan's papa was sure glad to see him. He picked him up at the station and drove as fast as the old truck would go, to get out to the Handley place. When they got out of the truck Nathan could smell supper on the stove. "Mama done made up a huge pot a chicken-n-dumplins," Moses told his son.

Nathan grabbed his bag from the truck bed and went into the house. His mother and sister smothered him with hugs and kisses, and bragged on him so that he thought he was, no, he knew that he was somebody special.

During their meal, Eula Mae told him how Althea had been singing in the church, and was planning to go up to Atlanta next year to sing there. Althea broke into, "Amazing Grace". When she had sung the full chorus, she told Nathan that it wasn't just hymns that she was singing, but she had been singing real black-folk music over at Jeb's on Friday and Saturday nights.

Nathan asked her teasingly, "What do you know about real black-folk music?"

"Why, Ms. Bea just loves it and lets me play her records all the time. I especially like Ella Fitzgerald. She was a orphan girl and ran away to make her name. And, Ms. Bea, she's got this new television. You've just gotta see it. It's really grand."

"I know of Ms. Ella Fitzgerald and I can tell you, the life of musicians and singers isn't always a nice life," Nathan warned her, "I saw a lot of them in Harlem, just trying to get by."

"So how are Isabelle and Irene? Are they getting along alright?" Mama changed the subject, "They don't write as often as they used to."

"Oh, everybody is just fine. They asked about you. Nobody can understand why you still insist on living in the country when there is so much more opportunity in the city," Nathan said casually.

He wasn't expecting to start WWIII. Mama got up from the table and Papa put his fingers to his lips to shush Nathan. Althea broke in, "Mama and Papa fight about this all the time. Papa don't want'ta do nothin but mope around this old place an run behind The Good Doctor an Ms. Bea, a fetchin fer'em like they was the king and the queen of Egypt."

"Althea, you is outta line," Papa interjected.

Althea wasn't finished, "Well it's all true Papa; we could go back to Atlanta even, ifin we don't go to New York or Chicago. We surely have enough money to get there. I think us slaving away for what little these white folks pay us is just sinful, is all. That's what they do, Nathan, they both act like servant people." Mama motioned for her to leave the room.

Althea said she was going down to Jeb's to see if Joshua and the band were playing.

Eula Mae told her, "They is things 'bout this you don't know, you need to be lettin well enough alone." Althea danced her way out of the door.

"Mama, Papa, there is a lot of money out there for education for black men. I have been talking to people in both Washington and New York. My grades are great and they can get me money on scholarship for medical school. You don't have to stay beholden to The Good Doctor and Ms. Bea on my account," Nathan informed them.

"We can talk about this later," Papa said. Eula Mae went about clearing the supper dishes.

"I'm taking the truck down to Jeb's and I'll pick up Althea on the way. Umm, Umm, great meal Mama," he added with a kiss on her cheek.

Nathan whistled for Althea and she came back down the drive to the truck and hopped in. He encouraged her, "So, you're singing in a band?"

"They ain't really a band yet, but they practice together. Joshua, he been playin the keys since he was 'bout two and he plays in the church now. Theo has a horn, what he learnt to play in the War, a trumpet, and it sure is a pretty instrument. A man from Tuskegee, he sometimes come all the way from Alabama on a hound just to play his sax with the boys. He's real good, and I just get up and start the bebop with them, not makin no words really, just like my voice is a instrument in itself, I do. They is even writin music now. They all love it. Folks come from all 'round, Friday and Saturday nights just to listen. Come all the way up from Albany to get shine and all, and sit, and listen, and clap. We mostly just practice on Sundays."

"Old Jeb, he must have the Sherriff in his pocket. I worry 'bout you so young and out here alone with these boys, Althea, it ain't a good place for you to be alone." Nathan expressed his concern and asked, "Are you drinking with these boys?"

It ain't like I'm the only girl in the place, Nathan, the Moody sisters, they are always out here, and sing with me sometimes, and Beulah, and Nadine , why they all come out," Althea evasively sought to give her brother some comfort.

"Are you drinking with these boys?" he asked again.

"I don't taken much to drink, but Sting, now he the man, folk come up from Columbus and come out from LaGrange, an Sting, he drive up in his flashy new Cadillac and all folks be gatherin 'round 'cause Sting, he can set'em up with a little blow. That can make'em work faster in the mills you know, keep'em goin. I like it 'cause it make me sing and all the better."

Nathan could hear the music when he stopped at Jones Crossroad. He was quiet until they reached the long dirt drive down to Jeb's. There was a low blue flag stuck into the ground at the drive. Nathan stopped the truck. "Honey, you have to promise me you won't be doing no blow. You get all hopped up on that stuff and before you know it you can't stop. It's real bad for you, Althea, as your only brother, you have to promise me." He added, "I love you little sister."

Althea looked down at her feet. She wouldn't give Nathan an answer. She smiled and hugged her brother around the neck, and they went on down the drive to Jeb's.

Nathan got to hear his sister sing her bebop, minus the saxophone. Theo and Joshua were both real good, also. Nathan sat in the back of the one room house and sipped a tall Schlitz malt liquor slowly.

Daddy-O Jeb came by and sat a spell with him and told Nathan that all were real proud of him. He asked him if he was planning to come back to practice in LaGrange. He told Nathan they needed a good colored doctor, "'Cause all the blacks, you see, they gotta wait on one side of the white doctor's offices, an the blacks, they sit on the other an wait til all the white's been seen. It just ain't right, you know."

Nathan wondered how long the Deep South would remain so very ignorant. After they got home and everyone was in bed, Nathan lay on his cot and thought of Sybil. She radiated the moonlight with her streaming waves of golden hair. Forbidden. She smelled of sweet and savory perfume, something expensive, he thought. Something, she treated herself to as a woman of privilege. Her skin was as white and creamy as the alabaster statues he had seen at the Smithsonian, chiseled into fine works of art. There were other white women in Washington and New York who could be had for a price, even for a black man's fantasies, but none with the lilting voice or the glow of Sybil. He drifted off to sleep with thoughts of her on his mind.

He woke to a bright sunshine, but it was cold in the bedroom. It was already Monday with Christmas only four days away. He had not brought gifts, except for his father, and needed to go into town.

After a hearty breakfast, he grabbed his coat, borrowed his father's truck and drove into LaGrange.
Mama already had lots of clothes, good store bought
clothes and some made from McCall's patterns by
her sister, Martha. He had bought his father a gold
pocket watch in Washington D. C., one with Lincoln
engraved on the case with the words "Freedom for
All" inscribed beneath. For his mama and sister he
had not yet shopped. Nathan had been doing light
maintenance at the University for spending money
and he had saved for over two years to buy that
watch.

Nathan took a right off of Hill Street, parked
on North Main, and put a dime in the meter. He
wasn't expecting on being in town more than a couple of hours. He walked past business row, across
the square, down the hill, and came to KayBee's
Jewelers. The prices were way out of his league, but
the clerk was kind enough to direct him to the pawn
shop. The pawn shop was right in front of where he
had parked. He strolled back to the square where
the gold tinsel tree stood tall over the fountain.
There were red ribbons wrapped around all of the
lampposts, wreaths hung on the store fronts, and
quilted Christmas banners of presents and candies
flew high at every corner. The sidewalks were beginning to crowd with shoppers and he was amazed at
how many people were out on the street.

He walked back to the pawn Shop. There was a sign that read, "Pawn, Radio and Bicycle Repair," and another beneath it read, "Certified Public Accountant." He had not noticed these when he parked, and the shop was down a few steps on what would be the basement level. There was a row of new bikes chained to a rack and adorned with red and green ribbons. He went inside.

There was a young man, a greaser, behind the counter. Model airplanes were suspended from the ceiling. Along the wall behind him were pictures of airplanes and war heroes. There was an American flag on the wall and beneath it a shotgun. Nathan noticed a resemblance of one young man in the pictures to the clerk. He looked up at the man, "Your brother?"

"No man, that's me, 11th Air Force, Alaska," the man said.

"I'm sorry, you look younger now than then," Nathan apologized.

"What can I do for you?" the man asked.

"I'm looking for Christmas presents for both my mother and my sister," Nathan explained, "And if your price is right, and I can find something, I would get a present for Ms. Bea and The Good Doctor."

"You must be Nathan Grier," the man went on, "Doc told me all about you, said he sent you up to Howard to keep you outta trouble."

Nathan mused, "Is that what he said, now?"

"I'm Trenton Stipes, call me Trent. I do the Doc's books. I know about where he puts his money. What sort of gifts are you looking for?"

"I had in mind a piece of jewelry for my mother and maybe something for my sister along that same line. Haven't thought much about the Doc and Ms. Bea, it just came to me that I ought to, they have been mighty kind to me."

Trent started his sales pitch, "I have the perfect thing for your mother, a lady brought it in just the other day, said she needed the money to bail her son outta jail, said it didn't mean so much to her anymore."

All of the glass cases were neatly organized and kept locked. Trent walked over to one and Nathan followed. Trent opened the case and lifted a gold plated book on a chain, "It ain't real gold, but it's pretty, made to look like a book and got an inscription on the cover reads, 'All that I am or ever hope to be I owe to my angel mother ~ Abraham Lincoln.' When you open it up," he demonstrated, "there are two glass plates where you put pictures into the frames here. It's the perfect thing like a proud mother would love to wear to church on Sunday, don't cha think?"

"How much are you asking for it?"

"Well, I was going to ask $6.00, I mean it's worth a day's wages for any man, but for you I'll say $4.00"

"I'll take it then, and for my sister?"

"I have these birthstone rings; do you know what month she was born?"

"May, she was born in May."

"That would be emerald, they ain't real, but they are pretty."

"I don't think I like them too much, I mean me, putting a ring on my sister. What else do you have?"

"Well, there is this brooch, it's Lily of the Valley, you know, that's the May flower, and the flowers, they are real ivory, well that's what I was told. It's old, but I don't think it is antique. The flowers are real white and it would look nice pinned to a coat lapel. The base is 14ct gold plated, not solid, and I can give it to you for $4.00 also."

"That will do just fine then. How much for these umbrellas? I don't think a lady can have too many umbrellas, for Ms. Bea."

"I'll give you one of those. I know the perfect thing for The Good Doctor… if you have the cash for it? He has a plane, out at the airport. Just came in here yesterday and bought a brand spanking new radio for it, top of the line. It's the best model I carry, and he was a lookin at the new microphones, and I know just the one he would like to have, right here." He locked the jewelry case and went back to the front behind the counter and around the wall. A few moments later he emerged with a box. "These just came in last week. I only have two. It is the best radio microphone money can buy on today's market. They aren't cheap, but everybody who's anybody has one and Doc said he'd be back in January to buy one."

"What's the price?"

"I'll give it to you for what I paid for it, and that's $15.00."

"Man, I could buy a whole radio for that price."

"You could, and I could sell you a used radio cheaper, but this here is the best microphone 'cause it blocks out all the background noise for pilots, you know, we have to talk clear and be heard with no static or interference. It has a self keying mechanism on it, so you can just hook it here and talk into it from four feet away. I could explain it all to you, but if you don't fly, you wouldn't rightly understand how it works best. I know that Doc, he would love to have it."

"Okay, I'll do it, like I said he's been real good to me."

"Great man, I know everybody will be real pleased. That'll be $23.05 total."

"There sure is a bunch of folk on the sidewalks today."

"The Christmas parade is at 10:00. All the roads on the square will be blocked off. It is a pretty big parade here."

Nathan took his packages, thanked Trent for his help, headed out and up to The Dime Store for wrapping paper. The girl at the counter said she could wrap them for 10 cents apiece, so he let her do that for forty cents. When he was done there, he went back to where the truck was parked. He leaned on the meter watching the crowd gather, knowing he couldn't drive away just yet. Ladies were lining along the curb with covies of small children pushing and squirming to get the best view of the street. A few fathers were present and hoisting the smallest onto their shoulders. Main Street was a one way going north and Nathan heard the first band coming up Church Street from the south, just across the square, probably from the high school.

The parade had a few colorful floats being pulled by tractors. The floats were covered in school children. There were a dozen convertible automobiles filled with waving homecoming queens, Miss Georgia, football captains and coaches. Marching Boy Scouts and Girl Scouts, and other club members held Merry Christmas banners. There were two or three bands, and clowns ran between them tossing candies into the crowd. Santa in his sleigh was on the tallest float at the end, also tossing candies into the crowd.

With the passing of Santa, the parade was obviously coming to an end as folk piled into their trucks and cars or walked away. Nathan noticed that there were no black people in the parade, child or adult, but many had gathered in the crowd to watch the festivities. He had propped himself against the parking meter for the parade and straightened to fasten his coat around him. He heard that lilting voice.

"Why Nathan Grier, what brings you into town?"

"Sybil!" Nathan exclaimed, very pleased to see her. "Last minute Christmas shopping, of course!"

She was beautiful in her dark green skirt and heels, with her red coat opened below her small waist, and her fur lined hood over her head outlining her fair face. Her step was graceful as she approached. She stopped beside him. Nathan breathed deeply to catch her perfume.

"Did you find everything you need, because we have some lovely ladies apparel at Behr's just up the hill there," Sybil offered thinking of his mother.

"No ma'am, thank you kindly, but I'm all done now," Nathan replied. Then continued, "What's a lovely lady like yourself doing out on a cold day like today, were you out to watch the parade?"

"Well yes, I saw it; my car was in the parade, with the Homecoming Queen. I got a break, because of the parade, and I needed to run an errand. I have to pick up my radio that was in for repairs here with Trent, Mr. Stipes."

They heard him shout from behind the bars around the well of steps leading down to his shop,

"Sybil, Sybil Hamilton, you come on down and get your radio now, I have things to do!" His voice sounded angry and uncivil.

"You are being summoned, Miss Sybil, I rightly ought to be going now. Have a nice day and a very Merry Christmas," Nathan said, tipping his hat.

"Merry Christmas and a Happy New Year to you too," Sybil shouted back over her shoulder. She descended down the steps to the shop.

Nathan watched her the entire way until she was into the shop with the door closed behind her. She had glanced back at him with a smile. He was sure of it.

Upon entering the shop, Sybil found Trent back behind his counter. He was quiet as usual. There were no customers.

"How dare you yell at me like I'm some sort of child?" Sybil demanded, "Who died and made you my papa?"

"Sybil, you were standing out there, in full view of God and everybody, carrying on a conversation with a nigger man like he was your neighbor."

"Last time I checked that wasn't against the law," Sybil quipped back.

"Some laws ain't written," Trent was shouting.

"You need not raise your voice to me. I wouldn't think you would care who I talked to. The proper term is Negro." Sybil was angry, but spoke in a whisper. She didn't want this to escalate into a blazing argument.

"Look, Sybil, men like him, citified Negroes, they are still niggers, but sometimes they lose their place, act like they think they are white folk, and all. There was a Negro boy soldier in the Army what carried a white woman's picture around with him and talked to it every night. Got some white boys real upset and they arranged to have him beat to a bloody pulp. You haven't seen the world, Sybil, like I have, is all. You're only twenty two years old, Sybil, there's a lot you don't know."

"You mean a lot I don't know about men? Don't be so sure of yourself, Trenton Stipes," she uncomfortably remarked.

"It just ain't respectable, Sybil, and you know it ain't," Trenton finished.

He walked into the back and brought out her radio, "I'll carry it for you. Where's your car?"

"What do I owe you?"

"You don't owe me anything, it was just a blown tube and I have plenty."

"The car is supposed to be pulled around back of Behr's, but I don't have my keys. I let the high school use it in the parade, you know, red and white, nice Christmas colors. Someone is supposed to drop them at the store. I think I can manage. Thank You, Trent."

She took the radio under one arm and said, "I wouldn't think you would be one to be too very concerned about my respectability either," as she turned toward the door.

8

BONNIE JEAN

Trenton Stipes had joined the service upon his graduation in 1944. He served two years as a radio operator and an aerial gunner aboard a B-52 Mitchell stationed in the Alaskan Aleutian Islands in the 11th Air Force. His older sister had died at the age of 22 years from complications of multiple sclerosis. Trent had seen a lot of suffering in his short life. He had planned to re-enlist when his parents were killed in an automobile crash. His father and his mother had both been heavy drinkers and Trent wasn't surprised at the news of their death, but it still pained him greatly.

Trent's parents had left him their small mill house, near the Dunson Plant where they had worked all of their adult lives. It was a clean and well maintained place, but nothing special. There was no note on the house when they passed. Like so many along the row, it was wood framed and painted

white. The floors were shiny hard wood and the
rooms were nicely furnished. No picket fence, but
well laid out gardens that his mother would tend on
better days. He could recall his sister sick and frail
and dying in that house. It had been remodeled
to accommodate her wheelchair. His father could
have afforded a bigger and better place, as he was
a Head Foreman, but they stayed in the small three
bedroom house for Lori, his sister. One day, he
would afford a nice brick house in the country.

In the Air Force, Trent had excelled at anything
to do with numbers and coordinates. He liked working with numbers and had always excelled, even in
grade school. With the money he had earned in the
Air Force, and some of his parent's insurance money,
Trent had opened the shop downtown to exclusively
cater to radios. Often people needed to barter in
exchange of goods for his services, and that's how
the pawn shop had gotten started. He worked on
bikes for local youth mostly. He enjoyed cycling and
did not even own an automobile until he bought his
1950 Chevrolet 3100 pickup truck new.

Mr. Handley had been his first client after getting his accounting license. Dr. Handley's downtown office was just across the street. He came over
to the shop the morning after Trent had put out his
sign. He told Trent that he was making more money
than he could rightly keep up with and neither

he nor his wife was good with the books. He gave
Trent some ledgers and a deal was made wherein
Trent would co-manage an account in both of their
names. Dr. Handley would come by every afternoon
when the office closed and give Trent the receptionist's log, and monies and checks received on a daily
basis. Trent had a huge safe in the back of his basement shop, and The Good Doctor was comfortable
with that arrangement. In the morning, Trent was
to make his deposits into the joint account. Ms.
Bea was never to be bothered with bills or money,
and Trent was to pay all the necessary bills from
this account, minus The Good Doctor's operating
expenses for the office. An allowance of sorts was
to be paid to The Good Doctor, and they would discuss possible investments once a month. Also, every
morning, The Good Doctor would come by with a
log and monies received from his home office, and
Trent was to keep this money separate, and keep it
in his safe for on demand needs and investments.
Trent knew that The Good Doctor did not plan to
report this income to the I.R.S.; after all, everybody
who was able cheated the I.R.S.. Trent was to keep
two sets of books; one was a thick ledger with all
transactions included, and the other set was a divi-
sion of Dr. Handley's downtown office patients and
his home office patients. He was instructed in keeping the confidences of a physician.

Trent, with The Good Doctor's permission, began making small loans for locals with interest. They were mostly small business loans and auto loans for which they would hold the title until such debt was settled. Trent established such a good reputation with Dr. Handley that it wasn't long after, Trent began to keep the books for many doctors, businessmen and others. The bookkeeping was almost all consuming and often Trent had to carry work home. The radio, bicycle repair became more of a hobby and the pawn shop flourished.

Sybil knew that Trent wasn't really a greaser, although he combed his slicked back hair into a Duck-Butt style, and wore his leather flight jacket everywhere he went, even in summer. He didn't much like working on automobiles. A group of greaser boys were almost always hanging around the shop, because Trent would order their parts out of his catalogs, and they would tinker with his tools in the parking spaces in front of the shop, or take them on loan for a fee. She also knew that Trent would sometimes set these boys up to seek his tardy collections, also for a fee.

Trent was a friend of her cousin Henry's. Unless he was trying to sell you something, Trent was a man of few words. Sybil had dated him a couple of times while in college. He was always a quiet one, not shy, but quiet. She would try to start a conversation with him and he would let her ramble without so much as a word in response. Twice, he had taken her all the way to Langdale, Alabama, for seafood. Twice he had stopped at Bartlett's Ferry Dam to look at the moon over the water. Twice he had tried to get fast with her in his truck, and twice he had come home disappointed. Twice, he had told her that she was the prettiest woman alive, but he had never made her any promises.

Sybil got the radio and her groceries out of the car. She hurried to the front door, and remembered that she had forgotten to call the milkman to let him know that she had returned from her week in Montgomery. Again, the telephone was ringing, and Melba was peering between her curtains. Sybil wondered why she didn't just take the curtain down. The phone stopped ringing before she could answer. She quickly rang up The Good Doctor's office number and made an appointment for Bonnie Jean to be seen at his home office on that very day at 7:00 pm.

Bonnie Jean rang her up to tell her that she was on the way over. Sybil put the coffee on the stove to perk and took a can of evaporated milk from the pantry. She tossed it into the freezer to cool. She thought about how her life was so different from that of her own mother's. She remembered what it was like to get the tepid milk out of the icebox. She was glad that she had a freezer, even if it was a chore

to thaw about once every two months. Trent said
that they were making new "frost free" refrigerators
that would be out on the market in just a few years.
He also said that in ten years they would be producing radios that would fit into a shirt pocket. Sybil
wondered if she would ever be able to afford such
things.

When Bonnie Jean arrived, she was already in
tears, and Sybil could do nothing more than console
her. She poured her a cup of coffee with cream. She
let Bonnie Jean cry it out; repeating most of what
she had told her last night on the phone. When she
seemed about done with it all, Sybil said, "So now
that you know your dilemma, what course of action
do you intend to pursue?"

Bonnie Jean continued to sob and offered no
answer.

Bonnie Jean had completed high school the
same year as Sybil, but was a year behind her in college. She sat at the kitchen table looking like a child
who had just lost her mother.

Sybil remembered a young lady who had come
into the store to buy her mother a dress for her
birthday. They were slow, so Sybil had talked her
into trying on a few dresses herself. In the course
of conversation with the young lady, Sybil learned
that the girl, not more than twelve or thirteen she

guessed, had missed a period and was curious about pregnancy.

As the discussion went on, the young lady admitted that her older brother, who had dropped out of high school in order to work to help pay the bills since their father had left them, had been molesting her since the age of eight. Last year, the young man had begun to rape her. She feared telling her mother, because her mother would be angry at her. She was afraid that her brother might leave and her mother would have no way to pay their bills. Her brother had also told her that he would kill her and their mother if she told.

Sybil immediately called the girl's mother to come to the store. The next day, Sybil rode with them over to Langdale, Alabama, where the girl saw a doctor. Within a few days the mother had called Sybil to say that the girl, only eleven years old Sybil then learned, was indeed pregnant. The mother had been given the name of a doctor in Birmingham who would perform abortions in cases of rape or incest. The lady had called to make an appointment, and the receptionist had told her that it would be $600.00 for the doctor's fee, up front, and the hospital would charge additional fees separately.

Of course the lady did not have that kind of money, but the receptionist was ever so kind to give them Dr. Handley's number, with all due discretion, of course. Dr. Handley was right there in LaGrange, and saw patients, discreetly, in his home office. Sybil had ridden with the girl and her mother to see The Good Doctor. He had only charged her $50.00, and had allowed the mother to stay with the girl throughout the procedure. Sybil never learned what happened to the girl's brother, if anything.

"There are places you can go for an abortion, Bonnie Jean, it's not like it's the end of the world," Sybil offered. "How much money do you have?"

"Gosh, Sybil, I just can't see me doing that, I mean I'm a Christian," Bonnie Jean professed.

"Of course you are, but a Christian with a very serious dilemma, now you need to decide in a hurry what you intend to do," Sybil insisted.

"These places, what do they customarily charge? I only have about $200.00, and to ask my parent's for anything more would certainly raise their suspicions."

"I think we should be able to take care of this for $50.00-$100.00, but you have to swear yourself to secrecy. The doctor that I am thinking of is about the only one outside of Birmingham or Atlanta that can help anyone in these parts," Sybil continued to insist.

"Oh God, of course secrecy, but how do you know of him," she asked.

Sybil, not willing to give up her confidence said, "Don't you worry about it, just go get into the car. I'll be out in a minute."

"You mean, just like that."

"Yes," Sybil concluded, "just like that."

Sybil changed from her heels to a pair of sneakers, but there was no time to change from her dress. She grabbed her coat, purse and keys, forgetting her gloves and made fast for the door. Again the telephone was ringing, but it would have to wait.

They rode out to Dr. Handley's place in Sybil's Studebaker. Bonnie Jean talked most of the way. Nervous energy, Sybil thought. They pulled down the drive to come around to the back of the house. Sybil saw Nathan outside. He was dressed in jeans, but despite the cold air, was wearing no shirt. Sybil imagined he had just cut the wood that he was stacking by the house door. Bonnie Jean got out first and tapped lightly on The Good Doctor's basement door and was promptly let in. Sybil waited in the vehicle. This time she had brought a book to read, but she was distracted.

She saw Nathan look in her direction and make eye contact. He waved, and took his shirt down from the hen box where he had it laying. He pulled his shirt on over his head. She waved back, and gave a slight smile. His back looked so very broad and his muscles were outlined even in his T-Shirt. He walked in her direction, and Sybil pretended not to notice. He went up the back stairs where he retrieved a bucket of scraps from his mother at the Handley's back door, and headed out to the pig sty to feed the two squealing hogs.

Sybil got out of the vehicle and began pacing the drive. Nathan came walking back with the slop bucket and took it back up the stairs. When he came back down he said to Sybil, "That's a mighty fine set of wheels you have there, but I would expect you would be driving something along the line of luxury rather than sport."

"Oh really, it's new, I mean I just bought it in spring. It was my graduation present to myself," she paused, then asked, "so, why would you expect luxury of me?"

"I don't know," Nathan pondered, "just seems that you would."

Sybil held her hands to her breath to warm them, and rubbed them together.

Nathan was to go on with the conversation, feeling a bit more comfortable out of public view, "So how is it that a beautiful lady such as you are, isn't already married?"

Sybil smiled, looking at her hands, "Well how would you know that I'm not, just by not wearing any ring?"

"Well?"

"No, I'm not married. Nope, don't have a beau, not now, well, never really had one to speak of, kind of like my privacy, don't know how likely I'd be to share, and give that up."

"I see. You brought a friend here to see The Good Doctor? I heard he has developed quite a business."

Sybil felt a bit uncomfortable. "Yes well, she's been to another doctor, and he recommended that she get an adjustment," she lied.

Eula Mae was coming down the steps with a large platter, "You best come on to supper, Nathan, it's Mama's fried chicken and mashed potatoes."

She shot Sybil a serious glance.

"Nathan excused himself and said, "I was just keeping Miss Sybil entertained while she waits for her friend."

"You come on now, Nathan; we ain't in the business of entertainin."

Nathan nodded farewell to Sybil, and dutifully followed his mother.

Sybil heard them in the house. Eula Mae was chastising him, "Nathan, you don't be talkin to them white women what comes out here. It don't matter what they do where you is from, it's where you is at that counts. You is in Jim Crow territory and all you have to do is look at one too seriously, or brush up 'gainst one and somebody be yellin rape. It don't matter ifin it's in public or in private. Sometimes private is worse, you never know what they is a goin to say 'bout it. It just ain't done here is all. Now let's say grace."

Sybil was left standing by the back door to the basement when out came Bonnie Jean. "It really wasn't as very awful as I had expected it might be. The Good Doctor treated me quite respectful and professional."

"Great, let's get you back home."

Sybil let Bonnie Jean out on the street where her auto was parked. She assured Sybil that she was just fine to drive, and not to worry about her, she was, "Peachy."

Sybil made Bonnie Jean promise to ring her up if she had any problems at all. She could call her at work or at home. She would be working Tuesday and Wednesday, but would be home all day Thursday and most of Friday. She planned to spend the afternoon of Friday, Christmas Day; at her Aunt Barb's and gave her that number as well.

Sybil went to work the next morning and was hanging up girdles in the lingerie department when in came Trenton Stipes. He was in a rush as he raced around the different departments searching for her. Sybil watched patiently from her spot in the lingerie department. When he spied her, he marched over like a man in control. "Where were you last night? I tried to reach you all evening!"

"I was out." Sybil decided to entertain herself at his expense.

"Out where?" he demanded, "and with who?"

"Since when should I have started reporting my whereabouts to you? I wouldn't think you would be concerned with whom I spend my time!" Sybil was furious.

"I'm sorry, it's just that I kept trying to reach you so late in the evening, I thought maybe something dreadful had happened," he tempered.

"Apology accepted. So what is your great need to reach me?" she asked.

"It's just...well, I don't know, I was thinking maybe we could take in a movie. I don't like how things ended so abruptly with us."

"There was no 'us' Trent. There were you and me on a couple of dates, is all. There is nothing for you to fret over."

"Well, I mean things just didn't work out for either of us, and I'd like to give us another chance. That's all I'm saying," he went on. Trent bit his lip and started fondling the bras on a table.

Sybil took them out of his hands, "You mean, things didn't work out for you, Trent, I am fine with how things worked out." He was getting clanked, and she hated to be the one to do it, but she had no desire for him.

Not to appear foolish, Trent smiled and said, "You know where I am if you should change your mind, Sybil, you know I'm quite fond of you." He backed away from the table to turn toward the door.

Sybil smiled and waved, "I'll keep that in mind."

Her working hours at Behr's seemed long. There weren't nearly as many last minute shoppers as the owner had thought that there would be, so he let Sybil go early. Wednesday was nearly as slow, so again she left early. Thursday hardly seemed a holiday. It was Christmas Eve, and not having any children, and being alone in her tiny apartment, she almost called Trent to see what he must be doing. She knew that he had no one, as well, to spend Holiday time. She could invite him to come out to be with her family at Aunt Barb's tomorrow. That would be the civil thing to do. It would also imply that she perhaps thought of him more seriously than she did.

Sybil had been reading magazines and chain smoking. It was getting late and she turned the radio off when the telephone rang. It was Bonnie Jean, "Sybil, I'm so glad I got you. I am having a horrible time. I'm cramping really bad and I'm running a fever. There isn't much in the way of bleeding, but I'm having a terrible discharge."

"Bonnie Jean, honey, what is your temperature?" Sybil asked.

"Last time I checked it was 102.4, but the cramping is awful. I surely don't know what I am to do. I've told Mama that I'm not feeling well, but the pain is so bad that I think I should scream and that is just going to set Mama off real bad."

"I'm coming over, Bonnie Jean, I've got your Christmas present, and your mama will be none the wiser if I drop by to deliver it," she suggested.

Bonnie Jean was glad as she didn't feel up to dealing with her parents alone and Sybil could always handle such things. Sybil got her coat, purse, keys and gloves and cranked up her Studebaker. She let it warm in the drive a bit. Then off she was for Bonnie Jean's.

Bonnie Jean's father answered the door and Sybil excused herself for the late calling. Her mother told her that Bonnie Jean wasn't feeling too good and must be coming down with a case of the flu. Sybil told her that she had spoken to Bonnie Jean and said that she needed to talk to her privately. She took Sybil into the kitchen where Sybil told Bonnie Jean's mother that she thought Bonnie Jean might have a urinary tract infection that could not wait to be treated. She told her that Bonnie Jean had described to her the cramping she was feeling and felt that they should take her to the hospital without delay. Sybil said that she wanted to see Bonnie Jean, and asked if she just might see her for a minute. She related to Bonnie Jean's mother that she had the exact same symptoms only a year ago, and the doctor insisted on a course of antibiotics and that if the infection was severe enough, she might need to be hospitalized.

She let Sybil go up to Bonnie Jean's room and Sybil told Bonnie Jean to insist that she must have a urinary tract infection, and to persuade the doctor in the emergency room not to suggest anything more. Her parents were just frightened enough to get moving on getting her to the hospital. Sybil followed in her auto behind them. Once at the hospital, Sybil waited with near breathless anticipation, for the doctor to come speak to the family.

It was two hours before the doctor came into the waiting room. The doctor was going to admit her. He told her mother that it seemed Bonnie Jean had a bit of an infection, and she would be requiring some I.V.s for both hydration and antibiotics. He praised them for making the decision to bring her into the hospital, even on Christmas Eve.

Sybil offered to stay with Bonnie jean throughout the night so her parents could attend to Christmas morning with her four younger brothers. She promised to call if there were any problems at all. Bonnie Jean had been put into a room on the maternity floor, and her parents were comfortable that she would be okay and that Sybil would watch her through the night.

After her parents left Bonnie Jean said that the doctor had mumbled something about a botched curettage. He had not said a word to her parents about abortion and for that she was grateful. She was clotting and the doctor said that she should be fine with a few days of antibiotics and some pain relievers. He was giving her codeine and already she was feeling a little better. She expressed that she felt much relief that Sybil had come.

Sybil stayed by her side for four days, except for what time was necessary to change clothes, bathe, and sleep. She excused herself from Aunt Barb's usual celebration and called in sick from work on Monday. By Monday afternoon, they were releasing Bonnie Jean with an oral prescription.

9

FRIENDS IN THE KITCHEN

Within a few weeks Bonnie Jean was feeling much better and girlfriends had gathered at Sybil's to have their hair done. Sybil was the expert at the new cold wave products. Sybil also had a special knack with her scissors. It was the Sunday before Valentine's Day and everyone wanted to look their best. This was a time when the girls could smoke, drink coffee, and share the latest gossip. They all chatted while they waited their turn.

The girls had been meeting about once a month for the last two years at one home or another, but they really seemed to enjoy meeting at Sybil's. There were no parents around to force silence upon them or to criticize their comments. Everyone could be at ease. She always had fresh baked cheese straws and tea cakes set on the tables to munch with the coffee. She also kept current issues of "Beauty and Make-up Guide", other books, and magazines. There were catalogs of the most current dos, which they scrambled over to find that one perfect cut which could be easily swept up into something glamorous for special occasions.

They had two portable hair dryers between them. Each girl brought her own Star-Brite correction treatment and cold wave, which could be bought for under $6.00 at Rexall Drugs, or Miss Clairol Hair Color Bath. They insisted on paying Sybil an additional $6.00 for her time. Sybil had declined the offers initially, but after a few times of standing for six hours or more, she gladly accepted their payment. It was a fun way to earn extra cash, and that was a necessary thing, especially for a single woman.

On this particular day, Peggy Sue McAllister, a strawberry blonde naturally, had brought with her a new Wella product; it was a colorant cream peroxide formula that promised to be less messy than typical dyes or bleaches. Peggy Sue had brought with her, also, a stack of magazines. She wanted Sybil to make her up as blonde as she could get her. She wanted to be like Marilyn Monroe. The conversation began about Marilyn having become the new "sex symbol" and Francine DeLoach, a deep brunette, was convinced that title should go to Elizabeth Taylor for her role in "A Place in the Sun".

Peggy Sue and Francine began to argue, with Francine stating that "Niagara", while filmed in

Technicolor with some gorgeous scenery, didn't really forecast any great talent of Marilyn for acting. Peggy Sue asked Francine if she had seen the picture show, "Gentlemen Prefer Blondes", which Francine had seen, and Francine said that Jane Russell made that film worth watching. Bonnie Jean and Sybil, both natural blondes, decided not to have any opinions and it was up to Francine to make her case. About the time Francine had finished forcing her argument regarding the seductiveness of Elizabeth Taylor's sultry look, Peggy Sue popped out a magazine that she had brought in her stack.

"My sister found this in my brother-in-law's box of 'Popular Mechanics' just yesterday," she said, as she pulled a magazine out of a dark brown wrapper. "She was ab-so-lute-ly livid, my sister. Claimed his brother sent it to him from Chicago as a belated Christmas gift. I told her that she should be glad it's just a magazine." She held up the 1st issue of "Playboy", with Marilyn Monroe on the cover. "There is a centerfold also, I'm not lying, just look at this!" she exclaimed, as she went about thumbing through the pages to find the centerfold.

The girls were all a gasp. Francine shouted, "You are all just a bunch of old biddies. I'm the only one of us who is engaged. I wouldn't want to be on the cover of a fifty cent magazine, I'm far more valuable than that!"

Francine was correct, she was the only one engaged, but Peggy Sue was determined to have the last word, "Well, it's obviously true that, 'Gentlemen Prefer Blondes,' really they do!"

Francine grabbed her purse. She slammed the door on her way out. The girls just giggled and said that Francine would just have to get over herself.

Peggy Sue was the one who put the idea into Sybil's head that she should open her very own beauty salon. "You very well should, Sybil, open your own salon. Not a beauty shop like Nadine has attached to her husband's auto shop out on the Hogansville Road, but a real salon where women can come for facials and manicures, spend the whole day, and feel pampered and well treated. LaGrange needs a local salon. Why, you could sell products, cosmetics and hair care products, and take the business right away from Rexall. They never know how to sell the products they carry anyway."

"I should," Sybil thought out loud. "That's a boss idea. I have a college degree, and I did all of the make-up and hair for the drama club. I know how to cut, and style comes easy to me. I'm sure there are product representatives and demonstrators that would jump at the chance to have their company's products promoted. All I would really need is a business license, and I'm sure Trent could help me secure one. I could take out a loan for the capital to get started. Men do it every day; how hard could it be?"

Bonnie Jean piped in, "Probably a lot harder than it should be, after all, you are a single woman. Doesn't matter that you have a college degree, you still might be destined to work at Behr's for 75 cents an hour for the rest of your natural life."

"Well, Bonnie Jean, you're a real pooper," Peggy Sue sunk in, "nobody said that Sybil would have it made in the shade, but she could cater to the younger, more sophisticated crowds and leave Nadine to dye away the gray of all the old ladies in town."

"You're full of illuminations, Peggy Sue. Well, I do think it's worth investigating, if not pursuing. It wouldn't hurt to try. I have either got to get engaged, like Francine, or I've got to come up with a way to earn more than I'm currently bringing in. Everybody is talking about televisions, and I can't even afford a pop-up toaster to see my own reflection in."

With only two girls to work on today, Sybil was finished with both in just a couple of hours. Peggy Sue offered to clip Sybil's hair, but Sybil declined. She was tired, and all of this talk about owning her own beauty parlor had her head spinning. She assumed she might be able to rent stalls and charge a fee to other stylists. It shouldn't be too hard to establish a client base. She really needed to talk with someone who knew about business plans. She would have to be able to sell herself to the bank first.

Sybil's next day at Behr's seemed like Nowheresville, and the next day was worse. She lilted around on her heels, trying to smile at the ladies who shopped; folding panties, bras and hanging up dresses all day. She was a regular housemaid, only she worked for Mr. Behr, and always with a pleasant expression on her face, and a nice compliment to whomever might purchase some garment tried on. "This dress style really flatters your figure," or, "These girdles are fifty percent off, you really must have two, they trim you down delightfully." She received a twenty percent discount on all merchandise, which allowed her to remain quite fashionable, but there had to be a better way for an honest woman to earn a buck.

At the end of her day, her feet throbbed. She hobbled to her car and sat there freezing in the February cold. Within a few minutes she was off for home and thought she might have a bowl of soup. It hadn't occurred to her that it was actually Valentine's Day until she reached her driveway to find the florist courier in her drive. "Thought I might have missed you Miss Hamilton, these are for you."

He held up a gorgeous arrangement of the largest, deep red roses Sybil had ever seen. They were fully opened, and as fragrant as a fresh apple pie. There was greenery and baby's breath interspersed in the blooms, which were arranged in a tall cut glass vase. She tipped the courier and took them inside. She set them in the center of the coffee table. There was a card, and she knew they had to be from Trent. She didn't bother with what he might have written. She knew he had been after her for his next date, and she hadn't decided that there should be one.

She made herself a can of chicken noodle soup and a pot of fresh coffee. She thought about ringing Trent up to thank him for the roses, but deferred to let him dwell a while. The coffee gave her the zorros, and she found herself restless. She got up and washed all of her hosiery and lingerie and set it out to dry in the bathroom. Her feet were aching and she drew herself a hot bath, adding oil to sooth her skin. She soaked for half an hour.

As she toweled off the telephone was ringing and she expected that it might be Trent. After all, it was getting late in the evening and he was probably wondering why he had not heard from her. She decided not to answer. By the time she was dressed in her nightgown, the telephone was ringing again. She doubted he would let it ring so very long so she answered.

It was Bonnie Jean, "I guess men do prefer blondes. Sybil, you'll never guess what just happened."

Sybil guessed, "Charles, he purposed to you!"

"Well, of course he did!" Bonnie Jean continued, "And it's a full carat diamond, much grander by far than Francine's. She's going to be so jealous."

"Well tell me all about it," Sybil encouraged.

"Mama and Daddy had taken the kids out to the Callaway Auditorium to see some play that was showing tonight. I think Daddy knew what was about to happen. I was planning a nice romantic dinner with Charles at our place, and daddy had said they would be out late. I had a white linen cloth and candles on the table. We had tenderloin steaks and asparagus with Hollandaise."

"I don't need all the details just get to the core, the suspense is killing me."

"I knew right off what he was about to do when he got down on bended knee and then he showed me the rock and said that he couldn't imagine living another year in his life without me by his side, 'Will you say that you'll marry me, my love?' he says."

"And you naturally said yes."

"Oh of course I said yes, and he placed the ring onto my finger and kissed me so deeply. I have to tell you that I did not at all think the evening was going to be so divine. He showed up with a bouquet of flowers that looked like something you would give your mother on Mother's Day, all pink and yellow with bows. Said the florist was all out of roses. I was just miffed. Then he hands me this Whitman's Sampler, and I'm thinking he really has no class, he should have made prior arrangements, after all, it is Valentine's Day."

"I'm sure he had other things on his mind, dear, I wouldn't take it personally," Sybil consoled.

"Oh of course he did, he's planning to have a wife, and I couldn't be happier that he finally popped the question. I'm on cloud nine, and he knows I'm delighted. He went on to tell me that we should look for a house right away, as he doesn't want a long engagement. My folks just love him, you know. My younger brothers are already taking dibs on my room. I'm entirely dazzled."

"I know you are, doll, and he is a lucky man, too. You get some good sleep tonight and know that you are loved."

Sybil was genuinely excited for Bonnie Jean. She had known it was a matter of time before Charles either popped the question or let her go. It had to be one or the other. Men get all funny when they are facing such decisions. Sybil wondered on Trent's intentions.

Wednesday and Thursday were just as laborious as the first of the week and Sybil still had not thanked Trent for the flowers. By Friday afternoon, she had made up her mind that she would approach him around quitting time. Although Mr. Behr had said she could go at five, she waited until six so she could catch Trent as he was leaving the shop.

She left by the front door, and proceeded up the sidewalk and just over the hill. There was Trent, helping Mary Jane Morgan into his Chevy. She was all smiles and looking all pleased with herself and Sybil was appalled. The audacity of the bastard to send her flowers and then hook up with this girl, only three days later, who couldn't yet be out of high school. She was a senior, Sybil thought, and Trent had to be ten years older, at least.

Sybil found herself fuming and turned to walk back down the hill to her auto. Although she was hot, she had to ask herself why she was so concerned when she had dismissed him so easily for having sent the flowers in the first place. It was a matter of principle, she thought, that he had not even given her chance to respond before whisking off with some little fuzzy duck. She knew she was drowning. Why hadn't she had the courage to simply confront the two of them? Well, she would confront him tomorrow for sure.

Sybil did not rest well at all that night. Her mind was boiling. She thought that she should just take her savings and go to Atlanta and buy herself a new television. Trent didn't feel like she could afford one. It was getting to the point that she couldn't carry on a normal conversation for all of the television talk.

Atlanta and Columbus both had broadcasting companies by now and people talked about the television characters as if they were real people living real lives on the screen.

There were soap operas where homemakers got so deeply involved with the characters that you would think they were talking about their very own relatives. Products were being introduced on television and demonstrations were filmed so that you need not go to the stores at all, except to purchase. It was better than the Sears catalog, because you could watch the workings of all the new appliances, and learn how to use them right from your very own home.

When she finally got off to sleep, she dreamed she was trapped in a house with the walls moving in and her world seemed to be getting smaller and smaller. Rhett Butler took her into his arms as birds circled around her head. He carried her out of the door and set her free, where she fell to spinning in a vortex of storm and debris. She awoke perspiring and dizzy. It was hours before she finally drifted off to sleep, alone in her cold bed.

When Saturday morning came she donned a pair of jeans and a white blouse and sneakers. She had slept in late. She wasn't in the mood to dress up and she wanted to get to Trent's shop before he left. He was usually in until noon on Saturdays. She hurried herself along, grabbing a stale doughnut and a cup of cold coffee. On her way out, she noticed that her box was filled with mail, as if she had not been home for a week, and it occurred to her that she had not checked her mailbox in days.

It was a sunny warm day for February, and Sybil was glad for the warmth. She parked in front of the shop and found Trent busy with a bicycle inside. "Hey Sybil, come on in. I'm almost finished here."

Sybil had not gotten in the door good. Trent seemed happy to see her.

"I'm riding out to the airport, in a few, The Good Doctor has a 1947 Cessna 120 he's rebuilding. You know a plane is like a good woman, dependable, but requires a lot of maintenance," he joked.

Sybil could barely find the humor to smile with what she was feeling inside. "Is that what you sent me the flowers for, maintenance?"

"What flowers?" he asked. "I have to be straight with you, honey, I probably should have, but the word from the bird is; I didn't send you any flowers. Guess you must have a suitor out there who wishes to remain anonymous. You won't even let me get to first base, why should I send you flowers?"

Sybil was stunned. She thought about the card. She had not even read it.

"I need to refuel. How about taking some change there from the register and run over to Charley

Joseph's for a couple of tube steaks with chile and cheese. Could you do that for me? I really have to get this done. Mary Jane Morgan pushed it all the way here yesterday with a broken chain, and her dad's picking it up directly so she can go on a bike ride with her friends at Callaway Gardens this afternoon. We should do that sometime, me and you."

"Yes, of course, we should." Sybil got some change from the register and left. She walked across the square, down the street, up to the window at Charley Joseph's and placed her order. Who in this world could have sent her flowers if it wasn't Trent? She had no clue.

When she returned with the hot dogs, Mary Jane Morgan waved from her dad's truck and Mr. Morgan was settling with Trent. How could she have been jealous of this sweet little school girl? Fact is, she was jealous, and that had to mean something. She wouldn't even let him get to first base. That was practically an insult that she was prudish, and that's not really how she wanted to be regarded.

Trent took the bicycle out to the Morgan's truck and Sybil followed. He asked Sybil to come along with him to the airport, but she declined, knowing it was only a half-hearted request. Men don't really want women around when they are talking engines and things of that nature. She told Trent that she needed to tend to her laundry, which was true. She really wanted to get home to see who had sent the roses.

When she arrived home she snatched the stack of mail from her mail box, unlocked the door, and tossed the mail onto the coffee table. She grabbed the small card from the roses, and opened the tiny envelope. It read simply, "Nathan."

10

An Idea Blooms

Sybil was shocked. She sat on the sofa with the card in her hand and read it again, "Nathan," how could she have guessed? She was angry, but why? Was she angry that Trent had not sent the roses? Or was she angry at herself for having thought he did? Or was she angry that a colored man had thought enough of her to send her such a romantic greeting, on such a special day? She laughed at herself for feeling such emotion. It was really a lovely gesture, and no small expense. Then it caught her eye.

There was a letter on the table postmarked, "Washington, District of Columbia, 14 FEB 54," with no return address on the envelope. For some reason, she felt compelled to get up and lock her living room door. She took the letter in her hand. It was fine stationary. Carefully she opened and read:

Dear Sybil,

As I am writing on Valentine's Day, I know by now you have received the roses. I hope that you were not offended. I do not believe a woman as lovely as you, whether she has a beau or not, should be without flowers on such a special day.

It is really tough to get through these classes of this last year before medical school. The chemistry is particularly challenging as I had no such classes before college. It is most fascinating, though, to learn about how the body functions on the microscopic level.

I have received my letter of acceptance into the medical school here, pending acceptable performance on my exams, and am looking forward to commencement in June. My parents, sister and many other family members will be here for the event. I plan to return home this summer and look forward to perchance see you again.

Fondly,
Nathaniel Grier

Postscript: You may reach me at the enclosed address if you should decide to write.

There was a small card with his address at the school. Sybil could not possibly entertain the idea of writing him back. It would not be fitting to encourage him in that way. She walked to the kitchen sink and set the lighter to the page. As soon as it was thoroughly burned to ashes, she started to burn the address card. She hesitated and put the card into her dresser drawer. There was no reason to keep it. Surely she would not be writing to this man. Regardless of his race, she barely knew him.

Sybil started going to the library almost every day during lunch and after work. She was determined to learn all that she could about finance and starting a business. Even though she had a college degree, she knew very little about the real world of business. She also went by the school and asked Professor Dunn if he could help her with a formal business plan of sorts. He agreed.

She had collected a world of beauty supply catalogs and knew the costs of everything to be purchased new and used. She had even found a shop in Atlanta that was moving into a larger and newer building and had a huge inventory that they wished to sell. They had commercial dryers, mirrors, work tables and caddies. There were two used manicure stations to be had for pennies on the dollar. The shampoo sinks and the plumbing would be the biggest expense.

It was May already, and the weather was fine on this day. The winds had died down and the flowers were all in bloom. It had been a stormy spring season, and the worst of the summer thunderstorms had not yet started. Sybil thought a nice drive to Atlanta would be a great way to spend the next Saturday afternoon, if the weather held. She went into Trent's shop to inquire if he would be willing to drive her with his truck to Atlanta on the upcoming weekend. She told him that she was looking to purchase a television. He begged her off of the television as he was certain, being such a frivolous item, he should have a couple in the pawn shop very soon. He told her to wait a while and new ones would be sold local for cheap. She told him that she had decided it was best to wait. She needed to focus on getting her business started anyway.

She shared her ideas with Trent about the business. He did not seem disinterested about it, but he wasn't nearly as excited as she. He said that he would agree to keep her books for a small monthly fee, *if* she got anything going. He wasn't the least bit encouraging. He told her that running a business was a lot of hard work...like she wasn't working hard already. She was always early to arrive, although she rarely stayed as late as Mr. Behr. Trent said, "No matter how you feel, you have to show up for work because people are depending on you to be there, even on bad days."

"Trent, if you are doing something you love, it doesn't feel like work. I'm tired of working for pennies for someone else to reap the rewards," Sybil insisted, "I want to work for myself."

Sybil left the pawn shop feeling a bit down, and second guessing herself. She walked down the street and took the telephone number of a building that was for lease. She thought it would be a grand location for her salon. It was an empty building diagonally across from the theater. It had been the home of a boutique that had gone out of business nearly a year ago. The front façade of the building was black marble tiles. It was spacious on either side of the entrance and Sybil could see through the windows that the building was very deep as well. The floors were tiled gray and appeared to be intact. She could imagine commercial dryers on either side of the back with four work stalls or stations toward the front. There was enough space in the front for at least two manicure stations, and a small waiting area. There was plenty of room in the very back for two sinks for shampooing, side-by-side. She would need a counter for the register.

Sybil purchased a copy of the Atlanta Journal and went back up the street to Rexall Drugs. She asked to speak to the manager and began to question him about wholesale prices. He told her that the company reps who brought merchandise in were always begging for more shelf space for their products, but he simply had no more room for large displays. He gave her the names and numbers for two such representatives.

She paused by the card counter and picked up a pack of small "Thank You" cards. She figured that this would be a more appropriate manner to express thanks for Nathan's flowers. It would be more formal and less intimate than writing a letter in response, while still acknowledging him in a respectable manner. In as much as it had been more than two months, she would not appear too eager. It had been bothering her that she had not acknowledged him at all, when he had been so very kind and thoughtful.

It occurred to her, once she was home and about to write out a "Thank You" note, that Nathan had to have recalled her address from that first chance meeting at the train station. Her name, address and number had been held private from the phone book that was published. She asked for the privacy because she is a single woman living alone. He had to have committed it to memory when she yelled it to the taxi driver. She made her quick note:

The roses were gorgeous. I know that your family will be very glad to see you come summer.

Sincerely,
Sybil

It was simple and kind enough and she was satisfied that it wasn't too very encouraging. She addressed the envelope and dropped it into the box. She poured herself some coffee and set about reading her paper.

The headline news for this Wednesday, May 17th issue was a huge and verbose article about a case in Topeka and its ramifications for the whole country. It was Brown vs. The Board of Education, and indicated that the Warren court's 9-0 vote was that, "Separate educational facilities were inherently unequal." It cited case studies of black children who had been given both black and white dolls to play with and how the black children preferred the white dolls and made negative comments associated with the black dolls. Basically, de jure racial segregation was ruled a violation of the Equal Protection Clause of the Fourteenth Amendment of the United States Constitution.

There were many articles and commentaries, and it appeared that Georgia lawmakers, legislators and the like were preparing to challenge this ruling. "Governor Talmadge remains a staunch supporter of racial segregation." Of course he would, thought Sybil.

She turned to the ads in the back of the paper. There were two listings for beauty supply companies. One advertised itself as the, "The largest warehouse for beauty supply in the country." Sybil doubted if such was really true, but they must have a huge inventory to profess such a claim. She made a note of the address and took out her Rand McNally to find the location. Sybil decided she would go to Atlanta on Saturday, with or without Trent.

Saturday came and Sybil was up early for her ride to Atlanta. She left LaGrange with the top down in a cool, but sunny 71 degrees. She had on her coat and hood, had tucked her scarves deep around her neck, and ran her heater at full blast. It did not matter to her, the cold; she was glad for the sunshine and hopeful for a fruitful adventure. She went off up the Atlanta Highway through Newnan.

As she was driving down Main Street in Newnan, she noticed a Beauty Shop by the name of Empress Creations. She turned her Studebaker around and went back to the shop. The proprietor was a red-haired lady named Edna and although she was very busy, she was more than happy to speak with Sybil about her shop. Her shop was set up much in the manner that Sybil had imagined for her own. Edna spoke with her about the intricacies of running her own business. She talked at length about the obstacles that she was able to overcome, mainly financing, which her husband was able to acquire.

Edna told Sybil that she should hire girls who could specialize in one treatment or another, and not limit herself to just those features which guaranteed a larger profit, because it was all about making the client feel completely pampered and not selectively attended to, even if those services didn't provide for a huge profit, they would bring the clients back in for more.

As Sybil was about to leave, Edna came to the front to see her out and leaned in to whisper, "The trick is to give them something that they could not possibly obtain at home, like a style that simply could not be managed from the kitchen sink. Look here," she pointed to some magazines that she held in her arms, "these are all out of Hollywood, they are screaming hairdos, bouffant, and styles that reach unobtainable heights without teasing or the hair pieces that come in all of the colors that the manufacturers are promoting with their dyes. You have to keep one step ahead of the game by watching what comes out of Hollywood and New York; I promise you won't go wrong. And listen, go to any expos you can, because those are the places to meet all the fabulous stylists who set the stage for the rest of us. There's one in July, six days long, I'll be having one of my girls run the shop that week, and here take this brochure and my number. There is an Expo prior to every season. This one is to prepare for the newest fall looks. The magazines are yours, review these, they show how the trends are being set. If you decide to go, we can ride up together."

Sybil thanked Edna for her time and she took her number, the brochure, and the magazines that Edna had insisted that she review. She already felt encouraged. Newnan was smaller than LaGrange and Edna already had a thriving business after just one year. As she turned to leave, she noticed the furniture store next door was advertising T.V.s for under $200.00. Zenith was supposed to be a good brand. It was a popular brand, and the same as Auntie's. The picture on the display model was clear, and sharp.

She stepped into the store. A gentleman was quickly by her side. He told her of all of the features of the small table top models that he had for $169.00-$199.00. Then he brought her attention to a 1952 Magnavox. It was a gorgeous piece of furniture, not merely a T.V. set. It had double doors and a large 22 inch screen, a radio/phonograph, AM/FM and 3-speed record changer. It was the most handsome set in the store and the gentleman promised the picture was far more superior to the smaller sets, as well as the speaker system. Since it had sat in the store for two years the salesman said that this fine piece of furniture had been marked down from its original price of $329.00 to just $280.00. If she could purchase today, he would include delivery for free.

Sybil knew this was a fair deal. She had been watching the prices on television sets for two years and a console piece of furniture at this price was a steal. Still, she bargained, "I'll offer you $250.00, and not a penny more."

"Ma'am, you'll not regret your purchase, the television is yours."

She went about writing a check and completing the necessary paperwork to assure delivery on the next Saturday. He told her that the check should clear in four days and if all was well the delivery would be by noon the next Saturday. She justified her purchase. She certainly couldn't keep up with the latest fashions without one. $250.00 was over two month's salary for her, and although she was frugal, she only had $720.00 saved up in the three years that she had worked, but she had not spent a dime on anything *frivolous*. She had paid cash for her car, from the monies she received from family for her two graduations, from high school and college. Why should she have to wait and settle for some small used set out of Trent's shop? God only knew how long that would take. She could buy a small one like that for her salon, in due time. The salesman promised not one little scratch on delivery. Trent would probably be furious with her. She could have cared less.

Rain was starting to drizzle, and the sky had become cloudy, so she put up the top. She felt that she had already done a day's work, and the day was only half over. She drove on to the Beauty Supply Warehouse. The warehouse was enormous and she was quickly attended. She was shown all manner of salon necessities, and was handed an inventory record twelve pages long. The wholesale prices were listed in a column along the side. There was every-thing from the simplest box of cold wave in bulk, to the most expensive shampoo sinks and dryers. They carried a variety of hair, skin and nail products. There were salespeople at every corner to explain all of the products. Marketing representatives for all of the major brands were present and she was given another brochure for the Expo in July. Some of these companies, she learned, would actually pay you money if you would agree to carry their brand exclusively in your salon, and give you huge dis-counts on all of their products.

Sybil spent hours rambling around in the sprawl-ing warehouse. It occurred to her that she had not even had lunch yet, and it was already suppertime. Without any clue to where she should dine in this neighborhood, she got into her car and drove to the nearest restaurant sign. She was way out on the west side of the city on West Hunter Street and saw a little spot that looked busy. She was at Paschal's Restaurant. When she went inside, she saw Negro and white dining in the same small building. They weren't at mixed tables. She asked the gentleman at the register if she was at Negro restaurant. The gentleman said, "Ain't no Negro or white in this restaurant, just satiated appetites." She was promptly seated. The menu was limited, but she was served the best fried chicken she had ever eaten.

She got back on the road in plenty of time to make it home before dark. It was a two hour drive on a good day and the traffic had not been very bad coming up. Although it had threatened to rain, there had been none. She was excited about her new television, and about all of the information that she had to work with on getting her business started. She knew that getting a loan would be the greatest hurdle that she had to jump. It was a man's world and she had no real property. In fact, she had no credit history what-so-ever. She was beginning to think that it was a futile and fanciful notion, this dream.

She saw his truck in her drive as she rounded the curve on Hillside. Trenton Stipes was parked in front of her apartment. She was certain that Melba had already called the police, and rightly so. The first thing out of his mouth was that he had been waiting for over an hour for her to come home and a local town cop had already taken his tag number and had a lengthy conversation with him about not needing any trouble in this neighborhood.

"You would think I had committed a crime," Trent went on, "I explained that I was waiting for you to come home and he questioned me like I'm supposed to know your business. I had to give him your name and number."

"I was in Atlanta all day," she curtly replied, and invited him in.

"So you bought a television anyway?" he asked.

Sybil nodded.

"I don't suppose you also bought an antenna?" Trent continued to inquire.

"Well, no, I hadn't thought of that. Auntie uses rabbit ears; I guess I just figured I'd pick those up somewhere." Sybil seriously had not given it a thought.

"Auntie's is near the top of the mountain and closer to Columbus. We are too far from Atlanta. You can use those things if you are in a city where the broadcast signal is strong, but they don't work too well here. I'll come over next week and erect a good one out back. It shouldn't take too long, but I'll need a tall steel pole. The hardware store should carry those. It's a good thing you are on the Hillside end of Doughtery Street."

"I'm glad you know all about that stuff, makes my life a little easier," Sybil smiled.

"Speaking of your life, I've been thinking about what you said about starting a business." Trent dove in, "You sounded serious and although it seems a bit grandiose, this idea of yours, I'm just wondering how serious you are about it?" Trent sounded as if he might even begin to be supportive.

"Oh Trent, I'm thinking it's a marvelous idea. I have been researching for months now and I have a good handle on what I'm going to need and how to get started. I'm going to an Expo on lady's fashions in July. See...I can get a letter of certification there, in cosmetology. It's a whole week long." She handed him the brochure. She also pulled out her papers from her work with Professor Dunn. They had set up lists for the first six months, and figured the antici-pated overhead expenses and income potential. She was genuinely excited to be sharing this with Trent.

Trent looked over the reports and asked, "Have you been to the bank?"

"No, I wanted to have as much pulled together as possible before I make any formal requests. There's so much more to it and I haven't even figured on taxes and insurance, and the cost of the business license. I thought maybe you could help with those,"

Sybil contemplated, as she went into the kitchen with Trent following closely behind.

Trent looked over all of her documentation carefully before he began, "Sybil, I know that you like to think big. I do not doubt that you could be successful, but I think you could cut your start-up expenses in half by going with no more than two stations and dryers, and one sink, etc…, then, as things improve and you establish a faithful clientele, you can add more, and hire in some help. As it is now, you'll be depending on too many other people who don't stand as much to gain as yourself. That's not good business. If you start this alone and hire in one girl part-time to answer your phone and maybe shampoo and sweep up, you'll be fine. If you have three or four stations to manage while you're trying to divide your attention, I think you'll run into big trouble. I mean from the start, take it slow and see how things go."

Trent was making good sense. She really had no other girlfriends as committed to this venture as she was, not even one who had agreed to work for her or with her. Everyone was thinking and saying it was a grand idea, but no one had stepped up to the plate. Sybil had somehow imagined they would come around when they saw how serious she was, but it did not seem to be working that way. She pondered Trent's words.

"Sybil, you get this in order, see where you can make some cuts and go see a loan officer at the bank. If you run into trouble, you come see me. I want you to try at the bank first. I am afraid you are going to run into some problems. Truth is, Sybil, you are the daughter of a poor dirt farmer and you have no real property, no spouse, no second party to hold accountable. I honestly don't believe they are going to give you a chance."

"That's not very encouraging," Sybil said flatly.

"I'm trying to be realistic, Sybil, and I want you to succeed. I just don't think that you'll get off the ground in the conventional manner. Like I said, give it a try. You know where I am," Trent said, as he headed for the door to see himself out. Sybil stayed at the table wondering how she could possibly do this alone.

11

SEEKING SISTER

Nathan knew there was something wrong with his sister. She had clung to him as a child, and some of her behavior could be attributed to hormones, he knew, as she was most definitely changed into a young woman, but there was something else. He thought about what she had said about cocaine on his Christmas visit home.

He was graduating with a B.S., and had four more years of medical school in front of him in Washington. He also had internships. How could he be his sister's keeper? When they got off of the train in D.C., everyone, even Mr. and Mrs. Handley, had shaken his hand or hugged his neck. Althea just hung in the background. She barely smiled at him.

At the commencement exercise, and the banquet that followed, Althea had stood off by herself. When he attempted to engage her, she shrugged her shoulders and pulled away from him. He didn't recall her ever serving a plate. He had approached her, asking her what was wrong with his baby sister, and she had rolled her eyes and said, "Nothing," crossing her arms across her chest, and defiantly pulling away from him. But he knew something was wrong even then. He had to practically force a hug good-bye.

Nathan had planned to come home in the middle of June. It was the middle of July before he had settled the scholarship and financial issues. He knew The Good Doctor would be glad of that. Then, just before he was to board the train to come home, Mama had called him to say that Althea was gone.

"Gone where?" he had asked.

"Just gone, Nathan, we don't know where or with whom, just up and gone," was all he had gotten from his mother.

There had to be more to the story than, "Just gone." How does a sixteen year old just up and disappear? He knew that he wasn't getting the whole truth. His mother had never really been good at lying or keeping secrets from him. She was not telling him everything. First there was all of this talk about her singing in church and planning to go to Atlanta to sing. Then what? She just disappears! Nathan wanted to get to the bottom of things and he would as soon as he was home. The train seemed to plod along slowly.

Sybil had gotten around to acknowledging the roses, nearly three months after they were sent. He really had not expected even that much after the first two weeks with no response. It was a humble excuse of an acknowledgement, an afterthought. Was it truly a ridiculous notion to think that this woman had his heart? Was she to be an impossible conquest? Is that how he regarded her, as a conquest, he wondered?

Nathan slept for the next two hundred miles. A baby crying awoke him. They were coming into Atlanta. Here Nathan had to board another train. To his surprise, the train had arrived an hour earlier than scheduled, which meant that he could board an earlier train for LaGrange. As he was walking across the platform, a group of young white boys came running past and pushed him aside. He nearly collided with a couple about to board another train, "Watch yourself Nigra!" the man yelled. Nathan gave no response.

It was hot and Nathan finally found the colored people's water fountain next to the white's only fountain. He drank long to quench his thirst. He thought about the Brown vs. The Board of Education ruling and wondered how many years it would really take for his people to have their Constitutional Rights.

The Independence Day parade in Washington had been quite a sight. There were marchers with

"Amendment Fourteen" banners, his people. How could someone like Sybil ever relate to his people? He boarded his train, with less than a hundred miles to go.

It was not yet 5:00 pm when his train rolled into town. His parents weren't expected before 6:00. Nathan decided to walk up to the Hardware Store or the Feed and Seed to see if he could find a couple of fishing poles for him and his dad. The Martins always opened the catfish lake the first week in July. They charged people a buck and a half to fish all day through July and August, then seined the lake in September.

Nathan was studying the poles and tackle in the Hardware Store when Sybil noticed him. Mr. Danson was filling her father's order while she waited. Nathan was dressed in a fine business suit and Sybil had a fleeting vision of Trent in his jeans, t-shirt and leather fly jacket. He looked marvelously swell, Nathan did, and he carried himself well. He held his hat in his hand as he handled the tackle.

She approached him, "Howdy stranger," she spoke.

He turned to face her and his heart nearly stopped, "Miss Hamilton, I didn't see you there."

"I know, sometimes I'm invisible like that," she smiled.

"No, it's not that, I'm preoccupied really, my sister, Althea, has gone missing."

"Missing? That's pretty serious," Sybil supposed.

"Yes, well, my folks seem to be taking it in stride. I planned to be here in the middle of June. Well, I guess you know that. I had to move out of the undergraduate dorm and well, wait on some financial matters to be settled. Didn't seem like there was any reason to hurry home"

"Of course, I did get your letter, I…"

"… Don't bother explaining. It's not necessary."

"Let me give you a ride home," Sybil offered.

"I wouldn't put you out like that. I mean, me being black and all, and you being white and single, people might talk," Nathan pardoned.

"I don't guess you know me well enough. I don't give a bloody rotten damn about what people in this town think of me," Sybil quipped. She could feel the anger in her own voice. She tempered herself, "I have to go out that way to carry my father some nuts and bolts and hinges for a new barn door he's constructing. It seems his mule, Lucy, is intent on running away."

"Althea and Lucy must know something we haven't figured out yet. Why, yes then. It will be a surprise when Mama and Papa see us drive up early," Nathan accepted.

He made his purchase and Sybil paid her father's bill. Nathan held the door and put the cane poles into the back of the convertible. He hoisted his heavy bag into the back seat, and commented, "Not being able to put the top up, are you sure you don't mind me riding along?"

"Don't be silly, get in." She already had the engine running and Nathan took his place in the front seat beside her. He had never been this close to her and the fragrance of her perfume was intoxicating.

"Did I detect a bit of animosity between you and the town folk?" Nathan started.

"It was that obvious?"

"You sounded upset about something."

"Oh it's nothing really, it's not anger at anyone in particular. It's the system of things," Sybil skirted.

"Do tell," Nathan encouraged, "I can certainly relate to that comment."

"I am starting a new business, a salon," she went on.

"Congratulations!"

"I wouldn't be so quick to congratulate. It isn't exactly a successful venture at this point. I am just getting my feet off the ground. I have rented a space in town, and have planned out every last detail. Banks and other financial institutions, they will pay a man for crops he hasn't yet planted, but won't give a woman the time of day on a sure thing.

They persist in discriminating against women in extending credit. Without access to credit, how can we develop sources of income, build an asset base, or develop a credit history. The loan officer tells me, 'We don't have the option to finance such *domestic enterprises* as these which are best served from a basement or kitchen.' I have had to accept the terms of a rather unconventional financing agreement, and I am not all that pleased with my situation."

"It's a white man's world, Sybil, and we are minorities, no offense fair lady, but black men have that same problem, and I couldn't imagine what it must be like for a black woman in this world today." Nathan solemnly added, "A woman like my sister."

Sybil asked, "So what has become of her? You said she's gone missing."

"That's the mystery of it. No one seems to know what has become of her. At least no one is saying. I fear that there is more to the story than my parents are willing to share. It's not like my mother to be so vague on such important issues. Normally she knows all about everything and all she will say is that Althea is gone, doesn't know where or with whom, just gone."

"That's so sad," Sybil comforted. "Was she seeing anyone? I mean girls sometimes do on the sly, without their parent's approval or knowledge."

"Not Althea, no, she was all about being discovered for her singing talent, there is only one boy that she has been remotely interested in and Joshua, a little guy in a jam band, is still around and Papa insists that he doesn't know a thing about Althea. Papa seems as elusive as Mama about the whole matter."

"Well, if you need work to keep your mind off of things you can come by my shop. I'm there twelve hours a day, from 8:00 am to 8:00 pm and then some. I have more painting to do and I'm having some interior walls done. The floors need polishing. The air-conditioning and plumbing are about finished. Once those are complete, I have to go to Atlanta to pick up a porcelain sink, three countertops, and a register. I have to make a second trip to pick up two hair dryer loungers and some odds and ends." Sybil handed him a card. "Here's my number at the shop, and the address. I had these printed at the Expo last week. It was a grand affair. I met a lot of helpful and informative people. Got to try out products and see hands on demonstrations on most everything on the market. I am more excited than you could possibly know!"

"Sybil's Salon," Nathan read. "Right on Main Street. You're a regular businesswoman now."

Sybil smiled, "Yes, indeed. I quit my job at Behr's last week, so it's imperative that I hustle this project along.

"I see, well thank you ma'am for your card and don't be surprised if I show up in my overalls wielding a hammer."

"I can use all the help I can get, and let me know if I can help with your sister, I mean, I know most everybody in three counties," Sybil offered in kind.

They turned into the Handley's drive just as his parents were about to board the truck, "Well look here what the cat's done drug in," exclaimed his papa.

"Tigress," Nathan whispered to Sybil.

Moses invited, "Come on in here, you two, and have you some home cookin!"

"Thanks for the invite, but I have to get to my folk's farm," Sybil excused.

Nathan grabbed his bag and the poles and tipped his hat to Sybil, "Thanks for the ride!"

He watched her speed away down the highway, with her thin scarf trailing behind her. "What a lovely creature," he whispered aloud.

His parents had stepped back into the house and his papa was standing in the threshold. He stopped Nathan at the door and said, "Don't be bringing up Althea to Mama tonight, just know that she is happy to see you."

"How can I not, Papa?" Nathan queried. "She's my only sister and she's gone, I can't just ignore it like nothing has happened." He handed his papa the poles.

"Ah then, we is goin fishin, I see," Moses said, as he took the fishing poles from Nathan's hand and set them into the corner.

Supper was quiet. Nathan had a hundred questions to ask, but he had no idea where to begin, so he said nothing. Eula Mae and Moses could feel the tension. Nathan had seen his sister's coat when he hung up his jacket by the front door. The Lily of the Valley brooch was still pinned to the lapel.

As his mother began to clear the table, she asked about his new off campus dwelling, and had he settled into it yet. Nathan had no intention of chatting about himself until he knew what had happened to his sister, "How can you ask me anything about myself, when you sit here in silence like my sister never existed?"

"Nathan," Moses started.

"No, Nathan, this is not about me. There is more to the story of Althea than you are revealing and I need to know," he demanded, "what happened?"

Moses and Eula Mae sat silent still with their eyes cast down, not looking at Nathan face to face.

Nathan shoved his plate in their direction. He scoffed, "Well, I see," and got up from the table. "I'm going for a walk."

Nathan left and headed quickly up the drive and down the long dark road. He felt a strong sense of remorse for not having come home sooner. He thought if he had, maybe he could have talked to his sister, been there for her as a support person, whatever her trial. Even in the night, the Georgia heat was unbearably hot, thick, and muggy. There was no movement in the air. He slowed his pace. He heard a night owl hoot.

By the time he reached the crossroad, he could hear the music. The gaiety of Jeb's Place on any night of the weekend was predictable. He imagined his sister could have connected with anyone, the likes of Sting, without his parent's knowledge. Nathan walked the distance to Jeb's driveway and paused only to decide his course of action. He went on his way down the drive to the old house.

He nodded at Jeb who was sitting on the porch playing checkers with another old man, "Daddy-O, what say has become of my sister?"

"Don't rightly know," said the old man, not looking up from his game. "She used to come down here to chat awhile with the boys and sing a little. She had a good voice on her."

Nathan questioned, "So you're telling me she just stopped coming?"

"Seems like, haven't seen her much at all since about May. She had a little birthday party of sorts

here, then she comes 'round once or twice, and
then she just stopped. I figured her mama got on
her, lots of women folk don't think this is much of a
place for the ladies."

"Have you seen her talking with any men, you
know, men like Sting, or strangers?"

Old Jeb looked up, "Can't say that I seen her
talkin to nobody much 'cept that Williams boy in
the band. Sting don't talk with the women folk
'round here. You need to know that. I wouldn't go
accusing."

Nathan stepped into the house. There were two
old dogs lying at the feet of an old guy leaning back
in his chair sipping a beer. The band was playing
loudly to a room of about 20 people, all of whom
had already had a few drinks. Nathan ordered a
malt liquor, but stayed standing. He downed his
drink fast. When the tune was over, he went over the
Williams boy, "I need to know what you know about
my sister, who she was with and what she was about."

The young man looked away and answered,
"Don't know nothin. Althea and me, we was just
friends. She wanted to sing with the band regular. We been goin 'round to different joints, and
couldn't take no woman, is all."

Nathan grabbed the boy by the collar, "Listen
slodge, if I find you are lying to me I'll make your

pretty boy face into a closet case. Do we have an understanding?"

The boy pulled back and straightened his collar. "You need to talk to the Moody sisters, over there, they know everybody's business. I don't know nothin!"

The room had witnessed the minor scuffle Nathan had with Joshua, and all eyes followed him around the room. He took another malt liquor and took a chair in front of the makeshift stage, where he could watch the Moody sisters in the corner of the room.

The Moody sisters were not twins, but they weren't far apart in age and dressed like twins. It was hard to tell them apart and they were collectively referred to by all as, "The Sisters." They were flirtatious and always wrapped around one guy or another, whoever would buy drinks. On Sunday mornings both would be seen at the church with their mother, who was most likely unaware of their behavior. Nathan watched them laughing and lifting their skirts along some guy's leg. He couldn't see his sister behaving like that, not Althea.

One of the sisters left the room by the front door. A few minutes later, Nathan followed. He found her talking with another girl in the yard, just off of the front steps. He went down the steps and took her by the hand, pulling her away from her companion, "This will only take a minute and she'll be right back with you."

He pulled her into the darkened shade of a nearby privet hedge. She stumbled along the hard red clay and nearly fell into his arms. Thinking he was being amorous of her, she placed her arms around his neck and began to kiss him about his face. He pulled away from her, "I'm not looking for affection." He demanded, "I want to know what happened to my sister!"

"Althea, well, we don't know." She felt rejected. She pouted and turned away.

Nathan took her by the nape of her neck and turned her to face him. "You do know, and you are going to tell me," he said angrily, holding her hard in his grasp.

"You're hurting me!" she snapped.

He let her go, "My sister just suddenly disappears and nobody seems to know where or why, and I think you know, and you're going to tell me."

"She left. That's what your mama said. She up and left to go up north to be with family. That's what your mama said, and we ain't heard nothin else from her. That's all I know."

Nathan wasn't satisfied, "That's not all. You know more. Tell me!"

"She was with child and didn't want to disgrace your mama nor your papa, is all, that's probably why she left. Joshua, he swears it ain't his, and I believe him. Now, that's the truth. And Sister Martha, she done give your mama a letter from Mayhayley, the fortune teller, and she were a goin to take Althea to see Swamp Witch Wilma, an old quadroon what can take care of things like that. She lives out near the river on the Long Cane. Althea must have changed her mind and just up and left, is all I know, and that's the truth."

Nathan was shocked. He turned from her and headed back down the drive, deeper into the darkness. When he reached the road, he was in a sweat. His heart was pounding heavy in his chest. He felt sick. He didn't know who they, Mayhayley or Swamp Witch Wilma, were, but he knew his parents were keeping a dark secret from him and he felt sick. The name Mayhayley seemed familiar to him, but he couldn't place it.

He wanted to go home, charge into the house and demand some answers. He wanted to know which family members Althea was supposed to be staying with. He wanted to know that his sister was okay. He wanted to know why she had not confided in him. Had Althea run off alone or with someone else to seek fame and fortune? Was she still pregnant? It was too much for him. He knew that he was going to confront his mother, but he couldn't do this in anger. She had seemed fragile, like it pained her immensely that she could not share what she knew. He slowly walked back to the Handley place, thinking of his sister and how it must be for any unwed pregnant woman, with or without a boyfriend to care for her. He prayed she was safe.

12

A TRIP INTO TOWN

Eula Mae was up early cooking breakfast and Nathan lay on his cot with the aroma of sausage and eggs bringing him around. He had a fitful night, tossing and turning. He fretted over his sister and how lonely she must feel, even if she had a partner. He had no clue who this Mayhayley or Swamp Witch was, or how they fit into the big picture of things concerning his sister. He seemed to recall the name Mayhayley, but from where he could not quite figure. What had they to do with her? He thought of Sybil, as he lay there half awake in his cot.

He imagined Sybil's skin as soft as the white cotton sheets, silkier, smoother. He could smell her fragrance above the aromas wafting from the room next door. He wanted to hold her face in his hands and caress her delicate features. He was dreaming again.

He heard his mother call breakfast. His father had come in from his chores. Nathan dressed quickly, came in from the bedroom, and kissed Mama on the cheek. The table was set, and a pile of hot biscuits and blackberry jam was placed before him. There was a plate of scrambled eggs, bacon and sausage. It seemed the best he had ever eaten.

"Ifin we are to go fishen, we got to get up earlier," his papa said.

"No doubt, Papa, another day. I'll be here til the 6th of September. Classes don't start for me until September 13th. I thought maybe I would go into town today and see Miss Sybil. She says she needs some help there to get things in order for her new business. She's opening a salon."

"You need to be careful how you hang 'round that white woman, Nathan, no good can come of it if people start to talkin," Eula Mae stated.

"Don't you be worrying about me Mama, I know my place."

"Well, see that you do. Things ain't like they are in the cities here, boy, and you need not forget that," she continued.

"Yes ma'am, Mama."

Eula Mae had the dishes cleared away before Nathan could get up from the table. He wanted to ask about Althea. He wanted to particularly let them both know that he knew of her pregnancy. Mama was off to the brick house and Papa was out in the barn before he could mention a thing. Nathan knew that they were deliberately being evasive. He walked back into the bedroom.

The big Family Bible lay on the night stand by his parent's bed. Nathan had never been one to pry into his mother's personal affairs, but he felt that he was entitled to see if there was any note regarding his sister. Mama sometimes kept letters in back of the Bible, for safe keeping. Nathan opened the back cover.

There were letters from all of her sisters, offering her prayers and hope for Althea's safety, but none mentioned any pregnancy. From the looks of what was written, Althea had not made her way to any of them, but they gave their assurances that if she did, Eula Mae would be first to know. Then he found it; Mayhayley's letter to Sister Martha. It was an old letter dated 1946, and the pen writing was faded and hard to make out, but Nathan read:

> *"...that your niece finds herself in such a way...I recommend that she see a lady that goes by the name of Wilma. She is skilled in the arts of such that will remedy your niece in a matter of days. However, I beg that you move swiftly as time is of the essence in such*

delicate situations as these…Mayhayley Lancaster"

Nathan knew that name. It all came back to him, this Lancaster lady. He recalled it from the year that he had first gone off to school. It was the year that John Wallace had been executed, and he remembered his papa and The Good Doctor talking about why it was necessary for Nathan to go a far distance to school. There was enormous racial tension in that year, and this white woman had testified in that trial where two colored boys had also testified against John Wallace.

This Wilma, she had to be the one the Moody sister referred to last night as Swamp Witch Wilma. He unfolded the map. He spread it out, got a sheet of paper from the nightstand and traced the map. He will find this woman and ask her what has become of his sister. He will take his sister's picture to her and have her tell him the truth. He did not know if all of what the Moody sister had said was true, but he was confident now that his sister had become pregnant.

Did his sister change her mind and run away to have her baby in secret? Or did she go out into the swamp to abort this pregnancy and then leave? He could not imagine his sister living with some of his family and him not being made aware. Mama and

Papa weren't being honest with him, and he would not pressure them further, but he will know if this lady has seen his sister. If she has, he might be able find out who she is with, a name maybe, some idea of her plans to give him some clue how to begin to search for her.

Nathan put the letters back in order, and into their place in the back of the big Family Bible. He folded the map he had drawn and placed it into his wallet along with his sister's photograph. He didn't know why, but large tears were rolling down his face. He was beginning to feel his parent's pain. What secret haunted them? Where was Althea now? How great was their loss? How could they accept this with some sense of peace, as if it were simply the Lord's will that they should not know anything, when he could accept nothing? He wanted to call the Sherriff and report her missing. Had they not done that, not found it necessary, why?

He placed the Family Bible back onto the night-stand. It was nearly noon and he wanted to get to town early enough to be of some use to Sybil. He borrowed his father's truck and headed for town. As he approached Main Street, he felt a cold chill and shuddered, as if a rabbit had run over his grave, like his mama would have said. He knew that he wanted Sybil. It was near to torture to be close to her and not be able to reveal his desire, and yet he found himself drawn to the flame. He wanted to feel the burn, to delight in the heat of it.

He went down the alley, parked the truck in the back, and went to enter through the back door. Two workers were making their exit as he was coming inside. They looked at him and then at Sybil. She shooed them away with her hand, "I'm fine here boys, and thanks again." They shot nasty glances at him as they left. He could almost feel their loathing.

"Miss Sybil, this is outstanding, what you have done with this place," Nathan complemented. "You are really moving along with a genuine transformation here."

"Oh the work has only begun, and I see that you did come in your work clothes and looking mighty smart in them as well," she returned with a wink.

"I have my hammer," Nathan said, holding the hammer up.

"Good then, you can start by getting these rods hung on that wall," she said, handing him a package of curtain rods and pointing to the freshly painted wall in the back of the large open space. "I put this wall up a couple of days ago and had it painted right away. I'm sure it's dry enough now. I want to hang curtains along here in the very center, so it looks more like a boudoir wall than a than a plain business wall."

"You're not going to waste any time with pleasantries are you?" Nathan asked, as he took the rods
from her.

"No time for pleasantries. I dropped and suspended
the ceiling before installing the air-conditioning, to
make it feel less like a warehouse and more like a room.
The air-conditioning already has it cooled in here, and
I'm really proud of that," she continued to explain her
accomplishments. "I've already cleaned up the dust
from this morning. They have the counter finished
in the front. They got the first phase of the plumbing
done this morning. I have a working bathroom in the
back there and the shampoo sink is going on this wall
here." She excitedly chattered on, "There are heavy
pink and silver Damask drapes for the ends and these
lovely pink shears for the center, each set will need two
rods, as if we are dressing a fancy window. That's how
I want it to look, very homey, and girly. I am using
pink and gray and silver as a color scheme. Even the
hair dryers are pink and silver and I can't wait to get to
Atlanta to pick them up. I've always thought pink and
gray are lovely together, don't you think?" She held
the shears out for him to see.

"It's wonderful, Sybil, I think you have good taste.
It's girly, quite feminine. I think you are doing a
grand job," he assured her.

"That's new Formica, the counter top at the entry,
looks just like real marble, not even on the open

market yet. I'm doing the manicure station and the stall work stations in the same thing. Everything's already cut to build, see." She pointed to the stacks of Formica leaning against one wall, "They just have to be assembled and mounted tomorrow. I have the neatest chairs for cutting hair. They are plush and soft faux leather, and they have hydraulics so they raise and fall gently to the touch of the foot pedal," she went on.

Nathan had a level and was already on a ladder marking the points for the drapes to be hung. He was glad she was dressed in slacks. Her gorgeous long legs were well defined when she walked and she carried herself with the grace of a dove, even without her high heels. He went about mounting the hardware, barely able to keep his attention focused on the task at hand, while she waltzed around the room explaining this proposed feature or that proposed feature. He was enthralled by her, and he could tell that she knew it.

Long dark canvas cloths hung in the store windows and over the front door blocking the view from the street and Sybil explained that she wanted to keep the design private until her Grand Opening. A girlfriend of hers was coming by next week to paint "Sybil's Salon" in large scripted letters to look like pink and gray ribbons on the window fronts. She had taken the liberty to paint Sybil in caricature, a quite becoming one, on a large sign with "Sybil's Salon" followed by a pair of scissors clipping the ribbon at its end, and this was to go onto the store front facade above the doorway. She was as excited as a mouse in a cheese factory, and Nathan adored her as she lilted around the room describing her visions of how things would be once the doors were opened and she had her first customers.

Nathan was aroused by the flush in her cheeks as he went about his work. He had just about finished mounting the hardware for the drapes when she announced that there were two more sets to go over the dryers. She was spacing them at some distance from each other, because she thought she might buy two more and wanted to leave enough room between them, just in case. The electrician had already wired the place for four dryers, another expense she had not accounted for, but she was still within her budget. She would place a table with a lamp and magazines between them for now.

Sybil prattled on about the financing terms she had established with Trent, and what percent he was charging and how he really wasn't using his own money to make this work, so she had to turn a profit soon. Once she started working her salon, she would really have no time for herself, and she knew that, but felt that everything would be worthwhile in the long run.

Nathan wasn't hearing the words, just the raspy sound of her voice. He loved the sound of it, with her long southern drawl. He thought he had been around the more northern women in D.C. too long. Although Sybil rambled on like a schoolgirl in her excitement, her voice was that of a mature and distinctive woman, and he felt that he could not contain himself long.

"There will be lights all around the mirrors that will be mounted once the work stations are in place. I think those lights will be dressing enough. Everything is already wired and ready. They tried to sell me some glass block to install between the stations, but it was exceedingly expensive, and I don't think it is all that necessary to have the stalls separated like that. I like the feel of it open and airy, yet cozy and comfortable, like someone's home."

"Sybil," Nathan paused, "I think that you have found your niche. Everything is coming along remarkably well."

"I agree, Nathan and thank you kindly," she smiled, and went about helping him slide the shears onto the first rod. "I know I'm babbling on like a child, it must not be very becoming of me. I'm just so excited."

"I love to see you excited, Sybil, and it does become you," he said smiling back at her.

She blushed red and quickly handed him the second rod for the first set of drapes, and those were hung. He moved the ladder and went on to mounting the second set, then the third. All the while Nathan was mounting the next sets of hardware Sybil was sweeping quietly. She came over to assist with the hanging of the shears and the drapes when needed, but remained quiet.

Nathan began to talk of the beautiful city of Washington, D.C., how it was laid out with monuments and the wondrous features of the city, the blossoms on the cherry trees in spring and the golden elms in fall. Sybil stopped her sweeping and listened attentively. All was about done and Sybil was helping him slide the last set of shears onto the rod, when he had to say, "You got awful quiet. I fear I've embarrassed you."

He stood on the lowest rung of the ladder, stepped down and took the rod from her hand and set it aside. "You must not be embarrassed on my account, excitement does become you and you should never have to be ashamed of anything you feel." He leaned in and put his arm around the small of her back, bent forward and let his lips touch hers. He felt her submit to him, and she drew his head close to her with her hands. Theirs was a kiss deep and passionate, rich and sweet and full. He breathed her in and knew that he would never get the taste of her off of his lips. He did not want to let go, nor did she.

When she released him he barely let her have a breath before he kissed her again. Her tongue was loose and relaxed in his mouth as she sought to drink from him. She found herself fully surrendered, willing to be with him, and powerless to pull away. It was he who backed away, apologetically, "I'm sorry, Miss Sybil, I've forgotten myself."

"Don't you ever say that you're sorry, I would not have let you had I not wanted it too," she replied. "Like you said, 'You should never have to be ashamed of anything you feel.' It's Sybil, not Miss Sybil. I can't imagine us not being on a first name basis." She took his hands into hers and placed them against her face.

"This is the moment I have dreamed about, to hold your fair face in my hands, so beautiful you are to me," Nathan went on without reservation, "I want to hold you here like this." He stroked her lip with his thumb, and ran his fingers down her cheeks. He felt the heat in her breath, he wanted to kiss her again, and softly stated, "I need you, Sybil, more than any other man has ever needed a woman, and I want you."

"We both have our wants," Sybil whispered back, "but I don't believe it could be that easy, you and me, we are worlds apart in so many ways."

Nathan asked, "Can we both think on this a while? I could never do anything that might hurt you, Sybil."

"I know, and yes we should." She let him go.

He picked up the displaced rod and shoved the last shear into place, climbed the ladder and hung it onto its hardware. She handed him up the last rod with the drapes secured and he hung the final rod into place. When he was done he came down the ladder to admire his handiwork with her. She gave him her hand.

She exclaimed, "Immaculate!" as she looked around the room.

He gazed more on her than onto the room, "Yes, immaculate is the word."

"Oh! I almost forgot. These valances, they drape over the top with the tassels hanging down and along the sides."

Nathan let go her hand, climbed the ladder again, three times, and finished the valances. "Now then, it is truly immaculate!"

She offered him coffee from a pot she had plugged in the wall, and poured herself a paper cupful. Nathan excused himself, "No, I can't really, I need to be getting along here, it's four o'clock and I have to get Papa's truck back."

She looked him squarely in the eyes, "You're troubled by what happened. You really don't need to be. I can see it in your face."

"I am troubled, Sybil, but not by what happened here. I'll go home longing for it to happen again. I have to know what has happened to my sister." Nathan was trying to divert, "I have a map here." He pulled out his wallet, opened the piece of folded paper, and continued, "It is supposed to be the way to a lady's house called Swamp Witch Wilma. I think she should know something of my sister."

"I have heard of her, yes," Sybil resolved. "She sees mostly colored girls who have become pregnant, but I've known of a few white girls who went to see her long ago. Was your sister pregnant?"

"I have cause to believe that she might have been, but I don't know the full story. I am hoping maybe this lady can enlighten me. I don't want to go out there alone. I mean, me being a man, it might spook her, and I don't take kindly to the thought of being shot."

Sybil took his hand in hers, "You want me to come along?" she asked, knowing that he did. "I can go late tomorrow afternoon. It will be after 6:00 pm, but it's light until nearly 9:00. I think we should be able to get there and back in less than three hours."

"That's great, Sybil, I'm much obliged. Should I pick you up here?"

"No, I have to go out to the hospital to see a friend. You can pick me up there, 6:00 straight up and don't be late."

"Will you be dressed for rambling around in the swamp after going to the hospital?"

"I'll be fine. Just don't be late."

Nathan said goodnight and kissed her gently on her cheek and then her hand as he let it go. His smile was difficult to conceal as he left the store by the back way. He looked around as he stepped outside, to see if anyone was in a position to be watching and felt as if he were a thief. He was angry that he had to feel that way.

13

THE SWAMP WITCH

Sybil had drawn herself a hot bath. She put a set of four Frank Sinatra 78 albums on the record changer. It was his second set of eight songs. She loved the sound of his voice. As she lay there in the tub soaking away her aches and relaxing into near slumber, she thought of her kisses. She had kissed boys before, but she had never really kissed a man with affection. Trent, yes, but his kiss was harsh and forced, with tightly pursed lips and a roving tongue. Nathan had kissed her fully, gently, lusciously taking time to softly bite at her bottom lip as he pulled away.

It was an experience not to be soon forgotten. Was it only his exotic allure that had her so very attracted? Sybil knew that he would be leaving in a month. Was it the taste of something forbidden and fleeting that caused her surrender? It did not matter. She was enraptured. She thrilled at the thought of him and found herself caressing her own body as if he were there with her in the water relishing every inch of her. She felt frustrated, and wondered if they would ever have time or place to satisfy their lust for one another. Was it merely lust, or had she come to love this man? She was infatuated.

She slowly shaved, inspecting her own fair colored skin and thought that it, too, must be exotic to him. She toweled off. Stroking her smooth skin with Jergan's, she breathed in the scent of sweet almonds. She put on her negligee and robe and seated herself in the kitchen for a pedicure, something bold, and red. The record changer had stopped. As she separated her toes with cotton, the telephone rang.

It was Trent. He wanted to come over to watch some television and she told him that she was dressed for bed already and offered him a rain-check, as she was most tired from her long day at the salon. She had no desire to entertain him and feared his advances were becoming too forward. She did not know if she would ever develop the sort of relationship with him that he seemed after. They were very close, as friends, but she was not at a place with him wherein she felt the desire for the sort of intimacy that he wanted from her. It was becoming more difficult to put him off since the loan was made. She knew he was feeling entitled to her, and that made her ashamed. It made her feel like a dedicated call girl, and she was beginning to have her regrets.

She so very much wanted to get on with the salon. She wanted her debt quickly settled. There was a likelihood that she could have Trent paid off in less than a year if all went well. Could she hold him off that long or would she indeed find him more worthy of her affection as time went on? Her friends all thought he was just swell. They encouraged her to pursue things with him. They could not possibly know where her love rested, whose arms gave her the comfort she longed for. Her affection for Nathan could never be revealed, and that truly pained her. She knew, for his safety and hers, things between them would have to remain clandestine.

The night was long. The moonlight brightened the room despite the blinds being drawn. Sybil knew that she had a hard day in front of her. She wondered if Nathan was as restless. After hours of staring at the ceiling she finally drifted off and dreamed.

The next day at the salon went far more quickly than she had expected. She struggled with the assembly of the manicure and work stations. The company rep had made it sound so very easy. She needed another set of hands or she was never going to get these mounted correctly. No sooner than she had the thought, Trent came in and offered his assistance. Things had been slow at the shop and he found he had time on his hands and knew that she could use all the help she could get. They quickly got the small counters assembled into place and screwed into the walls. She set a small stool by the manicure station. With the two work stations in place, it was starting to look like a real work space, not simply a room.

Sybil was delighted to have so much accomplished and Trent leaned in to offer her a kiss. She quickly turned her head, forcing him to land the kiss on her cheek, "I can't Trent."

"What do you mean you can't, or you won't?" he asked.

"It just seems less than spontaneous, contrived if you will," was the only way she could explain what she felt.

He continued to probe, "I see, so this is why you did not want me to come by last evening?"

"Sort of, yes, I suppose. If we are to develop much more than a serious working relationship, I mean, more than business, I need more time to consider," Sybil struggled with her words.

"You know that you razz my berries, but I'll back off, if that's what you really need right now," Trent remarked.

"It is, Trent, it's just the way I'm feeling right now," Sybil said to the floor. She could not look him in the eyes.

"Okay then, I'll see myself out." Trent left without another word, and Sybil was glad. She didn't want to argue with him.

Sybil went home at 5:00 and found a pretty yellow sundress. She put it on with bobby socks and sneakers. She felt that she had a schoolgirl look going on and that wasn't what she hoped to achieve, but she was determined not to show up in masculine slacks or jeans. She went into the kitchen and threw together a couple of peanut butter and jelly sandwiches, grabbed a couple of colas from the fridge, and tossed them into a brown bag with a bottle of Avon body lotion. As an afterthought, she grabbed a blanket from the closet.

She made it to the hospital by a quarter til 6:00 and parked far down from the building close to the road. She tied on a scarf, put on her largest pair of sunglasses, and walked to the front lobby of the hospital. When she saw Nathan drive up in his father's truck, she hurried out of the lobby door and down to the parking lot. He had parked beside her car. She looked around quickly to see if anyone was walking nearby. She gave a slight wave to him, and went to her car first to grab the blanket and brown paper bag. When she was certain that no one was around to see, she hopped into the passenger seat of the truck.

"You really weren't visiting a friend at the hospital, were you?" Nathan asked.

"No, I really wasn't. Am I that obvious?" Sybil returned.

"Yes, well, I would have to expect this to be rather covert," he added, "just makes me angry that it has to be."

"Oh please don't be angry, it's just the way things are. You know that, and that's not a way to start the evening," Sybil begged, "I know this isn't a pleasant adventure for you, there is a lot of concern for the safety of your sister, but it shouldn't be an angry time. Perhaps we'll find out something useful."

"You are right, Sybil."

They drove out of town in silence and Sybil could tell that his mind was a million miles away. She thought about her older sister and how she might have felt if she had disappeared without a trace. What an agony it must be for Nathan. She laughed inside at her own selfishness, and how she supposed this would be like a date. She wondered if he thought her silly to have brought along a blanket and picnic. He seemed so very serious and aloof.

As they turned down the red dirt road and toward the creek, Nathan said, "It is a very pretty dress that you are wearing, but I fear that you might scratch your legs something fierce."

"I'm a country girl at heart. I think I'll be quite alright. How about you, are you alright, you seem distant?" Sybil reflected his mood.

"I'm okay. I don't want to get my hopes up to be let down."

The narrow road was dusty and bumpy and there were great craters to go around that the logging trucks had carved out of the rocky red clay. The farther they drove into the forest and nearer to the creek, the rockier things got. The truck bounced and jerked. The stifling heat was almost unbearable with the windows rolled up to help keep out some of the dust. They stopped in a red cloud and sat for a moment for the dust to settle.

Nathan got out and came around to her door. He held to her hand to help her down out of the truck. They stepped off of the road and onto a well worn path to the creek. The water was low in its banks. They could see where the water had been much higher this year from the flood lines on the tall pines. They walked through the soft pine ticket, and Sybil pointed out a doe with twin fawns. They came onto the tracks and followed for some great distance until they came upon the trestle, a hundred yards long. They could see where the fast moving creek slowed to spread out into the marsh. The trestle was high up and the swampy creek water was far below. Already feeling dizzy, Sybil was afraid. She knew how swiftly the trains traveled in unpopulated areas. They made it safely to the other side and down the track yet a little ways further. In the distance, they saw the house in a dry clearing just under the start of the next set of trestles.   The place looked ominous. Nothing stirred except the mosquitoes.

Sybil caught her breath, and they descended the hill from the tracks slowly and carefully with Nathan holding to her arm. Before approaching the house, Sybil called out, "Wilma, I've come to see you about a friend."

Nothing moved. Sybil called out again. A raccoon came scurrying out of a window and up under the house. They walked closer. There was a mess of iridescent peacock feathers scattered around the base of the steps, its carcass long since removed by some other animal.   There was a sickening stench hanging in the thick air. Nathan motioned for Sybil to stay put. He ascended the steps and tapped on the door. He tried the latch and found that it wasn't bolted against him, so he went to enter very cautiously. Sybil ascended the stairs behind him. He pushed the door wide open to a well-furnished room. A putrid odor emanated from within, and Nathan covered his face with a handkerchief that he had retrieved from his jeans pocket. There was not a living soul to be found. He walked toward the back room where he pushed a second door slightly ajar. The sight made him withdraw quickly, and turn Sybil away.

"You don't need to see this, Sybil," he said, as he pulled her back toward the front door. Swamp

Witch Wilma lay dead in her bed and covered with flies and maggots. Nathan whisked Sybil through the front door and onto the porch where he wiped his forehead with his handkerchief, and offered one to her. She wiped the perspiration from her neck. The mosquitoes and gnats buzzed about their faces. Sybil fanned them away with her handkerchief. They felt and heard the train coming first, then saw it whizz past on its route somewhere out of the swamp.

"That bad?" she asked.

"The old woman is dead. There's no one to ask questions or to tell secrets. Whatever she knew she carries with her to her lofty grave."

"We should report it. We should tell somebody," Sybil said without thinking.

"That's not possible. Let the hoboes explain about the Swamp Witch, it's not for us to do."

Nathan was close to crying, and they spoke not a word as they carefully ascended the hill to the trestle. Far behind the train, they walked the trestle over the creek, back down the tracks along the creek bank. Nathan went down to the creek and wet his handkerchief, and hers, with the cool water. Off through the pine thicket, they hastily made their way. They were thirsty and Sybil was glad they brought colas. Nathan went to the truck and brought back the brown bag and blanket.

Sybil spread the blanket on the cool, dry forest floor, with the soft pine straw as a bed. The refreshing scent of pine was as thick as the moisture that hung in the still evening air. They sat, side by side, on the blanket. She offered Nathan a sandwich, but neither was hungry. Nathan popped the tops off the colas with his pocket knife. They were warm, but wet, and they drank them down quickly. The sun was setting. The air temperature was dropping ever so slightly. Sybil sat back on her elbows, while Nathan turned to lie prone, both breathing heavily. The full moon was already high in the sky, as darkness began to surround them. Sybil pulled off her sneakers and socks and began rubbing her feet. Nathan removed his heavy boots. There were no words to be found.

Nathan needed a vision to clear his mind from what he had just seen. After several minutes of resting there, he sat up, and put his hand to Sybil's face. "You are as delicate to me as a night bird, and I have brought you out here in the wilderness to face such dreadful unpleasantness."

Sybil could not speak. He was over her, as she watched the moon through the boughs of the trees over his shoulder, and thought the night nearly perfect. She turned from him, took the fragrant lotion from the bag, and began to smooth it across her arms and shoulders. Nathan joined her with his gentle touch. He whispered to her of the sunlight that stayed in her hair long after the sun had gone down. He told her that her lips were as luscious as fruit on a vine. He kissed her tenderly, then deeply, and deeper again. She felt as if she might faint, and let herself fall against the arm he had wrapped behind her back. He caressed her breast through her dress, and lingered there. Then he brought his hand down to her leg and up her thigh to caress a region that had never been touched by a man. "Am I to have you the way that I want to tonight, dear Sybil, full of light?" he whispered.

She hesitated.

"Do you want this?" he asked her.

"I do," she spoke.

"Talk to me woman, I need to know that you truly want me," he pleaded.

"I want you, Nathan, I want you, totally," she said, as she pulled her slip and dress over her head. He unfastened her bra, slipping it over her arms. He felt her softness, the flesh of her breasts laid bare before him. He bent to wrap his lips around her, and kissed her neck and her ear.

"I have so longed for this moment, Sybil. Since the day that I met you, I have longed to feel the silkiness of your skin against mine." He unbuttoned his shirt, unfastened his belt, and pushed his trousers off with his feet. He placed her hand low and forced her to hold him there with his own hand, "Feel my desire for you," he begged.

She felt his throbbing, and her own blood coursed hot through her veins with every beat of her heart. He gently caressed the flesh of her abdomen with his hand, and she saw the contrast of his dark skin against her light skin. She assisted him in removing her panties. He moved to put his body against hers. She felt him press himself into her. He thrust against her with his every breath. When she was about to scream out in pleasure, he forced his mouth over hers to stifle her cries. He swallowed her ecstasy, and continued to bring her over again, and again. When he was spent, he lay with his head on her chest breathing hard, fast, and heavy. Sybil felt such joy as she had never felt before, and her whole body pulsed with it. She felt his warm breath on the coolness of her damp skin as he spoke. "I don't think that I can ever let you go," he said to her.

"I don't think that I shall allow you to," Sybil offered in return.

"I'm sorry that it has to be this way, in the wilderness on a forest floor," Nathan apologized.

"Whatever do you mean? I think it rather beautiful. I'm sure I'm not the first girl who had her first time as a roll in the hay," she joked.

He smiled, "I mean that I couldn't, or didn't, take you someplace more civil, more comfortable and relaxing."

"There will be time for that. I wouldn't hope for this to be the only intimate time we can spend together," she assured him.

He smiled again at the thought.

"Promise me that you'll write to me when I'm gone. When I wrote to you, and you didn't write me back, that was painful," he frowned. "We know that I have to go back to Washington sooner than I would like, but you've got to promise that you'll write. I get so lonely up there. I'm going to be working long hours at Freedman's Hospital, and I know that I have hours of classes and study. I would like to know that I can expect to hear from you, from time to time."

"I will, Nathan, I will try to do right by you."

14

BUSINESS

The phone at the salon had started ringing off the hook once Marie had put the finishing touches on the window displays. Sybil had not expected to get quite so much interest right away. Her planned Grand Opening wouldn't be until Saturday, August 21st, and already she was booked through the second week in September. She had spent the last two weeks getting the work stations in order, but she really needed to get her dryers, chairs, mirrors, and sink from Atlanta and get them all installed. It was already the 2nd of August and she had barely three weeks for everything to be in order.

Trent had called to say that he wouldn't be able to go to Atlanta until Saturday, nearly a week away, and it was going to take at least two trips to haul back everything in his truck. Sybil was nearly beside herself.

There was a young lady named Kate who had come to the shop inquiring about a job. She had kept books for her father's business in Macon before she married and moved to LaGrange with her husband. She was only seventeen. She was quite personable, and Sybil had not thought to post the position of receptionist/bookkeeper in the paper yet. She was concerned that she would be inundated with high school girls wanting part-time. She needed a full-time employee and could not pay very well, at least from the start.

Sybil explained to Kate that she needed someone who could work the phone and the desk, as well as sweep up from time to time. She also needed someone who might be willing to shampoo client's hair when they were busiest. Kate agreed to the pay and the terms, and was eager to get started. Sybil put her to work right away. She was glad to turn over the phone to someone else.

Kate told her at the end of the day, that she had at least twenty calls from women wanting color or perms that she had to put off until the third week in September. She had the names and numbers of each of these prospective clients, and none of them were very happy about having to wait so long. Sybil knew then, she was going to have to get a partner, or someone willing to rent a stall. She thought that Francine, Bonnie Jean, or Peggy Sue might be willing to come in initially.

Francine was busy with her wedding plans, and neither Peggy Sue nor Bonnie Jean had the time or felt that they possessed the expertise to be of any use. Sybil promised that she could give them guidance, but she knew deep down inside that she probably wouldn't have much time to play instructor. The last thing she needed was someone to come in and get their hair ruined.

The next morning, as luck would have it, a young lady named Michelle came in by the back door. She presented her credentials from California and New York. She had attended a Marinello cosmetology school in California, and had letters from her school and her places of employ. She had worked as an apprentice in California. Most recently, she worked for two years at a salon in New York. Her husband, a radio programmer, was forced by his work to move every couple of years, but had just been relocated to the LaGrange area.

Michelle balked at the possibility of a small salary, but liked the idea of renting a stall for a monthly fee, and handling her own clientele. She had worked almost exclusively with the La Crosse product line. She was particularly up to date on current fashions and the "inside story" on the hair fashions that would be coming out of California in the near future. She gave Sybil a list of the supplies that she would need to get started and agreed to pay up front for her own supplies which would be kept separate from Sybil's. They developed a contract between them and Sybil was delighted to have her on board.

Wednesday morning Kate came to her and said that there was a man on the phone asking to speak with her. It was Nathan. The Good Doctor had purchased a trailer for hauling cows to market. He had already asked him if he could borrow it to pick up some supplies from Atlanta for Sybil. She was overjoyed. With Kate and Michelle there to mind the place she could take a day to ride with Nathan to Atlanta. She called the Beauty Supply Warehouse and told them to have her order ready immediately.

The next morning, Nathan met Sybil at the salon early with the truck and trailer and the two were off to Atlanta. Sybil was most apologetic for being so very busy the past few days, and Nathan had been glad to spend time fishing with his father. This was the first time they had seen each other since their experience in the wilderness. There was an uncomfortable feeling between them that they tried to avert with small-talk.

Sybil was chain-smoking. By 9:00 am it was already hot and humid, and even with the windows rolled down she felt that she was melting. Nathan offered to stop and buy ice cream or sodas along the way, but she was too excited, and anxious to get her merchandise.

They arrived at the warehouse about the time the doors were opened. Sybil left Nathan outside while she went inside to settle her order. She came out with four boys toting large boxes to go into the back of the truck. She handed a loading dock clerk her receipt and he sent the boys back inside to bring the remainder to the loading dock. He told Sybil, "Tell your nigger to pull that trailer along the side here."

Sybil was appalled at his lack of discretion and started in with, "Excuse me, he is Mr. Nathaniel Grier."

The man looked at her and said, "Like I said; tell your nigger to pull that trailer around, let's get this goin…"

Nathan shook his head at her and told her to be quiet about it.

"Well, they just might not get any more of my business. I'm writing the manager a letter tomorrow, I am."

Nathan pulled the trailer around as ordered and they got everything loaded with him tying down what needed to be. It took over an hour before they were ready to pull out. Sybil was holding her copy of the receipt and following their every move to assure that all of her merchandise was accounted for. She did a double check once the boys were done and the load was secured.

Now, Sybil was hungry. They decided to go through The Varsity on North Avenue to grab a bite to eat on the road. The Varsity had curb service, as well as sit down service. They didn't want any trouble with the college boys and pulled the truck with the trailer into the drive in parking lot. Although they received a lot of looks and stares from passersby. There was no trouble.

The traffic was stalled coming back through Atlanta and Sybil was upset with herself that her appetite had resulted in such a delay. They had passed several restaurants that served blacks on the way to The Varsity, which he had initially thought might suffice, but Sybil was quick to pass them by in favor of the drive in service of The Varsity.

"Sybil, you just can't understand what it is like to be a man of color," he said with an inflection of increasing anger. "You don't know what it is like not to be served at establishments because of the color of your skin. We can't try on clothes or shoes in your stores. We take the path of least resistance everyday of our lives in order to avoid conflict. We aren't even allowed to drink from your fountains or pee in your toilets, for Christ's sake, Sybil."

"You say that as if I'm personally responsible," Sybil quipped back, when she knew it really wasn't so.

"Would you prep a colored girl's hair in your salon?"

"I wouldn't even know where to begin, Nathan, it would be a disaster. Their hair treatments are different."

"Not 'their', Sybil, 'my,' my hair is different, the real question to ponder is; 'Would you be willing to learn?'" He waited for her answer.

"You wouldn't, Sybil." Nathan continued, "It's not on your agenda, as a white woman, to learn to treat black women's hair. That's my point. We don't matter."

Sybil paused to think on what he had said. She had never thought of offering to treat black women's hair. Seriously, the thought had not crossed her mind. She knew that she didn't have the skill set to do it. It wouldn't be fair to them and she couldn't take the time to learn. After all, she could lose a significant clientele if she brought in black women. And besides, black women probably preferred someone of their own kind treating their hair.

"It's not that you don't matter." Sybil concluded, "It's just the nature of things."

"Is it the nature of things? You know that's not it baby, I'm trying to get you to understand my position here. I want to be able to look into the eyes of the woman I love without any hesitation, anywhere I choose, and say it out loud without fear of repercussions."

Sybil hesitated, "Are you saying that you love me?"

"I am, Sybil, I do. I fell in love with you the first day we met," Nathan said, as he reached for her arm to pull her closer to him."

She pulled away, "Nathan, lust and love…"

He put his finger to her lip, "I want to make love to you, Sybil, today, now."

Sybil sat quiet. The delay in traffic had resulted from much heavy construction taking place on the roadway downtown. They were finally through the worst of it and had reached the edge of town near the airport. There was a small motor inn on the left side of the highway, just after the highway went back to two lanes, and Sybil told Nathan to pull into its drive. He let her out at the office on one end of the building and parked the truck and trailer at the very end of the other side of the building. Sybil went into the office to get a room.

The lobby was small but pleasantly decorated in tropical plants. Bromeliads bloomed colorful phallic plumes on each side of the front entry in the shade of low palms. The clerk was nice and asked if she would like to see the room first. Sybil nervously answered, "No, thank you, just the key, please."

She left quickly without any small talk and looked around the parking lot. It was quiet, and there was no one around. She knew what Nathan meant. It should not feel like such a sin to love another person regardless of their race, and though she was not necessarily a religious person, a sin is what she learned it to be. She adored him. Could it be love rather than lust that she felt?

She paced her step and approached the room with the key in hand, and in a matter of seconds Nathan was beside her. The motor inn had advertised air-conditioning, but it had not been turned on and the room felt damp and smelled rather musty. Sybil lit a cigarette as Nathan turned on the A/C. There was a small television bolted to the dresser and Sybil switched it on. Nathan took the cigarette from her, crushed it out, brought her into his arms, and cast her onto the bed.

Their love making went on for two hours. Sybil felt as if she were in a dream, on a movie screen, and not in real life. Nathan was tender and gentle the first time, and they lay quiet in each other's arms for half an hour. Then he was hard, fast, and rough with her. Afterwards, they napped in each other's arms, both feeling the heat and exhaustion. It was the bliss of serenity for Sybil, and she did not want to get up and leave, but she knew that they had to.

She went into the bathroom to freshen her cosmetics and hair as best she could. Nathan was the first to speak, "I wish you could come to Washington with me. I can say it, Sybil. I love you. Can you say it? Can you say, 'Nathan, I love you?'"

Sybil was dressing as Nathan lay prone on the bed with his back to her. "Nathan, I love everything about you. I do, but to say, 'I love you,' that carries with it a commitment that I'm not certain I can maintain."

"Sybil, things are going to be very different real soon. I can feel it. Already, at the University, they are talking about resuming the sit-ins that Howard students started in the forties. You know, they went and sat on stools in restaurants that refused to serve them. They only stopped because the administration told them they had to. The law was against them then. I'm not the only black man who feels the way that I do. There is talk of holding peaceful demonstrations in Washington, and other places. There are people, well educated black and white people, with the law on our side. Things aren't the same in New York and Chicago. People mingle. We don't have to stay in the South. We don't have to live in the hatred here."

"Hatred, Nathan, that's a little strong. I don't think everybody in the South has hatred for Negros, and I don't think all Negros have hatred for whites. They have differences."

Nathan rolled over to face her, "No, I know they don't, but most, even you, can't fully accept that people of color and whites can live together peacefully as one human race with their differences. You think blacks here in the South are happy being treated as second class citizens. Hatred brews on both sides."

"You are putting words in my mouth, Nathan," Sybil defended, "I can see things changing for the better, but I see it happening over generations; perhaps, not even in our lifetime. I worry that you look at the world through rose colored glasses, and I know that your people are going to struggle through some terrible circumstances before the South is resigned to accept what you are expecting."

"Resigned?" Nathan repeated. "I don't even like the sound of that." He grabbed his clothes to dress.

"The truth is prejudice exists all over the world. Indians don't like Arabs, Asians don't like Americans, and Muslims don't like Christians, these are centuries old battles that may never be totally resolved," Sybil insisted.

"But this country wasn't founded on prejudice, that's what Lincoln was saying those many years ago. Our freedom is guaranteed, but oppression is everywhere in this country," Nathan countered.

"You are set to have your M.D. in four years, how are you oppressed?"

"I'm oppressed that I can't openly and freely be with the woman I love. I can't take her to the theater, to dinner; hell, I can't even walk down the street holding her hand, or light her cigarette in public," he said as he lit her smoke. She turned away from him and opened the door.

They left the motor inn and walked to the truck. He opened the door for her and held to her hand as she stepped up. "It's not right, Sybil, and you know it. That I should have to steal you away like this."

They were back on the road for two more hours. Neither spoke much of a word to the other. Sybil had not been able to tell Nathan that she loved him. How could she? She knew that she felt something strong, but she had never known real love for a man, she supposed. There was nothing to compare this feeling to. There had been crushes in high school and even once while in college, but Nathan was the first man that she had ever surrendered so to. Was it that she loved him, then, that had forced her surrender? She shuddered at the passing thought that it might have been sheer curiosity. She felt shame that she might be toying with his affection. It was heartfelt and meaningful, the way that he spoke of his love for her.

The sun was beginning to drop in the sky. It was after 6:00 pm when they drove up behind the salon. Michelle and Kate were already gone. Trent's truck sat in the parking area but there was no sign of him. Then Sybil heard him call out, "Why the hell didn't you tell me you were going to Atlanta today? I could have driven you, you know."

"You said that you didn't want to go until Saturday. I thought we could get there and back and you would be pleased that you did not have to bother with the chore," Sybil responded.

"Let's get this stuff in, boy," Trent called to Nathan. Trent lingered at the truck inspecting the merchandise.

"Yes sir," Nathan said with a cutting glance at Sybil.

Nathan began lifting out the boxes from the bed of the truck and Sybil unlocked the salon door. Nathan passed her going into the doorway. "Don't you go saying a word, Sybil, I ain't nothin but a nigger to him. Do you understand?"

Nathan and Trent made short work of unloading the truck and the trailer, and Sybil was pleased. When all was done, Trent whipped out a ten dollar bill and went to hand it to Nathan saying, "For your gas, time, and work."

"Oh, no sir," Nathan declined, "I couldn't take your money. I did this for Miss Hamilton, sir, thank you for your offer though." He felt humiliated and Sybil felt it also. Trent pressed on, insisting for Nathan to take the money, and he did take it to prevent arousing any suspicion.

Trent added, "Thank The Good Doctor for me, too, for loaning the trailer."

Nathan left, head bowed, by the back door. Sybil heard the truck with the trailer leave. She scowled, "Trent, you didn't have to force the money on him so hard. That was rude."

"Of course I did. You don't pay 'em nothin and they go gettin high and mighty like you owe 'em somethin."

Trent said he would have two men come by over the next couple of days to get everything assembled and mounted into place; the chairs, sink, lights, and mirrors. The dryers could be easily set into place. Sybil, Michelle, and Kate had the boxes to unpack. They would have to organize the supplies and get the shelves, workstations, and caddies set up with all of the necessary items. It was really starting to come together and Sybil felt a strong sense of relief.

A short two weeks later, Sybil was ecstatic over the Grand Opening. She had run an ad in the local paper for three weeks, and already had appointments booked for both she and Michelle through the end of September. She was charging a fee for Michelle just shy of half her rent on the building and half of what she anticipated for supplies, power, phone and water. Michelle had no problems with Sybil being the namesake of ownership, but Sybil had Marie come by and add, "Hair Creations by Sybil and Michelle," under the phone number on the windows. The dark canvas cloths had been removed from the windows, and the place looked glorious in the light of the sun. The Saturday of the Grand Opening had finally arrived. The Mayor was coming out with a group from the local paper to help cut the pink ribbon she had strung across the front door.

There was to be an article in the paper about women business owners in the county and Sybil felt honored for having been selected as one of the interviewees and for the photo opportunity. The Grand Opening was to be at 10:00 am, and there was a small group of patrons and reporters outside. Sybil, Trent, Michelle, and Kate waited inside for the Mayor to arrive.

The hour approached. Standing by the counter at the front of the salon, Sybil could see that a rather large crowd had gathered on Main Street. She could see Nathan standing across the street. She gave him a slight wave and a smile.

An arrangement of two dozen pink roses had been delivered by the back door and Sybil was quick to grab the card. They were from Trent. He scooped her into his arms and planted a long wet kiss before she could realize what he was about to do. When she managed to turn and look over her shoulder, she saw Nathan leaving. Her heart sank. It was all she could do to keep from crying.

At the end of her day, Sybil was still exhilarated. Trent stopped by to pick up her cash and receipts. He offered to go pick up some beer and meet up with her back at her place, but she feigned exhaustion. She was glad that he left without any argument. She simply did not feel like dealing with him. Michelle and Kate had gone home. They all had a wonderful day. The salon was filled with chatter all the long day. The clients all expressed their joy at having such a fine salon to come to.

Sybil was feeling the energy, but her feet were aching and all she wanted to do was get home and draw herself a hot bath. It was Saturday night and she did not need to come back until Monday. She thought she might soak for two days. When she got home she filled the tub, adding bath oil bubbles, and put the record changer on, something laid back and intimate, Bing Crosby.

When the water became tepid, she decided to get out. She toweled and robed. She lay on her sofa listening to the music, when she heard a light tapping at her back door. She got up and peered through the kitchen window to see Nathan with a bouquet of hollyhocks and snapdragons standing on the back patio. She quickly let him in. He presented her with a bottle of Champagne. He had parked at The Heart of LaGrange Hotel and walked to her apartment in the night. Her celebration was just about to begin.

15

GRIEF

The next two weeks were but a blur. Business at the salon was so very intense that Sybil barely had time to think of anything else. She had spent the prior Sunday with her parents. Her father wasn't doing very well. The doctor had told her mother that her father had hardening of the arteries and things were going to get worse. He had been forgetful and misplacing regular household items, but otherwise seemed okay to Sybil. He was still working their small farm and had a large pumpkin patch that he would be harvesting next month.

Sybil was working six days a week. She could scarcely believe that it was September already, and then it occurred to her as she was closing her books for the day, it was September 4th and Nathan was leaving for Washington, D.C., on September 6th. She had not seen him since the weekend of the Grand Opening. He had not called the salon and

Sybil had never given him her home number. She couldn't just drive out to the Handley's to see him. That would most certainly start talk.

Sunday was a long and boring day that Sybil spent mostly in tears. For most of her day she was doing laundry and watching television, between crying episodes. She regretted that they had not thought to take Labor Day off as a holiday and were booked solid for tomorrow. Sybil was longing to see Nathan, or at least to speak with him. She knew in her heart that she did love this man, she truly did, but she could never be honest with him.

Sybil knew also that she was pregnant, but she could never tell Nathan. She remembered Bonnie Jean's plight and thought more than once that she should confide in someone, maybe Bonnie Jean. She picked up the phone a few times to do just that, but lay it back in its cradle, time and again. She could not confide in another living breathing soul, except The Good Doctor, and even he could never know her whole truth. She would go to him as soon as Nathan was gone. She couldn't possibly tell Nathan and have him start planning their lives together. He had medical school in front of him and she had just started her business. It was a brief summer romance and it was painfully ending.

Sunday night was fitful. She lay in her bed and wished to hear a light tapping on her back door, but it never happened. She did not rest well. Monday morning's light came too early and she forced herself out of bed and dressed.

Kate and Michelle were already at the salon by the time Sybil arrived. She poured herself a cup of coffee and prepared for her first client. She called the station to find out what time the train bound for Washington would be arriving. She asked Michelle if she could cover for her for half an hour around 11:00 am and Michelle was agreeable.

She prepared a small paper with the words, "Call me," and her home phone number. A few minutes before 11:00 am, she left the salon and went to the station. She parked on the colored people's side and waited for Moses' truck to drive up. Her auto was conspicuous. Nathan spotted her immediately, and walked over. Her top was down and she handed him the small paper as she shook his hand. "I'll write," he said. There was little time for much else to be said. He could tell she had been crying, even through her large sunglasses, and they had so much more to say, but his parents were waiting on the platform and the train had arrived.

Sybil drove away before the train left. She had to collect herself and go back to work. She parked behind the salon. She had refreshed her face in the mirror when she saw Trent drive up. He had taken the day off. He was spending the day at the airport with The Good Doctor and other friends, but wanted to know if she would like to take in a movie at the Drive-in Theater on Saturday night. At first, she thought not, but on second thought, she really did not want to be alone this weekend. She needed the company of someone and she knew it. A movie might help take her mind off of the worst of her worries, so she agreed. "Great, we'll take your car," Trent said with a smile.

Nathan was on the train bound for D.C., and was still grieving the loss of his sister. He had confronted Jeb on numerous occasions over the past couple of weeks, but was getting nowhere. If his parents were being honest, then Jeb, and everybody else at his place, was lying. He still had the feeling that his parents were not telling him everything that they knew. After several inquiries on the matter, his father had finally pulled him aside and asked him not to say anything else to his mother as he was upsetting her.

He had told his mother that he had found out that Althea was pregnant. She would not confirm nor deny. She simply told Nathan that she was not at liberty to discuss certain things and that Althea herself would let him know, in due time, what she wanted him to know, "In the meanwhile, you need to let it go," was all she would say. "Let it go!"

Neither Swamp Witch Wilma nor the letter from Mayhayley was mentioned. All he had was what the Moody sister had told him, and she insisted that she knew nothing more. He had felt that she was lying and knew more than she was about to tell, but he wasn't able to get any more from her with kindness or force, and he had tried both.

Nathan had promised his mother that he would try to come home for Christmas, but he wasn't sure if that would be possible. He had taken a paying job at Freedman's Hospital and his studies were about to take on a whole new character. The next four years of his life promised to be dramatically different from the last four. He wasn't expecting to have time for much of a social life. He was also becoming increasingly interested and involved in what was emerging as a serious Civil Rights Movement.

Sybil would never fully understand nor appreciate where he was coming from on certain issues. He did not blame her. Her family was on land that had been in her family for more than a hundred years. Although they were not wealthy, her life had been stable and wholesome. He wanted so much to be able to give her the same or better. With his M.D., there was a chance that he could. Things were going to change for the better, and he could make a place in this world for Sybil as his wife, and for their family. He looked at her note, "Call me," and thought; she must know how deeply I feel for her, I can't possibly let her down.

Sybil was finished at the salon before 5:00 pm on Saturday. She let Michelle lock up and took her cash and receipts with her. It was a good feeling to know that the salon was doing so well. She remembered what Edna had told her, "Give them a look that they can't achieve at the kitchen sink, that's what keeps them coming back to you." It was working for her. She already had repeat customers who were calling to schedule to have their hair styled and set and who were asking for weekly appointments. She thought tonight she might ask Trent for the money to put in additional chairs and dryers.

The movie would not start until 10:00 pm. Sybil had plenty of time to unwind and change clothes. She had been unable to take her mind off of Nathan all week. She wondered how long the trip from LaGrange to Washington was by rail. She had never traveled that far on a train. Her high school class had gone to Washington, but she had not been able to join them. The most she had traveled by car was a trip with her girlfriends in college to Florida one summer. They drove all the way to Miami, and it took them two days one way. It occurred to her that the largest city she had seen was Atlanta, and she had never been out of the south. Nathan was right; there was a whole other world that she had not begun to explore, and now she was tied to this business.

Trent drove up at 9:30 and tooted his horn, announcing to the world that he had a date with Sybil. She wondered if she waited long enough would he have the decency to come to her door. Rather than have him toot again, she grabbed her purse and locked the door behind her. He had decided to take his truck. He was out of the truck and holding the door for her. He took her by the hand and helped her step up.

On the way to the Drive-In Theater, Sybil asked Trent about money to add more chairs and dryers. He told her that it had only been three weeks and she needed to at least wait and see how things went in the near future before she started investing anything else. "You don't have it to invest. You have a huge debt on this place, Sybil. I don't see how you can even think of spending more. You've got to at least wait until you are out of the red."

Sybil thought she could get out of the red quicker with more to work with, but he was right, more chairs would mean more costs. She was only one person, and already had more work than she could do alone.

The movie, "Dial M for Murder", starred Grace Kelley, and Sybil thought her to be a fine actress and very beautiful. She absolutely adored her. There were so many movie stars who made her wish that she had found a way to succeed in theater. She thought about what Nathan had shared about his sister wanting to be discovered for her singing talent. She seemed a brave woman, Althea.

Although Troup County was a dry county, Trent had secured a bottle of I.W. Harper bourbon in Columbus and set about pouring off half of their colas to fill their cups with the golden fluid. Sybil had never been much of a drinker and the first cup was enough to make her head swim. By the time they were back at her apartment, she was inebriated. Trent took her keys from her and unlocked the door. She sat at the kitchen table while Trent foraged through the refrigerator for something to eat. He pulled out the quarter of a bottle of Champagne that was left, and asked, "You've been drinking alone?"

"My Grand Opening celebration," she answered.

"I offered to come and celebrate with you, and you were too tired, if I recollect correctly."

"You are right, Trent, I was too tired to entertain you," she slurred with a thick tongue.

"Looks like you entertained yourself quite well. Let me entertain you tonight," he offered.

"I can't move," she admitted.

"Then I'll just have to move you," he insisted, and bent to lift her from her chair. She didn't resist. He took her to her bed and pulled off her shoes. He massaged her feet and she felt it divine. He had her clothes off before she was fully aware of his intentions, but still, she did not resist him. She felt lonely, even in his presence. He was awkward and rushed with her. She didn't feel as if she were a part of his experience with her. She was like a mannequin in a department store window, cold and not at all alive. There was no reciprocation on her part that she was aware of. When he was done, he rolled over and lay beside her. He didn't speak a word, and for that she was grateful. She had nothing to say. In the morning, he was gone. Again, she was grateful.

Sunday was a God awful day. Sybil spent most of the morning hugging the porcelain throne. By mid-afternoon her headache was beginning to subside. She knew that she had sex with Trent, but didn't recall much about it, except that she didn't feel at all like they had made love. In fact, she was feeling disgusted with herself and ashamed that she had even accepted that first drink from him. He had to know what he was doing, even if she didn't, or didn't she?

Was she attempting to throw herself away because she couldn't be with the one she longed to be with? She looked at her calendar. Had it only been three weeks since they were last together intimately? Nathan had not been gone a week before she surrendered herself, however unwillingly, to the arms of another man. Why had he not called, just to say that he was safely in Washington? She had not heard a word from him. If he called, could she keep her pregnancy secret? She knew that she had to.

There was a part of her that wanted to tell Nathan everything. She missed him terribly. She wanted to tell him that she missed him, and she wanted to say, without hesitation, "I love you, Nathan, and I'm carrying your child," but she knew that she could not. With a tortuous realism she knew that she would not leave her business to go to Washington. She would never be with Nathan. She had to abort this pregnancy.

Over the next few weeks, she found herself submitting to Trent on a regular basis. He was coming by her apartment from time to time and always brought booze. She found herself going by his house after work and lingering with him, even when he had not asked her over. It seemed his affection was better than none at all. They were becoming an item whether drunk or sober. She felt ashamed. She really had no love for him.

It was the end of October before Sybil had finally found the courage to set an appointment with The Good Doctor. She called his receptionist and made an appointment for a "home office visit" under the name of Mary Brown for 8:00 pm on Friday night, October 29th. She didn't schedule any salon appointments for Saturday, Monday, or Tuesday. It was a dreary evening and drizzling rain as she drove herself out to the country house. Mr. Handley was in his office in the basement when she arrived. He looked at her and said, "I'm sorry, Sybil, Trent's not out here, I have an appointment at 8:00. What can I do for you?"

"I'm not looking for Trent. I am Mary Brown," she revealed as she seated herself.

"I see," said The Good Doctor. "Are you sure that you want to do this, Sybil?"

"I'm not here for counseling, and I'd ask for your utmost in confidence. I'd rather not have Trent to know that I have come here, if you will."

"It is entirely up to you. Of course, you have my confidence. I just hope that this would be a decision made well."

"It is a decision that has been carefully thought through, I beg let us get on with things," Sybil confirmed.

The Good Doctor persisted, "You know, Sybil, I can easily take you in as a client, but knowing Trent as I do..."

Sybil interrupted him, "Forget it! I'll take my business elsewhere, and I'd kindly ask you not to mention a thing to Trent about my visit here. It doesn't concern him." She rose from her seat and started for the door.

"I'm just asking you to seriously think through what you are about to do. For people that I don't personally know, things are a bit different for me," he went on as he followed her outside.

Sybil was furious, "You need not recall that I was ever here!" She wasn't about to explain herself to him. She left in a heat of spun gravel.

When Sybil returned home, she found the letter in the box from Washington, D.C. It was dated 15 OCT 1954:

Dearest Sybil,

I have been back here a mere month and a half. It seems like only days in that I have been busier than ever, and yet it seems like an eternity since I held your face in my hands. I wish I could hear your voice. There is a phone in the super's office, but there is no privacy there. I do not have a phone in my apartment. It is shared with another young man who is also in medical school. We spend our nights over our books and barely speak.

There is a little coffee shop down the street, and when I can find the time, I meet up with other students from the University. They are from all disciplines and are male and female, white and black. They share letters calling for like minds to come together for the common cause of civil rights. I have to be brief here, but I do hope that you will come to understand that our love is not lost.

You have my new address. Please write to me when you can. I am certain that your new salon keeps you very busy. I know that even when my attention is occupied by my work, I have thoughts of you constantly on my mind.

Yours Truly,
Nathan

Sybil took the letter and read it over and over. She could not possibly write back to him. She had waited so long to hear from him, yet knew that the decision for the abortion rested with her and her only. She could never tell him her truth. Her heart was heavy. She prayed over her dilemma and went to bed.

When she woke up, Sybil's plans for the day included getting the doctor's phone number from

Birmingham, Ala., that the young lady and her mother had been referred to when she worked at Behr's. She couldn't afford $600 +, but it might be possible that the Langdale clinic had other referral sources bedsides The Good Doctor.

Sybil did not subscribe to the newspaper, but had told her neighbor, Melba, that she would bring in her papers while she was away visiting her sister in Macon. She stepped outside and retrieved the paper. She opened it to the shopping ads in the back.

There was a bold printed full page advertisement that promised discreet legal services for adoption or divorce placed by a prominent attorney in Columbus. The ad offered free telephone consultation. She thought about her own sister who had been trying to get pregnant without any success. She knew that her sister could never raise a mulatto child, and she could never tell her sister about this pregnancy. Surely there were other couples who would be happy to raise this child and give it a loving and caring home. She wondered what sort of arrangements could be made for an expectant mother of a child that would be adopted out. She was already near three months along.

She knew that she would not start to show until the sixth to seventh month. The smocks that she wore to work would most certainly help obscure any show at least until that time. What were two or three months of her 23 years of life? Sybil decided at that moment that she would deliver this child. She had not a clue where, or how, but she knew that this was what she needed to do. The baby would be due around the end of April and she expected that business at the salon would slow after Valentine's Day in February.

Trent would be easy. It was Michelle she worried about. Could she manage the salon on her own for two months? Sybil would have to feign some excuse for being out of town through March and April. She thought about Edna in Newnan. Edna knew all about the business, the expos, and beauty schools. She knew all about what was happening, when, and where.

Sybil picked up the phone and dialed Edna at her salon. Edna was glad to hear from her. Sybil told her that business was good but that she felt she was in need of more training. She was taking a couple of months off and was wondering if Edna had any info on where she could go. Edna suggested one of two Expos that were being held in Atlanta around the time of Sybil's planned *vacation*. Sybil felt that Atlanta was too close. Trent could drive up in a couple of hours. It simply wouldn't do. She asked if Edna knew of anything a little farther away. Edna told her that there was a new beauty school opening in Miami around the first of March, but their program was 12 weeks long. Sybil asked her to mail her the information on it.

Sybil knew that she wasn't going to Miami, but she had to have some way to keep Trent at bay for two months. She had been spending a lot of time with him over the last two months and he was deeply involved in her business affairs. She thought about telling him that her Aunt Minnie was ill, but again, Montgomery was too close for comfort. If she told him that she was going to Miami for business, he might well accept her plans.

Monday morning she placed a call to the attorney office. She was fully expecting a secretary to answer and have the attorney call her back, instead, an attorney answered and it was a woman. She said that she had entered partnership with the prominent attorney whose name was in the paper. Sybil inquired about adoption proceedings and the lady said that she was handling all of the adoption cases. At the attorney's request, Sybil related some biographical information about herself.

The attorney asked if Sybil had anyone selected to parent the child and Sybil told her no. She explained her circumstances further and let her know that this would be a mixed race child who had a Negro biological father that was in school at Howard University and studying to become a doctor.

She also explained that he was unaware of the pregnancy. She told the attorney that she preferred a family that was not local due to the sensitive nature of the pregnancy. The lady told her that she would need to review some files and call her back. She told Sybil that she had several couples who might be interested and was most certain that arrangements could be made to accommodate her. Sybil felt a flood of relief that she wasn't carrying her burden totally alone. God had heard her prayers and sent her an understanding attorney.

There was nothing on the television that held Sybil's attention on Tuesday afternoon. Sybil had turned the stations between the soap operas and the drama was too much for her, so she switched off the tube. Her anticipation was enormous and she jumped when the phone rang. The attorney had three couples who were interested in adopting her child, the terms of which Sybil would have some control over. Sybil asked if she would be able to meet the couples and the attorney told her typically not, but she could speak with them and see how they felt about it.

The attorney called her back later that afternoon. Two of the couples were white couples who already had other adopted children, some of mixed race. Neither was interested in actually meeting the birth mother. The other couple was mixed, a white

American woman and a Hispanic American man who was in the military. They had no other children, and had been trying for 10 years.

The woman was 28 years old and the man was 32. He had been in the service for 14 years and considered himself career military. He had joined the Army at the age of 18 and served throughout WWII, and was currently stationed at Ft. Benning. The couple had married in 1944, just after he returned to the States. The woman was from Texas, and they had met while the young man was stationed there after the war. She was an only child and her parents longed for a grandchild. She had spent four years with her parents, stateside, while he was stationed in Guam, during the Korean War.

This couple was very much interested in meeting the birth mother and they had offered a room in their home for the expectant mother. They wanted to share in the experience of the pregnancy, if possible. The man had come from a large Catholic family, and the woman was devastated that she had not been able to bear a child. She had already had three miscarriages and the doctor told her that she would never be able to birth children. There was small clinic on post where Sybil could receive prenatal care and know that her privacy was protected. Although they were interested in meeting Sybil and sharing in the experience of the pregnancy, they wanted no contact after delivery.

At first, it bothered Sybil that she would have no contact with her child or the child's parents, and then it occurred to her, this was not to be her child. The couple was willing to assume the cost of all attorney fees, medical care, and to pay Sybil's rent, electric, and water so that she might keep her apartment. They also wanted to "gift" her $2000.00, which meant that she would have some cushion against her debt with Trent and his investors.

Sybil agreed to meet with them the next day and called the salon to tell them that she would not be in until Thursday. Wednesday morning she drove to Columbus to the attorney's office. She tried not to cry for fear of wrecking her face, but her tears ran in a constant stream.

She found the couple to be very pleasant and liked that the lady had a southern accent, though different from her own. She was as blonde as Sybil and her husband referred to her as his, "Yellow Rose." Her parents owned a cattle ranch and frowned on a woman working outside of the home. She would be home for the child every day. She spoke Spanish fluently. She went on to explain that most military families were large, and they received many benefits. Living on post, with its many playgrounds for children, her heart ached to be a mother. She saw the mothers tending their young ones every day, and she so very much wished to be a part of that experience.

The gentleman assured her that his child would be well educated and most certainly bi-lingual, as he had many siblings with many cousins for his child to come to know. Trying not to get too very technical, he explained that he was from Puerto Rico, and had trained in the 65th Infantry there. He later was schooled in engineering, and primarily worked on building bridges and waterways. He admitted that he preferred a son, but acknowledged that a daughter would be a most blessed welcome also. He said that his family was huge, with black, white, and Hispanic from many countries, and race wasn't a concern at all. His own mother was a black woman from Brazil, and he was fluent in Portuguese, as well as English and Spanish. Sybil envied their lack of bias.

Most importantly, the couple seemed genuinely affectionate toward each other, and promised that this child would grow up with love and affection to spare. They were also planning to adopt a second child of the opposite sex of this child. It did not matter to them which came first, the boy or the girl.

Sybil was very pleased with the couple and they were pleased with her. They had the attorney draw up the contract, and made their commitments. The couple was moving into a larger home with three bedrooms. Sybil would be staying with them in their home on post through March and April, until the birth of the child. The child was to be delivered at St. Francis Hospital in Columbus.

Although Sybil had volunteered the information that the biological father was a medical student, the couple did not ask for any information about their relationship. For that, Sybil was grateful. She expected that the topic might come up during the two months that she would be residing with them, but for the time being she was under no pressure for discussion.

16

KEEPING THE SECRET

Business was booming and Sybil, Michelle, and Kate stayed busy working twelve hours on most days. At work Sybil found it easy to be artificially cheerful. They had worked long hours for Francine's wedding, as well. In addition, Sybil had served as Bride's Maid. The make-up and hair was all done by Sybil and Michelle. The wedding was most beautiful at the First Baptist Church downtown in the second week of November. The morning sickness had abated. It had been a blessing to be so involved, yet it had been a tiring and a most emotional experience for Sybil.

Thanksgiving came and went. Trent had joined her at Aunt Barb's. Her aunties, uncles, and cousins, except for Moe who had joined the service, were all there. They had a big feast and all that Sybil could think of was whether or not Nathan had made it home for the Holiday. She had not heard a word from him since October, but she had not written him back.

As the Christmas Holiday neared, Sybil found herself more and more emotional. It was okay to cry at a wedding, but she was finding it difficult not to break down in tears at gatherings of family and friends, especially if children were present. She always felt as if her heart was someplace else. Her depression was deep. Trent knew that she was often on the edge of tears and aloof. He told her that he felt that the business at the salon was taking too much out of her and that she should perhaps cut her hours. She took this opportunity to explain about the beauty school in Miami, and how she might take a couple of months in March and April, after the Holiday rush, to enroll for a course. At the same time, she could relax in the sunshine and most certainly come back refreshed. He surprised her when he offered no argument. He thought it would do her a world of good.

Sybil prepared her Christmas cards and wrote one out for Nathan. It was simple, no different from the rest that she sent out, wishing him a Merry Christmas and a Blessed New Year. She signed it merely, "Fondly, Sybil," and dropped it into the box with the rest. Although she had helped Trent set up a small tree at his place, she had not bothered at hers. She was busy with appointments right up through December 23rd.

She had told Trent that she was going to be leaving for her Aunt's home in Montgomery on Christmas Eve, even though she planned to stay home alone. They had been to numerous parties for the past two weeks and she wanted some time to herself. She insisted that she preferred to take a cab to the train station and told Trent that she would call when she returned.

When the phone rang, Sybil started not to answer it; for fear that it might be Trent. It was Nathan and she immediately brightened, "Well, hello, and Merry Christmas handsome!"

Nathan said, "Hello to you too beautiful! I tried to call a couple of times, but you must be having a busy Holiday season. You haven't written a word and then I get this card like I am just one on your list, you have been a naughty girl."

"I'm sorry, Nathan, but I have been horrifically and yet wonderfully busy. Business has been frantic throughout the entire Holiday season."

"I'm calling from Washington," he responded, as her heart sank. "I did not make it home for the Holiday this year. Things have been outrageously busy for me as well. I know already that I won't be home next summer either. I have a job at

Freedman's Hospital, and it will be a year before I am given enough time off for travel."

"I see, I know your parents must be sad at the thought of not having you home," she said, knowing that it was she who was sad.

"Yes, this is the first year ever that I have not spent with them, and they don't have me or my sister. No one in the family has heard a word from her," Nathan continued, "I am simply beside myself with grief over the thought of her being away from our family over the Holidays, and can't begin to understand why she would not have at least called to say that she was okay. I really don't know what to think on the matter."

"That is so very strange," Sybil agreed, "that she would not even call. I'm glad you called me, Nathan."

The operator broke in to ask the caller to deposit more money for the next three minutes, and Sybil heard the familiar clicks with the dropping of coins.

"Sybil, I don't have much time here. I am on a pay phone. In all honesty, there is a particular reason that I have called you. Of course, Happy Holidays, but I have something to tell you as well. You have not been able to express with words that you feel any love for me. I'm not asking you to, if you cannot do so, but I cannot hold my heart for you either, if you tell me that you can't be mine."

"Nathan," Sybil interrupted. "As much as I would be true to you if I felt it possible for us to maintain such a relationship. I cannot and will not profess a love that can never be allowed to flourish. I fear that we are both kidding ourselves to think that we can make the world as we know it accept us, when the world, at large, isn't prepared for such a love as ours. There are so many barriers for us to begin to overcome that I feel we would weary to even begin. It would almost be like attempting to cross an ocean on a raft. You have to agree, do you not?"

"I needed to hear how you are feeling about things. I appreciate your honesty. I have met a young lady at the coffee shop. I haven't pursued any sort of relationship with her, and absolutely will not if you offer me any hope that we can somehow find a way to be together, but I cannot deny that my loneliness is unbearable without you. I am certain that the time is coming soon when we, as a people, will peacefully and harmoniously resolve our racial differences."

"Nathan, I do not doubt you," Sybil responded, with a crushing pain in her chest, "but I have to let you go so that you will feel the freedom to pursue your own happiness. That is the greatest gift that I can give you."

"Sybil, you have to know that my happiness would be best found in your arms, but I cannot force you to hold me. I will never forget the summer we spent together, or the scent of you on my clothes."

There was a long silence as Sybil fought to maintain her composure through tears.

"I have to go now, Nathan," was all that she could say.

"Sybil, please write to me if you have any word of my sister. I have to ask of you that one kindness."

"I will, Nathan, good-bye."

Sybil hung up the phone and cried into her pillow. She was glad to be alone. She prayed that Nathan would find his happiness, even if he did so in the arms of another woman. She could not be for him what he needed her to be. She would never be available to support him in his life or his causes and she knew this, but knowing didn't cause her pain to wane any at all. There was no way for it to be any other way other than as it was. She knew by his own words that Nathan was getting on with his life and she had to do the same.

She poured herself a very tall glass from Trent's bottle. She did not want for this to become a habit, but tonight she needed the drink to be at peace with herself. The apartment seemed small. Her life seemed small. She turned on the television to watch Casablanca. "…he's just like any other man…" It was one sentence, out of context, but it resonated in her mind for hours until she fell off to sleep.

Sybil was awakened by the National Anthem, and the piercing sound of the television signing off the air. She got up and turned the set off. She went into the kitchen for a cold glass of water. She thought she heard someone knocking at the door, and dismissed it. Then she heard it again, distinctly. She quickly went into her bedroom and peered through her curtain. It was Trent. She debated over whether or not to answer. He had most likely seen her light on, but he might have been there long enough to know that she had turned off her television set. She turned on her bedroom light and went to open her front door. "Trent," she said, "I was just about to go to bed."

"I saw your lights on, and your television, and thought you might be up." He asked, "Did you not make your train to Montgomery?"

"So what are you doing? Stalking me now?" she returned.

"No, not really, well yes, sort of, I guess…I'm worried about you. We need to talk," he implored.

"Good God Trent, it's after midnight. Come on in. It wouldn't do for us to be standing on the front porch talking at this hour," she relinquished.

Trent came inside, "Sybil, I know that your heart is heavy and I know why. I have seen you on the verge of tears and the life seems to have faded from your eyes. This is so very much not like you."

"Trent, whatever are you talking about? I have a bad case of Holiday blues. My father's health is failing and I am not in a position to give my parents the assistance they need."

"Sybil, this is not about your parents. I spent the evening with the Handleys. Their sons are both home for the Holidays."

Sybil's posture stiffened. She immediately felt a flush of anger. She turned away from Trent and asked if he would like a drink.

He didn't want a drink. He followed her into the kitchen, "I'm not here to drink with you. I need for you to know that I am here for you. Please don't be angry at The Good Doctor. He is like a big brother to me. Surely you have to know that. He would not have told me anything except that I shared with him how I am so very worried for you, and that's when he told me that you had an appointment with him."

"Yes, well, my back was out from standing for such long periods at work, and I needed a minor adjustment, that's all," Sybil attempted to lie.

"No, Sybil," Trent said. "You cannot tell me that. I know this man. I know what he does. I keep his books, all of them. I know why you went out there and I only wish you had confided in me. I would have made you an honest woman, Sybil, if only I had known."

"Where did you go for the abortion, Sybil? I know that you left The Good Doctor in anger." He took her into his arms and turned her face to his own, "I would have married you, Sybil. You didn't have to do that. Don't tell me that you didn't. I have known for years what The Good Doctor does, hell, half the county knows."

Sybil pulled away from him, but he held to her, "I should tell the authorities what he does," she threatened, "he cannot keep a confidence. He is no real doctor. It doesn't matter where I went or to whom, it's done now."

"He is a good doctor, he knows that I care about you, and he knows that I feel your pain. I love you, Sybil." Trent turned her head to face him again, "I'm going to make this up to you, Sybil, really, I am, if only you will let me. I promise that you should never have to go through something like this alone again, not while I live and breathe."

Sybil let herself relax in his arms. Truly, she did not wish to be totally alone in the world. "...I cannot hold my heart for you...I've met a young lady...my loneliness is unbearable without you..." Her mind played these words over and over. And Trent, "...I would have made an honest woman of you..." Poor Trent, how much and how little he knew.

"I can't be with you tonight, Trent. I have so very much on my mind," she insisted.

"I understand, baby, I do. I'll call you in the morning and we can go out to your Aunt Barb's. It will do you some good to be around family. You'll see." Trent let her go. "I don't want for you to be feeling despair. You call me any time. I mean that. We can talk, anytime."

Sybil let him out the door. They shared a light kiss.

Christmas passed, and business in the 1955 New Year was slow in starting. The entire month of January, Sybil had offered Trent a multitude of excuses on why they could not share time. She was doing inventory, the salon needed cleaning, and she had pre-study in preparation for her trip. Business picked up just before Valentine's Day as expected. A bouquet of red roses was delivered to her at the salon from Trent. The card read, "I hope I did this right this time." She could not help but smile.

Sybil knew that she held Trent hostage with a lie. There was no other way. The secret they shared with The Good Doctor was theirs alone. It was better this way. She could never tell Trent the whole truth. He would hate her forever. She had been able to hold him at bay with more excuses throughout the month of February. Her bags were packed, and Trent saw her off believing that she was bound for Miami.

On her way to Columbus she stopped by her parent's home to let them know that she would be gone a couple of months and she would call them. She phoned Michelle and Kate at the salon and they wished her well. There was nothing to do but press forward. She had her fears, but she had her faith. She knew that the chosen couple would welcome her with open arms.

Passing through the gate at Ft. Benning, Sybil felt as if she were leaving the country. She followed the winding road until she came to the residential area. She had never been on post and the tree lined streets surprised her with a charming home-like atmosphere. The greatest difference was that the houses, row after row, all looked the same. They were modest, new, ranch style homes differentiated only by the gardens and landscaping that varied from address to address. There were little parks on every corner with see-saws, swings, merry-go-rounds, and slides. There were children on skates and bikes, and mothers pushing strollers and buggies. Sybil began to understand the grief of this adoptive mother. The young woman wanted to belong.

When she reached the address, she found the young woman in the front yard planting marigolds. She warmly received her, took her inside, and showed her to her room. Next, she showed her the nursery that she and her husband had prepared. There was a bassinet and a baby bed all quilted in yellow and green, with Winnie-the-Poo characters painted on the walls. Sybil felt comfortable that this couple would cherish the child.

In the first few weeks, Sybil and the young woman began making weekly visits to the military base clinic and were assured that the pregnancy was coming along fine. She also joined the young woman at the base PX to purchase items to complete the nursery. They had intimate moments wherein they shared in the movement of the baby inside of her. In these moments, Sybil was reminded of her courage. The woman repeatedly remarked on the many ways that their lives were being enriched. Sybil felt very much satisfied that she had made the right choice.

It helped to see how the military mothers related to each other, and how their children played together. There were several mixed race families and there did not appear to be the undercurrent of racial tension that Sybil felt in civilian life. The mothers swapped recipes and household management suggestions as they blended into their community. Sybil could not help but feel that she was affording this child a sense of protection and inclusion in an accepting society that she could not provide elsewhere.

The arrival of springtime seemed to bring life to all things. Gardens were all abloom, and the smell of fresh mown grass began to fill the air. The baby had dropped and Sybil knew that the day was nearing. She was seeing the clinic doctor weekly and he told her that she had already started to efface. The young couple could barely contain their excitement. Sybil was having Braxton-Hicks contractions, and having never been pregnant, these were the cause of a couple of false alarms. The anticipation of the actual delivery was frightening to her.

April had come and gone and Sybil started to worry. She had been with the family for two full months and her almost daily calls to Trent, her parents, and Michelle were getting costly. It was long distance to LaGrange from Columbus. She began to feel like she was imposing, but the couple assured her that everything was okay. They accommodated her in every way.

When the first true labor pain hit her on Friday, May 6th, she knew there was no mistaking it. It was early morning, around 5:00 am, and it sat Sybil straight up in her bed. When the couple awoke, Sybil shared her news with them. They set about timing the contractions. It was more than twelve hours before they were five minutes apart. By 6:00 pm, they were at the hospital. As was customary, Sybil was almost immediately put into a twilight sleep.

Sybil had no recollection of the delivery, except that she heard them exclaim, "It's a boy!" It was hours before she was fully awake and the couple had already left the hospital. She wandered down to the nursery where the neonate slept, swaddled in his warm crib. The nurse told her that the baby had weighed 6 lbs. 12 oz. and was 19 ½ inches long. He was taking his bottle readily and had a strong cry. She returned to her hospital bed and dreamed of Nathan.

The next morning, the attorney arrived shortly after breakfast with more documentation that had to be signed. Sybil was told the baby's name. She had been permitted to hold him once. The couple had arrived to sign their paperwork, and Sybil held the baby while they wrote. She passed him over to his new mother and she sat on the bed with tears in her eyes, while holding the newborn in her arms. Their gratitude was expressed over and over again, while they adored their new son. They stayed at the hospital all day and into the night.

The next day, they were allowed to take their baby home with them. Sybil would stay at the hospital a few more days. Although the couple had not pressed Sybil for any information concerning the father, on this day that she was to take her newborn home, the new mother asked Sybil, "Did you love his father?"

"Yes, I did, and he expressed his love for me. It was a relationship that was ill timed," was all that Sybil could say.

A few days later Sybil took a cab from the hospital to the home of the couple. They said that they would have come to get her if she had called to say that she was ready, but Sybil knew that the mother would be busy with her new child. She watched as the mother tenderly attended to the baby in the nursery, and then she packed her bag to return home. The couple had a few days to become accustomed to parenthood before Sybil had arrived. They were already joking about the feedings every few hours and the diapering every couple of hours. They both seemed very happy. Sybil loaded her car to leave. She kissed the infant on the forehead, and hugged both mother and father, while saying her last good-byes.

Trent was expecting her home, as she had called a couple of days earlier and told him that she was leaving Miami. He was calling her number when she walked into her small apartment. She brushed his inquiries about the beauty school aside with a remark that it wasn't really anything exceptional, and was, quite frankly, a waste of time and money.

When she returned to the salon the next week, she told Michelle and Kate as much as she had told Trent, hoping that would quell any excitement or interest. She didn't wish to fabricate anymore on the subject.

❦

Days turned into months. Summer of 55 was a busy summer for Sybil. Work was demanding. Sundays were often spent in the company of Trent. Sometimes, The Good Doctor and Ms. Bea joined them. Sybil took a week off from work, and they spent a lovely time at a resort in Florida together. The summer soon passed, and it seemed the seasons were ticking by like hours on the clock.

Months turned into years, and still Sybil had not agreed to marry Trent. She spent a lot of time at his house, attending to him as if he was her spouse, but marriage seemed such a final thing. She insisted that she wanted her debt settled with him before she would consider becoming his wife. Trent started paying on her debt to settle it early.

The money to investors had been returned with interest by spring of 1958, and Trent pressed Sybil hard for her hand in marriage. He promised that he would love her forever. On bended knee, at the top of Pine Mountain, at a quiet little place overlooking the valley called Dowdell's Knob, he presented her with a most beautiful engagement ring on the first day in May. Sybil finally accepted his offer.

Sybil enjoyed her work in the salon. The ladies who came in seemed to appreciate their professional appearance. Sybil had insisted on white smocks, pants, and shoes. They treated their customers with respect and never had complaints that could not easily be resolved. They had both young and older regular clients. Women brought their children in for haircuts and styles every year just before school started. She particularly enjoyed the young people.

It was a joy to her that people felt relaxed enough in her salon to talk freely, and Sybil could not deny that it had become a regular rumor mill. They almost always knew who was getting married, often before the bride had been asked. They learned who was dating whom, who was cheating on whom, and who had been caught skinny-dipping in the square fountain. Every initiation and every tissue paper rolled lawn got explained in her chairs.

The Handleys had received a card and letter from Nathaniel that he would be receiving his M.D. Friday, 06 June 1958. The Handleys planned to attend. Of course, Moses and Eula Mae would be making the trip. The Good Doctor suggested to Trent that they go up to Washington D.C. a week earlier, and take in the sights of the Capital City. Sybil took a week off from the salon to join them. Although she had mixed feelings, she also had a secret desire to meet with Nathan. She hoped to steal away some time with him, but she had not a clue how to reach him, except for an old address.

They arrived on May 28th. On their first tour of the city the next day, The Good Doctor was pleased to be able to see a ceremony in the Capitol Rotunda, unknown soldiers of World War II and The Korean War brought home and laid to rest. They toured the White House grounds and took in many monuments over the next few days. They explored many collections at The Smithsonian. Sybil could see why Nathan had said Washington, D.C. was a beautiful and fascinating place. They rode street cars around the city, and wined and dined in its many expensive and historic restaurants.

Wednesday, June 4th, they were to meet the Griers at the train station and Sybil knew that Nathan would be there. She spotted him in the crowd before anyone else had taken notice, and he returned her glance but looked away and remained still until The Good Doctor brought everyone's attention to him. Congratulations were offered all around. He shook hands with the men folk, and hugged his parents.

Nathan seemed a stranger to her. He had lost his boyish innocence and appeared to be a man of stature. Although he had hugged his mother and father upon coming together, he spoke with them as if they were at a formal meeting of some sort. He talked with his parents of the Montgomery Bus Boycott of 1955, and of Martin Luther King, Jr. and his founding of the Southern Christian Leadership

Conference. Sybil commented that she had seen the news of the bus boycott on television. Nathan seemed to barely notice her presence. He raved over the, "Small book with big ideas, 'Strive Toward Freedom'."

Speaking most directly to his parents, he insisted that theirs would be a changing world, and that solidarity of their people was coming. Their people would be united with liberal whites for the common cause of equal rights under the law. He insisted that there were to come many more protests, marches, and peaceful demonstrations that would turn around the fate of the black man, forever changing the way he was able to function in everyday society. He sounded almost like a preacher.

Nathan told them that he was particularly concerned for the plight of black women in society, who were deeply and profoundly oppressed. He was completing an internship in obstetrics and gynecology. He wanted to open a specialty clinic for women at some point, either in Atlanta, New York, or Montgomery. He told them that his thoughts of Althea had become an inspiration to him. He said that he wanted to honor his sister, because they had never learned of her fate. His mother was in tears.

The Good Doctor assured him that he had connections that could get him set up with a nice family practice for colored folk if he decided to return to

LaGrange, but Nathan thoughtfully declined. He was still working at Freedman's Hospital, but he and another physician were looking into the possibility of a partnership. Nathan asked a few questions about how business was with The Good Doctor, Trent, and herself, but there was little more interest expressed. Sybil wondered if he had noticed her ring.

Nathan had arranged for his parents to stay in an apartment at the Whitelaw Hotel. He promised them a night of delight on U Street. They would celebrate together at the best clubs in town. The Good Doctor, Ms. Bea, and Trent were hailing a taxi-cab. Sybil had a moment alone with Nathan as his parents were gathering their bags and preparing to go to their hotel. It was a brief encounter. Nathan said, "I see you have a fine new rock adorning your lovely hand, you and Trent, I suppose."

"Yes, Nathan, I so want to see you alone. Your lady friend…"

"That didn't last," he interrupted, "seems she had more friends than I could become accustomed to."

"I'm so sorry, Nathan."

"Don't be. I have plenty to keep my time occupied, and I wish the two of you the most happiness. As to us being alone, I don't think that would be proper, surely you can understand my position."

Nathan left her to attend to his parent's bags. They boarded a bus together, and Sybil returned to her group. She had a feeling of emptiness. It had been a long time and he seemed a very changed man.

In the cab, Trent remarked, "Eight years of education seems to have given Nathan quite a big head for a Negro."

"These city boys, they all talk with a big head, Trent, color doesn't make much difference," The Good Doctor returned.

"I know," Trent went on, "but he's all grandiose about how the black folk are going to do this and that. I don't like it."

Sybil remained quiet.

On Thursday, Sybil feigned a mild headache. While the group went out for more sightseeing, she stayed back at their hotel, knowing that Nathan was aware of their location. She had a slim hope that he would have a change of heart and call, send a note, or come by. Would he take that sort of chance for her? It did not happen.

Friday evening, there was not to be a formal commencement. Instead, a small banquet hall had been prepared for guests and honorees. A light dinner was to be served. The honorees and guest speakers were all seated at one broad table and their guests had been seated at smaller tables around the room.

There was a podium at one end of the broad table where speakers were to gather and awards would be presented. It was to be a much smaller event than Sybil had expected.

There were few white people present and it did not appear that any whites would be receiving awards. The table of honorees, both male and female, was abuzz with chatter, while most of the guests spoke softly or not at all. Sybil could hear Nathan's voice, a cantor above the crowd.

There was a debate over medical journal articles regarding biochemical research on female hormones. These hormones had the potential to be marketed as birth control in pill form. The debate began as one person indicated that the pills, not being readily available to people of lower socio-economic status, would have no effect to improve the lives, or the standard of living, among that group. Another person insisted that such a form of birth control was comparable to mass-sterilization, when mass-marketed, and accompanied by propaganda, could effectively and would ultimately result in annihilation of entire races of people.

Nathan argued that no one was advocating sterilization as the pill was surely a much safer long term alternative than most current forms of contraceptive, and would possibly eliminate much of the unsafe, back street abortion market if properly administered, in a properly executed program, accompanied by education. He said that the American Birth Control League, changed now to the Planned Parenthood Federation of America, was gaining the support that it needed to get the proper education out to young people. He was filled with passion and determination when he spoke.

Sybil was amazed at how loudly and candidly they spoke on what she regarded as most sensitive issues. They expressed no reservations in the company of their peers. It was as if others were not present in the room.

Once dinner was served, the crowd quieted and the guest speakers had their turns commending the honorees, and speaking to the educational process that each would continue throughout their lives. The awards were presented, one by one, and each honoree was allowed to express their appreciation to faculty and guests.

After the presentation, Nathan came by to say good night, and to let everyone know how he appreciated all coming up for the ceremony. He made his excuses, and left with several of his colleagues. He told his parents that he would take them to church Sunday morning and see them off Sunday afternoon. This was to be the last time that Sybil would see Nathan for more than three years.

17

EULA MAE AND
HER SORROW

The coming of the decade of the sixties promised prosperity. Roads, even in rural areas, were being paved and construction was underway everywhere. Bridges were being replaced. Whole new communities of houses were being built. New industry was moving into the area lured by local tax exemptions. The textile industry in the area was still thriving. Two new high schools, one for coloreds and one for whites, had been built. There was talk that these would have to be integrated soon, but that had not yet happened.

It seemed that everyone Sybil knew was getting married and starting a family. Her own cousin, Henry, six years younger than she, had married in 1958, and by November of 1960 already had two baby girls. His brother Moe had married a woman who already had one son and was expecting another baby. Their older brother in Atlanta already had five children. Sybil was beginning to feel like an old maid, but she still wasn't sure that she wanted the responsibility of family. She and Trent had been engaged for more than three years, and he was pressing her hard for a commitment to set a date for their wedding.

They had been busy in the salon with young girls all spring, summer, and into the fall. There were debutante balls, weddings, receptions, and banquets, numerous occasions to have one's hair, nails, and makeup professionally done. The coming of Christmas had brought so very many by the salon to have their hair styled for parties that Sybil was pleading with Trent to hire on another girl. Trent had finally consented for the purchase of two more chairs and dryers. She had not hired on any new staff, but she and Michelle could work on two clients each at one time. They made a really good team, and it looked as if her husband was planning to stay at the local radio station in LaGrange permanently.

In 1960, John F. Kennedy, democratic candidate for President, passed through town as school children lined the route. Politics became a subject that fascinated women, as well as men. Gossip was still rampant in the salon. They often learned who was pregnant even before the father had been told. They knew who was about to be engaged, and whether or not the bride should or should not be wearing white. They knew who was being hired and who was being fired. They knew who was sick and who was well, and who had been diagnosed with this malady or that.

The week after Christmas 1961, a young woman from LaGrange College had come into the salon to have her hair styled in preparation for a New Year's party. She was Michelle's client and Sybil was paying little attention to their conversation until she heard Eula Mae's name mentioned. The girl said that her family's maid had told her mother that Eula Mae Grier had a severe stroke and wasn't expected to make it. The girl found the news particularly disheartening as, "The Handley's maid is not but 47 years old; why, my own mother is only 47 years old, and I could not bear the thought of losing her!"

Sybil hurried her last client out, and headed out of the door to go straight from the salon to the hospital. When she arrived at the hospital, there was utter chaos. A gypsy queen of some profound stature had been admitted to the hospital. Her band of followers was camped about the hospital grounds and between the two parking areas in front. There were police and armed guards, who were attempting to keep the peace as various groups pushed for entry into the hospital. Sybil assumed it was her white uniform that resulted in such easy passage through the front doors to the lobby.

She learned that Eula Mae was in a special care unit on the second floor. The nurses on the unit would not let her pass and she seated herself in the waiting area. She went to a pay phone and called the Handley residence. Beatrice told her that they had just come from the hospital, Moses was with Eula Mae, and Nathan was on his way down from Washington. She told Sybil that Eula Mae was standing in the kitchen on the previous day, when she suddenly collapsed and could not speak, and before the medics had arrived with the ambulance, Eula Mae was already fading in and out of consciousness. The doctors said that she had a severe stroke and things did not look good.

Sybil called Trent, who had already heard the news, and told him that she planned to stay a while at the hospital. She waited for hours. She had seen Moses once, and had gotten him food and drink. He told her that Eula Mae could speak a few words, but she seemed focused on her lost daughter and it was tearing him apart to hear her grieve in her final hours. He said that the doctors told him that her brain had swelled, the damage was massive, and there wasn't anything else they could do for her. They told him that they would be moving her from the special care unit to a regular ward the next day, if she made it through the night.

It was near midnight when Nathan arrived. He was distraught and went straight into the special care unit. Perhaps because of her uniform, and perhaps because of his despair, he had not noticed Sybil standing at the door when the nurses led him in. She waited for another half hour before he came out alone. He saw Sybil seated in the waiting area and she stood. "Mama has passed," he said through his tears. "Papa wants to stay with her until the mortician comes."

"I'm a doctor," he continued, "and I know how these things go. There is nothing anyone could do for her, but the pain is immeasurable."

"I'm so sorry for your loss," Sybil said.

"When I first got here she was vacillating, in and out of consciousness. The only words that I could clearly understand were, 'Althea is here.' Papa said that she was delirious. She had been this way all day, grieving over her lost daughter. I still believe that he knows more about it, but he's not giving it up. I don't know what to think, or even if it matters what I think. I can't wait in there with them. Thank you for coming, Sybil."

Sybil had no words. She felt awkward. It was a reminder of their day in the swamp. There was Nathan's anguish at finding Wilma dead in her home. There was their passionate interlude on the pine forest floor in the mix of things. There was

Nathan's persistence that his parents were not being forthright with him regarding his sister. Of course, Sybil had her secret, as well. They sat in silence for a considerable time.

Sybil inquired, "How are you doing? I understand that you are still working in Washington."

"Yes, Baltimore mostly, in Public Health Services, but I am still on staff at Freedman's," his answer came from his lips, but his mind was clearly elsewhere. "I've been to a couple of sit-ins with some students. I have become quite active in the Civil Rights Movement. There is much more organization to it than most people realize. I come to Atlanta quite often."

"Sounds dangerous, you could be arrested," Sybil replied.

"Not as dangerous as the *Freedom Rides,*" Nathan responded. "I've been on a couple of those, too. Blacks board the buses and trains in the 'whites only' sections and ride for long distances. Sometimes the locals assault them, or they do get arrested and jailed for disobedience along the way somewhere."

"It seems to me that you are just looking for trouble, and it still sounds even more dangerous," Sybil stated.

"Can be, but that's not the objective. The objective is for you to assert yourself as one of the human race who deserves to be treated as such and not as an outcast of it. Don't worry, my job is to ride along in the 'blacks only' sections to help deal with any trouble, if there is any, and so far I haven't had to," he spoke, with a hint of resentment. "In October, I was with the hundreds of students who participated in the sit-in at Rich's Department Store's Magnolia Room in Atlanta. Martin Luther King, Jr. himself was there. He was arrested along with about 50 others. Robert Kennedy intervened on his behalf. "

"I see," Sybil confirmed.

"No, Sybil, I really don't believe that you do, but I thank you for asking. I'm getting along quite well. Don't you watch the news?"

"I'm so busy that I scarcely have time to watch Lawrence Welk or the Ed Sullivan Show on the weekends," Sybil answered.

"I see that you are still wearing your engagement ring, but no band. Have you not tied the knot yet?" Nathan asked her.

"No, not tied the knot. We probably will soon though. No fancy wedding planned. We'll have a small ceremony somewhere. I can't see putting my parents through all of the pomp and circumstance of a large affair," Sybil explained.

Sybil felt that Nathan was changed. Not only matured, but hardened in a bitter sort of way. She admired his sense of purpose in life, but she feared for him also. They quietly waited together for the mortician.

The mortician came and Nathan followed him into the unit. Nathan and his father came out a few moments later, and they told Sybil that they would have Ms. Bea call her once the arrangements were made. They walked down to the hospital lobby together, and Nathan walked Sybil to her auto in the midst of the gypsy din, and said good-night.

The Handley's had taken down their Christmas tree and put away their decorations. They moved into a hotel for the week, and opened their home to the wake. Eula Mae's open casket was displayed in their living room. The locket that Nathan had given her for Christmas several years earlier lay open on her chest displaying the photographs of Nathan and Althea. Nathan could not bear to look on her.

The church ladies came and went with their offerings of food, tears, and prayers. It was not a solemn affair. The ladies made music on the piano and sang hymns. There was much joy expressed that Eula Mae had been released from all of her earthly burdens and had gone to her heavenly home.

Over the next few days, many of Eula Mae's family members came from out of state, from Chicago, Houston, New Orleans, and New York. Some old friends, white and black, had driven down from Atlanta. There was no mention that the house belonged to anyone other than the Griers. Ms. Bea told Sybil that Moses had asked her if he could borrow the home as his own for the wake, and Ms. Bea and The Good Doctor had thought it was a kind gesture on Eula Mae's behalf. Sybil thought it a rather noble thing to do. There was much talk of what could have possibly become of Althea. Moses was distraught. Nathan, preferring the solitude of the old house, barely showed himself. He came out to greet new arrivals every evening, and then he quickly retreated.

On the day of the funeral, a cab company from town was hired to bring guests from their hotels in LaGrange. The January air was frigid and most had their furs and mink stoles wrapped tightly around. It was a surprisingly long procession. There was to be a church service, followed by a graveside service at the little country church cemetery. The church service was lengthy, and many family and friends spoke of Eula Mae's dedication. At the graveside, Sybil stood in the back with other friends, and the family was gathered under the tent for the brief service.

The pastor mentioned Althea, "Who had been lost to the world at the age of sixteen, never to see her mother again." He begged of the congregation to, "Take heed, for when they are gone from us, we may not see them again until joined in that heavenly host." Sybil lingered by her car after the services were over.

All had gone except Nathan and his father, who stood by the grave as the first shovel of hard red clay was tossed over the vault where the casket lay. Eula Mae's family had paid for the funeral arrangements and there was a truck load of flowers in the hearse which would be taken back to the house. They turned to go toward the hearse when Sybil heard Nathan's voiced raised, "She's dead and buried now, Papa, and I need to know the truth about Althea!"

Moses said nothing and went to enter the hearse. Nathan got him by the arm, "I need you to be straight with me Papa!"

Sybil saw Moses jerk his arm from his son's grip. He shouted back, "There ain't nothin fer me to tell you, Nathan!"

"Papa, I don't want to be cruel, but as her brother, I need to know the truth."

Moses said nothing. He sat down quietly in the hearse with Nathan standing at the door.

"Damn you to hell, Papa! I wouldn't care if I never saw you again!" Nathan slammed the hearse door.

He walked back to his mother's grave, which was now covered, stooped and crumbled a handful of the red clay onto the mound. He wiped his hands on the green cloth that had been pulled back from the grave site and stood. He saw Sybil standing beside her flashy new Oldsmobile sedan and walked over to ask, "Can you take me to the train station?"

"I can, but I think you should try and make some peace with your father. Those were very harsh words," Sybil offered.

"I have nothing more to say to him."

He went around and got into the car. Sybil asked, "What about your clothes and personal effects? Should I stop by the house?"

"There is nothing there that I can't replace. I don't want to speak to him, not now, not ever. Just take me to the station."

Sybil drove away with Nathan into town. He sat silently beside her the entire way. When they arrived at the station, Sybil asked him again to try and make some sort of peace with his father before leaving town, and again, Nathan would not accept that such was possible. He stroked her hand with his one last time, and got out of the car. She did not wait with him for the next train north.

18

PROSPERITY PASSES

Trent and Sybil were married in February of 1962, in a small private ceremony. She was 30 years old by the time she spoke her vows, and Trent was 36. By popular standards, they were an older couple. Girls at that time were marrying in their late teens and early twenties. One reason for the long engagement was their dispute about starting a family.

Four years prior, Sybil had decided that she did not want children. She was a working woman with a business and career. Having children would have been a serious commitment that she did not feel prepared to make. She felt that she would want to be a stay-at-home mom if she had children. She did not feel that she could balance both. Trent also needed to complete his accounting degree, which was very time consuming.

Trent had initially insisted that he wanted children, but later recanted saying that he had only said

that he did because it was what he thought Sybil
needed to hear. It took a long time for her to believe
that Trent loved her, and not just the idea of having
a family.

When she traded her sporty little convertible
Studebaker in 1961 for a 1959 Oldsmobile Ninety
Eight Holiday Sport Sedan, Trent teased her that
this was her form of nesting. Hardly, this was a
rocket V-8 with a hydramatic transmission, and a
real eye pleaser. It was a black beauty with flashy
red, white, and charcoal interior. It had factory air-
conditioning. The dash was ultramodern and the
car featured power windows and seat, Wonderbar
signal-seeking radio with power antenna, autotronic
eye automatic headlight dimmer, deluxe wheel covers, and of course, power steering and power brakes.

Nesting was never on Sybil's mind. She knew that
she did not want the responsibility of children. She
had been on Enovid since 1960 and changed over to
Ortho-Novum in 1962. Trent never learned that she
was on *the pill.* Birth control was her responsibility.
She felt that he secretly wished for her to become
pregnant, again.

On November 22, 1963, Kennedy was assassinated in Dallas, and the whole country grieved the
loss of one so young and full of promise and hope.

Sybil put a television in the salon so the women
could keep up with current events. Women in the

salon spoke openly of equality and women's rights and responsibilities. They were becoming more conscious of how politics affected them directly. They knew that major changes were on the horizon.

Most monumental, the Civil Rights Act of 1964 prohibited any State or Local government or public facility from denying access due to race or ethnicity. This was to bring about the most drastic and radical change of the century. No longer could there be "whites only" public establishments. Sybil knew that Nathan had to be rejoicing. The South continued to resist. Many restaurants and businesses closed their doors rather than serve the black population. Lester Maddox, Sr., a staunch segregationist who ran for Governor in 1962, gained valuable recognition, although he lost that race. He received much publicity when he closed the doors to his restaurant, the Pickrick, in 1965, rather than serve African Americans. Some called their businesses "Private" or "Members Only" in an effort to skirt the law.

Sybil tried not to think about politics. To do so only served to put her loss of Nathan's love on the front burner. Her love for Trent grew out of familiarity. She had known him for most of her adult life. He knew almost everything about her. After her obsession with thoughts of Nathan had subsided, she found that Trent really did respect her, and he treated her nicely. He managed her business affairs and took care of all of her finances, even before they were married. He had become a smart investor and his accounting business had become the mainstay of his pawn, radio, and bicycle repair shop, which had become mostly a hobby.

Trent's relationship with The Good Doctor was solid. He had been Trent's first customer in accounting after receiving his C.P.A. license. Trent completed his degree in accounting and passed the SRO securities qualifications exam. A local investor who maintained a small firm had also taken him under his wing to teach him the basics and to sponsor him.

Trent frequently brought his bookkeeping home. He had made an office in one of the spare bedrooms and worked there into the morning hours, especially during tax time. He did the books, including quarterly reports, for many businessmen in town. He was buying, selling, or trading stocks on nearly a daily basis. Financially they were becoming very well off.

Business at the salon stayed steady throughout the early to mid-sixties. As predicted, the styles out of Hollywood set the precedent and everyone wanted height. They learned teasing and styling techniques, and learned to set hairpieces to give the hairdos the sought after lift. Their reputation regularly brought in new and repeat customers. Trent had consented for her to hire on an apprentice at a rather meager salary. Sybil had her trained and ready to work on her own within twelve weeks.

By 1965, Sybil and Trent were feeling very comfortable with their position in the community. Sybil traded in her flashy Ninety Eight for her first "new" car, a luxury Cadillac Fleetwood. Trent was driving a new Ford F100 pickup truck. They had bought a new house in the country and sold their place in town. They had many friends, other couples, in addition to Ms. Bea and The Good Doctor. Trent was always helping someone tinker on a boat or a plane. With the new hire at the salon, Sybil was able to leave more often and they vacationed with friends in Florida, Jekyll Island, Ga., Hilton Head or Myrtle Beach, S.C., or in the Tennessee Mountains. They threw dinner parties for The Good Doctor and Ms. Bea and other clients that Trent entertained, as well as Sybil's circle of friends.

Sybil was far removed from the violence of the anti-war protests and the marches for civil rights that she saw on the television almost every night, but she could not cease her worry over Nathan. On March 7th, 1965, Bloody Sunday, she knew that he must be in the crowd somewhere between Selma and Montgomery, Alabama. All that she could do was say a prayer for him.

In 1966, things were beginning to change for the worse. Trent had set up a nice office in the spacious den of the new house. He worked there tirelessly into the night. Sybil claimed the sunroom for her morning room, took her coffee there, and read her mail before going off to the salon.

One morning in May a long black sedan pulled up in their driveway. Trent had already left for the shop. Sybil did not recognize the two men in suits who pounded on the door. She stayed quiet for several long minutes while the men walked around the house and yard. She feared that they might try to break into the house and she got her gun from her purse, switched off the safety, went into a back bedroom, and locked the door. She called Trent at the shop and told him what was going on. She was trembling and could barely speak. He told her to stay put, not to answer the door, and he would explain more when he got home. She called the salon to tell them that she was running late.

The two men rummaged through their trash cans. They collected bags of papers. They pounded on the back door, came around to the front door, and pounded hard again. One man yelled out, "Mrs. Stipes, we're with the F.B.I., we would like to ask you a few questions."

Sybil remained silent. She could hear her own heartbeat and the sound of her fast breathing. The two men got back into their car and sped away. She stood still for what seemed a half hour. She walked over to the window and carefully peered through the sheers. There was no sign of the black car. She switched on the safety and put the gun back into her purse. All she could do was to wonder aloud, "Why would the F.B.I. need to question me?"

Sybil called Trent again and told him what had happened. She pleaded with him to tell her what was going on, and why the F.B.I. would be coming to their home. He told her not to worry, that it was strictly a business issue, and he would tell her more about it, but not over the phone. He told her that he needed her to do something for him immediately. He asked her to look on his office desk at home and find the Ledger for The Good Doctor.

Trent said that he needed the Ledger to remain intact but he needed her to hide it away some- place very safe. He wanted her to transcribe all of the names and information on the clients that The Good Doctor had seen in his office, and only those clients, into another blank Ledger that she would find in the bottom drawer of the cabinet. He also needed her to take several files out into the woods and burn them as soon as possible. He told her to make sure to cover the burn pile with dirt and leaves. He advised her not to burn them in the fire- place. He promised to tell her everything as soon as he got home.

Sybil took the Ledger and hurriedly transcribed the names and client information of all of the office visits from The Good Doctor's book into the fresh Ledger. It seemed a mountain of material, but she knew it must be important so she wrote as fast as she could. It took her over three hours. She called the salon and told them that she had to go out of town for supplies and would not make it in. She asked Michelle to get Kate to try to reschedule her appointments and apologized for leaving them in such a predicament.

Fearing that the agents would be back, she grabbed a couple of magazines, the old Ledger and the files, and decided to go out to her parent's at Hamilton Farm. She drove slowly down the back roads, knowing that she couldn't draw attention to herself. She was constantly watching in her rear view mirror to see if she was being followed. When she arrived at her parent's, they were just finishing their lunch. She ate a quick bite and set about helping her mother clear the table.

The kitchen was a room connected to the main house by a narrow breezeway that they used as a dining area. This breezeway had never been completely finished on the inside. There were missing boards in some areas of the tongue in groove wall where the higher interior wall had not been completely covered. Her mother stepped out to feed the dogs.

Sybil reached high and dropped the Ledger into a gap between the wallboards. She heard it come to rest out of sight. She kissed her parents good-bye and set off down the Hopewell Church Rd. for Pine Mountain, the new name for Chipley.

It was a warm and sunny day. Sybil had thought of a place that she knew she could set a fire without arousing any suspicion. She stopped at a market and purchased a pack of wieners and buns. She drove to the Roosevelt State Park and turned down the little dirt road to Lake Delano where the camping grounds were. She made her way to the most obscure site and reviewed the files.

The files were all about various accounts for various people with whom Trent had been doing business. She didn't understand very much of what she was reading, but she knew that her husband had to be engaged in some sort of illegal business. She gathered enough tinder to build a small fire in a pit. She set the pages ablaze, making certain that they were all burned to ashes. She tossed sand over the ashes. No park ranger had come by. She felt relieved that her task had been accomplished without having to interact with another person. She was shaking with fear, knowing that she had most certainly just destroyed evidence of some sort.

She took the back roads over the mountain, through Pine Mountain Valley to Columbus. In

Columbus, she went to a small beauty supply store to buy shampoo and hair spray. She tossed the wieners and buns into the garbage. Chain smoking with trembling hands, she drove back to LaGrange. She felt as nervous as a cat on a hot tin roof. By the time she reached the salon, Michelle and Kate were closing up. The new hire had already gone. She went inside and put away her purchases. Michelle said that two men in suits had come by asking for her, and she had told them that Sybil was out of town for the day making purchases for the salon.

Sybil tried to call Trent at his shop but there was no answer. She went home and tried him again, still no answer. Ms. Bea called to say that men from the Internal Revenue Service and the F.B.I. had come to her home with warrants, and had been all through her home looking for documentation. She had told them that The Good Doctor did not keep his business records there, but they didn't rest until they had made a mess of everything. They left empty handed but, Ms. Bea said, "They said terrible things about my husband, things that simply aren't true." She was gravely worried and said that she had not seen nor heard from Trent or the Good Doctor since noon. About the time that Sybil hung up the phone, Trent called to say that he was in a meeting at the Moose Lodge and probably would not be home until late.

He insisted that she should not worry, "Everything is going to be fine," he promised.

Everything was not fine. For the next six months the revenuers and federal agents made their lives a living hell. They questioned friends, neighbors, and relatives weekly. They initially brought charges of tax evasion against Trent, The Good Doctor, and other businessmen in the county. Though it was never made public record, there was an effort to apply even more pressure by threatening to accuse The Good Doctor of criminal abortion, a felony crime at that time, even for licensed physicians. Trent was devastated. He could not see his mentor going to jail. This man was like a big brother to him.

Trent had made a good number of men large amounts of money and nobody wanted to see Trent go down on felony charges. Though some of the illegal accounts were discovered in the investigation, many of the off shore accounts remained hidden and were never revealed during the investigations. There was a Securities Exchange Commission investigation, as well. In Trent's favor, this did not reveal any wrong doing.

In the end, at a tremendous cost in attorney fees, and after months of haggling with the Feds, Trent alone was brought up on two felony counts of willfully committing tax evasion and using illegal methods to avoid paying taxes. He was also brought up on charges of conspiracy to commit fraud, but this charge was later dropped. They temporarily froze his accounts. Much of the evidence was not accepted by the court due to illegal seizure. The charges against Trent's clients were eventually dropped. He forfeited his accounting license, and he worked out a deal to turn over his remaining client accounts to the owner of the investment firm that had taken him under his wing. No charges were brought against The Good Doctor for criminal abortion.

There was a trial and Trent had initially pled not guilty. He had numerous character witnesses, but the prosecution also had a pretty sound paper trail and they had The Good Doctor's secretary, and her testimony could be more than damaging. After much consideration, Trent changed his plea to guilty. The Judge said that Trent had a history of contempt over time and sentenced him to five years in prison and a $10,000.00 fine. He was arrested and originally sent to the Troup County Work Camp, and later transferred to a camp for minimum security males adjacent to the United States Penitentiary in Atlanta. The newspaper articles were most damning. The journalists made Trent sound like an extremely wealthy man who had gained his fortune by stealing from the pockets of the working class.

Sybil was an emotional wreck by the sentencing date in June of 1967. Trent told her that he would much rather go to jail right now than to Vietnam. He didn't seem to be terribly troubled, though Sybil knew that he was worried about her. He gave her instructions on how to manage his affairs at the shop. She would keep paying the rent and utilities and he would keep up his business license. He had given her the name of a younger man who would be hired to manage the shop. He was an old friend, a greaser who Trent had worked with years ago. Sybil didn't feel that she could trust him, but it was how Trent wanted things to be done. He told her, "Honey, I spent two years off the coast of Alaska, surely I can do a couple of years in Atlanta."

Trent was certain that he would not do more than two years time. Sybil visited every opportunity that she had. During every visit he professed his love for her, and her for him. Most of their old friends shunned her, the couples they had once entertained. Thanksgiving Holiday was the hardest. She spent a great deal of her free time with the Handleys. They seemed to be the only close friends that could offer her emotional support. The girls still came by the salon and their friendships weren't over, but Sybil was certain that she and her husband had been the best gossip in town for the past year. People were casually friendly enough, but there always seemed an undercurrent of tension.

On a visit with Ms. Bea, Sybil learned that Moses had cut his leg on barbed wire. The cut had gotten

infected and gangrene had set in. He had to have a
leg amputated. He was still in the hospital and The
Good Doctor and Ms. Bea didn't know what they
might be able to do for him. Ms. Bea said that they
never heard from his son, but occasionally received
letters addressed to Moses from Eula Mae's kin
that she would read to him. Sometimes Nathan's
activities were mentioned, but Ms. Bea doubted that
Nathan would do much, if anything, for his father.
Moses was being fitted for a prosthetic, but most
definitely could not stay in the old house any longer
walking around on crutches. The Good Doctor no
longer raised cows, pigs, or chickens, and they had
only kept Moses on as a hired hand because there
was nowhere else for him to go after Eula Mae had
passed away.

Sybil visited Moses at the hospital. She spoke
to the nurses about his circumstances and they put
her in contact with a Social Services case manager.
The lady was very attentive and said that she would
make arrangements for him to move into an apartment in the housing projects on Whitesville Road,
and to have meals delivered to him until he was up
and around. She did not feel that he was in need
of nursing home care. He would have some home
health services until he was strong enough to manage his personal care on his own. She could also
help him apply for financial assistance. Sybil was

greatly relieved for him and overjoyed to tell him the news.

Moses was glad to know that he was to have follow-up care and a place to stay. He told Sybil that he had a letter from Nathan's Auntie Martha in Harlem that Ms. Bea had delivered to him. Ms. Bea had left it with him for the nurses to read to him, but they had not had the time. He asked Sybil to read it to him. She read aloud:

"…Enclosed is a Xerox of a most recent letter from Nathan. I worry for his safety each and every day. He has always been and continues to be an activist for the causes that he believes in. We remain proud of him and hope that he can find his peace in the world. I hope this finds you well.

Love,
Sister Martha.

The enclosed letter read:

'27 November 1967

Dear Auntie Martha,

I want to wish you all Happy Holidays. Please tell the other aunties that I am well. There is not a day that goes by that I am not frustrated by the anguish of racism, yet I am convinced that I cannot keep up my alliance with my NAACP colleagues. I have argued my case both privately and publicly and fear that it is to no avail. The Pittsburg branch of the NAACP has issued a public statement with which I, as a physician, cannot agree.

It is my position that birth control offers the poor, both black and white, an opportunity to relieve themselves of undue burden at will. If that is not permitted to happen, we will surely be further oppressed. It is the wealthy white man's idea to perpetuate the poverty of which most black females suffer in order to maintain a poor working class comparable to and not much better than the class of slavery.

I have been working with Planned Parenthood in an effort to make birth control easily accessible to these women of little means. The statement issued by this branch is one that the NAACP seems willing to embrace, calling birth control and Planned Parenthood, "An Instrument of Racial Genocide."

Auntie, you know my position on things. This sort of oppression is no different than the illegal drugs that government officials and crooked law men allow to infest our

*neighborhoods. Will we ever get them back?
As soon as funding is available, and I do think
it soon, my partner and I will be relocating
to Atlanta to proceed with our plans to open a
clinic. I believe this should occur within the
next two to three years. I will try to write
more often, free time is scarce right now. Give
everyone my love.*

Truly Yours,
Nathan'''

Sybil handed the letter to Moses. He didn't have
much to say except, "Well, I guess he knows what he
means to do. I should just be glad he's not about on
the streets somewhere unheard from." Sybil begged
Moses to let her write Nathan on his behalf but the
old man just waved her away. He asked her to write
a brief letter to Sister Martha explaining about his
leg and that he was selling out to move into a smaller
apartment in town. He told Sybil to be careful how
she worded things, "Because they think I'm a right
smart better off than I am." Sybil read him the letter
when she was done and he approved it. She placed
it inside of a Christmas card and dropped it in the
outgoing mail box at the nurse's station.

By February of 1968, Sybil and Ms. Bea had Moses
comfortably situated in his new home. He had learned

to walk on his prosthetic leg and was beginning to walk short distances without his crutches. Sybil stopped by his apartment every two weeks to pick up his grocery list, and made certain that his needs were met. She also read him his letters from Eula Mae's kin. There was rarely a mention of Nathan.

April 4, 1968, Martin Luther King, Jr. was assassinated and again the whole country grieved. Politics were the hot topics. The women who came into her salon thought that the blacks were about to riot any day. There was serious talk that the National Armed Guard would be called in to force integration if local government didn't comply soon with the orders to desegregate schools. The women spoke of establishing a private school with a college prep curriculum, "For surely the black children would trail behind, resulting in a decline in the educational process of white students." Lester Maddox, Sr. had become Governor of Georgia in 1967, and had a four year term. Maddox would not allow King to Lie-in-State at the Capital. Sybil thought of the son she had placed in the care of the military couple, and knew that he was much better off than he would have been in this community. She wondered if the gentleman had stayed in the service throughout Vietnam. Did the child still have his father? She wondered also, if Nathan remained engaged in the Civil Rights

Movement, most surely he would. She doubted that he would ever come back to Georgia.

Trent had managed to avoid a lien being levied on their home with the large cash fine. His shop was producing barely enough money to pay the hired manager and the rent. There was a dramatic change in hairstyles with the coming of the counterculture that occurred in the late sixties. Younger ladies were letting their locks grow long and natural. Most of her customers were established repeat customers her age and older ladies. She had to let her apprentice go. Michelle's business had dropped off, as well. By June of 1968, Sybil also had to let Kate go. Bonnie Jean, her dearest friend had been diagnosed with breast cancer. Her cousin, Henry, was in the middle of a divorce. It seemed that things were going from bad to worse.

The Good Doctor had stepped up to help Sybil manage her financial affairs. Sybil knew from the gossip at the salon that The Good Doctor had resumed seeing clients at his home office. He was also seeing black girls now. His business was as good as, or better than, it had ever been. The court proceedings and the investigations had briefly dampened his business. Without easy access to birth control for younger girls, and with the "free love" mentality of the youth, things had actually become rather brisk of late for The Good Doctor's business.

He gingerly spoke of this one night when Sybil had joined them for dinner.

By June of 1969, Trent had been incarcerated for two full years. He was certain that he would soon be paroled. Sybil tried hard to hold onto her faith. She felt as if she had been through one trying tragedy after another. She had seen Moses through his relocation, with thoughts of Nathan constantly on her mind. Her cousin Henry had gotten divorced and remarried, and his day old son had died. His former wife had committed suicide by overdose, leaving the three girls to be cared for by his new wife. Her best friend, Bonnie Jean, had died of breast cancer leaving her young sons in the care of their father. Most significantly, according to The Good Doctor, her business was going down fast.

The gossip had become morbid in the salon. Boys were coming home from Vietnam in body bags. There was hardly a family unaffected. Elvis and Little Richard styled rock and roll were replaced by Beatlemania and that seemed to be evolving into a subculture of drugs, and psychedelic rock music. Large populations of young people were leaving their homes to join groups of beatniks and hippies, hitch-hiking across America, living in communes, protesting the war, and demanding Equal and Civil Rights. Some of the women at the salon suffered news of family members or their very own children overdosing on one drug or another. Large chain department stores were moving into town on Commerce Avenue connected by strip malls of shops. The businesses downtown were beginning to suffer. Sybil was aware of the financial stressors and was becoming increasingly concerned.

The Good Doctor explained that Trent's shop was staying afloat, in part, because there was little overhead. Her business at the salon was entirely different. Her fees, while comparable to many salons, weren't high enough to keep up with the rising operating costs. Her rent had been raised. Another salon had opened up in town, and although she had not wanted to admit it, she had lost a large customer base after the trial. According to The Good Doctor, her business was losing hundreds of dollars each month. He assured her that Trent had accounts that paid dividends that the Feds had not been able to touch. There was enough money from those accounts to pay her living expenses and keep up the house. There simply wasn't the money to keep up her business. Trent agreed that she should close up the salon. They debated the issue for months while she tried to sell the salon as it was.

Sybil was heartbroken. She had a sit-down discussion with Michelle, and Michelle had been losing money as well. She was pregnant and had no interest in buying the business. Sybil tried advertising the business for sale as a whole but had no interest after three months. She did manage to find a buyer in Columbus for all of the salon supplies; the dryers, chairs, shampoo sink, and other miscellaneous items. Finally, she agreed to close the salon. She took down the pink and silver curtains that Nathan had helped her hang, and moved out the furnishings. On September 19th, 1969, she locked the door of Sybil's Salon behind her one last time.

The next three months were challenging. Without the salon, Sybil was at a loss to find ways to spend her time. She would sometimes spend time at Trent's shop, but felt that she was a nuisance to the young man who worked there. Her father and mother were having a really difficult time. Her father had about lost his mind. He was wandering at all hours of the day and night, carrying a rope and bridle, and calling for his old mule, Lucy, who had been dead for years. After a few times of having to get search parties out to hunt for him in the surrounding kudzu patches and creeks, and having to call for helicopters to come out from Ft. Benning in an effort to locate him, it was decided that he would be put in Royale Elaine Nursing Home. It was one of the toughest decisions that Sybil had ever had to make, but it was necessary. Her mother simply couldn't manage him alone anymore.

The decade that had promised so much prosperity at the start, was ending in a vortex of decline. Sybil was still trying to process the loss of her business. Christmas was coming around, and she was not going to bother with a tree. Sybil thought she was in the worst state of despair and depression that she had ever encountered. She was lonely and afraid, crying herself to sleep night after night. There was still no word on Trent's possibility of parole.

19

ON PAROLE

Three weeks before Christmas 1969, Trent finally received notice of his parole hearing. Sybil was allowed to come, and to bring letters from friends and associates. After serving 30 months of his sentence, he was given probation for the remainder of his next 30 months. He was to be paroled on Christmas Day. They called The Good Doctor with the news.

Sybil brought Trent home on Christmas Day. When they pulled into their driveway, there sat The Good Doctor in his Chevy pickup truck, and there sat a brand new 19 ft. Sportmaster ski boat with a Johnson inboard-outboard motor. The Good Doctor told Trent that it was his gift to him for all of the trouble he had been through on his account. Of course Trent insisted that The Good Doctor did not have to gift him anything, but The Good Doctor insisted and told him that it was already a done deal.

He also told him that there was an AA-1 Yankee
Clipper waiting for him in a hanger at the airport,
paid in full.

Sybil, who had given up her business, felt a
twinge of jealousy. She was happy for Trent that
The Good Doctor had been so very kind to her husband. She was also upset that The Good Doctor had
indicated that she was practically broke, except for
a small living allowance, after expenses...then he
shows up with a boat and an airplane for Trent. The
Good Doctor told Trent that his sound investments
in Standard oil companies and Caterpillar heavy
machinery were making tons of money for him. He
wanted to share the wealth with the man responsible
for his good fortune.

Trent and Sybil threw what was to be a small New
Year's Eve party at their home. All of the people
that she had felt shunned by when Trent was incarcerated showed up for the event. Droves of people
she had not seen for more than three years came
out to celebrate. Trent had to go out for more
food and drink twice. Sybil wasn't impolite, but
she wasn't particularly attentive to their guests. She
felt a strong sense of resentment that these people
had not found it necessary to include her in their
lives for the past three years. Suddenly, they were
all gathered together like a big happy family. She
wanted to scream at them all. She had spent many

lonely days and nights waiting for them to return her calls. Their return calls never came. They slapped Trent on the back like he was some sort of lost hero returned to the fold. Sybil sulked in the shadows.

For Valentine's Day Trent took Sybil shopping in the Lennox Square Mall in Buckhead. He watched as she tried on expensive outfits at Rich's and Davison's. They went downtown to the relatively new Regency Hyatt House Hotel. The atrium hotel was stunning with its draping green foliage and glass elevator. They dined atop the hotel with a breathtaking view that took in the Atlanta skyline, while the Polaris Restaurant slowly revolved. Trent had secretly purchased a diamond studded heart for her to wear around her neck and he presented it to her at dinner. They took a room on the 19th floor. He was treating her like a princess, and yet she held to her resentment.

On the way home from Atlanta the next day, Trent told Sybil that he was concerned for her. He said that he felt that she was holding something inside that caused her great pain and that she was too quiet. He wanted her to talk. He asked, noting an observation on her behavior, "What's eatin at ya babe? You barely spoke six words last night at dinner and you've been quiet all day."

"I can't help but feel I have been duped," Sybil said without explanation.

"Duped by who, me?" he asked innocently. "You know that I'll love you forever," he added with a smile.

"I struggled so terribly when the salon was in trouble. I truly wanted it to thrive. You don't know what it was like for me, with you in jail. I felt so all alone in this world. Bonnie Jean was sick and I couldn't dare confide my troubles to her. Both you and David were telling me that I had to close up shop. Then you come home and all of a sudden there is money for expensive toys, clothes, and jewelry. Our friends, whom I felt had abandoned us, suddenly return to our lives as if nothing has happened. These people, who wouldn't so much as return a call while you were away, come patting you on the back without so much as an apology to me."

"I'm sorry babe. It's not that they mean you any ill will. I believe that they simply regard us as a couple, and it was my doings that made them uncomfortable. I am the one who should apologize," he blamed himself.

Sybil didn't want to hear excuses. She knew that all of those men, his friends, including The Good Doctor, should have been jailed, and they knew it, too. It was her husband who had taken the fall for all of them.

"You can excuse them, if it makes you feel better," Sybil pouted, "but I'm still angry. They ignored me for years, Trent, as if I didn't exist, and through the worst of my agony. I can't find it possible to call them 'friends' now, and that you can only drives a wedge between us. And the money, Trent, I know that David claims that these expensive items are gifts, but how can he gift you now, when he could have helped me with the business? That would have been a real gift. That salon was my life. I think I could have turned things around and gotten it to make money if I had been given enough time. Adjustments could have been made in my fees, I could have located more affordable suppliers, and I could have managed alone without Kate or Michelle if need be."

"Honey, we talked about this for months," Trent reminded her. "That business was stressing you out. You told me that it was many, many times. It was bleeding us red, and David and I both agreed that it was best to be done with it. You're a wonderful housewife, Sybil. I don't expect you to have to be anything more. It's not necessary."

"It's obvious that you don't understand at all where I am coming from on the matter," Sybil concluded.

For the next three months Trent collected all sorts of boating and camping gear. He was buying water skis, life jackets, tents, dining canopies, stoves, and lanterns. He was studying maps of the

Chattahoochee River and had big plans to take the boat on an extended trip down from Columbus, through the locks to Lake Eufaula, and to the Gulf. Sybil's cousin, Henry, had made the trip once in his similar boat, and came by to help Trent map out his course and to locate the best spots for overnight camping along the way. He took Henry up in the plane to fly over the river. The next day, he took Sybil up to repeat the course. He seemed happy, joyous, and free. Sybil wanted to be happy for him, and outwardly expressed happiness that Trent had his freedom, and he had found a way to release himself from the resentments that he could have been bound by.

While Trent gloried in his new found freedom, Sybil secretly continued to sulk. It ached her that she seethed inside, unable to let go and be free in the way that Trent had been able. Little petty annoyances irritated her. She snapped at Trent constantly until finally he would blow up and the two would argue over nothing at all. He wanted her to join him on his excursion down the river, and she had no desire to fight the heat and mosquitoes for two weeks.

Trent was supposed to leave on his trip on May 29, 1970, about five months after his release from prison. A male friend was to join him on his adventure. He never got to put the boat in the water. On May 23rd, Sybil came home from grocery shopping to find him dead on the sofa where she had left him napping. There was no one to hear her scream. The coroner said that Trent had a massive heart attack. Sybil recalled him telling her that he wasn't feeling too well when he lay down on the sofa. She had no idea that she would come home and find that he was gone from her forever.

Sybil instantly regretted every cruel word she had flung his way over the past five months. She was deeply grieved. Trent had been her best friend. He was the only person in the world that had put her first and expressed a genuine and lasting love for her. He was a young man, at forty-four, and Sybil tried to make some sense out of what had just happened. She felt that the Gods were surely punishing her for her selfishness. She had been so very concerned for her own feelings without giving Trent the good grace to have someone care for his.

Trent's interment was three days later at Meadow Lawn Cemetery. There must have been well over a hundred people present. Sybil had opted for a closed casket funeral with graveside only service. People that she didn't even know were there expressing their condolences. Flowers by the truck load had been delivered. She had the flowers delivered to Nursing Homes and the hospital. The hearse took her home. Her friend, Francine, offered to stay the night, but Sybil insisted that she return home to her family.

The house seemed far more enormous than it did while Trent was behind bars. There was a hope then that did not exist anymore. Sybil had never been much of a drinker, an occasional social drinker, but she found that the only reason she left the house now was to drive to the Muscogee County line to refresh the bar. This went on for about six to eight weeks. She woke up not knowing when it was that she had gone to bed. She went to bed not knowing when she had awakened. Her mind was lost in fluids of gold that warp the soul, only to be found in dreaming without meaning. She had no interest in anything except the contents of the bottle. One hot night in July, she stared at a bottle of Tylenol and the only reason she could think not to have taken the whole damned bottle was the fear that she might die a slow and painful death, rather than the sudden death that she desired. It was Ms. Bea that put a stop to the descent of Sybil.

The Good Doctor had called early in the day to ask Sybil to come over to discuss finances, as he was executor of Trent's estate. When Sybil did not show at the scheduled hour, Ms. Bea called her on the phone. Sybil answered the phone, but she wasn't herself, and Ms. Bea wouldn't let The Good Doctor rest until they drove over to see to her. They found both her and the house in a mess. Ms. Bea packed a bag for Sybil and they drove her directly to The

Bradley Center, a private mental health treatment facility. They explained about the recent loss of her husband and her current state of drinking and depression. Sybil told them that she felt she had no reason to live.

The doctors started her on antidepressants, and told her that it would be a few weeks before she felt much improved. She learned that alcohol was a central nervous system depressant and it only served to deepen her depression. She also started into counseling, both group and individual. The facility was splendid and comfortable. She was treated very well. There was a swimming pool and a TV lounge, as well as a dayroom and other rooms for meeting with visitors. She also found comfort there in both the staff and in other patients with similar situations, or worse. She learned that reaching out to others was helpful to them and to her. They went out for walks, for bowling, to art shows, and the theater. During the day, between meetings, she had art therapy where she learned macramé and needlepoint, or painted ceramic bisque in dry brush. At night she would read. She basically learned to busy herself. The Handley's visited weekly and complimented her progress.

In three months she was home and Ms. Bea had hired a lady to come in and clean the house. There was a chill in the night air, and she was able to set the fireplace alight. She could see, again, the many ways that Trent had cared for her and it gave her internal warmth. She made a habit of lighting a fire every night and curling up in front of the fire with a book. She would make hot chocolate, and sometimes roast marsh mellows, just because she could.

At Thanksgiving, she joined the Handley's, and then went by her Auntie's house. She visited with her mother and her mother expressed a desire to join her father at the Nursing Home. She said that her loneliness was too very intense and she longed to be with her husband even if he could not recognize her. Sybil could relate to her feelings and wondered why it had taken her so long to approach her mother about the matter. By Christmas her mother was admitted to the Royale Elaine, and seemed happier to be with people again.

Sybil took her lesson learned from her mother and joined a local book club. She also joined the Pine Mountain Women's League, and started going to the Sunnyside Community Clubhouse. They had a covered dish dinner the first Saturday night of each month in the little schoolhouse where her eldest auntie had once taught. Aunties and cousins and other community members met there to discuss the local happenings. With her mother, she started attending the little country church that she had attended as a child. Sybil no longer felt alone. She also learned that it was as much her responsibility to reach out to others as it was for others to reach out to her. Instead of hiding away and feeling resentment, she reached out to the mutual friends that she and Trent had and found them receptive. She continued in her therapy.

Determined not to fall into such a sad state of depression again, Sybil took a part-time job in a salon in one of the strip malls on Commerce Ave. It was only three days a week, she paid a monthly rent on the stall, and a monthly supplies fee based on her usage. She quickly established a client base and many had been her former customers at the salon. She did not do it for the money.

Trent had left her enough in insurance and investments to carry her for the remainder of her years. She spent hours each week with her attorneys, The Good Doctor, and the owner of the small investment firm that Trent had worked with, until she felt comfortably aware of and in control of her assets. The house was transferred to her name, and the promissory note on the house had been satisfied. A trust was established, and she had a moderate amount as an allowance each month that would adjust for inflation. Her financial security was guaranteed. Her emotional security was not. By June of 1971, Sybil had survived her first year without Trent.

Sybil watched her father quickly decline. He died in July of 1971, and was buried at the little Methodist

Church she and her mother had attended. Her sister, who remained childless, had moved to Ohio with her husband. They came down for the funeral. Sybil and her sister were no longer close, and barely spoke to each other. Although her sister helped with her mother's finances, it was Sybil who saw to her mother's needs.

She visited her mother twice a week at the Nursing Home, but her mother's memory soon began to fade and she did not seem to recognize her anymore. Her mother fell and broke her hip. Confined to a wheelchair, she sat in a corner no longer able to interact with her peers. Sybil felt some regret at having given up her child. There wasn't a day that went by that she did not think of him at least once. The support that she received in therapy helped some, but it did not fully relieve her pain. In depriving herself of children, she had also deprived her parents of the joys of grandparenthood. She felt ashamed.

Sybil's thoughts turned to Nathan. She was still meeting with the support group that she had connected with during the worst of her depression, but had not mentioned her past relationship with Nathan. She knew that a big part of her depression was related to her experience with him, but it was not something she could talk about to anyone.

Sybil was still attending to Moses in his apartment, but letters from Eula Mae's family were far and few between. If she had moved to Washington to be with Nathan those many years ago, her life would have been dramatically different. There would have been no one to care for her parents or his father. She wondered who would care for her in old age. Their child had turned sixteen years old this year, old enough now to be driving. She wondered if Nathan had realized his dream.

20

MOSES HAS A PROBLEM

In mid-November 1971, the temperature highs were in the low sixties with lows in the forties, and there was fog, rain, and drizzle almost every day. Sybil had central heat and air in her modern home, but was also keeping a fire going day and night. There was a warm comfort to it that she couldn't get from electric heat. She had just settled down to read a controversial book, "The Bell Jar" by Sylvia Plath, a posthumously published sort of autobiography of young girl who suffered depression before taking her own life. It was around 8:30 pm when the phone rang. Sybil answered the phone. The caller hung up. Calls like this made her nervous being alone in her house so far out in the country. Moments later, the phone rang again. She let it ring quite some time before answering. It was Nathan.

Nathan had looked her up. He had heard through the notorious grapevine that her husband had passed the previous year. He apologized for taking so long to express his condolence. He was in Atlanta at a hotel where he would be staying for the next two or three weeks while he secured an apartment and located a site for his new clinic. He said that he and a partner had finally gotten the go ahead to proceed with a women's clinic and he was very excited to be moving back to Georgia. He spoke as if there were some urgency.

He wanted to see her, and asked if she could come to Atlanta. He admitted that he had not made any peace with his father. He asked if she was involved in the Women's Rights Movement, and she told him that she had not been particularly involved. As a businesswoman, before it was the cool thing to be, she had asserted her rights in many ways, but acknowledged that she had lost her salon. She told him of her part-time job three days a week.

Nathan asked if she could take the next Friday off and join him for dinner at Paschal's Motor Hotel and Restaurant. She remembered the little diner near the Beauty Supply Warehouse, but did not recall the hotel. She agreed to drive up. She looked forward to seeing him, but her anxiety was immense. It is a strange thing to fear love, and stranger still to deny. It was easy to get the day off. A few appointments were cancelled, and the girls were glad to cover for her.

Friday, November 19th it was rainy and foggy all day. There was much new construction on the roads to Atlanta. The drive was taking much longer than expected and Sybil feared that she might get lost with all of the detours to make. She finally arrived on West Hunter Street near Clark College where she expected the restaurant to be, but the small place was closed. The rain that had been falling in sheets had subsided, at least for the moment. She stopped a young boy in a rain slicker riding past on a bicycle. He told her that Paschal's had moved right down the street. She felt much relieved.

Paschal's Restaurant was in a much larger brick building than it had been previously, and the hotel stood behind the restaurant several stories high. Sybil parked her car and went inside. The place was crowded. There were men, black and white, in suits everywhere. A few ladies were interspersed in the crowd. It had been so many years, she wondered if she would recognize Nathan. A gentleman tapped her shoulder, she turned and there he was, as handsome as he had ever been. She couldn't help but hug him, and he hugged her back with as much vigor. He excused himself, spoke briefly to two other couples at another table, then held out a chair for her at a nearby empty table. Nathan seated himself across from her, ordered two bowls of soup, and began talking as if there was no one else in the room.

"It is so very wonderful to see you again, Sybil, it is hard to believe that more than a decade has passed. You are as lovely as the day when we first met," he said.

"Of course, you flatter me. You look marvelous, as well. When you called, you spoke as if there was some great urgency," Sybil recalled.

"There is some urgency. Tomorrow I am, well myself and my partner there, Dr. James Johnson," he said, pointing at one of the gentlemen nearby. "We're going to meet with a man about buying office space on the west end, just south from here. Freedman's is closing in a few years. Howard University is building a new hospital. My time in Baltimore is over."

He continued, "Me and Dr. Johnson have been saving for years, and we've pooled our resources. We share the same dream. We plan to establish, with the help of the Planned Parenthood Federation of America, another clinic for women's health here in Atlanta."

Sybil sat quietly while he continued to explain his intent, "We placed an ad in the paper for property last week when we arrived. I got a call yesterday from a black man by the name of Amos Oglethorpe, who is here in Atlanta. Says his deceased father had insurance offices in a stand-alone building on Lawton Street. He has this property and the vacant lot next door for sale. He wants to sell the property, cheap, and move on. We are prepared to go out to see the property tomorrow and if all looks well, we should be able to settle right away."

"I hear what you are saying, and it all sounds so wonderful for you and your partner," Sybil responded with some confusion, "but what does this have to do with me?"

"I want you to come out with us tomorrow to see the property. Of course, it will be some time before we have the clinic set up," he continued, "I don't know yet what sort of remodeling will be required on the building, but from the way it was described to me there shouldn't be much but the interior that will need work. I think the vacant lot next door can be paved to accommodate parking. We have to get permits and other such formalities. We'll hire help for any construction that needs to be done. Any way that we can save money would be helpful. I was wondering if you would be able to help us plan out the clinic space, you know, lay out a plan for the interior walls, provide the design, and décor. I remember how well you did with your salon."

"It all sounds magnificent, Nathan, but I'm sure you can find someone more qualified than me for this remarkable endeavor." She questioned, "Why me?"

He sounded excited as he spoke, "Sybil, this is my dream about to be realized. I want you to be a part of it. I know that your husband has been gone but a year. He was a good man for caring for you, but I can't say that I'm sorry. I'm sorry for your loss, of course, but I have thought about you every day of my life, and I know that there is supposed to be a time that we can come together again. Sybil that time is now. I have never stopped loving you." He took her hand in his, and she quickly withdrew it. Her head was reeling and she felt faint. How could he profess such a love after all of these years?

The server had brought their soup. Sybil couldn't begin to eat. She felt as if she were about to tear up. She could hear the voices from the tables around her, some students, maybe. There was conversation about political, professional, and educational equality for women and the promotion of economic justice. She looked around the room and couldn't make out one person with whom she could identify. They laughed, and then they argued. They spoke of the National Organization of Women, oppression, and racism. Sybil had a deep and sudden feeling that she didn't belong. She was happy with her simple life. The cacophony sounded troubled and sad, even angry, yet amused. Nathan was speaking to her, but she wasn't hearing a word. She had to excuse herself. She went to the restroom and locked the door. She wiped her neck with a cold, wet paper towel. She was consumed by confusion and conflict.

Sybil wanted to be part of someone's dream, Nathan's dream. She had felt love and longing for him. She admitted that she was lonely and filled with regret. She had never been honest with herself, or with him. To accept him now would surely mean that she would have to confess her lies. So very many years had passed, could she possibly tell him the whole truth? Could they, or should they, attempt to rekindle their relationship? Nathan seemed so very complex. Could she possibly tell him how much she had missed him? She had denied her love for him once. She felt a sudden need to escape.

The room seemed quieter when she returned. Nathan stood as she approached their table, "I have to go now, Nathan, really I must," she said as she started for the door.

Nathan followed her to the door and out to the parking area. He pleaded, "Sybil, I know this is a lot to take in. I do. Tell me that you will stay, at least through the night with me. I have a room here in the hotel. We can be together. I don't want you to go. Let me explain my heart to you."

Sybil went straight to her car and opened the door, "I can't, Nathan. It has been really nice to see you again. I care for you, and always have. I know that I always will, but we can't be together now, or ever. The world as we know it isn't ready for us. You'll have to come to understand that."

"Then why did you come?" Nathan asked, "Why did you drive eighty miles in the pouring rain to see me if you don't want to be with me?"

"I suppose that I just needed to see for myself that you are okay. You have your dream, but I can't be a part of it. To think that we can be together is but a delusion," she concluded. She didn't wait for him to respond. Sybil drove away as the tears began to fall like the rain.

It was a long ride back to LaGrange. After the rain, the fog was like a blanket of cotton, so very thick that even with her headlights dimmed she could see no more than fifteen to twenty feet ahead. She followed the taillights from the vehicles in front of her for most of the way home. Her nerves were on edge as she let herself into the house. She hung her raincoat into the closet, and kicked off her shoes. She was glad that she had not stayed any longer.

Nathan had wanted her to stay the night. How impulsive to jump at the opportunity to see him, to ride eighty miles on a whim in the pouring rain, and for what? She questioned her own character. She went for a glimpse of a man whom she had not seen in more than ten years, an old friend, no, a forbidden lover. How could she not have thought that he might wish to rekindle that romance? He seemed as passionate as he had ever been. What was her cold and lonely simple life in comparison to his? He lived for a cause, and she merely lived.

"Why did you drive eighty miles in the pouring rain to see me if you don't want to be with me?" he had asked. She laughed at herself. She was labile and tried to make some sense of her own actions. There was no sense. She was lonely, and besides the man that she had married, she had laid with no other, and Trent was gone. Nathan had probably been with many other women. Of course he had, he's quite handsome. He's only forty-three. How he had remained single was a mystery. She hoped it wasn't because of her.

Their lives had taken two very distinctly different pathways. How could Sybil begin to think of starting over at 40 years old? Nathan needed a young wife and a family. She could never be for him what he expected her to be. She didn't know what she might do or say if he called. She felt foolish and embarrassed. She shoveled the ashes from the fireplace, lit a fire and a cigarette. She drew a hot bath, and soaked herself warm again. Safely back on her sofa in her simple life, she thought she would make herself a drink and then thought better of it, placing the bottle back onto its shelf. She made some hot chocolate, instead.

The next day Sybil tried to put the incident out of her mind. She went shopping for clothes at Mansour's and treated herself to lunch. She picked up a few books from the library. She went grocery shopping and got home late in the afternoon. The phone rang and she could not bring herself to answer it.

What could she say to Nathan today that she had not said last night? She was not ready for what he offered her. Would she ever be? "We can't be together now, or ever," her own words stung her ears.

As she went about preparing her supper the phone rang again. Again, she did not answer it. When she sat down to her meal, the phone rang yet again. Fearing there might be something wrong with her mother, she answered the phone. It was Moses Grier, "Lawd, Ms. Sybil, I been callin all day. I'm so glad I finally reached ya! The Handley's, well they is out of the country on some sort of trip again, and I just gotta ask you a favor. You know, I wouldn't be askin nothin of ya ifin it twernt important, but I gotta call here from a detective in Atlanta. He says I be needed to come up there right away. Says it's 'bout Nathan, my son, but won't say no more."

"A detective," she asked, "is Nathan in some kind of trouble?"

"I suppose he is, but this here Mr. Roper, he wasn't 'bout to tell me nothin, says I got to find me a way up, and he can't tell me nothin on the phone. Why, Ms. Sybil, I ain't heard nothin from that boy in ten years. I know it has to be some big trouble for them to be a callin me. Says I'm supposed to meet him at Grady. That can't be good, Ms. Sybil."

Sybil asked, "Did he say what time to meet him, or where at the hospital?"

"He tol me to go to D-Wing. I tol him I don't drive anymore since I lost my leg. He says he's on duty til midnight. He give me a number to call from the pay phone when I can get there, says it won't take him no time to be there. He's right downtown."

"Moses, I'm going to eat a bite and then I'll be over." Sybil hung up the phone and immediately called Grady Hospital. There was no patient admitted there by the name of Nathaniel Grier. The girl went on to say that a patient by that name was treated in the E.R., but there was no disposition noted. Sybil didn't know whether to sigh with relief or panic. She hurried through her meal.

Moses was sitting in a chair on his front porch when Sybil arrived. He had his prosthetic leg and brace on and went to lock his door. Even though he got along well on his fake leg, Sybil insisted that he bring his crutches along in case they had to walk a long distance. She asked how the detective got his number. He told her that the detective had Nathan's auntie's number, and she had given him Moses' number. He said that The Good Doctor paid him a little each month so he could keep a phone, but he never expected to get a call like this. He said that Nathan's auntie had told him just last week that Nathan was getting along right well and was moving back to Atlanta to open a clinic. Sybil didn't tell Moses that she had seen Nathan the night before.

The rains had passed, a front had moved in, and the air was cold. Sybil had the radio playing on an FM station of easy listening all the way. They didn't speak much. It got dark early. They arrived at Grady by 8:00 pm. She dropped Moses off at the front entry and went to park the car. Emotion grabbed her again, like it had last night as she left the restaurant. She felt dizzy and dazed. She held back her tears. She met Moses at the front door and they proceeded to D-Wing. It was a long walk and Moses was glad she had made him bring his crutches. Pay phones lined the hallway. Moses called the detective. He told them to wait in the lobby.

It did not take him twenty minutes to arrive. Detective Roper was a large man. He seemed impatient and brusque. He carried a stack of files with him under his arm. He introduced himself, not waiting to shake hands, and told them to follow him. He walked a fast pace and it was all Moses could do to keep up with them. They boarded an elevator. The detective had a key and took them to "B" for basement, a place not freely open to the public. Sybil cringed. The man showed them into a small conference room. After Moses was seated he said, "Mr. Grier, your son is dead. He was alive when he arrived at the hospital but died a few short minutes after his arrival."

Moses stared at the man, he was visibly shaken, and his eyes filled with water. "Are you sure it's him?"

"Well that's what you are here for, Mr. Grier. We need a positive I.D. on the body. Had his Maryland I.D. on him, and a number to call in case of emergency. I understand that was his Aunt who gave us your number."

Moses asked, "Well, who are us?"

"Atlanta, P.D., I am with a special drug task force."

"So it weren't natural, what killed my boy?" Moses inferred with awe, as the tears began to spill.

Sybil stood in the back of the conference room, her legs went weak and she took a seat. She couldn't hold back the tears that ran down her face. She held to her purse with trembling hands. How could this be? Special drug task force, please God, she silently prayed; don't let this be an overdose on my account.

"No, it was a gunshot, through the car windshield and into the right side of his head," the detective calmly stated.

Moses asked through his tears, "Who would want to shoot my son?"

"That's what we are trying to find out. A passenger, we presume, was shot in the chest. He died on the scene. The car was parked with the engine running, and the passenger was found on the ground with the passenger side car door open, as if they were to meet someone. The two shots were fired at some distance, some twenty feet away, M-14 assault rifle, standard military issue. Only two shots were fired and they both made their kill. It had to be a professional job. Somebody knew exactly what they were there to do. Nathan wasn't conscious when we found him. I hardly think he knew that he'd been hit."

"It's doctor, Dr. Grier, if you please," Sybil pointed out. She expressed her shock, "This was not some neighborhood thug! This was a man of respect, and I don't like the sound of things that I am hearing. You think drugs were somehow involved?"

"Ma'am, the passenger had on his person just shy of an ounce of cocaine, and some $150,000.00 in cash was found in a brief case in the back seat. We don't know who did it, or why these men were shot, or why the money wasn't taken, but we do know that somebody wanted those men dead, both of them. Mr. Grier, if you'll come with me." Moses rose to his feet slowly and held to his crutches.

Sybil asked, "If this was a drug related crime, why would the money have been left behind? Detective Roper, may I see you in private?"

"As soon as we're done here," the detective said as he led Moses down the corridor.

About twenty minutes later the detective led Moses by the arm to a seat in the lobby. He was given some tissues and did not try to contain his grief. Sybil knew that she had to contain hers. She had to tell the detective all of what she could recall from the night before.

Detective Roper came back to the conference room. Sybil knew that she would be telling this man intimate things that could become open record in a court. She wanted to do anything that she could to help find the killer. She owed it to Nathan to be honest.

Detective Roper sat across from Sybil. She told him that she and Dr. Grier were friends from way back, when Nathan was still an undergraduate. She knew him well. They had a brief romantic relationship, but remained friends. She said that Nathan would never be involved in drugs. Moses had letters to prove that Dr. Grier was adamantly opposed to drugs and the continued oppression that illegal drugs caused for communities. She told him of her phone call, wherein Dr. Grier told her that he was staying in Atlanta at Paschal's Motor Hotel, while he looked for an apartment. She told him of Dr. Grier's dream to open a women's health clinic. He was working closely with the Planned Parenthood Federation of America to get the Atlanta clinic established. She told him that she had just met with Dr. Grier the night before, for dinner at Paschal's Restaurant, and his partner, Dr. James Johnson was there also. They were supposed to meet with a Mr. Amos Oglethorpe, a black man, about a piece of property, two adjoining lots, that he had for sale. He wanted a quick sale. The property was on Lawton Street or Avenue...Sybil could not recall.

Roper sat quietly listening, and then he asked,
"This Planned Parenthood, same outfit that pro-
motes birth control and abortion?"

"The organization is dedicated to women's
reproductive rights, yes," Sybil rephrased.

"Lawton is where they found them, Peace
Officers on patrol. Nobody in the vicinity claimed
to have heard any shots. Man who owns the property is a white man, and not by the name of Amos
Oglethorpe. Can you write down a statement for
me? What you just told me, and sign it?"

Sybil blushed, "Need I explain my relationship?"

"That won't be necessary, just a note that, as a
friend, he asked you to meet him for dinner, etc..."

"What happens to the money?" Sybil asked on
Moses' behalf. "I'm sure it was Nathan Grier's life
savings. This was his life's dream, the clinic. His
father isn't well off and I'm sure he could use it."

"For now, it's evidence. If the money is traced back
to legitimate income from Dr. Grier or Dr. Johnson, it
will get back to its rightful heir."

Sybil finished her statement and signed it. It
seemed such a small thing to do. "What do we do
from here?" she asked.

"Not much we can do. Bury them. To the department it looks like two black men from out of state in
a drug deal gone bad. For whatever reason, turf war,
bad deal, and involving whom, we don't know. We

know there was cash and cocaine at the scene. It doesn't matter that they were physicians. We have no suspects."

"It does matter. It was two prominent black physicians going to see about the purchase of a piece of property for a clinic. That can be substantiated, I'm sure," Sybil defended.

"Yes Ma'am, thank you for your statement."

"They weren't looking to buy drugs. I know that they weren't," Sybil insisted, "I'm sure that Dr. Grier was unaware that Dr. Johnson possessed cocaine."

"Yes Ma'am, like I said, thank you for your statement."

"Dr. Grier was estranged from his father. There are letters from Dr. Grier to his Aunt that were forwarded to his father explaining his involvement with Planned Parenthood, his intentions with the clinic, and his detest for illegal drugs. He was actively engaged in the Civil Rights Movement. There was also some sort of serious falling out that he had with the NAACP over his involvement with Planned Parenthood. I can't help but feel that it's all related somehow."

"Here's my card with my address and phone. They move us around a lot, so you may want to keep in touch fairly regular. Go ahead and send the letters to my office. They'll be filed with the case. Dr. Grier and Dr. Johnson were from Baltimore.

They had established no residency here. From what I can see, this is a case for the F.B.I. It may be out of my hands soon."

Sybil joined Moses in the lobby. The detective waved them good-bye and left. Moses could hardly walk away from his son. He kept turning back to look over his shoulder. "Lawd knows, Ms. Sybil. This is some hard thing to do."

Sybil was patient with him. Outside the front of the building, she had Moses take a seat on a park bench while she went for the car. When she reached her car, with no one around she cried hard and loud. Her whole body shook with grief. Her words came back to her, "We can't be together now, or ever." She knew that if she had stayed with Nathan last night, she could have ended up with them at that property on Lawton, witnessing these murders. She would never love again. After all of the denial, she deserved to die in his arms.

Conclusion: Hannah Makes Her Greatest Discovery, *2012*

As a Hamilton, I was very sad for Sybil and Nathan, that they could not have found a way or a means to be happy together. I also felt that their story should be documented for the sake of posterity. It was not likely to be one included in Family History books, but their story did not end with Nathan's life.

As a nurse, I have worked most of the past decade in pediatric extended care, primarily with medically complicated and/or neurologically impaired children. Although working with complicated and impaired children carries with it some degree of grief in that these children will never be "normal", they also develop their "norms" and radiate their joy. Unlike adults, who scream, "Why didn't you bring me that blanket yesterday when I really needed it?" The children would curl up in their blankets and coo in their comfort. It was a much needed change for me to come to work on the other end of life's spectrum.

Prior to that position, I had worked as a Palliative Care Liaison (PCL) for a large Hospice organization on the other end of the spectrum of life. It was my job in that position to explain Hospice services and admit patients to Hospice care. I interfaced with both patients and their family members in hospitals, nursing homes, and their own residences. In that type of work, being as it is most emotionally charged moving from crisis to crisis, you can't help but remember each and every case. Practiced in other cultures for centuries, Hospice as a well-defined service was relatively new in this country at that time. Often, in the admissions and marketing position that I held, I was also explaining our services to physicians and other service providers.

By far, Hospice was the most challenging work that I have ever done in the field of nursing. In the E.R., C.C.U., I.C.U., and other such specialty units, I was working with empathy for emotions, pain, and other subjective components. The work could be grueling; yet, the actual work was most often dictated by objective data. Somebody is bleeding, you stop it, someone has an infection, you use an antibiotic, you titrate a Dopamine drip, administer packed red blood cells, give injections, change wound dressings, and so on. In Hospice, there is a degree of empirical data required to qualify the dying patient, and the team nurses do provide some hands-on care, but in admissions, the subjective and emotional components are always in the forefront.

There really were no "typical" days. Every day was unique. I might have three or four nursing home cases in one day, or three or four hospital cases. Then again, I might have a home case, a hospital case, and a nursing home case all in the same day. I might have three home cases in one day. I covered three large counties, Osceola, Orange, and Seminole. I could be as far west as Ocoee, or as far east as Christmas. I could be as far north as Sanford, or as far south as Yeehaw Junction. Regardless, each case was a crisis in which someone had just been determined to be terminally ill, with six months or less to live. They either already knew that they were dying or I was there to tell them that they were. Although a patient's doctor should always be the one with such news, sometimes the doctors would leave that nasty detail to the Hospice team.

The way that my organization operated, faxes were sent to my home from the referral center. A physician, friend, or facility representative had called the referral center to indicate a need for assessment. My job was to assess the patient and their records to determine if a candidate met the qualifications for Hospice and would be admitted. If they did not, I called in my report, notified their primary physician, and went on my way. If they did, I would process the admission; get orders, do the paperwork, order the necessary durable medical equipment for services, report my findings to the team doctor and team nurses, call in the crisis continuous service nurses if necessary, notify the primary physician, social services or clergy, depending on the circumstances, and go on my way. I was not involved with the long term care of the patients.

There were five or six of us PCLs covering the same area, and we wore casual dress clothes, not scrubs or uniforms. Sometimes we ran errands for team members who had patients that needed some service while in route to our appointments. For example, someone might be out of their pain med, and the team nurse could not see them that day and they had no caregiver who could pick up their meds from the pharmacy, so we would do that for the patients. Or a patient needed wound care but the team nurse was otherwise occupied, so we would pick up that task. Some days we had no appointments at all and would visit the nursing homes or hospital units with cookies or doughnuts, passing out notebooks and pens with our logo, marketing our services so we would not be forgotten at the patient's time of need.

On a trip to Washington D.C., for a national conference, I was asked by a panel of interested women to describe a day in the life of a Hospice nurse. I gave a rather vague description of what we do. I was told to give a specific example of a "typical" day in the life of a Hospice nurse in admissions and marketing. I recalled one from the previous week that seemed fairly representative.

I had gone to sleep with no faxes on the machine, and expected the next day to be a slow day with marketing to hospitals and nursing homes. When I awoke, there were still no appointments. My Supervisor called and said that a man in Yeehaw Junction needed his pain med delivered and his team nurse could not get that far south in a timely manner. I was living in Kissimmee on Lake Tohopekaliga in Osceola County at the time. About 8:00 am, I map-quested his address and set about in the pouring rain to pick up and deliver his Morphine.

After picking up his prescription, I arrived at my destination on the other side of the county about 9:00 am. I knew that I was inappropriately dressed for this assignment, but there was nothing to do but to forge ahead. I stopped my car on the sandy wet road, and waded my way through the knee deep swamp, where a little shack sat about thirty yards from the road. There, I found a 400 lb. Haitian man sitting on the porch smoking a doobie the size of a Cuban cigar, and holding an alligator on a leash. You may be wondering if I would be reporting his illegal activity to the police or the humane society, and the answer to that question is no. After all, he was dying and I was there to deliver his Morphine. What difference was it to me that he was smoking marijuana? If he found some pleasure in holding a two foot long alligator on a leash, who was I to tell this dying man that his choice in entertainment was unacceptable? I made my delivery, and waded back to my car.

I returned to my home to find a fax on the machine for a 12:00 noon appointment at the Winter Park Towers, far north in Orange County. I quickly showered, dried my hair, and changed clothes. The Marketing Director had faxed me some information that I was to review and present to a group of administrators and physicians regarding the feasibility of instituting a general inpatient bed unit in their facility. They provided lunch at this meeting, for which I was grateful. I made my formal presentation to this bunch of suits and doctors seated around a highly lacquered desk, and called my report to the Director.

Shortly after, I was paged by my Supervisor and informed of a home case. She sent the address via text messenger on my pager and I was on my way to the center of Orlando's downtown area. Home cases were almost always the most difficult. Sometimes it was necessary to phone the patient's primary physician to get further information than the family or patient could provide. That could be very time consuming. Frequently, there were many family members at some level of emotional distress asking multitudes of questions. Often, the patient was actively dying upon my arrival. Getting them signed on for services was a race against the clock, working frantically while maintaining an overt manner of calm and composure, sincerity and empathy.

This same "typical" day was the same day that came to mind after hearing Sybil's story and reading the pages of her diaries. In this one particular case, the patient's family member also happened to be a doctor. The name was Manuel Rivera and my Supervisor had told me that it would not be necessary to use the AT&T translator, as the son spoke English. I arrived at the home around 02:00 pm, and expected the appointment to take about two hours.

It was a large two story historic home on the cobbled streets of Thornton Park. The rain had stopped. Spanish moss dripped from the looming live oaks that lined the walkway to the double front doors. I pulled my rolling office behind me, approached the doors, and rang the bell. The gentleman who invited me in was tall, very handsome, with dark skin, bright green eyes, and a slight curl to his smile. He introduced himself as Dr. Miguel Rivera.

Dr. Rivera appeared to be middle to late forties, soft-spoken, and very polite. There was no notable accent. We talked downstairs in the den for a while as I explained our services. I noticed a wedding photo on the mantel. The man, whom he said was his father and my patient, was in dress military attire and the lovely bride had golden locks draped around her shoulders. He explained that his mother had died from cervical cancer in 1971, when he was sixteen years old. His father was retired military, having served in both WWII and Korea before Vietnam, and getting out of the service after twenty four years in 1964. From 1964-1987, he wrote military contracts. He had moved to Orlando to live with his son in 1991. At eighty years old in 2002, he was dying from organ failure, the result of a large tumor that involved the major blood vessels of the liver.

Dr. Rivera showed me upstairs to meet his father. The older gentleman was in obvious distress. His breathing was labored and wet and his pulse rapid. Dr. Rivera told me that he had been semi-conscious for three days and he knew that the end was near. He said that he had thought, being a physician, he could handle his father's death alone. His wife had taken their two children, a son age seven and a daughter age ten, to Puerto Rico to visit her parents, as she could not bear to have them see their grandfather in such a way. There were photos of these two beautiful children placed all around their grandfather's room. The doctor had called Home Health Services and they had referred him to Hospice.

I went about explaining our services. Dr. Rivera's sister was in Puerto Rico also, but he had Power of attorney. The son signed the necessary paperwork. At the son's request, I spoke with the sister briefly over the phone to indicate to her the serious nature of the circumstances and she was most agreeable, having already spoken with Dr. Rivera's wife. I notified the Hospice Continuous Care Crisis Team, as I knew that his father's next breath could be his last and I did not want to leave them alone. As I waited with the son, completing the assessment of his father, he told me that he was adopted at birth. It was a very emotional experience for him in that he had also lost his adoptive mother at such a young age. He held his father's hand, stroked his face with a cool cloth, and thanked him repeatedly for being the best father a man could have ever dreamed of having in his life.

When the Crisis Team Nurse arrived to care for his father, the son and I returned downstairs. Usually, I would leave after the Crisis Team Nurse's arrival, but Dr. Rivera seemed to have a need to talk. I was about to take my leave when he insisted that we have a cup of coffee or tea. We went into the kitchen and sat at the table with the tea set to steep.

He told me that he was born in Columbus, Georgia, in Muscogee County, when his father was stationed at Ft. Benning. Of course, I told him how close to Ft. Benning I had been raised, joked that I was related to nearly everyone in nearby Harris County, to one degree or another, and we were likely to be cousins.

I asked him to tell me about his adoptive father. He said that he had been career military and that he had lived with his adoptive mother and father in the Panama Canal Zone, until the age of nine. In 1964, the riots in Panama and the general feelings of animosity toward Americans made his father afraid for his family and he retired from the military. They moved to Puerto Rico where his sister was adopted in 1965, when he was ten. His sister was only six years old when her adoptive mother died. His father had been working out of an office in their home throughout his adoptive mother's illness. He was a dedicated husband and father, but the demands of a girl child so very young at the time of her mother's death were too much for him. Although his father continued to provide financial support, his sister was raised by other family members in Puerto Rico, but they saw her often. His father never remarried. He brought Miguel to Miami in 1973, after he had graduated high school.

Dr. Rivera had attended University of Miami and the Miller Medical School. He received further training and worked at M. D. Anderson Cancer Center in Houston, Texas, from 1981-1991, and was able to spend a significant time with his adoptive grandparents, the parents of his adoptive mother, while in training to become a research physician. He specialized in Gynecological Oncology, primarily as a result of his mother's illness. He moved to Orlando in 1991, with M.D. Anderson Cancer Center Orlando.

He met his wife and married while he was in Texas, and one thing they shared was that they both had family in Florida at that time, so their visits to Florida became quite regular. When they moved to Orlando, his father came from Miami to live with them. His wife was also very career oriented and was a pathologist. They had put off having children, but with his father around they decided to go ahead. The next year, his daughter was born, and three years later they had a son. His father greatly participated in their lives. They loved their "abuelo" and were very close.

We had finished our tea and he asked me about myself and how I had come to Florida. I told him that I had lost my mother when I was a couple of years older than his sister at the time she lost hers. A few years later, with my father being so very involved with his other relationships, which included a few wives, my younger sister and I were placed into foster care, being considered too old for adoption by that time. I told him that I was divorced and had cousins who owned a resort in Kissimmee, so I moved down in 1997.

I began to gather my paperwork and pack it away in my bag, and asked Dr. Rivera what he knew of his birth parents. He said that he knew that his father was black, and had been a medical student, and his mother was white. He said that her last name was Hamilton, but he could not recall if he had ever known her first name. He didn't know much about her but assumed that she was military or worked on post. He had thought once about looking her up after his adoptive mother had passed, but he had nowhere to begin.

I joked again with him, that my maiden name had been Hamilton and we really could be cousins. I stepped back upstairs to let the Crisis Team Nurse know that I was leaving. I returned downstairs. Dr. Rivera showed me to the door. I went by the office to turn in some paperwork and then I drove back to my home in Kissimmee. I thought about how hard it is for anyone to lose a parent at any age. This man was losing a parent that had brought him into his home at birth, not knowing if his biological parents were living or deceased.

❧

Having recently heard Sybil's story and having read the pages of her diaries, the story of Dr. Rivera recalled seemed so familiar, even ten years later. That this doctor's father had been at Ft. Benning, and had adopted a son at the same time that Sybil Hamilton would have been giving birth seemed too coincidental. That his biological father had been a black medical student also, and his adoptive father was Hispanic with a white wife from Texas, it all seemed to come together in my mind. I thought it rather fascinating that Dr. Rivera had chosen to specialize in Gynecological Oncology in that; perhaps, his own biological father had been so similarly inclined. I also thought it rather fascinating that he might indeed be my cousin.

I emailed Sybil to ask her if she knew the names of the couple who had adopted her son. She e-mailed me right away that the names were Manuel and Violet Rivera. That was almost a confirmation in my mind, but I did not know Dr. Rivera's adoptive mother's name. I asked Sybil if she would wish to meet her son after all of these years had passed, and she told me that she would only want for her son what he wished for himself. I did not mention the appointment that I had been to some ten years earlier. I wanted to speak to Dr. Rivera.

In June 2012, I finally got up the courage to call Dr. Rivera. I had already written up what I knew from my own experience growing up in Georgia, from my experience with Moses Grier and Beatrice Handley, and what I knew from Sybil. I wanted to share this with him if he wished to know more.

As a research physician, Dr. Rivera did not have a private practice, and I doubted if his number was listed in the phone directory, but it was there. I called and left my number with his housekeeper, a Spanish lady who informed me that she would have him call me. I had told her that I had been his father's Hospice nurse when he had been admitted to the program ten years ago. I was excited that he was still residing in Orlando, but when he had not returned my call after four days, I was afraid that he might not ever call me back.

On the fifth day, I received a call back. We spoke briefly about his wife and children. His children were now seventeen and twenty, and both were in college locally and living at home. I spoke with him about his adoptive mother and father, and asked him his adoptive mother's name. As expected, he said that her name was Violet, and her parents had owned and operated a ranch in Texas. He said that his adoptive Grandparents had both passed away in the 1980s, but his cousins still operated the ranch where they sometimes vacationed. I asked if he would like to meet his biological mother and told him that I was convinced by a family member's confessions that we really are cousins. I told him of my family name and how it had struck a chord with me after hearing my cousin, Sybil's, life story, and that she was still living in my hometown of LaGrange, Georgia. He said that he would have to give it some thought. I invited him and his wife over for dinner the next night, and told him that I had something that he might like to read. He accepted my offer.

My husband had been an Army brat, and I knew from our many discussions about the Old South, that it might be difficult for Dr. Rivera to relate to the era that I had grown up in and the era of Sybil and Nathan. I had my notes from the meetings with Moses Grier, his biological grandfather, and my manuscript ready to share with him.

When they arrived, I put the steaks on the grill. It was cool enough to sit on the back porch so we took our chairs there. It had been ten years since his adoptive father had passed, and I started the conversation about that day. He was very proud of his adoptive father and spoke in detail about his life.

His adoptive father had joined the all volunteer Army's 65th Infantry in Puerto Rico in 1940. In 1943, he was sent to Panama to protect the Atlantic side of the isthmus. In 1944, he was briefly in New Orleans, where he met his adoptive mother who was from Texas, but was visiting relatives in Louisiana. They fell immediately in love and were married right

away. Very soon after, he was sent to Virginia, then
to North Africa, and on to Italy. They kept in touch
by mail and he worried that he would leave her a
young widow. He had told his son that thoughts of
her were what kept him alive and fighting in France
and Germany during WWII.

His father returned to Puerto Rico in 1945.
His mother joined him there and they lived there
together until he was sent to Korea in 1950, where
he fought in that war. His mother had had three
miscarriages during their time in Puerto Rico. After
the Korean War, the 65th Infantry was embroiled in
a serious controversy, but he was not involved, so he
was sent to Ft. Benning, Ga., where his wife, who had
been staying in Texas, with her family, rejoined him
in 1954. He had been selected to participate in a
specialized military training. It was while he was stationed at Ft. Benning that he and his wife adopted
Miguel in 1955. Miguel had been born on May 6th.

His parents were at Ft. Benning a couple of years.
While many soldiers from the 65th Infantry returned
to Puerto Rico to serve in the Armed Guard, his
father, along with him and his mother went to live
in the Panama Canal Zone. His father was highly
decorated, had combat experience, language skills,
and engineering skills. They lived in Panama for
seven years as a family while his father trained men
in jungle warfare and served to protect the canal.

In 1964, when riots broke out over a disagreement about flying the Panamanian flag, his father felt it best to retire from military service and bring his family home to Puerto Rico.

He spoke of his mother as a very happy but quiet woman. She was very tender and loving. Her adopted daughter was only three years old when she was diagnosed with cervical cancer. She had a hysterectomy, but the cancer had already spread to vital organs. Her last three years were not good years. Her depression was severe and Dr. Rivera watched her go from a mother filled with life and vitality to a sad, easily fatigued, despondent woman. He was staying with family when she actually passed away. He concentrated on his school work and caring for his younger sister to fill the void left in his life, until his father sent her away to live with other family in Puerto Rico.

Not unlike my husband, who spent his early teen years in Ecuador, Dr. Rivera did not have a personal connection to how things were in the period of time prior to integration in the Old South. His mother from Texas had spoken of the time before integration mostly in reference to the Mexicans from her area, and little was said about the Old South with its Jim Crow Laws. Dr. Rivera had missed the peak of the Civil Rights Movement, and the Black Power Movement of the sixties and seventies. By the time he moved to Miami with his father in 1973, the area of Florida that he was living in was far more blended than other southern states. He was aware of the anti-war protests and spoke with his father about them, but he was focused on his education and felt somewhat removed from the discord.

I told him about our cousin Sybil, and how she was at the age of eighty years, youthful and spry for her age. I gave him a brief synopsis of her circumstances with regards to her pregnancy, how she had loved his biological father, but both were actively pursuing careers and the racial tension was even more severe in the South than the hatred that his father had removed them from in Panama. Sybil had wanted him to have a wholesome life and felt that his adoptive parents could give him a better home than she could at that time.

After dinner, I explained about The Good Doctor and shared the manuscript that documented the story of Moses Grier and told of the demise of his Aunt Althea, and how proud his grandfather and grandmother had been of his father. He read it and was moved to tears. This was family that he had not known, a history that he had not been aware of existing. He noted that the manuscript did not speak of what had become of his father. He asked if I knew whether his father was living and I had to tell him that he was not. I gave him my complete manuscript and asked if he would read it and then make his decision regarding whether or not he wished to meet our cousin Sybil.

A couple of weeks later, I received a phone call from Dr. Rivera. He said that he and his family would like to meet Sybil. At this point, I felt that Sybil needed to know that I had possibly located the adopted son of Manuel and Violet Rivera, and how that came about. Her emotions were mixed. There was joy in that her son was doing well, and there was a sadness that she had not been available to him all of these years, particularly during the time following his adoptive mother's death. She also felt guilt and shame concerning the prejudice that she had been indoctrinated with in her youth, that she could not accept her own son in the manner that his mixed race adoptive parents had been so very happy and eager to do. She had regrets that she had not tried to look his parents up through military records, but she had intended to honor her contract with them. They were both gone now, and Sybil wanted to meet her son.

We discussed the best way to get together and it was decided that we would all go up to Ga., rather than have her come down to Florida. My husband, daughter, son-in-law, and granddaughter were in our car, and the Riveras were in their SUV. We had reserved a couple of chalets in Pine Mountain, at

Callaway Gardens, for the week of the Independence Day Holiday. My daughter was thrilled to meet her cousins and they were thrilled to meet her and her family, more cousins. I did not tell my family in Georgia about our intentions as I felt that would be at Sybil's and Miguel's prerogative. The trip to Georgia from Florida seemed shorter than ever because I was very excited to bring together Sybil, her son, and his family.

I was also very glad that Miguel's daughter, Rita, age 20, and son, Victor, age 17, were coming along on the trip. I had thought it would be difficult for them, but they seemed happy for their father. We stopped for dinner in Valdosta, Georgia, and Dr. and Mrs. Rivera seemed as excited as my husband and me that the cousins were getting to know each other. My son in Georgia, and my other son and his wife from North Carolina, were also joining us at the chalet in Pine Mountain, Georgia. We planned to have Sybil join us the next morning.

We never know why God puts us in any place at any given time, why He introduces us to anyone at any point in our lives, or what lessons He chooses to teach, but God always has a plan. It might be a plan not well understood, but the design is most definitely divine. He chooses the time and the circumstances to make it right for the fulfillment of His plan. I may not be a religious person with a specific doctrine, but I have felt the hand and heart of God in my life many times. I have seen Him working through myself and others. I have felt His love.

After breakfast the next morning, the younger cousins all went to rent bicycles while Mrs. Rivera and I prepared the food for our lunch picnic, and looked after my granddaughter. Dr. Rivera and my husband took a walk along the mountain laurel shaded trail to the chapel. Sybil was on her way.

When Sybil arrived, I introduced her to Mrs. Rivera. The three of us, along with my little grand-daughter, walked down the trail toward the chapel. The trees were a wall of beautiful, bright green reflecting off of the still lake in front of the chapel. We came around the corner to see the little chapel, feeling the solitude of its stature in this woodland setting. The air was fresh and cool in the shade. A fast running stream trickled over rocks under the arched stone bridge near the chapel door. Stained glass windows, showing the seasons, splashed the colors of the rainbow onto the stone walls. Dr. Miguel Rivera stood in the arched doorway with my husband. He held out his hand to Sybil. "Our son," she said, as she walked slowly toward him, took his hand, and then hugged his neck. They shared their tears in an embrace. We left them alone and walked back to the chalet.

AFTERWORD

08 July 2012

This book is the product of a compilation of stories related to the author over time, and her own personal experiences. It is both a fictional and historical account loosely based on fact. Any likeness of the characters to anyone living or dead is coincidental.

Mark Twain said, "Racism, chauvinism and religion are the three greatest evils of mankind." The blood shed by racism, chauvinism and religion is what makes them tangible evils. This book is to serve as a reminder of our progress away from these evils, and how hard fought this progress has been. It is not enough to have good intent if the outcome is evil. The author focuses on two primary issues; racism, and women's reproductive rights and responsibilities.

Racism spans generations, and takes generations to overcome. To know the hatred of any era involving any culture, one would have to live through it.

The pain of racism will exist until we are all one kind, speaking in one tongue, with one collective spiritual presence and consciousness, and poverty is no longer a threat. Until we totally cease to perpetuate racial hatred through our children and theirs, no ground can be gained in social harmony.

It is not the author's intent to choose a side, pro-life or pro-choice, regarding abortion with the writing of this book. The purpose is to enlighten those unaware of the conflicts that women have historically faced with regards to their reproductive rights and responsibilities. There is more of an attempt to avoid absolute or relative poverty than an attempt to exercise selfishness influencing any woman's decision in any direction. Abortion, whether medically aseptic or not, has always been and will always be an option for women. Legal and clinically safe abortion by trained professionals has not always been an option. No abortion is without liability and risk for the mother. That liability and risk can be minimized. All successful abortion terminates a potential life. Women bearing the brunt of responsibility in birth control, and being faced with the chauvinism that is perpetuated by our society and its religions, exercise their rights under the law. Oppression, poverty, and ignorance are our greatest foes.

S.K. Nicholls, R.N.

Author Bio

Susan Koone Nicholls is an R.N. who lives in Orlando, Florida, with her husband, Greg. She was born, raised and educated in Georgia, where she also raised her family. She has three children, a step-son, and two grandchildren. Orphaned from her mother at an early age, she spent time in foster care and in a children's group home in the North Georgia Mountains, The Ethyl Harpst Home. She loves to hear from her fans.

She can be found at S. K. Nicholls on Facebook, and you can visit her at:

www.redclayandroses1.wordpress.com

Email: redclayandroses1@gmail.com